# MAGGIE GALLAGHER LEGAL THRILLER

*The Midwest Lawyer*

*The Bloodied Client*

# THE MIDWEST LAWYER

## PETER KIRKLAND

MAGGIE GALLAGHER LEGAL THRILLER SERIES
BOOK ONE

This is a work of fiction. Names, characters, places and incidents either are the product of imagination or are used fictitiously. Any resemblance to actual persons, living or dead, events or locales, is entirely coincidental.

RELAY PUBLISHING EDITION, APRIL 2025
Copyright © 2025 Relay Publishing Ltd.

All rights reserved. Published in the United Kingdom by Relay Publishing. This book or any portion thereof may not be reproduced or used in any manner whatsoever without the express written permission of the publisher except for the use of brief quotations in a book review.

Peter Kirkland is a pen name created by Relay Publishing for co-authored Legal Thriller projects. Relay Publishing works with incredible teams of writers and editors to collaboratively create the very best stories for our readers.

*Cover Design by Deranged Doctor.*

*Print and ebook formatting by Lori Colbeck.*

www.relaypub.com

# BLURB

*A terrible accident could send an innocent man to prison…*

Returning to her hometown after years of practicing law in Chicago, Maggie Gallagher is determined to put her family first—no more cases that could put her or her loved ones in danger. But when her childhood friend is arrested for the murder of a high school football coach, Maggie has to take the case. She knows Troy better than anyone, and she's certain he wouldn't hurt a fly.

But the evidence is stacked against him. The murder weapon, clothing fibers, and more all point to Troy. The Prosecuting Attorney is hungry for a win, and convicting Troy looks like a slam dunk.

As Maggie digs deeper, trying to find the truth, she uncovers a twisted trail of rage and broken lives surrounding Coach Schafer. And Troy has secrets of his own. Unless he comes clean about his past, there's no way Maggie can mount a proper defense.

If she fails, Troy will go to prison. A shattered family will lose everything. And the real killer may strike again…

# CONTENTS

| | |
|---|---:|
| Chapter 1 | 1 |
| Chapter 2 | 5 |
| Chapter 3 | 14 |
| Chapter 4 | 22 |
| Chapter 5 | 29 |
| Chapter 6 | 37 |
| Chapter 7 | 44 |
| Chapter 8 | 52 |
| Chapter 9 | 58 |
| Chapter 10 | 66 |
| Chapter 11 | 72 |
| Chapter 12 | 78 |
| Chapter 13 | 85 |
| Chapter 14 | 90 |
| Chapter 15 | 97 |
| Chapter 16 | 105 |
| Chapter 17 | 111 |
| Chapter 18 | 115 |
| Chapter 19 | 122 |
| Chapter 20 | 132 |
| Chapter 21 | 136 |
| Chapter 22 | 143 |
| Chapter 23 | 150 |
| Chapter 24 | 159 |
| Chapter 25 | 167 |
| Chapter 26 | 180 |
| Chapter 27 | 186 |
| Chapter 28 | 194 |
| Chapter 29 | 200 |
| Chapter 30 | 209 |
| Chapter 31 | 214 |
| Chapter 32 | 225 |
| Chapter 33 | 232 |
| Chapter 34 | 238 |
| Chapter 35 | 244 |

| | |
|---|---|
| Chapter 36 | 250 |
| Chapter 37 | 257 |
| Chapter 38 | 266 |
| Chapter 39 | 271 |
| Chapter 40 | 278 |
| Chapter 41 | 285 |
| Chapter 42 | 291 |
| Chapter 43 | 297 |
| Chapter 44 | 306 |
| Chapter 45 | 314 |
| Chapter 46 | 321 |
| Chapter 47 | 328 |
| Chapter 48 | 338 |
| Chapter 49 | 347 |
| Chapter 50 | 353 |
| Chapter 51 | 359 |
| | |
| *End of The Midwest Lawyer* | 367 |
| *About Peter Kirkland* | 369 |
| *Sneak Peek: The Bloodied Client* | 371 |
| *Sneak Peek: Small Town Judgment* | 377 |
| *Also by Peter Kirkland* | 387 |

# 1

Sirens pierced the early morning peace growing louder, coming closer while I was on my morning run. I crossed the street and glanced left as an ambulance turned the corner and raced past, down two blocks before turning left. A younger woman with her baby stroller joined me on the corner as the siren stopped.

"Looks like someone in our neighborhood," she said. "I hope things are okay."

"Me too." Even though we hadn't lived here for long, I'd already become acquainted with some of our neighbors. That was definitely something that was more typical of small towns than my previous life in Chicago. But then, this was my *previous* previous life—the small town where I'd grown up.

"I'll say a prayer."

I nodded. "Good idea. I'll go see." I raced the two blocks and turned the corner. My heart sank. The ambulance had stopped in the driveway of a close friend from high school. More like a brother than a friend, though after I moved away, we'd drifted out of regular contact. The only time we'd spoken recently had been at a garage sale a few weeks back. Was it a heart attack? Surely Troy was too young. He'd be my age—forty-two.

I slowed to a walk. The paramedics were already inside, the front door open. What should I do?

A next-door neighbor in his bathrobe was outside holding a mug of coffee. He came toward me. "Do

you know what happened?" he said.

I shook my head.

He motioned with his thumb toward Troy's house. "I heard a gunshot. Just one."

*Suicide*? I didn't say it out loud.

"They've been fighting lately. Cops came a couple of months ago…"

Troy was not an angry person. At least twenty years ago, when I'd spent every moment possible with him and his family, he wasn't. I was relieved to see him appear in the doorway, even if he was staring off into space.

"Excuse me," I said to the neighbor and walked up Troy's driveway. He had sunk down on the front porch, sitting with elbows on his knees, hands over his face. He looked devastated, and I could feel my dread growing. What happened? Who was hurt? Was there a chance it was just an accident…or was it something worse?

"Troy," I said, "Are you all right?"

He mumbled something and shook his head.

"Out of the way." Appearing in the door, a paramedic was leading the gurney back outside. He was holding an IV bag over a young man. With a jolt, I realized that the victim must be Troy's oldest son,

Benny. He looked to be about the age of my own son, Ian. I felt queasy. I'd seen more than my share of crime scene and homicide photos in my years as a prosecutor—but seeing it in real life, real time, happening to the son of my friend...

Another paramedic in gloves held a white gauze pack against Benny's left side, under his arm. It was red with blood. A gunshot wound—and not in a place where you would expect a suicide attempt. Who had pulled the trigger?

Pushing the gurney was another paramedic, and then came Troy's wife, Denise. She held a small boy in her arms: their other son, Charley. The boy was sobbing.

The paramedics moved quickly but carefully down the driveway, loading the gurney into the ambulance with Benny in the back. Two climbed in with him and the third turned back to us. "Allegiance hospital ER." Then he rushed to the driver's seat and pulled out of the driveway.

Denise looked at me with no recognition. Then she grabbed Troy's hand and forcefully made him stand. "I'm taking Charley to my mom's. I will see you at the hospital." She looked at me again, then started for the open garage. Without looking back she said, "You go there *now*."

Troy turned to me. "Maggie..." was all he said.

"What happened, Troy?"

"My boy, Benny." Troy looked past me, like the answer was out there somewhere. "He got shot."

"An accident?" I said, feeling a rush of relief. Why had I let my imagination get the better of me? Of course it had been nothing more than an accident. Troy wouldn't have shot anyone. He didn't answer, still staring off with a distant gaze, clearly in shock. I'd always been told I was good in a crisis, but I had no idea what to do here. What did he need? Was there something I could do to help, or was I just in the way? "Are you okay to drive?"

His eyes came to mine. "I can't believe this, Maggie." Then he turned to the door. "I've got to go," he said and disappeared inside.

I stood there for a minute, staring after him. What would I do if I were in his shoes—if something happened to Ian? I could barely stand to even think of it. Ian was part of the reason my husband and I had recently moved back here, to the hometown I thought I left behind after high school. Over a lot of long, hard talks, Sean and I decided that we needed a change. Instead of focusing so much on my career, I needed to put Ian first and give him a home that was peaceful, stable. Safe. I thought we'd find that here in Kerry, Ohio.

But nowhere is ever fully safe.

## 2

I took a sip of my coffee and grimaced. I wasn't sure how long I'd been sitting at my desk, lost in my thoughts, but it was long enough that the coffee had turned cold. I kept drinking anyway. *Waste not, want not*—the theme of my hardscrabble childhood that I'd never fully shaken off. Anyway, if I kept my thoughts elsewhere, I barely even noticed the taste. Poor Troy and Denise. I should have done something. I was the first one there. I could have driven him to the hospital. After twenty years away from town, we finally reconnect and what do I do? Let him down.

There was a knock in the reception area of my office. I didn't have a secretary, so I walked out and opened the door to an explosion of color in the form of an eye-searingly bright flower-print shirt that hardly anyone could pull off. But my aunt Louise wasn't just anyone. "Auntie El!" I stepped into the hallway and hugged her.

"Hi, Margaret," she said. "I thought I'd bring you an office-warming gift." She held forward a loaf of Irish soda bread.

"Awesome," I said, taking it from her. I loved her Irish soda bread almost as much as I loved her.

Auntie El was my favorite aunt. Mid-sixties, plump, with red hair like me, although her color was fading into gray now. We had bonded over our red hair when I was young and self-conscious. She taught me to be proud of it. "Come in," I said, leading her into the small reception area that made up the front room of my office suite. I put the loaf down on the desk meant for the secretary I didn't have yet and headed over to the little kitchenette area in the corner, complete with a sink, a cabinet, a row of electric outlets, and a drawer that *might* hold some utensils.

"I think I have a knife somewhere…" I said, pawing through the drawer. It looked like the person who had used the office last hadn't gotten around to cleaning it out—but rather than anything useful, all I found were soy sauce packets, some paper napkins, and a crumpled menu for the local Chinese restaurant, which might come in handy later.

"Good luck finding it," she said and laughed. I let out an embarrassed chuckle, knowing that she had a point. My office was a mess. I had moved in two weeks ago, and boxes and books and files and office supplies were still strewn everywhere. I had furniture, thankfully, because it had come with the lease, but the pieces were all solid wood —heavy, mid-century pieces that were impossible for me to move around and rearrange on my own. She pointed at the coffeepot next to me, the only kitchen appliance I'd bothered to plug in so far. "You unpacked the most important thing, at least. Coffee will go great with the soda bread." She headed for the pot.

A voice came from the door. "Excuse me." I turned to see a shorter man, about my age, in an ill-fitting suit, standing in the hallway. "Are you Mrs. Gallagher?"

I stepped toward him and smiled. "Yes, I am *Ms.* Gallagher. You must be Mr. DeNuzzio." We had an appointment for 11:30 a.m. I held out my hand and we shook. I pointed at Auntie El. "Um, this is my Aunt Louise."

He laughed. "Hello, Aunt Louise."

"I know you," she said. "I'm Louise O'Brien. I dropped my daughter at your shop a few years ago. You put a new muffler on her pickup." She walked over and shook Mr. DeNuzzio's hand.

"I hope it's still working for her," he said.

She smiled and nodded, then turned to me. "I see you are busy, so…"

"Thanks so much for coming, Auntie El. It means a lot. I'll call you later with my review of the bread," I said with a smile. Then I led Dominic DeNuzzio from the reception area to my inner office and closed the door. It was a *little* more organized in here. There were still plenty of boxes sitting around, and I hadn't hung anything on the walls yet, but my desk was set up with my computer, and I'd cleared the junk off my guest chairs in anticipation of this meeting.

"Thank you for seeing me, Ms. Gallagher. Tyler down at the shop said he knew you in high school and you were really smart, so…"

"That was nice of Tyler. I'll have to thank him." Referrals would be important now that I was in private practice. I'd buy Tyler lunch or a drink or something. "And you can call me Margaret or Maggie. Please, have a seat, Mr. DeNuzzio."

"Thanks. And you can call me Dom."

I sat behind my desk and pulled up the reports I had reviewed last night. "Okay, Dom. Sorry about your son, but I think I can help him."

"That's great to hear." He pulled nervously at the collar of his white shirt. He probably didn't wear a tie very often. "It was just an accident," he said. "I mean, yeah, we were drinking, but not that much…"

I leaned back in my chair. "Start from the beginning and tell me what happened," I suggested, trying to sound as calm and reassuring as I could.

"So we go out to Lefty's. You know, the bar and grill? They were showing the Reds game on the big screen."

I smiled and shook my head. "That changes things, Dom. I don't help Reds fans. You see, I root for the Guardians." I thought I'd see if he had a sense of humor.

"Maybe you're not as smart an attorney as Tyler thought. Cleveland sucks." Then he smiled to let me know he got the joke.

"I guess I can overlook your bad taste," I said. "A spring training game?"

"Exactly." He loosened his tie and crossed his legs, relaxing. "They hardly ever show a spring training game on TV. We were pumped. I probably had four or five beers, but Frankie had only two, maybe less than that."

*Only two beers.* One of the oldest clichés in the business. Every defendant in a driving-under-the-influence case claims he only had two beers. "Did you pay with a credit card?" I said.

"Umm... Does it matter?"

"It could. That would create a record of what you purchased, or at least how much you spent. Cops rarely go after the bar bill, but if it helps our case, then I might want to see your receipt at some point."

Of course, there was always the chance that it wouldn't help our case if he was lying about how much they had. Only time would tell. Dom nodded, turning serious again. He unfolded his legs and nervously rubbed his palms down his pants. "You should probably know...I've had a couple drunk drives myself."

I nodded to show that I wasn't going to be judgmental. "So you know how it works," I said.

There was a knock at the door before it cracked open, revealing Aunt Louise. "Sorry to interrupt," she said, "but I thought your client might like some soda bread and coffee." She had apparently found paper plates and a knife somewhere in my office mess, and she offered a piece of bread to Dom.

"Thank you, ma'am," he said and happily took the plate.

"And some coffee?"

"Yes, thank you."

She handed me the second plate, then briefly left, returning with two mugs. "One with cream, one without," she said.

"I'll take the cream, ma'am, if you don't mind," Dom said with his mouth full. He had already started on the soda bread. He raised the mug to me. "You run a nice shop here."

Auntie El backed out of my office and I mouthed a "Thank you" before she closed the door.

I sipped my own coffee. Strong. I remembered my aunt liked things strong. Coffee, jokes, Irish whiskey… As my mom would say, back before she died, "Louise is a corker."

"Where were we?" I said.

"We were at Lefty's." Dom set the empty paper plate on my desk. "We both had dinner. Frankie had the rib plate and I had a burger, if that matters." I nodded for him to continue. "So we left at about the sixth or seventh inning. They took out all the starters, and there's no point watching minor leaguers play, you know? Frankie says to me, 'Let me drive.' He knows about my record, which is why he didn't drink much." Dom seemed more animated now, like he was trying to persuade me of something. It seemed a little suspicious, but for now, I'd give him the benefit of the doubt.

"Anyway, we're in my F-150. We come around the corner there on 16th and this car comes out of the parking lot of that apartment building on Cherry. It looks like it's gonna hit us, so Frankie swerves to avoid a collision and we run into the side of a house. Actually, it was a garage."

I took out my phone and pulled up the satellite image on the maps app. I walked around my desk to Dom and had him show me where it was.

"Right here," he said, pointing. "I can tell because the garage is right next to the road. Shouldn't there be a setback from the street? Maybe that's something you can argue…the builder committed some kind of code violation."

I ignored him and returned behind my desk. "You probably don't remember any details about the car that pulled in front of you. Make? Model? Any part of the license plate?"

"Sorry, didn't notice the license plate." He smiled sheepishly. "It was a Honda Accord. Gray. Couple of years old. I don't remember much else."

"Were you or Frankie injured?" I asked. "Did you have your seat belts on?"

"Um, yeah, to the seatbelts. I hurt my ribs pretty bad." Dom reflexively rubbed his sternum. "I thought about going to the hospital. But Frankie was all right. The cops were there almost immediately."

"The report said nothing about field sobriety tests."

"Yeah, that's right." Dom sat up a little straighter. "When I got popped, they made me walk a line, touch my nose, stuff like that. Frankie didn't do any of that. They screwed up, didn't they?"

"I don't know. We might be able to use that." I sipped the strong coffee. "Anything else?"

"No, the cops arrested him, no tests or anything." Dom leaned forward, excited, like he was helping me uncover Frankie's innocence. "I don't think he even blew."

"No, he did," I said. "But not at the scene. They took him back to the station for the breathalyzer. He blew an .08."

"Oh, shit." He shook his head and leaned back. "Maybe he's screwed, then."

"Not necessarily. They didn't give him the breath test for over ninety minutes. They have to prove Frankie was above a .08 at the time he was *driving*. But alcohol takes a while to affect a person. It's possible he was a .07 or less while he was driving, before the beers fully kicked in." I already knew this was going to be our main defense.

"Okay." Dom nodded, encouraged.

"What happened after the crash?" I asked.

"The owner of the house freaked out. He was in the doorway yelling at us, and then something happened to him, and he ended up on the ground. Frankie and I didn't touch him," he assured me. "We couldn't have even if we wanted to—the cops were already there by then. A cop went to the guy, and then a few minutes later, an ambulance showed up. They took Frankie to the police station, but I hung around waiting for the tow truck. I guess the owner had some kind of panic attack or something. That's what the cops said. They took Frankie to jail and that little guy to the hospital."

"Did *you* talk to the police at all?" I said.

"Just small talk, joking around, you know? I'm in the Elks with the dad of one of the cops, James Carpenter. His boy Jimmy was taking pictures of my truck and the garage, telling me they were pissed because they were supposed to be off duty, but the call came in just before their shift ended."

I looked at the time on my phone. "You should probably head over to the courthouse. Frankie's arraignment will be at 1:30 p.m." I stood to signal we were done. "I'll see you there."

I opened the door and led Dom to my outer office. Auntie El stood near the formerly empty bookcase, smiling. She had moved half of the boxes off the floor and unpacked some of my supplies. It was beginning to look like a real law office.

"Thanks for the bread," Dom said. "It was unbelievable. I might have my girlfriend get the recipe."

Auntie El laughed and shook her head. "Sorry, ancient Gaelic secret. My own kids don't even know it."

Dom turned to me and held out his hand. "Thanks for your help, Margaret. If we can get Frankie out of jail and keep him out…that would be great."

When he had left, I turned to Auntie El. "Thank you so much," I said, waving my hand around the office. "This looks great. I feel like a real lawyer again."

She handed me a piece of paper. "You got a call while you were with your client. A woman who said she needs a good lawyer."

"Thanks." I took the paper.

"You can't get clients, Maggie, if you don't have someone answering your phone."

It was a fair point, but hiring someone was going to be tricky until I built up enough of a clientele to have a steady cash flow. I wasn't used to all of this—finding clients on my own, building up an office from the ground up. I'd worked as a prosecutor for my entire professional career. Switching to private practice was a huge change. But I had to believe it would all be worth it. That this town, this fresh start, was exactly what my family and I needed.

With my aunt smiling at me and a loaf of soda bread on the counter, it was pretty easy to believe.

## 3

Downtown Kerry, Ohio, looked impressive, in a touristy kind of way, like the town was auditioning to be the quaint community on a movie set. In the center of town was the old courthouse, currently home to the Donahoe County Historical Society. It was a beautiful early 20th century wood structure surrounded by lawn and hundred-year-old oak trees.

Thrift stores and antique shops circled the town square, along with some restaurants and a microbrewery, but the new businesses were mostly housed in the old brick buildings that gave Main Street its character. My office was on the second floor of one of them—looking south across the street at the old courthouse. The best, and worst part of my building, was the French patisserie on the street level. The pastry smells taunted me every morning when I came to work and sometimes I gave in.

But today, I needed to look pristine, so when I left for my court appointment, I didn't stop to check out the display cases. I couldn't risk any croissant flakes or crumbs on my perfectly pressed suit. I might be a native daughter, but I'd been away a long time, and it was important to make a good impression. The court officials needed to look at me and see someone to be reckoned with—someone they could respect. That was why I'd dressed to impress…mostly. The power heels wouldn't go on until I actually reached my destination: the nondescript pair of brick buildings two blocks away that housed the new courthouse and the jail. Sneakers would do just fine until then.

When I moved back to Kerry, I wanted my office to be in the center of town where I could get to know business owners who might someday need a lawyer. And I liked the idea of walking to court as a kind of continuing physical therapy for the injuries I'd sustained, weather permitting. On beautiful spring days like this, the walk felt perfect. But of course, I would drive to court during the brutal Ohio winters. I wasn't a masochist.

One block down Main Street, I passed the old marble statue of Paul Brown, towering over a small park. Brown was a football icon in the state of Ohio, having founded the NFL team, the Cleveland Browns, who were named after him. I noticed some cracks in the old guy, like he had been patched up recently. The statue reminded me of how big football was here in my hometown.

I reached the modern courthouse and started up the steps when I saw my cousin Liam coming toward me. He was tall and clean-shaven with sandy brown hair, casually good-looking and he knew it. But his smile was sincere and warm. We'd always gotten along, though our version of "getting along" included a lot of playful arguing. Growing up, we had a kind of intellectual rivalry whenever our families got together. Debating just about anything, like politics or even sports trivia. I could argue any side of an issue, which would frustrate him. "You're gonna be a lawyer, aren't you?" he would say.

"Hey, cuz," he said and hugged me. I could feel the badge and holster on his belt bumping up against my side—Liam was a detective with the Kerry PD.

"I just saw your mom," I said. "She brought me an office-warming gift…" I delayed a moment to build the drama. "Irish soda bread. It was almost as good as that bread I made when we were kids." I had once helped Auntie El make some bread, and it came out heavy as a brick.

"I chipped a tooth on that," he said. "I hope she made some for me."

I shook my head. "But she made two loaves for your brother."

"That's not funny," Liam said. His older brother Patrick was a patrol officer in the same department, and they had an interesting rivalry. Whenever I had only-child envy for them having each other *plus* a sister, I thought of the pranks they'd play on one other and thank my lucky stars that my parents had stopped at one.

"Come check out my office," I said. "I might have a piece left for you," I said and walked up the stairs.

I got through security and headed for Judge Blankenship's courtroom. He was handling arraignments this month. I pushed through the doors, hoping they had brought my client up early so I could talk to him, but the courtroom was empty. Even his father, Dominic, who hired me, wasn't here. Frankie had been in jail all weekend and I had not yet met him.

There were three courtrooms in the courthouse and this was the largest, with four rows of wooden benches behind the bar separating the lawyers' tables. Oak-paneled walls and judge's bench gave it a 20th century feel. Not a classic courtroom like the old one downtown, but not a cement block, bullet-proof glass monstrosity like some modern courtrooms I frequented in Chicago.

"Hey, Margaret."

I turned to see Assistant Prosecutor Oliver Altman. "Hi there, Oliver." I had met him a few times since I moved back to town. He wore the prosecutor's best friend: a navy blazer with gray slacks and a club tie. He was a nice enough young guy, maybe twenty-eight. I tried not to judge him for his hipster black glasses. As a new defense attorney in town, I needed good relationships with the prosecutors. "Do you have the DeNuzzio case?" I said.

"I do. Pretty scary fact pattern, if you ask me."

"Really?" I said. Time to work him. "I was a little surprised you even charged him. A .08 blow that was taken ninety minutes after the accident. You'll have a tough time showing he was intoxicated while he was driving."

"Your client smashed into a guy's house!"

"Into a garage that was practically on the street. His insurance will cover that."

"The crash is pretty good evidence of intoxication. And the victim is in the hospital, by the way. I was looking at the assault statutes to see what else I could—"

"Come on, Oliver. He's not a victim and you know this wasn't an assault. The police report said he had a panic attack." I held up the report, as if he hadn't seen it. "Look, my client swerved to avoid a speeding car coming out of the apartment complex. Do you really think a jury is going to hold that against him? But just to make everyone's lives easier, we might plead to a careless driving charge."

Oliver stepped back. He didn't like me pressuring him. "I will talk with the officers, but I think a jury should decide this." He walked through the gate to one of the lawyers' tables at the front of the courtroom.

I had suspected that he wouldn't agree to a deal right now, but I wanted to plant the seed. A driving under the influence charge came with a suspension of Frankie's driver's license, mandatory alcohol treatment and extra fines, in addition to more jail time, and maybe community service. Having him plead to a lesser charge would help immensely.

As a young prosecutor, I would have been happy to convict Frankie for intoxicated driving, but that wasn't me anymore—and not just because I was a defense attorney instead of a prosecutor. I also wasn't fresh out of law school and looking to make a name for myself. I was old enough to understand that the system worked best when laws were practiced with a little humanity.

Eventually they brought up my client, along with three other men in orange jump suits who had spent the weekend in jail. Frankie DeNuzzio must have taken after his mom. I'd been expecting someone wiry and dark-haired like his dad, but he was a little chubby and had blondish red hair and large eyes with long eyelashes. I sat next to him on the bench. "I'm Margaret Gallagher. Your dad hired me to help you with this."

"Yeah, he told me." Frankie wouldn't even look at me, apparently not impressed with his new counsel. He looked around the courtroom. "Where is he?"

"I don't know. I was expecting to see him here. He stopped by my office and we talked about your case."

"Oh he did, huh? What did he tell you?" It sounded like Frankie wasn't too happy with his old man either.

"He said you swerved to avoid a reckless driver coming out of the apartment complex and that's why you crashed."

"Is that what he said?"

I frowned. "That's what happened, right?"

Frankie shrugged, still not looking at me. "It doesn't matter. I just want to plead guilty and get this over with."

I turned my body to face him and make sure we had eye contact. "I understand wanting to be done with this. But if you plead guilty, your license will be suspended, probably for a year. You'll have a large fine and will have to do more jail time."

"I can't do any more time."

"How about this? We'll enter a not guilty plea today and sort this all out. I might be able to get a deal for reckless driving or something better. Okay?"

"You just want to get paid more," he said and looked away.

Where was this attitude coming from? I never imagined it would be this hard to get a client to listen to me. Did he honestly not care about the consequences? "Is your driver's license important to you?"

He turned back, angry. "I drive a tow truck. Of course it is."

There was some movement among staff at the front of the courtroom and I sensed the judge would be coming out. I had to find some way of connecting with Frankie, and fast. "Just trust me on this, Frankie. Ginger to ginger."

He looked at me a long moment and then huffed out a laugh. "All right."

I hoped I had won him over—if not completely, then at least enough for him to take my advice and plead not guilty. The bailiff called, "All rise. The Donahoe County Court of Common Pleas is now in session. The Honorable Victor Blankenship, presiding."

Blankenship in his black robe took his seat. A former criminal defense attorney with grayish brown hair and wire-rimmed glasses, he had a reputation as the most reasonable of Donahoe County's judges. He banged his gavel. "Let's get this going. Who's first?"

Oliver stood, "Your Honor, the first matter is, State versus Crandall. He is represented by Mr. Gates."

The first three defendants were those who had hired private counsel. Later, jail staff would bring up the other inmates who were arrested over the weekend and couldn't afford their own attorney. They would get court-appointed attorneys.

The Crandall case was processed quickly, and then our case was called next. Frankie joined me at the front table. Oliver handed me the charging document.

"Hello, Ms. Gallagher," the judge said. "Nice to see you again. Does your client waive reading of the charges and advice of rights?"

"We do, your Honor."

"Very well. Mr. DeNuzzio, how do you plead?"

Frankie looked at me and said, "Not guilty, judge."

I tried to be discreet about my sigh of relief. Thankfully, no one seemed to notice. The judge paused a moment to look at his calendar. "I'm setting this for a pre-trial conference in four weeks. April 12. If you have any motions, Ms. Gallagher, file them before then. Is there anything else?" He looked at Oliver. "Any reason Mr. DeNuzzio can't be released?"

"Judge, this wasn't just an intoxication case. The defendant crashed his pickup into a house and there is a man still in the hospital."

"Objection," I said, standing. "It is true there was a minor accident, but according to the police report, the reason the man went to the hospital was because he had a panic attack, not because he was injured." I wanted to grab Oliver by the collar and give him some prosecutorial advice. No case was worth tarnishing your reputation for integrity. Especially a run-of-the-mill drunk driver. I'd thought better of him than this. Was he really so desperate for a win that he'd edge this close to lying for it? But instead of asking, I bit my tongue, reminding myself to play nice.

Judge Blankenship said, "Go to the release office, Ms. Gallagher, and fill out the paperwork. I will sign it. Next case?"

Oliver called the next matter, not making eye contact with me. Frankie and I walked back to the benches where Dominic greeted us after arriving late. I smelled beer on his breath. "Hang in there, Frankie," he said.

An officer tapped Frankie on the shoulder. "Back to the jail." Frankie turned and gave him a defiant look.

"Don't make trouble, Frankie," Dom said. Frankie's frown deepened, but he didn't say anything—and eventually he walked off. Dom turned to me. "What are his chances?"

"If we can't get a plea deal, I have a few good arguments."

"You have a lot more experience than that young prosecutor, don't you? Your website says you've tried over a thousand cases."

I put my arm in his and walked him toward the door. "I've seen a thing or two, Mr. DeNuzzio." And while I didn't say it, because you can never guarantee how a trial will turn out, I was very confident we could win this case.

# 4

Driving home after putting in a few more hours at the office, I flipped on the local AM news station and got a bit of a shock when I realized they were talking about the shooting at Troy's house this morning. The broadcaster and a local attorney I didn't know were discussing an Ohio initiative from a few years ago. It would have required gun owners to safely store their weapons or face civil and criminal penalties. The initiative didn't pass. "I don't want to jump to conclusions," the lawyer said, "but this case illustrates why we need this law. Parents should be required to lock up their guns."

This was bad for Troy and Denise. Their tragedy might become a political issue, which would draw a lot of unwanted attention. I made a mental note to check in with Troy tomorrow and see how his son was doing. How the whole family was doing.

I had been feeling good, heading home for dinner at a reasonable hour, unlike when I was a prosecutor back in Chicago. Now I had a knot in my stomach. I knew too well how tragedy could impact a family. Almost two years ago, I had been walking to my car after work when a former defendant I had convicted ran me over with his

1998 Mercury Sable. I was left with a shattered ankle, a broken femur, and a whole slew of stresses and strains cascading along the rest of my leg and my hip. After that, something changed in our family. I spent a couple of weeks in the hospital, and then underwent a painful rehab regime that lasted months. My husband, Sean, carried the family through that period, doing all the cooking, all the driving, including taking Ian to band practice and all his other school activities. And Ian, well, he seemed to withdraw from me. He only visited the hospital a couple of times. According to Sean, Ian said it "freaked him out." He would excuse himself from the dinner table when I talked about my injuries, so I stopped talking about them.

After a lot of soul searching, Sean and I decided to move from the city, back to my hometown. The injuries weren't just affecting my home life. I was struggling to manage my heavy workload in the Chicago prosecutor's office. Rehab, doctor's visits, and the constant, base-level pain were making the job a struggle. Sean had agreed that maybe a slower pace for me might allow me to spend more time at home, more time with Ian. Perhaps then he would accept my injuries, or at least accept me. And Sean had grown up in the country. He said he missed that special sense of community you find in a small town, and he'd thought that maybe it would be good for Ian too.

I pulled into the garage before 6 p.m. and found Sean in the kitchen making chili. "Hey, babe," he said as I came in the door. I went to the stove to look at his creation in the big pot.

"Smells good," I said and pecked his cheek.

"It's missing something." He wrapped his arm around my waist and squeezed.

*Human touch*...it's a good thing. I rested my head in his neck and said, "If you made it, I'm sure it's great."

"Don't make me ask for it," Sean said, playfully pushing me away.

I put my hands on my hips and cocked my head. "But I want to hear you ask for it, baby. I want to hear you beg."

Sean Gallagher was the sexiest English teacher I had ever met. Black, wavy hair, piercing blue eyes, and a swimmer's lean frame. And even better, he had a cheerful happiness about him that was a beautiful counterpoint to my tendency toward self-criticism. He even had a positive spin on that. "It's because you're a lawyer. You're always looking for weakness in your cases, and in yourself, whether they're there or not."

He turned back to the pot on the stove and said, "Black pepper, onions and garlic…plenty of chili powder…"

"Cumin," I said. "For a pot that size, maybe a teaspoon, not too much."

"Cumin." He nodded. He pointed the wooden spoon at his laptop on the counter. "It's right there in the recipe, but I managed to look right past it." He shook his head, "You fixed it without even tasting it."

I smiled and shrugged. "How long 'til we eat?"

"Maybe fifteen. Could you tell Ian?"

"Yeah, I'll have him set the table." I walked down the hardwood hallway and knocked on Ian's door. I knew enough not to bust in on a teenage boy. "Hi, honey. We eat in about fifteen minutes. Could you set the table?" I heard a grunt in acknowledgement, and I went to change out of my pant suit.

When I returned to the kitchen in jeans and a sweatshirt, the dining table was not set. Sean pointed to a glass of red wine on the counter next to the small TV. "Time to relax, Maggie."

Back in Chicago, I had come to rely on that first glass of wine to dissolve the stress that had built up from dealing with criminals, judges, and whiny defense attorneys. I had met more than a few trial lawyers who found their only relief in a bottle and I had been worried that was happening to me. But not here in Kerry. There was no stress, at least so far. A little generic California red was just a nice complement to dinner. It wasn't something I needed—not like before. I took a sip and said, "What can I do?"

"Cornbread is baking, but could you make the salad?"

I pulled the romaine lettuce out of the fridge and shook in some Caesar dressing. I glanced at the TV, which was tuned to the news. When we bought this home, Sean had insisted on putting a small TV on the counter. "I need to stay on top of the news while I prepare your nightly feast. Otherwise, I'll have no idea what the kids are talking about," he said, referring to his job teaching English at Kerry High School. "These kids know what's going on. It's not like Chicago."

Kerry was too small to have its own news broadcast, but both Dayton and Columbus stations would sometimes cover local events, if they made enough of a splash. As I put the salad plates on the table, I noticed a shot of our brick courthouse on the screen. I turned up the sound. "Charges, if any, will depend on whether the child survives." The anchor paused a moment, and then said, "I am told we have fixed our connection. Let's go live to Allegiance hospital in Kerry, where our Alison Brantley has the latest developments. Alison?"

The screen shifted to a reporter standing outside our local hospital. It was dark out, but flashing emergency lights gave the scene an ominous glow. Sean came next to me to watch, but said nothing.

"Dave, it has been a tense day here at this small Kerry Ohio hospital, where a nineteen-year-old male is in critical condition after suffering a gun-shot injury, apparently inflicted by his five-year-old brother. Minutes ago, when the father of the two boys reentered the hospital, we attempted to ask him questions. This is what happened."

The view shifted from the talking reporter to a shot of the sliding glass door into the hospital's ER The camera showed Troy exiting, walking fast. The camera moved in and someone put a microphone in Troy's face. "Is it true the nineteen-year-old victim was shot with your gun?"

Troy back-handed the microphone away and the video turned shaky, showing the night sky and then a sideways view of the parking lot.

The camera returned to the reporter. "The man who shoved our cameraman has been positively identified as forty-two-year-old Troy Weaver of Kerry, Ohio. We have learned that police are actively investigating this shooting. Potential charges include child endangerment, and if the shooting victim does not survive, I have been told that homicide charges would be considered."

Anchorman Dave was back on the screen. "Let's hope it doesn't come to that, Alison. Alison Brantley reporting live, from Kerry, Ohio."

"Poor man," Sean said. "It's got to be hard enough having your kid in the hospital—having to deal with reporters shoving microphones in your face must only make things worse."

"I know him. That's Troy Weaver, my good friend from high school. You met him last month at that garage sale, remember? They live about five blocks north of here. I heard the siren when the ambulance came this morning. I saw them wheeling Benny away."

"My God," Sean said. He put his arm around my shoulder and hugged. "Are you all right?"

No, not really. I'd been battling against flashbacks of my own accident and worries about Troy all day. I'd thought about reaching out a dozen times, but I couldn't figure out what to say. I wasn't going to let myself off the hook again. He deserved to know that he had friends in his corner. And that meant I needed to get over whatever angst I was feeling and focus on what I *could* do.

"Yeah, I'm fine," I lied. "I should check on Troy." I took out my phone. "I don't know if I have his phone number." I walked into the living room to scroll through my contacts. Even though we'd run into Troy at the garage sale, I hadn't had a real, long conversation with him in at least ten years. We had grown apart when I joined the Army for a two-year tour after high school.

But there was a time that he was like a brother to me. I owed a lot to Troy and his family. And after all he'd done, I hadn't even bothered to keep in touch enough to have his number in my phone. With a huff of self-directed disgust, I opened up Facebook and sent him a quick private message, letting him know I was around if he wanted to talk. I wondered if he'd even see it. Who'd be checking Facebook at a time like this?

I walked back into the kitchen, where Sean was putting a chunk of cornbread on Ian's plate next to his chili bowl. His latest growth spurt had left Ian pretty lanky—he needed all the calories he could get, preferably not from junk food, given that he had inherited my teenage acne problem. He tried to hide it with shaggy brown hair that covered his ears and angled down over his forehead, sadly obscuring the piercing blue eyes he got from his dad.

Sean said, "Ian asked to eat in his room so he can study for his math test." Ian didn't look at me, quickly heading down the hallway.

I pointed my phone at Sean, my frustration boiling over. "That's why we moved to Kerry, to slow down and spend time as a family." I was pissed and stepped closer. "I come home early for dinner because eating dinner together is important. We agreed to that."

"Don't raise your voice with me." He set down his wineglass, like he wanted his hands free. Sean took a deep breath, and then in an overly calm voice, "Everything's a balance, Maggie. Ian has been struggling with his math…"

I hated it when he did that, when he tried to pacify me like I was a child throwing a tantrum. "Don't give me that, 'everything's a balance' crap. He's got all night to study. He's growing more distant from me, and eating in his room isn't going to help. And you know he's not studying. He's playing video games."

"I can hear you," Ian yelled from his room.

Sean stared at me for a long moment. "That's great. Very helpful, Red." His nickname for me when I lost my temper. It was not a term of endearment.

I stalked off to our bedroom and grabbed my keys and coat, and I came back to the kitchen. "I need to go to the hospital, see if I can help Troy."

"So much for family dinnertime."

I ignored Sean and walked out to the garage, slamming the door.

# 5

On the way to the hospital, I drove by Troy's house, afraid of what I might find. My heart sank when I saw three police cars on the street and one in his driveway. I slowed down next to a uniformed officer and asked what was happening.

"Keep moving," he said.

"I'm a lawyer friend of Mr. Weaver's, and I'm going to see him at the hospital. Is there someone in charge I can talk to?" I tried to sound calm, but my anger with Sean and Ian—and my frustration with myself—had not yet settled. The officer told me to wait and he walked back to the house. A plain clothes detective came back. She was short with fake blond hair. It was too dark to make out her face.

"You're Mr. Weaver's lawyer?" she said.

"I'm a lawyer *friend* of his. Are you executing a search warrant? Do Troy and Denise know about it?"

"Nobody was home when we arrived. We will leave the proper documentation when we are done. Anything else?"

I could have asked more questions, but she wasn't likely to give me any answers I couldn't figure out for myself. They had a search warrant to look for evidence from the shooting this morning. They wanted to charge Troy with a crime. I drove off.

Our subdivision was southwest of downtown Kerry and the hospital was northwest, so it took about eight minutes to get there.

I parked and walked into the ER through the sliding glass door I had seen earlier on TV. No reporters now, however. The check-in counter was straight ahead, but I went left toward a large seating area interspersed with oversize ferns and indoor palm plants. There were at least ten people there, including Troy and Denise in the corner behind a pile of McDonald's wrappers. Troy stood, looking haggard and disheveled, dots of mustard he didn't seem to have noticed drying on his high school lettermen's jacket. I gave him a hug. Then I hugged Denise and tried to think of something to say. Lawyers were supposed to be fast talkers, weren't they? Smooth, eloquent, always knowing what to say.

In a courtroom, I *did* know what to say—because I worked like hell to be as prepared as possible. But there was no preparation for something like this. Every parent's nightmare was their child getting hurt. And this was so much worse, since it sounded like Troy might end up facing legal consequences, as if he wasn't already suffering enough.

"You're Troy's lawyer friend," Denise said. "Thanks for coming."

"I'm so sorry." I motioned for them to sit, and Troy cleared the wrappers from the table for me to sit on. "How's Benny?"

Denise said, "He's in a coma. They're still trying to figure out why. Maybe loss of blood is affecting his brain. They're talking about taking him up to Columbus, to the university hospital. They have a neurology department there, but Troy's worried about the transport."

Troy said, "If something goes wrong in the ambulance…"

"What do you think?" Denise said. I sensed she wanted me to help persuade Troy.

I didn't want to get between the two. "Tough call," I said. "If it were me, I would defer to the experts here."

"I guess so," Troy said. I noticed his eyes were red and swollen. Denise seemed more composed. He said, "Thanks for coming."

"I saw you on TV. I don't like being the one who brings bad news, but this has become a story. You need to be careful how you deal with the media."

"What did you do?" Denise said, turning to glare at Troy.

"Nothing. Just…these reporters got in my way when I was coming back from getting dinner."

Denise shook her head.

I said, "I drove by your house and the cops were there. They were searching it."

"For what?" Troy said. Then he slapped the arm of his chair. "They can't do that!"

"They can if they have a search warrant, and I suspect they do."

Denise put her head in her hands. "Can't they just leave us alone? Don't they know what we're going through?"

"Can you help us, Maggie?" Troy said.

I thought of the twelve-year-old me, crying on Troy's couch, his mom hugging me. I owed Troy and his family so much. Back then, he hadn't hesitated to help me. I wanted to come through for him now. "Why don't you tell me what happened this morning."

Denise huffed out a breath before she said to Troy, "You're the dumbass. You tell her."

"I don't know how it happened." He looked off past me, not making eye contact. "I mean, I was sleeping and I heard a gun go off. I go out to the kitchen and there is Benny lying on the floor." Troy touched a spot beneath his left armpit. "He was bleeding here. Charley was holding a gun, looking up at me." Troy's eyes welled up.

Denise said, "I came running out from the bedroom. Troy got there first because he had been sleeping on the couch." She wanted me to know that. "But Troy did nothing. I took the gun from Charley and gave it to Troy. I told him to call 911, but he just stood there." Denise shook her head. "I had to make the call."

"Okay," I said. I had a lot more questions, but I could tell that this wasn't the time to ask them. Denise was blaming Troy and getting her angry wouldn't help.

But Denise kept going. "Benny was making breakfast for Charley. There was cereal out on the table. I guess Charley got one of Troy's guns and must have been playing with it."

Troy shook his head. "I don't know how. I keep 'em locked up."

"Bullshit," Denise said. "How many times have I found your guns sitting out?"

"Once. Just that one time when I came home from the range." Troy looked at me. "I have a gun safe."

"It's more than once," she said. "What about that time you left the handgun in my car?"

"Okay, twice."

"There's more than that."

I broke into their argument, wanting to keep them from getting worked up. Yelling at each other wouldn't help anything and it might get hospital security on their cases. "You both should know, the police are probably investigating this as a child endangerment case. And with the media on it...I want you both to be careful about what you say." I looked at Denise to make sure she got it. Blaming her husband was something they needed to work out between the two of them or maybe with a therapist. But talking in public about how it was all his fault would not do any good.

Through the glass door, I saw my cousin Liam. He was walking with another detective, likely the one I spoke with at Troy's house.

I said, "Excuse me a moment," to Troy and Denise and went to head off Liam and the other detective. Liam was visibly surprised to see me.

"Maggie. Why are you here?"

I stood in front of him, blocking his way. "Probably the same reason you are."

He introduced me to his partner, Janice. She was definitely the detective I saw earlier. Now that I could see her clearly, I noted that she was younger than both of us—maybe mid-thirties. "We'd like to talk with Troy," she said. "Give him the search warrant return."

"I can take that," I said, not moving out of the way.

Janice said nothing and walked around me to Troy and Denise.

I looked at Liam, who shrugged and said, "It's her case."

We followed her toward Troy. "Mr. Weaver? This is a search warrant which we just executed at your home. And here is the receipt for the items seized. We would like your cooperation in opening your gun safe so we don't have to destroy it."

Troy looked at me over Janice's shoulder.

I said, "We want to cooperate, of course, but I will need a chance to discuss things with my client. Did you take the safe?"

"We did," Janice said.

"Then there is no rush. We can give you an answer tomorrow."

"We would also like to ask each of you some questions." She motioned to Denise. "How about you first, ma'am? Would you join me outside?"

I said, "I think we are going to pass on making a statement right now."

Janice didn't like that. She turned and faced me. "I'm assuming you represent the husband."

"I represent the family, for now. At least until we can get some more details. What is it you are interested in?"

Janice said, "This case could end up a manslaughter." Then, realizing how horrible she sounded, she looked at Denise, who visibly paled. "Of course, I hope it doesn't come to that."

I handed her my business card. "For any future communication, please go through me. And we will get you an answer tomorrow about that safe."

Janice looked at Liam, then back at me. "We are going to need to talk with the little boy, Charley."

Denise stepped forward and pointed her finger. "You are not talking to Charley. Stay away from him or I will…You will not talk to my boy."

Whatever trace of sympathy had been on Janice's face before was gone now. It was clear she was not on board with Denise telling her what to do. "He's not the one we are investigating here. And we *will* talk with him, whether or not you cooperate."

Keeping my voice calm, I said, "Is there anything else we can help you with?"

Janice held up my business card and read it aloud, "Margaret Gallagher." She turned and walked past Liam, mumbling something under her breath to him. I thought I might have heard the B word. Clearly we would not be doing spa treatments together.

"Pissing off the lead detective isn't going to help things," Liam said.

"She came *in* pissed off," I pointed out. "It's like she was looking for a fight. Do you really think that's any way to talk to a grieving family? Is she always like that?"

He grimaced, looking torn between giving me an honest answer and defending his colleague—which meant the answer was yes: she was always like that. Great, that was *just* what Troy needed.

Liam took my arm and pulled me a few steps away from Troy and Denise. "Are you actually taking this case, Maggie? This one could get ugly."

"I know," I whispered. "And thanks. But Troy and his family took care of me after mom died. I owe them."

Liam nodded. "Loyalty is a good thing. Just don't let it blind you." He stepped back and looked at me a moment. "I'm sorry we weren't there for you back then. I mean, we tried, but…"

I stepped closer and gave him a hug. "You tried. You were all great." After my mom died, Auntie El and her family had swarmed our house, cooking and cleaning and even mowing the lawn. My dad resented it. I was pretty young, but I remember him getting drunk a lot, and one time swearing at Auntie El to "Get the hell off my property." She and her family pulled back after that—which meant they weren't around to realize when things got really bad. "It's good to have you back," I said to Liam. He squeezed me once, and then headed for the door.

I turned back to Troy and Denise. "Thank you so much," she said, hugging me. "I don't know what we would have done if we'd had to deal with that woman on our own."

"Is it okay that I stepped in like that? I didn't really ask you if you wanted me to be your lawyer."

"I couldn't think of anyone better to represent us," Troy said, and he hugged me too.

I nodded. "Okay. I'll draw up an agreement later, but for now, I'm your lawyer.

Before I left, I reminded them, "Don't talk to anyone about this. Not even your family. They could be called as witnesses against you."

"Do you think they are going to charge me?" Troy said.

"I don't know," I lied. "We'll have to wait and see."

# 6

By the time I got home, Sean was asleep, so I slept in the guest bedroom. I didn't want to wake him or take responsibility for being a jerk last night.

Nothing had caused me more trouble in my life than what my dad called my "Irish." He blamed himself, saying I inherited the explosive temper from him.

I could usually control it in court. Even harness it to focus my energies and sometimes use it to get under the skin of opposing counsel. But I had also harmed more than a few relationships in my personal life. During my stint in the army, working as an intelligence analyst at a base outside Tacoma, Washington, an incompetent, arrogant sergeant set me off, and I ended up with a temporary demotion for "borderline insubordination." I loved my time in the service, but I learned a lot about myself. Like, I couldn't work for idiots.

I had gotten better over the years. Most of the time, if I felt like I was about to go too far, I could walk away—get some space until I could calm back down. When my temper *did* get the better of me, I'd learned to make amends, most of the time. For some reason, though, when it came to my nearest and dearest, it was a lot harder to smooth things over after it happened. Half the time, I didn't even know what we were really fighting about. The other half of the time, I knew all too well. Sean and I both loved our son so much and wanted what was best for him, but more and more lately, it felt like we couldn't agree on what that should be. Sean was adamant that we needed to give Ian his space while I wanted to wrap him up in bubble wrap and protect him from everything.

That was the difference between us. As a teacher, Sean could still see the good in everyone. As a lawyer, I was constantly dealing with everything that was wrong in the world. Up until my accident, I felt like we were a counterbalance to each other. Since then, I felt more and more as if one of us always had to be on top and that was no way to coparent much less function in a committed relationship.

In the morning, rather than going for a run, I snuck into our bedroom, gathered my courage and crawled into bed to apologize. Sean didn't move. "Are you awake?"

"No."

"I'm sorry about last night." I'd had to say that many times in my life and it never got easier. But I knew that nothing would get better until it was said. "It just seems like Ian is pulling away. I don't know what to do."

Sean rolled over on his side to face me. I could see his face in the faint dawn light. "I know," he said. We lay there in silence a moment. "The move might have been more traumatic than we thought it'd be. He's tall, but he's still just a kid." Sean's foot slid over and rubbed against my leg. "At that age, I was kind of pissy with my parents too."

I reached my hand over to touch his face. "I hope that's all it is."

Sean moved close. "Do you need to get to work early this morning?"

I smiled back at him. It was always good to apologize.

---

I arrived late to the office and indulged in a croissant and coffee from the patisserie downstairs. A potential client was coming in later this morning, a middle-aged woman arrested for the thirteenth time for shoplifting. And then later this afternoon, I was meeting a couple that had their Tesla rear-ended. It would be my first civil case. There could be a lot of money helping people with their civil problems, but they rarely went to trial. And I love going to trial. That's why I became a lawyer. But I needed to build my practice, and that meant taking civil cases, even if it was a little boring sometimes. It would be worth it if it meant I'd have more time for Sean and Ian.

Before my prospective clients arrived, I reorganized some of the clutter of boxes and files. I needed to make the office look more professional.

---

It was a little before 5 p.m. and I was thinking of heading home early when my cell phone rang. "They took him." It was Denise. "I was at the hospital and Troy just called me from jail. He was home when they came and got him. He asked me to call you."

"Okay, I will head over there now." That meant the prosecutor had taken the case to the grand jury and gotten an indictment today. And an arrest warrant. The justice system never worked that fast. Was the prosecutor doing this for political reasons?

"I'm gonna stay here at the hospital," Denise said.

"How's Benny doing? And Charley?"

"Benny's responding to stimulus, the doctor said. A flashlight in his eyes and pinching his arm. They said it's encouraging. They're not going to move him to Columbus. For now. Charley is with my mom. We haven't told him anything yet. Honestly, I don't even know where to begin."

"I'm so glad about Benny, Denise. That is great news. My husband and I are praying for you." I didn't know what to say about Charley. How would someone go about explaining what happened to a child?

"Thank you." She seemed touched. "It's like my world has been turned upside down. We need all the help we can get."

I called Sean and told him I would be late, then headed down the stairs for the walk to the jail, which was next to the courthouse.

I made it through the metal detector. The officers didn't recognize me, so I showed him one of my business cards. "I'm here to meet with my client, Troy Weaver."

"It's almost dinnertime," the officer said. "I don't think they will let you see him."

As a prosecutor, I did all my fighting in the courtroom—I never had to fight for a client. But I was a fighter all the same, and for Troy's sake, I needed to fight now. "He will want to speak with me," I insisted, then forced myself to take a breath and try to find a way to ease the mood. I already had Janice aggravated with me—I didn't need to tick off these officers too. If we stayed in Kerry, I would be working with these officers long after Troy's case was over. I needed to balance my fighting instinct with a more gracious attitude. I said, "I heard you have a five-star restaurant here. Maybe I can get a table?"

That seemed to work. He laughed and then escorted me down the concrete hallway to one of the legal visiting rooms. Bare white walls, only large enough for a small table and two chairs. "It could be a while," he said, and walked away.

He wasn't kidding. Much later, the door opened and in came Troy in his orange jump suit with his hands shackled. "Hi, Maggie," he said with a scared voice. Jail did that to people. "I can't believe this is happening. I didn't leave a gun out." He shook his head. "I don't know where Charley got it."

I reached across the table and grabbed his hand. "Look at me, Troy." He did. "You have to stay strong. For your kids and your wife—and for me. I need you to listen to me and do what I tell you. Okay?"

"Okay," he said with wide eyes.

"Let me tell you how this is going to work. Tomorrow you will be arraigned, which means we go to court and they tell you what the charges are. We should be able to get you released, but you may have to post some bail." Troy nodded.

"Should I plead guilty?" Troy said.

I shook my head. "We haven't even seen the discovery. We don't know what evidence they have. I think they are going to charge you with child endangerment. You will plead not guilty and then we will sort this all out."

Troy leaned forward and put his head on his arms. "I don't even know if he's going to live."

I patted his hand again. "When Denise called to tell me you were here, she said he was doing better, responding to light and touch."

"So you think he'll be okay?"

I wanted to say yes, to give him something to smile about—but I wasn't just here as his friend. I was here as his lawyer, and he needed to know that everything I told him was the truth. This wouldn't work if he didn't know he could trust me. "I can't say for sure, but it certainly seems like a good sign. By the way, how old is Benny?"

"Nineteen."

"Okay, good," I said. Benny was an adult. That meant if they were looking at child endangerment charges, it would be for endangering five-year-old Charley. I was already thinking how this might play out. If Benny was still a child, it might be a tougher case. "Why was Benny up so early?"

"He's got a job down at the Honda plant. It's been great for him." And then Troy broke down all the way. I rubbed his forearm as he cried into his cuffed hands. He pounded the table. "I didn't do anything…"

"Troy," I said. He took a moment to gather himself and looked up. "Remember when my mom died?" He nodded. "You told your mom that I was alone, that my dad was a drunk and I was making dinner for myself. Remember?" He nodded again. "So you guys had me over." I was tearing up myself. "I think we had meatloaf that first night," and I chuckled. "My world was ruined, and you guys took me in. I must have eaten with you a thousand times, all the way through high school. Your parents always made sure I felt welcome." I was crying now. "But that first time, you were a twelve-year-old boy and took a lonely girl into your house. You watched TV with me, played video games with me." I took a tissue from my purse and dabbed my eyes. "My point is, I thought my world had ended and you gave me hope. That's who you are—a good person who cares about the people around you. That's the guy I'd do anything to help. We're going to get through this. Okay?"

I took out another tissue from my purse and gave it to Troy. He wiped his eyes and blew his nose, which made me laugh for some reason, which then made him laugh.

"Just one more question, and I'll let you get back to your fabulous meal."

"Yeah, right," he said. "Chipped beef and biscuits."

"When the cops arrested you, you didn't talk to them, did you?"

He hesitated a moment and then looked away. "I might have said something, I'm not sure."

Which meant that he had, and he knew it was dumb, so he was embarrassed about it. Oh well, nothing we could do about that now. "Whatever you do, don't talk to anyone in the jail. There are guys in here who will try to get you talking so they can trade info with the cops and get themselves a sweeter deal."

He nodded.

"Tell me you understand."

"I understand, counselor."

Good. Publicity or not, I was hopeful that we'd be able to get past this fairly quickly. Troy was a good man and a loving father. The shooting had been nothing more than a horrible, chance accident.

Surely this would all be over soon.

## 7

Troy's arraignment was scheduled for 10 a.m. That was when we would find out the charges and get discovery from the prosecution to see the evidence they had. Not that there would be much. The handgun from the incident, anything Troy had said when they arrested him. I would try to get any of his statements suppressed. At the hospital, I told the cops I was his lawyer and not to talk with him. I would have to research whether that was a sufficient invocation of his Fifth Amendment right to counsel. If it was, his statements he made when I was not present should not be admissible.

It was about 8:30 a.m. when I walked up the stairs and unlocked my office. And there was Aunt Louise!

She smiled, poured me a cup of coffee, and brought me the mug. "I know your landlord, Gus," she said. "We went to high school together."

"Okay." I glanced around the room. The reception area had been cleaned. I went into the small conference room where I had moved my files and boxes. Empty. I turned and looked at Auntie El. Just how early had she gotten here? And why had she taken it all on herself? If she'd come during my regular hours, I'd have been happy to tackle all of it with her.

"I have a proposition for you," she said.

I took a sip of coffee and held the mug up to my face, enjoying the warmth and enjoying my aunt and her surprises.

"Ever since I retired from my bookkeeping business two years ago, I've been so bored you wouldn't believe it. I gave it up when your uncle stopped farming because I thought it would mean we'd have more time to spend together, but…frankly, Carl and I are spending *too much* time together, if you know what I mean. All day in the house with him?" I started to speak, but she cut me off. "Hear me out. It is obvious you need some help. It's hard running a business and practicing law at the same time."

Did I want to have my aunt as my employee? What if things didn't work out? "I can't pay you much," I said.

"I don't need much," she said. "Social Security only lets me make a small amount. And it's not like I'll be doing hard labor. Filing, greeting clients, answering the phone… You need someone to answer the damn phone."

I did. And I loved Auntie El, although she could be a handful. She was like an older, more colorful and volatile version of me. I'd probably end up firing her.

"Done," I said. "But where did you put all my stuff?"

She poured herself a mug of coffee. "It's filed away. If I told you my system, you wouldn't need me."

———

It was a beautiful March morning for a walk, the trees leafing out, birds chirping. I did catch a few looks on the sidewalk for wearing my knee length navy skirt with sneakers, carrying my heels in a bag to put on when I reached the courthouse. I refused to feel self-conscious about it, telling myself that if people ever needed a lawyer, they might remember the wacky redhead walking to the courthouse in her tennis shoes.

I arrived about 9:30 a.m. There were two TV trucks parked in front of the steps, their satellite link poles rising into the sky. The blonde reporter from the hospital stood next to one truck. She glanced my way, clearly trying to decide whether I might be involved. I kicked off my sneakers and converted to my black heels. I walked carefully up the stairs and through the metal detector.

The arraignment would again be in Judge Blankenship's courtroom, so I turned left and made my way there. The same young prosecutor, Oliver Altman, sat on a bench across from the courtroom, where a crowd of about ten people stood waiting to go inside.

When I looked at him, something in me snapped. I knew the legal profession had its flaws. It could be too slow to adapt to the times, too open to manipulation by interested parties, too fallible in many ways. But it didn't have to be cruel. That was a *choice* that the people in the system made. And today, it was pissing me off.

I sat next to Oliver. "Troy Weaver's son is fighting for his life, and you take this case to the grand jury? You don't think his son being shot is punishment enough?" I had gone into fight mode again, even though I *knew* it was a stupid thing to do. Antagonizing him before we even stepped into the courtroom wouldn't do me *or* Troy any favors, but I couldn't help myself.

This was why most lawyers understand they should not represent family members. They are too close and too emotional. And here I was representing Troy, who had been like a brother. "Do you have kids, Oliver?"

He held up his hands. "It wasn't me. I have nothing to do with this one." Then he pointed down the hall. "It's Carol's case."

A shorter brunette woman in a tasteful black pencil skirt and white blouse had stopped near the exit, looking outside at the TV trucks. She waited a moment until the TV reporter approached her and they had a brief conversation. *Great.* Carol the Prosecutor was working the media. I'd heard her name in passing, but this was the first time we'd meet face-to-face. I had a bad feeling about her right from the start. The woman was more concerned about her political aspirations than helping victims. The hardest part to stomach was that if I'd stayed in Chicago, that might have been me, too.

After a moment, they separated and Carol came toward the courtroom, carrying a file folder. I walked up to her. "Carol? My name is Margaret Gallagher and I represent Troy Weaver."

She stopped and looked at me. "Good for you," she said, and started walking again.

"So it's going to be like that," I called after her. She waved her hand dismissively and kept going. I looked over at Oliver, who shrugged.

"Welcome to my world," he said.

The bailiff had opened the courtroom for Carol, and the crowd filtered in behind her. I was glad to see no cameras in court. I had handled a few high-profile cases back in Chicago, including the shooting of a city alderman by a mentally ill owner of a dry-cleaning business. Media attention could impact people's motivations in unpredictable ways, making everything more complicated. In that case, the alderman hired a PR firm from his hospital bed to help advance his political career. That made it much harder for me to convict his shooter.

I took the left table at the front of the courtroom, since Oliver and Carol were to the right. Oliver had a stack of files for the other defendants in jail awaiting arraignment. Carol had one file: Troy's. There was noise from the back, and I turned to see about ten men in orange jail garb entering from a rear hallway that connected to the jail. Troy was last, looking scared. An officer escorted him up front to join me as the bailiff announced, "All rise. Donahoe County Court of Common Pleas is now in session. The Honorable Victor Blankenship, presiding."

"Be seated." The judge banged his gavel and looked at me. "Hello again, Ms. Gallagher. Two appearances this week. Looks like your practice is picking up."

Carol stood. "Your Honor, Carol Becker. I am the new Chief Assistant Prosecuting Attorney for Donahoe County."

"Yes, Ms. Becker. I heard you were starting. Down from the Attorney General's office, right?"

"Correct," she said. "I ran the cold case homicide unit there. But I am glad to be in Kerry and back in the courtroom."

"Well, glad to have you. Call the first case, Ms. Becker."

"The only represented defendant we have this morning is State versus Troy Weaver."

I motioned for Troy to stand. "Your Honor, I have not yet received a copy of any indictment." I turned to Carol and held my hand out, but she made a point of setting the paper on my table. I stared at her a moment, letting the judge see my displeasure at her rudeness. Then I picked it up and read it. Child endangerment, one count—as I'd expected. It wasn't for shooting Benny, but for Troy not securing the handgun to keep Charley from being able to play with it. "We have received a copy of the indictment and waive reading and advice of rights."

"Very well. Mr. Weaver, how do you plead?"

Troy hesitated, and I said under my breath, "Like we talked about. Not guilty."

He looked at the judge. "Not guilty."

"Okay, anything else?"

I had remained standing and said, "Yes, I ask that Mr. Weaver be released on his own recognizance, Your Honor."

Carol Becker stood again. "The State opposes that. We ask that the defendant be held without bail. He is responsible through his conduct for the shooting of his own teenage son. There is another son in that household and the defendant's release could pose a grave risk to that five-year-old boy."

I'd expected some showboating, but this was beyond what I'd imagined. Carol knew as well as I did that the jail was overcrowded, and Troy was no threat to anyone. "Your Honor, there certainly has been a tragedy that resulted in my client's son being placed in critical care at the hospital. You can imagine the impact on Mr. Weaver and his family. His wife and sons need him at home and also to provide a round-the-clock presence at that hospital. He has never been needed more."

Carol cut me off. "Our society needs him where he can't do any more damage."

If she thought I'd lie down and let her bulldoze me, she had another thing coming. "Your Honor, Mr. Weaver has no criminal record, he has a full-time job and a strong network of friends, and relatives and the State has seized all his firearms, so we're fine with a no weapons term in his release agreement."

"But Judge—"

"Hold it, Ms. Becker. I can't have you two talking over each other." Judge Blankenship was getting annoyed himself, and as much as Carol seemed to love the sound of her own voice, she was smart enough to realize when to shut her trap. And so was I. "I am going to set bail at $10,000." Troy would only need to post ten percent, or one thousand dollars. "Can you post that today, Ms. Gallagher?"

"Yes, Your Honor." If Troy couldn't, I would.

"Fine. Is there anything else?"

Carol said, "Your Honor, this case has attracted some significant media attention. In fact, two TV stations are here and wanted to film these proceedings." She turned and motioned to the blonde TV reporter and a couple of other media persons in the audience. "I asked them to hold off until I had raised the issue with you, to see if you have concerns with cameras in the courtroom."

"I appreciate that, Ms. Becker. I am okay with having one pool camera in here, but we will have to work out the details for any future hearings. My courtroom is not a circus." He looked at me. "Anything else?"

"We have received no discovery," I said, holding up the one-page indictment. "Usually the prosecutor's office provides at least some discovery at the time of arraignment." I glared at Carol.

"Ms. Becker?" the judge said. It was clear he disapproved.

"We are working on it, Judge," Carol said. "We moved quickly on this case because of the risk to the public, but we will have materials to counsel by the end of the day."

"All right," the judge said. "Anything else? No? Then let's set this for a pre-trial conference one month out—April 17th. Will that work?"

I had my calendar out. "Yes," I said, as did Carol.

"Very well. Next case."

Oliver stepped up and called the next defendant to the front. I turned to Troy. "They'll take you back to the jail, I'll post your bail, and then I can take you home." I patted him on the shoulder as the officer came to get him. I headed for the door, but Carol cut in front of me. "You're pretty excited about the media," I said.

She turned and faced me. "I didn't ask them here."

"But you rushed the case through the grand jury while it was still in the news cycle."

"I'm just a humble public servant," she said with a smirk, and then walked out of the courtroom. We definitely weren't going to become BFFs, and I was okay with that.

# 8

I wrote a check for Troy's bail, figuring I'd get paid back when his case resolved. Not exactly a good business practice, but I wasn't defending this case for the money. I walked back to the office and got my car, an older Ford Escape, and came back to the jail. Troy climbed in and said, "Thanks for the lift. Denise is still at the hospital."

"Charley still with Denise's mom?"

"He is."

We were quiet a moment as I turned left onto Highland Avenue. "How are your folks?"

"They're doing great. They moved to Sun City about six years ago and they're living the life." He looked out his window. "I haven't told them about this…any of it."

"It's tough," I said, not knowing what else to say. "How are you and Denise doing?"

Troy let out a sigh and stared out the window, avoiding looking at me. "I think you already know the answer to that. She blames me for all this—for having guns in the first place, for leaving one where Charley could get to it. And we weren't doing very well beforehand." More silence. I stopped at the light to turn into our neighborhood. "Things have been tense for the past few years—since not long after Charley was born. I made some friends on a softball team, and she doesn't like them. She said they're 'loudmouths.' She said they treat their wives like shit."

"Are those your shooting buddies?" I said.

"Yeah, a couple of them."

"You really weren't a gun guy, were you?"

He shrugged. "I wasn't into hunting, or anything. But the guys invited me to come shooting at the range, and I found out that it's fun. So is going to the gun shows. It's a little like collecting. Remember, I used to collect baseball cards?"

"Yeah. I thought that was a waste of money. You spent hours with those cards, spreading them out on the floor, trading with those O'Loughlin boys down the street."

Troy laughed. "I should have been doing my homework, like you." Then more seriously, he said, "Denise never liked the guns, but she didn't say anything when I only had a few. But then…well…"

"You ended up with more than a few, right?"

He squirmed in his seat, looking embarrassed. "Yeah, I guess you could say that."

I pulled into his driveway. "How many do you have?"

"I don't have any now. The police took them all," he said, but I just gave him a look, waiting out his deflection. His shoulders slumped, and he finally answered me. "I had twelve, now thirteen. I just bought a .300 Winchester Magnum. I was thinking about going deer hunting, get some meat for the family. Denise doesn't know about that one."

Suddenly the garage door came up. Denise, holding a suitcase, came storming toward us. Troy climbed out, looking wary.

"I don't want you in this house," she said.

"Come on," he said. "Let's talk about it."

"We'll work out a schedule at the hospital to sit with Benny. I don't want you around Charley…or me."

"Denise…"

She set the suitcase by my car, returned to the garage, and went inside as the door descended. Troy stood there watching, letting her go. Then he leaned down to look at me through the open window. "Do you think you could drive me to a motel?"

———

Our house was empty when I arrived back home. I changed clothes and felt an urge to check my own gun. I only own one, a Beretta M9, the pistol I was trained on in the army. Also in the case were two fifteen-round magazines. I hadn't fired it in a while, too busy to make it to a range in Chicago very often. But I took it out every now and then to oil it. I spun the combination on the case lock and put it back underneath a pile of my sweaters.

Sean and Ian had arrived home, and I could hear them in the kitchen. I went out front. "Hey, guys."

"We got some takeout," Sean said. "I didn't feel like cooking."

"Thai," Ian said.

"That sounds great. I'll get some plates." I quickly set the table. Sean said a quick grace and we dished out the food. Standard stuff—pad thai and some green curry with tofu over rice. Sean had been talking about going vegetarian and he was trying to get us used to some different things, like tofu.

We ate in silence for a while as I fought the urge, but eventually I gave in and asked the stupid parent question. "Ian, how was your day?"

"Fine."

"Anything interesting?"

"I already told Dad. This school has a mock trial team. That's why we're late. I was thinking of trying out, but—"

"Honey, that's great," I said.

"If you'll let me finish… They told me I missed the deadline. It was last week."

"Oh, shoot. Maybe I could talk to someone…"

"No! I don't want you sticking your nose in my business." He picked up his plate and looked at Sean. "Can I eat in my room?"

*Great, here we go again*, I thought.

Sean looked at me, then said, "Do you need to study for a test or something?"

"No."

"This is the only time in the day when we can all be together, so…"

"I don't like sitting here getting grilled about everything. I'm sorry I missed the deadline, *okay*?" He took a bite of pad thai and chewed and sulked. "It wasn't like this in Chicago," Ian said with his mouth full.

"Well, we're not in Chicago," Sean said, showing a little edge himself.

"You don't have to tell me," Ian grumbled, eyes down on his plate like Sean and I weren't even worth looking at.

"Fine," I said. I felt like I'd spent all day fighting, and now that I was home, I didn't have it in me to fight anymore. "If you want to eat in your room, go ahead."

He rolled his eyes, then picked up his plate and walked down the hall.

Sean ate three or four bites before he broke the silence. "Family time, huh?"

"I know," I said. "And it's not that I don't appreciate you taking my side, it's just…family time with an angry teenager who resents us for making him sit with us might be worse than no family time."

Sean let out a sigh. "How about a glass of wine?" He didn't wait for my answer, getting up and pulling a bottle of white from the fridge. As he poured us each a glass, he said, "I thought it was pretty cool he wanted to do the mock trial thing. That's the first time he's shown any interest in extracurriculars since we got here." He handed me a glass. "And it's something you do, Madam Attorney."

"I know. That's encouraging." Even in Chicago Ian hadn't been involved in too many activities. He played soccer and basketball when he was younger, and then joined the marching band in high school. He played the baritone sax, for some reason, carrying that big instrument up and down the football field at half time. So it was a pleasant surprise to learn he had an interest in the law. He had never wanted to hear about my work before, and he would actively change the subject when I brought it up.

I sipped my wine and said, "It's just that, every conversation is so difficult. I can't seem to break through." I raised my glass in a toast. "But you seem to have the magic touch. He'll talk to you."

Sean laughed again. "On the ride home I asked how his day went, and he said, *'fine,'* with the same attitude. Then he played on his phone until we got to the restaurant. He didn't even bring up the mock trial thing until we were almost home." Sean took another helping of pad thai. "Sixteen is a tough age, and he's a sensitive kid. Besides, it can't be easy on him moving here like this. Most of the kids in his class have known each other their whole lives. It makes it tough for him to find friends. We just need to be patient."

"You're right, of course." My husband, the calm, wise one. I appreciated that about him, I really did—but it could make it hard sometimes, knowing that I was the difficult one. The one who made everything harder than it should be. The one who couldn't connect with our son. But I tried hard to push away any feelings of resentment. I cleaned my plate, gave Sean a smile, and said, "I love you."

# 9

Thankfully, the media attention over Troy's case died down over the next two weeks. And in the meantime, with Auntie El handling the phones and arranging my appointments, I'd managed to pick up a few more clients. Sean seemed to enjoy teaching English here in Kerry. "I haven't had an AP class in years. These kids actually *like* reading." And most importantly, without any help from me, Ian had made a real effort to talk his way onto the high school mock trial team. The coach did not give in on accepting a late application, but he was encouraging about Ian trying out his senior year. We were proud of him for making the effort. Slowly, we were settling into Kerry.

On Easter Sunday, we went to the church near the middle school. We hadn't been since moving to Kerry and I expected Ian to fight me, but he didn't complain, which surprised me. As a kid I had some wonderful memories of our church youth program and going to summer camps—that is, until my mom died. Dad never talked about it, but I think he blamed God for her death. We never went to church after that.

In the afternoon, we went to Auntie El's, who always hosted the whole family for Easter Sunday dinner. It was the kind of family time I had been hoping for in moving back home.

Auntie El and Uncle Carl lived five minutes outside of town on two hundred acres. Uncle Carl stopped farming two years ago, and now leased his land to his nephew, the latest farmer in the family. His two boys had never had much interest in farming and went into law enforcement. That meant Carl had nothing to do, which was why Auntie El came to work for me.

On the ride out I said to Ian, "Auntie El is planning on an Easter egg hunt for the kids…"

"Mom, I'm sixteen."

I looked to the back seat where Ian was staring at his phone. "You don't have to do it. I just wanted you to be ready when she asks you."

Ian looked up from his phone. "I hardly even know your cousins' kids. And most of them are little."

"If I know Auntie El, it won't be any old Easter egg hunt."

"What do you mean?"

I grinned at him. "Well, you'll just have to participate and find out." Ian grunted in response and went back to his phone. I fought the urge to ask him what was so important, he couldn't put it away.

We turned down the long gravel driveway and parked in front of their white, two-story farmhouse. There were kids outside everywhere. In addition to police officers Liam and Patrick, there was also their sister, Bridget. And all of them had at least two children. All of the kids, except Ian, would be grandchildren to Louise and Carl.

Two younger boys came up to our car. "Hey, Ian," one of them said, as we climbed out. "We got our BB guns. Want to come shoot?" Auntie El must have prepared the boys for their older cousin.

Ian put his phone away and looked at his younger cousins before springing into a trot. "Race you!" The brothers squealed in delight and raced after him. I heard Ian laugh at something one of them said.

Sean smiled at me. "He gets to be the cool older boy for a change." I smiled back, happy to see Ian shed some of his attitude and be the sweet boy I remembered.

After getting the obligatory glass of iced tea, and after saying hi to my aunt who was busily cooking up a storm and spending some time catching up with my cousins, we settled down to Easter dinner. The kids were in the family room eating around a bunch of folding card tables, and us adults squeezed around the large family dining table. Liam and his wife sat across from me, but we hardly talked. He spent a lot of time on his phone. And he made a lot of eye contact with his brother Patrick.

So I struck up a conversation with Bridget, their younger sister. She was up from Athens, Ohio, where she was a biology professor at Ohio University. I remembered her as a little girl with pet hamsters and frogs and snakes.

"Look at the two brainiacs over there," Patrick said, "plotting against us."

She pointed her fork at him. "The two with doctorates against the two dumb cops. Remember that, boys. Now pass the potatoes, officer," Bridget said.

Back before Mom had died, I remember sitting at the little kids' table, listening to the banter at the grown-up table. The loud talk, the laughter, the occasional heated arguments over crop prices or politics. Of course this was before Dad cut off contact with the family so he could stay home and drink. This was what I was after, moving back to Kerry.

Bridget told me about living in Athens, another small town, with her twin girls. "I turned down a job at University of Cincinnati because Dave and I don't like the city. We love it in Athens." One of Bridget's daughters came up to her. "Mom, Danny called me stupid." She lifted the girl on to her lap. "Honey, look around this table." Everyone's conversation stopped. "You see everyone here? You are smarter than all of them. Isn't that right, Dad?"

Uncle Carl was at the head of the table. He said, "Sweetheart, I'd trade Liam for you, right now."

Everyone laughed, and the girl ran back to the kids table shouting, "You hear that Danny?"

After stuffing ourselves with ham and cheesy potatoes and green beans and Jello salad, Auntie El brought the kids into the dining room. "We'll have the pies after the Easter egg hunt. Unless you kids don't want to…"

"No," the younger kids shouted. "We want the Easter egg hunt now!"

Auntie El looked at Ian. "You're probably too old for this…" She winked at me. I had told her about my challenges with Ian.

Bridget's twins pleaded with him to join the hunt. "Come on, Ian. You're not too big," they insisted, tugging on his arms.

Ian didn't do a very good job of hiding his smile as he said, "If you have enough eggs, I guess I can."

"Great," she said. "Here are the rules. You can only collect five eggs yourself. I want the younger kids to get their share. Some have chocolate, some have money, and some have very cool surprises. Let's all go outside, adults too, and Grandpa Carl will start the hunt."

We stepped into the April afternoon sunshine, a perfect day. Auntie El had spread the eggs across a two-acre section of the farm off to the right of the driveway. "Covering all that ground will wear them out," she said to the adults after the kids had scattered.

I sidled up to Liam. "What's going on? You've been weirdly quiet." He usually loved holiday get-togethers and was the loudest, most energetic person there. But not today.

He looked at me a long moment. "I can't talk about it."

"Work?"

Liam glanced around to make sure no one could hear. He took my arm and gently moved me away from the other adults. Then he leaned in, "There's a new twist in your client's case."

"You're talking about Troy Weaver?"

Liam nodded. "That new prosecutor, Carol Becker? She took the case back to the grand jury."

"For what?"

"The shell casing we found at his house. We ran it through NIBIN. You know what that is?"

I nodded. The National Integrated Ballistic Information Network. It was a system operated by the Bureau of Alcohol, Tobacco and Firearms that contained data from millions of shell casings found in criminal cases all across the country. Back in Chicago we had solved a gang shooting through NIBIN, proving that the same gun had been used in two different attacks.

"So Troy's gun is connected to another crime?"

Liam nodded solemnly. "And not just any crime. Murder."

A cold shock ran through me, and I froze where I stood. *Murder? No, it can't be. There must be some mistake.*

"About a year and a half ago, our high school football coach was murdered. Grant Schafer," Liam explained. "It was New Year's Eve. He was home alone and someone shot him—a single gunshot. The case was never solved. No one was even arrested. We didn't have any viable suspects…until now."

"You're saying the football coach was murdered with Troy's gun?"

"Well, it was a hit in the database. They're trying to get a forensic expert to confirm it."

"And Carol is taking this to the grand jury?" I couldn't believe this. Just because it was the same gun didn't mean Troy committed murder. There had to be an explanation. People buy and sell guns all the time. He must have gotten it *after* the murder. There was simply no way Troy could kill someone.

Liam said, "The prosecutor used to work with the cold case homicide unit in Columbus, you know. Coach Schafer's case went there once we stopped our active investigation. This is her baby."

"So she's taking this new info to the grand jury?" I asked again. I could feel the anger rising inside. Carol Becker seemed like the worst kind of prosecutor, one who was after publicity. Why else would she rush such an old case?

"She already did, and she indicted your client. There's an arrest warrant out."

I stared at the kids scrambling across the field, thinking about Troy and Denise and Benny still in the hospital. "A ballistic match isn't enough to indict," I said, trying to reason this out. "There must be more."

"Your client was one of our original suspects. Apparently, they had a beef after the coach cut his son from the football team."

"Cutting his kid from the high school football team was his motive for murder? Come on."

Liam shook his head. "Well, we didn't arrest him for it back then. On its own, it wasn't enough. But the gun changes things. You know, I shouldn't be telling you this. You need to keep it to yourself."

"I have a duty to my client," I said. If he had an arrest warrant out on him, I needed to go find him. Let him know what was coming so he wouldn't be blindsided by it. I looked up at Liam. "I won't tell anyone what you told me." I patted him on the arm. "Thanks." Then I headed over to Sean. He was watching the kids return with their plastic eggs.

"Honey, something's come up. It involves Troy Weaver. It's bad."

Sean glanced behind me at Liam. "Do we need to go?"

"I'm sorry," I said. "This has been the best day. Ian is getting to know his second cousins…"

Auntie El blew a loud whistle and announced the egg hunt was over. "Bring all your eggs into the house," she yelled.

"Can it wait until they finish going through the prizes?"

"You guys don't have to leave. I'll take the car, and maybe you can get a ride home from Patrick."

Ian came up to us. "I found twelve eggs, but I let the twins take the ones with the chocolate. But look at this." He held up one egg and pulled it apart. Inside was a note.

Sean took it and read it out loud. "Bearer entitled to one hunting trip with Grandpa Carl."

"Do you want to go hunting with your great uncle?"

Ian looked between me and Sean. "I mean, sure. I guess."

"That sounds like fun," I said. I was happy that Ian might build a relationship with my Uncle Carl, but I was too focused on Troy at the moment. "Listen, I was just telling your dad, something at work has come up and I have to go. You guys can stay, though. I'm really sorry."

Ian's face closed off, going back to the sullen, stony look I'd gotten way too used to. "Your job sucks," Ian said, and he walked into the house.

I kissed Sean and said, "Bring me home a piece of pie." I headed off toward our car wondering if I could find Troy before the police did.

# 10

I found Troy in Benny's room at the hospital. They had moved him from the ICU to the general wing. Troy stood to greet me. "The doctor said we're still in 'wait and see' mode, keeping an eye on his vitals. It's up to him now, whether he wakes up or…or not." Troy looked beaten down, unshaven, with his hair uncombed, still wearing the same mustard-stained letterman jacket.

"Why is it so cold in here?" I said.

"The doctor said it's good for Benny for some reason." He looked down and shook his head. "He's stopped responding to stimulus. I'm starting to think he might not make it."

I hugged him, patted his back, and gave him an extra squeeze. "We have to keep up our hope." I came to the hospital a little angry, feeling betrayed about what I had learned from Liam. Was Troy a murderer? But that feeling was now overwhelmed with sympathy for my long-time friend. He was a dad, suffering over his child. And I didn't believe he was capable of murder.

"I know this isn't a great time, Troy. But we need to talk. Can we step outside for a minute?"

"We can talk here."

"Okay." I pulled a chair closer to him and we both sat. "Tell me what you know about Grant Schafer."

He stared at me a moment, looked at Benny, and said, "Okay. Let's go outside."

We walked out past the nursing station, down to a small waiting area with a vinyl chair and couch. I sat in the chair and said, "Coach Schafer."

"I got a call about him last week," Troy said. "What's going on?"

"You got a call? From whom?"

Troy swore. He ran his hands through his hair and sat there with a stricken expression on his face, looking at me. "Can things get any worse?" Then he stood and walked over to a window looking out on the parking lot. The sun was setting, and it was getting dark outside.

I needed to be patient. It was a hard part of my job, letting witnesses tell their stories in their own way. Eventually, Troy walked back to me. "I don't know where to begin."

"Have a seat." I patted the vinyl couch. "Start from the beginning. I'm told you didn't get along with the coach?"

"Yeah. We had some words over Benny." Troy swallowed hard and shook his head. "This is tough, going back over it."

"Take your time," I said.

Troy nodded. "Benny was good. Really good. He played outside linebacker, the same position I played. He started getting calls from colleges his sophomore year. I mean legit calls. The head coach at

Bowling Green called him after the playoff loss that year, said he was at the top of their recruiting list."

Troy leaned back. "We were excited. Junior year he got hurt, sprained his ankle week two. He missed about four weeks. We missed the playoffs that year, but in the final game he had two sacks and made a diving interception." Troy stood up, getting agitated, reliving it all. "Northern Illinois actually gave him an offer. A full ride…" He shook his head, then sat back down on the couch.

Troy looked at me and said, "Benny had everything going for him, and then Schafer cut him. Four weeks into his senior year, and he cuts him. Said Benny was failing his health class, which was bullshit. That's not why he cut him."

"Why did he?"

"Because Benny was one of the team leaders and he didn't like the way Schafer was treating some of the players. He was pretty abusive, embarrassing kids in front of the team, berating them in front of the stands. You had to see it. Benny came to me and asked what he should do. I was like, 'you're all kids. You shouldn't have to put up with that.' Anyway, I'm sure that's why he flunked him in his health class. And, by the way, Schafer's nephew was a sophomore—and he took over playing Benny's position. Such bullshit."

"Okay," I said. "So what did you do?"

"I went to talk to him. He denied his choice to kick Benny off the team was about anything other than Benny's grades, so I went to the athletic director, other parents… I complained to everybody, but it didn't do any good. The team was going to make the playoffs, so nobody wanted to stand up to Schafer and tell him he was being a dick. They all just told me to let it go."

"And did you?"

Troy looked me straight in the eye. "Yeah. I did."

"When did all of this happen?"

"When Benny was cut from the team…I guess it was October. I spent the next few weeks raising Cain, trying to get someone to listen to me, but I suppose I'd given up by the time November rolled around. The season was over by then, anyway."

November. And the coach was killed on New Year's Eve. No wonder the police had considered him a suspect.

"What do you remember about the night he was killed?"

"Denise and I went to a New Year's Eve party at Lefty's."

"People saw you there?" I asked.

"Sure, plenty of them. There are pictures of me too." I made a mental note to myself to get copies of those pictures. "We left after midnight, went straight home, and went to bed. It wasn't until the next morning that we found out the coach had been shot. The police asked me some questions, but nothing came of it. They never found whoever did it. Everyone figured it was a robbery gone wrong—maybe some guy passing through."

I nodded. "Okay. Now tell me about the phone call."

"It was this investigator from Columbus, guy by the name of Cameron Hykes. He works for the cold case unit with the state Attorney General's office. I guess when the Kerry police couldn't solve it, they gave it to them. He first contacted me about a year ago. He said his job was to check my alibi. I told him I was at Lefty's, sent him some of the pictures. He told me I was in the clear."

"And this same guy, he called you again last week?"

"Yeah." Troy held up his phone. "He texted me first, asked if he could call me. He said every year they have to take a look at their old cases and he wanted to confirm some things with me."

"Okay. This is really important, Troy. What exactly did he say?"

"We talked about that night at Lefty's. Who I was there with. I told him Denise. How long I was there. I said we got there about 10 p.m. and left around 12:30 or 1 a.m."

"Anything else?"

"No. Just...he asked if I ever left."

I leaned forward. "Did you?"

Troy looked away from me, out the window. "No. I was there the whole time." His eyes shifted back to me. "What's going on? Why do you want to know about that, anyway?"

I hated doing it, but I needed to tell him. "The police did some preliminary forensic testing on the gun that shot Benny. They are saying it's the same gun that killed Coach Schafer."

Troy turned and stared at me as the words sank in. "That makes no sense. I didn't kill him." He went silent as some people came off the elevator. When they had moved on, he said, "I'm not gonna kill someone over football. And besides, I was at Lefty's."

"Did you buy any used guns over the last two years? Did you go to a gun show and buy a handgun?"

"Yeah. I've bought most of my guns at gun shows."

"So maybe that's where it came from."

We sat in silence for a moment as I tried to make sense of it all. But there was more to tell him. I reached over and grabbed both his hands. "The prosecutor now thinks you killed the coach. They have a warrant for your arrest."

He pulled back from me. "I didn't do it. You gotta believe me."

More than twenty years had passed since I'd spent any real time with Troy. Maybe Liam was right and Troy was dangerous now. It was possible—people could change. But was I ready to believe that about him?

"Give me a dollar," I said.

"What?" He shook his head, confused. But he handed over a five-dollar bill. "It's all I got."

"Good enough. I'll consider this your initial retainer. Now I'm officially your lawyer on both cases." I stood up and hugged him. "This might be your last night out of jail, so I can give you a ride home if you need one."

Troy stared at me a moment, then shook his head. "If it's my last night out, I'm going to spend it with Benny," he said and he walked down the hall.

## 11

The plan was for me to meet Troy at his house so he could drop off his car. Then I would drive him to the jail to turn himself in. But he was late, and I began to worry that I had made a mistake. If he decided to run, he could have left last night and be halfway to Mexico. I knocked on the door and Denise answered.

"Have you heard from Troy?" I said.

"He texted me last night and said he was staying at the hospital." She stepped back from the door. "Would you like to come in?"

"Thanks." It was the first time I'd been inside since the day after the shooting. I'd come back to visit the scene, taking in the sight of the dried blood that had pooled in a thick, ugly stain on the floor. I arranged for a bio-hazard contractor to come clean up the kitchen. A mother shouldn't have to clean up the blood from her son.

I closed the door and glanced around for little Charley. He wasn't there. Time to break the news, since Troy apparently hadn't. "There is a warrant to arrest Troy for the murder of Grant Schafer."

"The football coach?" She shook her head like the news wasn't processing. "That was a long time ago."

"The police traced the shell casing from the gun that shot Benny. It matches the gun that shot the coach."

Denise sat on the couch next to the door. "There must be some mistake. He was with me that night—at a party. It was New Year's Eve. We've been through this before." Her reaction was strange, like she was almost expecting this.

"And you were together all night?"

"Yes. He was with me the entire night." She stood and took out her phone. "I have pictures of us together. We gave them to the police when they questioned us."

I heard a car out front and peered out the window. Troy. So he hadn't decided to run after all.

"Troy's here," I said. "I am going to drive him to the jail to turn himself in. He's not likely to get bail this time. Do you want to talk with him?"

"No," Denise said.

"Okay." I opened the door and started out.

"Wait. Yes, send him in here. I need to talk to him. Alone."

I walked over to Troy's gray Toyota Corolla as he got out with the suitcase Denise had given him the day she kicked him out. "I told Denise."

He nodded.

"She wants to talk with you inside. Leave your wallet and phone and all your valuables."

He nodded again and walked into the house. It was a cool, cloudy morning, so I waited in my car and turned on the heat.

What were they talking about? I should have told Denise about the spousal privilege rule in court. She didn't need to worry about the prosecution calling her as a witness. But if she was Troy's alibi, *I* might need to call her, which would open her up to questioning by the prosecution.

There was no hurry to get to jail, so I left them alone. After about twenty minutes, Troy came outside. He had changed clothes, wearing jeans and his letterman jacket over a gray T-shirt. He climbed in the passenger side. "Ready?" I said, and he nodded. The first time I had ever driven someone to jail, and it was horrible. Was this part of being a defense attorney?

I got off the main drag and drove slowly through town. Troy was silent, staring blankly outside. As we drove by the high school he said, "I didn't do this. I want you to know that."

"We'll see what evidence they have." I turned down the road for the jail. "The prosecutor seems to be interested in publicity. I bet she's setting this case up for a big press conference. You turning yourself in might take some of the wind out of her sails." I parked across the street from the jail. "Ready?"

We walked into the public entrance, made it through security, and headed for the front desk. My cousin Patrick was there in uniform, sitting on a bench. I waved. He didn't wave back. He looked from me to Troy, who he clearly recognized, and then he stopped his conversation and pulled out his phone.

I made my way to the desk officer and said, "This is my client, Troy Weaver. I believe there is a warrant for his arrest. He wants to turn himself in."

She said, "Just a minute," and typed something into her computer. "Yes, I see it here." Then her eyes went wide. "Oh my gosh... I need to make a call."

I turned to see Patrick coming my way. "What are you doing, Maggie?"

"We heard there might be a warrant for my client, so we're checking in."

Patrick said, "That new chief prosecutor told our chief she was planning a press conference. She had some specific timing in mind for when she wanted the arrest to happen."

"Is that why they didn't arrest him over the weekend?" I said.

He smiled and shrugged. "Above my pay grade." Patrick was two years older than Liam and me, and easily the most relaxed of the cousins. We were all shocked when he became a police officer. With a head nod he motioned for me to step toward him and away from my client. "You always did shake things up, Maggie. You sure you know what you're doing?" He leaned closer. "I don't mean just this case. I mean, being a defense attorney, helping the bad guys."

I glanced backward to make sure Troy couldn't hear me. "No, I'm not sure, Pat." I had expected this from my cop cousins. It was known as "going to the dark side," if you were in law enforcement. I'd gone from a public prosecutor, putting criminals behind bars, to a defense attorney who was—in Patrick's eyes—helping criminals go free. I had shared the sentiment in my younger days, but over time I had learned the importance of good defense attorneys. I said to Patrick, "The thing is, I don't think Troy's your guy. We go way back. I *know* him. He's not a killer." I made eye contact to make sure he got it. "I am going all out on this one, Pat. By the way, do you know where the prosecutor's office holds their press conferences?"

"I don't know," Patrick said. "I don't remember ever seeing one before. Word is, this new chief prosecutor is gunning to be the AG or governor or something." I'd figured that out from the moment I'd met her, and my cousin had just confirmed it.

Another visitor had arrived and stood behind me as if I were still in line. The officer behind the counter said, "It will be just a minute. You can wait over there," pointing off to the side.

So we waited. Patrick stayed with me. "Why don't *you* arrest Troy?" I said. "It's a court order and you have a duty to enforce it."

"Be patient," Patrick said.

Finally, I saw what they were waiting for. Carol Becker came charging through the front door, straight at us. "What the hell do you think you're doing?"

"I heard there might be a warrant for my client's arrest, and we wanted to clear up any misunderstanding."

Carol wore a silver silk blouse with black slacks and she had a smear of cream cheese above her lip. We must have interrupted her morning bagel. I said, "So, is there a warrant?"

She hesitated.

"If not, we will gladly leave." I grabbed Troy's arm as if we were going.

"There's a warrant. Aggravated murder. He is not going anywhere for a long time." To the officer behind the glass she said, "Can we get someone out here to take him into custody?"

Patrick stepped forward, not giving Carol any say. "I'll take care of it. Mr. Weaver, come with me." He put his hand on Troy's shoulder and gently nudged him toward a side door.

He looked back at me and I mouthed a "thank you." I knew Patrick would treat Troy well. I turned to Carol. "We can probably get him arraigned this afternoon."

"You don't dictate my schedule," Carol said, trying to take control of the conversation, but I knew what cards to play.

"Then you could hold a press conference just in time for the five o'clock news," I pointed out.

I'll give her credit. Although she looked like she wanted to curse me out, she said nothing.

At that moment, I had an idea what to do next, and I needed to get back to my office. But I couldn't resist getting in one more blow. I turned to face her. "If there are cameras present, make sure you wipe the cream cheese off your face."

## 12

From the jail I headed straight to my office and drafted my own press release:

*Today, Troy Weaver of Kerry, Ohio, turned himself in to the Donahoe County Jail on an arrest warrant for aggravated murder. The County Prosecutor's office alleges that Mr. Weaver is responsible for the death two years ago of former Kerry High School football coach, Grant Schafer. Mr. Weaver's defense counsel, Margaret Gallagher, expresses confidence that a full examination of the evidence will be sure to exonerate Mr. Weaver in due course.*

I spent an hour searching the web for contacts at TV and print media outlets in Columbus and Dayton, then sent off the presser. It was a trick I had seen good Chicago defense attorneys use to blunt the impact of any law enforcement press conference. If I could break the story on my terms, the media would be less interested in the prosecutor's later press conference. Not that I ever held pressers myself, but my bosses over the years—the Cook County State's Attorneys—would sometimes want publicity. Especially in an election year.

Now that I was on the other side, I could use the trick myself.

Auntie El had connected my thirty-two-inch TV in the reception area and when I explained what I'd done, she turned the TV on to Dayton's Channel 7.

"You should do a live interview," she said. "Get yourself on TV. It'll give you a chance to really get Troy's side of the story out there, and it might help you get more clients too." It was a good idea. I would keep it in mind going forward. The media was going to be all over this case.

Sure enough, at noon we made the news. It was the third story. They used old footage from the murder investigation two years ago and some video of the coach's memorial in the high school gym. The anchor closed the story by saying the prosecutor's office had planned a press conference for 4 p.m. Hopefully, my little gambit would reduce the impact of Carol's show later.

Auntie El grinned, rubbed her hands together, and said, "This is going to be fun, working for you."

---

Sean and I watched the evening news while he seared the tofu in the cast-iron skillet. They had video footage of the prosecutor's press conference, but they followed it up with my statement, which at least introduced the idea that charging Troy might have been a mistake. At the dinner table, Sean explained my strategy to Ian, who gave it a little head nod, like my plan met with his approval. "Do you think he's guilty, Mom?"

This was the most interest he'd shown in my work in a long time. If he was actually curious to learn more about the case, then I wanted to encourage that in any way I could. "He says he didn't do it, and I believe him. But even the guilty deserved representation. It's the only way to ensure the government doesn't abuse its power."

"You used to *be* the government," Ian said.

"Yeah. And I had a lot of power. But there were plenty of defense lawyers who kept me from abusing it. They made me a better lawyer."

"What about the lawyer you'll be going up against?" Ian asked.

I didn't think Carol Becker was dirty. But she certainly was out for herself and any benefit that would come from publicity. "Let's just say, I'm going to enjoy keeping her honest." Ian smiled at that, and I felt as if I'd scored a major victory with my son. We had a nice family dinner, I had helped Troy's cause, at least a tiny bit, and I went to sleep feeling good.

---

The next morning, the clouds and rain came. I put on a raincoat for my 6 a.m. run, only to slip at the end of our driveway and do something to my right hip. I walked back to the house in significant pain, hoping this wasn't an omen for the day. After some oatmeal and a couple of Advil, I showered and dressed, taking my time. Sean drove himself and Ian to the high school and I wanted them to leave without seeing me limp. I had made so much progress since the accident. I didn't want them to have to keep carrying me.

I drove straight to the courthouse—between the rain and my still-throbbing hip, I was in no shape to walk from my office. The arraignment was at 10 a.m. Entering Judge Blankenship's courtroom, I noticed a TV camera in the back with power cables running out the door into the jail.

Media types filled the front bench, including the blond reporter from the last appearance. She stood and approached me. "You're Ms. Gallagher. Thank you for the heads-up on this. Will you be making a statement after the arraignment?"

"Is Ms. Becker?" I said.

"Yes. On the courthouse steps, fifteen minutes after we are done here. Although with the rain…"

I said, "I'll have a statement in the hallway right after we finish."

"Perfect." She handed me a card. "I'm Julie Garrett." We shook hands.

Carol Becker had entered the courtroom and saw me talking with the reporter. She glared at me and muttered something about "hypocrisy."

Two officers brought up Troy, by himself. I guess the judge wanted to handle this case, then clear out the camera and media for the rest of the arraignments. I gave Troy a thumbs-up. He blankly stared back, then looked around the courtroom. Besides the media, there were about fifteen young men. I could only guess they were former football players from the coach's team. Many were in their letterman jackets. They all stood when Troy entered, trying to stare him down. A couple said things I couldn't hear, but it was clear they shook up Troy.

In front of them was an older, gray-haired woman and a bald man. Grant Schafer's parents, maybe? The man had his arm around the woman, who was dabbing her eyes with a handkerchief.

Denise wasn't there.

Judge Blankenship appeared in his black robe and the bailiff had us rise. The judge was all business. "Be seated. Ms. Becker, let's get to it. Call the case."

She remained standing. "State of Ohio versus Troy Weaver."

Troy came forward past the bar and joined me as Carol handed me the indictment. There were two counts. The first was aggravated murder for the coach. That would make this a capital case, carrying the possibility of a death sentence. The second count was child endangerment.

Carol had re-indicted Troy for the shooting of Benny so she could try both cases at the same time.

I stood. "Your Honor, we have received a copy of the indictment and waive reading and advice of rights. In addition, we will be moving to sever the charges in the near future since they are not of the same course of conduct."

"Very well," the judge said. "Do you wish to address custody, Ms. Gallagher?" His tone made it clear he thought it would be a waste of time. Defendants facing the death penalty don't get released.

"Yes, I would." I glanced sideways at Carol and then said, "I have not received any discovery. No reports or documentary or forensic evidence. I would like to reserve the right to challenge Mr. Weaver's detention based on no clear and convincing evidence of guilt. However, at the moment, I would like to request bail to be set at one million dollars." I knew that would sound like a lot to the media, but court rules only required the posting of ten percent. I hoped Troy and Denise had that much equity in their house to put up as collateral.

Of course, Carol knew what I was doing and didn't like it. "Your Honor. Regarding the discovery, this is a two-year-old case, so you can imagine gathering all the evidence for discovery purposes has been a challenge. However, we will provide it to counsel by the close of business today. Concerning the defendant's release, we are requesting no bail. The defendant faces the death penalty for this case, which obviously makes him a flight risk. In addition, we have re-indicted the defendant on a separate charge where the same gun used to kill Grant Schafer was also used in the shooting of the defendant's own son, Benedict Weaver."

Blankenship said, "Ms. Gallagher? I am going to deny your request for release at this time. The defendant shall remain in custody without bail. However, you are free to renew your request once you have received discovery."

"Thank you, Judge," I said.

"Now, let's talk scheduling. Assuming the defendant remains in custody, Ms. Becker, will you be prepared to go to trial within sixty days?"

"We can be ready in that time, Judge."

He looked at me. "Ms. Gallagher?"

"We don't anticipate waiving any rights at this time."

"Then let's set this for a status hearing in two weeks. Ms. Gallagher, you can raise any bail issues you would like then and decide whether you will waive your speedy trial rights. Anything else?"

Carol and I both said no. "Very well. Let's clear the courtroom and then we can bring over the rest of the defendants." He banged his gavel and withdrew into his chambers.

Troy turned to me. "I have no idea what's going on."

I squeezed his shoulder. "It's confusing, I know. I'll come see you in about half an hour and explain everything." I wasn't used to this. As a prosecutor, I never had to explain what I was doing. But Troy was my client, and I didn't just need him to understand things, I needed him to approve of any strategic decisions. Like asserting his speedy trial rights, or even holding a presser.

But we couldn't talk about it now. Not when there were two officers waiting to escort Troy back to the jail. I gathered up my calendar and evidence book and put them in my leather satchel. Should I talk to the media? I'd told that reporter that I'd have a statement, and if I backed out now, it might sour our rapport, making things harder for me if I wanted to reach out later on. On the other hand, I didn't want to do anything that would piss off the judge—or my client. Now that charges were filed, the judge would be concerned with a fair trial and that meant getting a jury pool that wasn't tainted by things they had seen in the newspaper or on TV. And I hadn't talked about it with Troy. These were all factors I'd never had to consider before.

Carol stepped toward me. "I'm not hiding anything. We'll try to get you discovery as soon as we can."

"Good luck with your press conference," I said and brushed past her.

Yeah, I would talk with the media.

## 13

My press conference had been a mistake. At least the way I handled it. I'd wanted to point out how the prosecutor had rushed this, and remind people to keep an open mind and wait for the evidence. But as the questions came, I found myself getting angrier at Carol. "It's hard for me to even comment on this case when the prosecutor's office is failing to comply with basic due process and turn over their evidence."

Behind the media were some of the young men in letterman jackets. As I finished and started to walk away, someone yelled, "Your client killed our coach!"

I turned back. "My client is innocent. This is a rush to judgment and you're all going to eat your words." As soon as I said it, I regretted losing my cool and making a threat. I knew the TV stations would play it.

Oh well. I walked over to the jail and had to wait almost two hours, until they brought Troy to the small legal meeting room in the jail. He squeezed in behind the table, still wearing handcuffs. "How are you doing?" I asked.

"I'm okay." His voice was shaky. "I talked to a couple guys inside and I think I understand what happened today."

"Troy, remember what I told you? Don't talk about your case with anyone. No one is your friend in there."

"I didn't talk about what I did. Just…the process. This one guy said he's been arrested thirty-two times."

"Okay. Good." I leaned back in my chair, trying to exude calmness. Troy was clearly stressed. "Let me tell you what happened today. As long as you are in custody, you have a right to have your trial within sixty days. In cases like yours, defendants usually waive their right to a speedy trial because they need time to do their own investigation. That's really what I want to talk with you about."

"If I waive my rights, how long will I be in here?"

"I've seen cases take over a year."

"I can't do that, Maggie," Troy said. "I can't be away from my family that long." I noticed his hand trembling slightly.

"Here's what I'm thinking." I leaned closer. "The prosecutor and the police rushed this case. I don't think they have all their evidence together. I will know tonight when they deliver the police reports, but I'm thinking we don't waive your speedy trial rights. We force them to trial before they're ready."

"Is that what you recommend?"

I nodded. "For now. We can always change our minds later if we need to, but let's put the pressure on them." Because I was just starting a practice, I didn't have that many clients, which meant I could spend more time on Troy's case. And because I had done murder cases before, I was reasonably confident I could be ready in sixty days, while maybe Carol couldn't.

Troy said, "The judge also mentioned bail."

"We can still ask the court to release you on bond. I've got to be honest, I don't think it's likely. But if it does happen, it's going to be expensive. You'd probably have to put your house up as collateral. How much equity do you have?"

Troy rubbed his forehead like it would help him think. "Not much. We just bought it five years ago when Charley was born and Denise stopped working."

"Do you think you could come up with a hundred thousand dollars?"

He shook his head.

"What about your parents?"

"No." Troy suddenly was angry. "I don't want them to know." He raised his handcuffed hands and pointed at me. "And you don't tell them. No one tells them. I can do the sixty days."

I held up my hands in a surrender pose. "Okay, I won't."

This helped him relax a little. "Sorry," he said. "It's just...they've been through a lot. I don't want to get into it."

"It's up to you," I said, pushing back from the table. But I had one more thing to cover. "I should get the police reports this evening. I will make copies of the important stuff and bring it to you. It's very important that you don't show it to anyone. With your help, maybe we can figure out the mistakes the police and the prosecutor are making." I wanted to give him some hope.

"Thanks, Maggie." He smiled for the first time since they'd brought him in. I stood to leave, and he said, "Sorry again for getting mad there. I know you are trying to help. Do you think I have a chance?"

"Yes, I do. Like I said, I think the prosecutor rushed this, which will make it easier to challenge their case." I couldn't tell Troy what my plan was, because I hadn't formed one yet. It would all depend on the evidence Carol was supposed to deliver today. But I knew I'd be interviewing numerous witnesses. I knocked on the door to tell the officer we were finished. "Hang in there." I gave Troy my business card. "You can call me collect if you have any questions, okay? Don't ask the other inmates."

He nodded and waved the card. "Got it."

―――

Carol Becker did not send over the discovery that night. The next afternoon I got a call that I could come pick it up. The prosecutor's office was on the second floor of the courthouse, in the back, behind the upstairs courtroom. The elected prosecutor, Daniel Jackson, had been in Donahoe County for fifteen years, and he no longer tried cases. He was more of a figurehead, handling administrative matters like budgets and hiring and working with other governmental agencies. I had heard a rumor that he was thinking of retirement, and I was afraid he had turned over the prosecutorial decisions to his new chief, Carol Becker. I asked the receptionist if he was in.

"I'm sorry. He's meeting with the county commissioners today."

"My name is Margaret Gallagher. Do you have some discovery for me?"

She laughed. "Do I have some discovery for you?" She pointed to three cardboard boxes stacked on the floor. Each was filled with files full of documents, about the volume I expected for an aggravated murder case. I asked the receptionist if she had a hand truck.

Nope. So I made three trips down to my car. On my bad hip.

Back at the office Auntie El helped me bring the files in. "Let's put everything in the conference room," I said. "We can spread out there."

We set the boxes on the large oak table. The off-white walls were bare, like the visiting room at the jail, except for one whiteboard. I needed to buy some pictures or something. A window at the end of the room looked across at the old courthouse where a man was out in the rain lowering the American flag. It was five o'clock. Quitting time. "You go home," I said to my aunt.

"And you?" she asked.

"I have fifty-eight days to get ready for trial."

"Okay, I'll be back in the morning to help you." Auntie El started out, and then turned back. "Margaret," she said, to focus my attention. "Don't forget your family."

## 14

I came to the office early, wearing jeans and a University of Illinois sweatshirt, since I had no court appearances and wasn't meeting with any clients. Auntie El was already there holding a bucket that sloshed as she scrubbed furiously at my door.

I looked over her shoulder. Someone had graffitied something that looked like a giant dick along with some words. As a result of the scrubbing, they were now reduced to "urder defend" but it wasn't hard to figure out what they'd originally read.

"Well, that was quick. Would you like some help?" I offered. It wasn't uncommon for people to express their dislike of lawyers, but I had to admit that I hadn't expected to see this in Kerry.

My aunt tossed the sponge back in the bucket and her dour expression shifted to a smile. "I've already called maintenance, and they'll send someone up to paint the door. I just couldn't stand to see it there."

I took the bucket out of her hand and gave her a side hug. "Thank you for trying. It was probably just dumb kids." My mind went to the courtroom filled with football players and I made a mental note to check to see if security caught anything on the building's cameras.

She squeezed my hand. "You're right. Come on. Let's get to it," she said.

As quickly as that, my aunt had shaken off her mood. Her energy and enthusiasm were just what I needed. Last night I stayed at the office late, calling Sean to apologize. "We understand, hon," he had said. "I've talked with Ian about what Troy means to you."

"Thanks. How'd he take it?"

Sean chuckled, "Let's just say it's a work in progress."

So I had felt guilty all night. And then, I'd returned to the office to find vandalism, none of which helped my concentration as I read through the reports, took notes, and continued to think about possible defenses. I had left the house this morning before Sean and Ian were even up, with no run again, because of my stupid hip.

Aunt Louise gave me a mug of black coffee and took a bite of her soda bread. "What can I do to help?" she said.

I had brought some dry erase markers for the whiteboard and handed them to her. "I'm going to tell you what I learned last night. You write it on the board." I took a bite of my soda bread. "First column, write HOW. How was Grant Schafer killed?"

"A gunshot, wasn't it? That's why Troy's gun is relevant. They think it's the same gun, right?"

"That's right. Gunshot, upward trajectory through the neck." I pointed to a spot just below my Adam's apple. "It lodged here, in the skull above the occipital bone," touching a spot on the back of my head. "Slightly left of center."

"Where would the gun have been?" Auntie El said.

I smiled at that. "Exactly. That is the right question. You should have been an investigator."

"I'll leave that to my sons." She came over to me and pointed her finger like it was a gun. "It must have been down here," she said, holding her gun hand down around my stomach, aiming up to my neck. "Either very close to the coach, or the shooter was very short." She pointed at the police reports strewn over the conference table. "Does it say how tall the coach was?"

"The autopsy said 5'10", without shoes. But he had shoes on when the body was discovered."

"Where was the body?" Auntie El said.

"He was lying on the floor in the entryway to his house, which was west of town in Cumberland Heights. The door was open a couple of inches." I sat down, trying to get as comfortable as I could. Going over the evidence this carefully was going to be a long process. "The forensic report indicated there was gunpowder residue on the sleeve and chest of the coach's shirt."

"Any chance it was suicide?" Auntie El said.

I pointed to the spot below my Adam's apple. "Not typically where a person would shoot themselves. And we'd still have to explain how the gun got out of the house. But let's not rule it out."

"You were in the army," she said. "You've shot guns. You know that all kinds of things happen when a person pulls a trigger. He could have flinched at the last minute."

"That's good," I said. "Make a note up there," I said, gesturing to the whiteboard. "*Suicide*. There was no residue on his hands, but that doesn't mean much. I can get an expert to explain that away."

"But the open door," she said. She sipped her coffee and finished her bread. "It makes it sound like someone else was there. And of course, the gun wasn't there when they found the body. It didn't walk away on its own."

"Right." It was nice having a smart person like Auntie El to help me flesh out the facts. As a prosecutor, I would brainstorm with other prosecutors in my office or with the cops. An extra set of eyes or ears could help me avoid mistakes. Here I would be all alone, except for my precious aunt.

"No damage to the door," I said. "If someone entered, the coach probably let the person in."

"Did Troy know the coach?"

I shook my head. "He knew him, but they weren't friends. Troy tried to get him fired."

"Why would he let Troy in?" she said, and made another note on the whiteboard. *Not Friends*. She turned to me. "What's next?"

"The only other piece of forensic evidence came from the autopsy. They found three small yellow fibers under the fingernail of the coach's left middle finger."

"What do you make of that?" Auntie El said.

I shook my head and pulled out a folder containing 8x10 photos of the scene. The coach's body lay on a Turkish style rug, a dark blood stain under him. I showed one of the photos to my aunt. "He landed on this carpet, which is mostly brown and gray. I don't see any yellow fibers here."

Some people flinched at the sight of a dead body, but not my aunt. She came over from the whiteboard to look more closely. "You're right. No yellow in that carpet. So he didn't get the fibers from the rug." She looked up at me. "Maybe a struggle with the shooter? The coach is fighting with the guy...both of them struggling over the gun, and somehow the coach gets some yellow fibers from the shooter's clothes under his fingernail? Then the gun goes off."

I nodded. "Possible. Or the fibers were from some other fabric in his own house." I held up a report. "Just because he isn't wearing anything yellow in the picture doesn't mean he doesn't *own* anything yellow. There's no indication the investigators made any effort to match the fibers with fabrics in the coach's house." I shook my head. "Sloppy police work."

"They don't have a lot of resources," Auntie El said, bristling at my comment. She motioned to all the paperwork. "It looks like they did a decent job for a small-town force." I needed to remember that her two sons were cops and she would defend them.

"They did," I conceded. "But my job is to look for any weakness in the case." That had *always* been my job, though before, I'd looked for weaknesses in my own case as a prosecutor so I could address them before the trial. Now, I was looking to exploit them. The end result was different, but thankfully the skills remained the same. For all that I found strange about being a defense lawyer, this was something I knew how to do. I motioned to the whiteboard, "Write *yellow fibers*, with a question mark."

She did and then turned to look at me. "Anything else?"

I shook my head, and we sat in silence a moment. "So far, I see three possible scenarios. One, a possible suicide. But as you pointed out, the gun didn't walk away. Two, coach lets in an acquaintance, who shoots him, for some unknown reason. Three, coach lets in a robber who shoots the coach after a struggle."

"It's only three scenarios, but it doesn't really narrow anything down, does it? Anyone could have done it," my aunt said. "Was anything stolen from his house?"

"Not that we know. The coach was a bachelor, so no wife to say if anything was missing. The detective asked his parents, but they couldn't say for sure. He still had his wallet on him."

I motioned to the whiteboard. "Let's focus on the *when*. A neighbor said he heard a shot around midnight, but at the time, he thought it must have been New Year's fireworks. The body wasn't found until the next morning. That same neighbor was out walking his dog and saw his door open. The autopsy pegged the time of death as sometime between 10 p.m. and 3 a.m."

"And where was Troy then?"

"He was at a New Year's Eve party at Lefty's from about 10 p.m. until after midnight. Then he went home with his wife."

Auntie El sat down in the chair across the table from me. "He's got an alibi." She was quiet, thinking. "Why did they arrest him?"

"You're asking about the *why*," I said. "What was Troy's motive? The coach was flunking Troy's son in his health class, and he cut him from the football team."

"You don't kill someone for that, do you?"

We stared at each other a moment. "I guess Troy's son was good and had a shot at a college scholarship until he got cut."

Auntie El wasn't buying it, and neither was I. "From what I can tell, all they have tying Troy to the killing is the gun found in his house. The serial number came back to a man from Dublin, Ohio, who bought the gun twelve years ago. It was later sold through a gun show to a woman in Toledo who died three years ago. No records after that."

"How did Troy get it?" Auntie El said.

"I still need to talk to him about that. The gun is the key. We need to know where it came from." But how?

My cell rang and I looked at the number. "Hi, Denise," I said.

"The cops are here," she said, sounding scared. "They're searching our house. Can they do that? They said I could leave or sit here on the couch…"

"Okay. I'll be right there. Did they say what they were after?"

"No. It's that woman from the hospital. That mean detective. She gave me some paperwork. Said they were looking for some clothing." *The yellow fibers.*

"I'm on my way."

## 15

Detective Janice Evans would not let me in the house, so Denise came outside. She handed me the warrant, which said the judge authorized the police to search for evidence of the crime of aggravated murder.

"Can they do this?" Denise said. We stood in the driveway out of earshot of the cops walking in and out of the house. She wore sweatpants, flip-flops, and a fleece pullover, but she had her arms wrapped around herself like she was cold, even though it was a pleasantly warm day.

"Yeah, they can do this. Although they usually do it before they make an arrest. I think they are realizing they moved too fast—indicting Troy before they had enough evidence."

"What are they after?"

"My guess is, Troy's clothing. The coach had some yellow fibers under his fingernails. Did Troy have any yellow clothing?"

Denise looked up to the sky, as if trying to remember. "Sure, I guess. He has a yellow-and-green plaid shirt."

"But he didn't wear that New Year's Eve, did he? I think I remember a black shirt from the pictures."

"Yeah, he wore a black-and-white plaid shirt."

We stood in silence a moment as a cop came outside with something in a clear plastic bag. "That's his underwear," Denise said. "Why are they taking his underwear?" It had some yellow in the fabric, I noticed.

I grabbed her arm and walked her across the driveway and around the garage. "Where's Charley?"

"Still with my mom," she said. "They've been bugging me to talk with him, so I thought he'd be safer if he stayed there. I've been calling him in sick to school, too." She shook her head and pointed down the driveway toward a police car. Eyebrows furrowed, she whispered, "Nobody's talking to my Charley."

"That's right," I said. "You don't have to let them unless they get a court order. And remember, nobody can make *you* talk."

"I know."

We stood in silence some more. I noticed the unkempt neighbor's yard and asked about it. Denise said, "Mr. Cross," and she shook her head. "Nice old guy. He lived alone until he fell and broke his pelvic bone. He's been in a rehab facility for a long time, and Troy's been mowing his lawn." She began to cry, covering her face with her hands. "This is so hard." I wrapped my arms around her shoulders and hugged, wishing I could do more. Her son was in a coma and her husband in jail. How could she even sleep? She said, "There's so much to be done and I can't do it all." She wiped her eyes and straightened herself, pulling away. "I'm sorry. I should be stronger…"

"Nobody's that strong," I said. "Your son and then your husband…" I squeezed her again and rocked gently. I began to tear up myself. "We're going to get through this."

She whispered, "They suspended Troy at work, and our mortgage payment was due so I had to get a job." Then laughing at the apparent absurdity, "I'm the new hostess at Denny's. Come by tonight and I'll get you a free Grand Slam."

---

The prosecutor's discovery included two reports documenting police call-outs to Troy's home. I had wanted to ask Denise about those incidents, but she was dealing with enough at the moment. The reports only documented shouting matches, loud enough for the neighbors to complain. But nothing physical, and no arrests. None of that would be admissible at trial, so I decided to wait.

I stayed around until the police finished their search and Detective Evans gave me the inventory form detailing all the items seized, which wasn't much. A pair of underwear, Troy's yellow plaid shirt and some other fabric items from the garage and Benny's room. None of it seemed important, other than it showed the police hadn't been able to find a connection between the yellow fibers and Troy.

Based on what I had seen so far, I was feeling pretty good about our chances at trial. The primary evidence tying Troy to the shooting of the coach was the gun. I still didn't know how it had ended up with Troy, but there had to be an answer out there somewhere. So when the police finished, I left Denise and drove to jail to talk with Troy about it.

"How are you doing?" I asked when the officer brought him in.

"Hanging in there." He rubbed his wrist where the cuffs had been. "I haven't heard from Denise. Do you know how Benny is doing? And Charley?"

"I just came from your house. Denise said Benny's about the same, and Charley is staying with your mother-in-law."

Troy shook his head. "I want to see Benny. Do you think they would let me out for that?"

"No," I said. "I've never seen that before." Then I got mad at myself when I saw how crestfallen he looked. Maybe I could have been a little gentler in how I framed that. And for that matter, maybe I was being too quick to say it wasn't possible. This wasn't the big city—there might be a little more flexibility to work with here. "Let me give it some more thought," I suggested. "The judge might be sympathetic and agree to have the police escort you there." What did we have to lose by asking? "I'll see about filing a motion. By the way, the police searched your house."

"For what?" He slapped the table and stood up. "I didn't do this. There's nothing in my house for them to find." He balled his fists, turning like he was looking for something to punch. I didn't remember Troy being violent.

"They took some clothing and fabrics. The coach had yellow fibers under his fingernails."

"Don't call him *coach*." Troy was almost shouting at me. "He was a piece of shit for what he did to Benny."

With my palms out, I motioned for him to settle down. "Have a seat. I need to go over some things with you." He didn't seem to hear me, so I stood and grabbed his forearm. "Troy. Look at me. I need you to calm down."

It took a moment for him to gain control. Then he nodded, and we both sat. "I have some questions about the gun."

"I don't even…" He sighed. "Which gun was it?"

This took me by surprise. "You don't remember?" I thought back to when Denise laid out what happened. Hadn't she said that she'd handed Troy the gun after taking it from Charley?

"I was in shock," Troy said. "I couldn't stop staring at Benny. At all his...his blood," Troy's voice shook, "pooling out across the floor. I... I remember holding the gun after Denise handed it to me. I remember taking out the clip and checking the chamber. But the gun itself...no, I don't remember which one it was. I don't even know if I really looked at it."

"It was a Sig Sauer M17."

Now it was Troy's turn to look genuinely startled. "An M17? That can't be right."

"Why not?"

"Because I don't own an M17."

For a second, I just stared at him. "Troy, the gun was in your house. Are you really saying you didn't buy it?"

He'd seemed sure of himself a moment ago, but now some uncertainty started to creep in. "No, I...I never bought an M17. I'd remember that, wouldn't I?"

"Is there any chance you borrowed it from a friend?" I suggested. "You have some gun buddies, right?"

"You sound like Denise. Like they are bad guys." Troy glowered at me.

"Maybe they came over and left it?"

"No. Denise doesn't want them in the house. None of the guys have been there in months."

I took a tablet and pen from my leather satchel and slid them in front of Troy. "I'll need their names and contact information, if you know it."

He took the pen and scribbled out some names. Then he set the pen down and looked at me. "I mean, it doesn't make any sense. Maybe I bought it and completely forgot about it. I've bought a couple of guns at a time at these shows, especially if the dealer was offering a decent discount for paying in cash." He shook his head. "But I don't think so."

I said, "Have you been having any memory issues?"

Troy snapped at me. "Did Denise tell you that?"

*Shit.* That meant he *had* been having memory issues. If Troy was forgetting things, who knew what else he'd forgotten? Had he had arguments with the coach that he didn't remember? Arguments that could be brought up in court?

"She thinks I've changed. She thinks it's stress at work, since I got that promotion last year. She's always saying that I'm too distracted, that I don't pay enough attention to what's going on with her and the boys."

"What do *you* think?" I asked.

Troy sat there looking at the floor for a long moment. "I don't know. It *is* stressful." Troy worked near the county line at a brake pad plant. "I run the inspections unit now, and it's a lot to keep up with. I've got my ass chewed a couple of times." He looked up at me. "I guess it's possible that gun was mine, but I would almost swear it's not. I have similar handguns and wouldn't see a need to own an M17."

My job had just gotten a lot harder. How could I prove that the gun hadn't been in Troy's possession on the night of the murder when even *he* didn't know where it came from? *Work the problem*, I reminded myself. *One step at a time.*

"Where do you get your guns?"

"Gun shows. I go with the guys. There are gun shows all the time."

"Do you know who you bought them from? I mean, are there certain dealers you use?"

"Yeah," Troy said. "There's this guy out of Toledo. I bought most of my guns from him. Good guy. I don't remember his name." He tapped the tablet in front of him. "These guys will remember." He pointed to a name. "Walt helped me buy my first few guns. He might know more."

"I'll start there," I said. I looked at Troy playing with the pen. "How are you doing, really?"

He set the pen down and rubbed his hands down his thighs like he was wiping away sweat. "This place is scary. I can't do a year in here waiting for trial."

"Okay," I said.

"This morning a guy said he played for Coach Schafer. Said he was gonna steal a knife from the kitchen and cut off my dick."

"Did you tell someone?" I thought about the graffiti left on my office door.

"Yeah, right." Troy shook his head. "But I met this kid who hated Schafer too. He said he knew Benny in high school."

I stood. "Don't talk to him about your case, even if it seems like he's on your side. Remember what I said about not having any friends in there?" I picked up the tablet and put it back in my satchel. "Anything I can do for you?"

Troy shook his head, stood, and gave me a hug. "Thank you so much, Maggie. I don't know what I'd do without you." He stepped back. "I guess…the only thing I really want is to see Benny one more time." And he started to cry.

I walked to my car, my stomach in knots. Working as a prosecutor was never this gut-wrenching. Sure, there was pressure to win a case and keep dangerous criminals locked up, but I didn't have clients that brought me to tears. And I never felt the heavy burden of a person's entire future. Troy could spend the rest of his life in prison, or even get the death penalty if I failed him.

Troy needed something to go his way, and Benny was the answer. If I could persuade the judge to let Troy see his son, that might give him hope. That was my next mission.

## 16

Driving home, I was thinking through my strategy when I noticed Village Subs ahead on the right, so I pulled into the parking lot. Maybe Ian and Sean would like a pizza tonight. On Friday nights when I was a kid, Troy's mom often brought home a pizza from this place, and I was always invited to stay. She would usually get a Margherita pizza with no meat and Troy would complain about it. Then his dad would look at me and say, "There's no such thing as a bad pizza, is there, Maggie?"

"No, sir." And Troy would give me a dirty look.

I walked into the restaurant and ordered a large Margherita, then saw my cousin enter through the glass doors. "Hey, Liam," I said, smiling. But my smile faded at the sight of the scowl on his face.

He came quickly toward me at the counter. "What did you say to Carol Becker, the prosecutor? I got my ass chewed."

"What? Why?"

"The chief accused me of telling you about your client's indictment."

"I didn't say anything about you." I glanced behind me at the counter clerk watching us. "I took Troy to the jail and asked if there was an arrest warrant. Ask Patrick. He was there. In fact, he was the one who arrested Troy."

He rolled his eyes. "That makes it look even worse. If I can't trust you…"

"Wait a minute," I said, getting pissed myself. "I have an ethical duty to my client. And I said nothing about how I learned Troy had a warrant. I can't believe your petty little chief gets angry over something like this—"

"Wait a minute." Liam held up his hand. "He's not a bad chief."

"—when what he *should* care about is his detectives running a crappy investigation. I have never seen such poor work."

"You mean, since you went to the dark side?" He stuck his finger in my chest. "Funny how you changed once you started helping perps." I knocked his hand away, and he glared at me. Then he stepped to the counter and asked for his order. While he waited, he looked back at me and shook his head, saying nothing.

When he finally had his bag of sandwiches, he walked out, but not before saying, "Guy kills our football coach and then lets his own kid get shot…and you're helping him."

I was too mad to say anything, so I just stood there in silence, fuming, watching him walk across the parking lot. My own cousin turning on me.

"Your pizza's ready," the clerk said. I handed him my credit card. "Are you defending the guy who shot the coach?" He was about nineteen years old, still with some acne. "My bro played for him." I said nothing. "He loved him, but I thought he was an ass. I had him in health class and he was the biggest jerk... Not that I wanted him killed or anything."

I got back in my car and practically tossed the pizza onto the passenger seat. Starting the engine, I was clicking my seatbelt in place when headlights flashed in my face. A truck was heading toward me driving on the wrong side of the street. I honked at the driver in warning, but it kept coming toward me. Before I could dive into the backseat, it veered away and accelerated down the street—but not before I caught a blue sleeve leaning against the open window. It looked a whole lot like a letterman jacket.

Blowing out a harsh breath, I let loose a string of profanity before putting my car in gear. I had gone over to the dark side, as my cousin said, and it was clear that some members of the Kerry community weren't okay with that.

I drove home with the overpowering smell of the pizza giving me a headache—or maybe the headache was from my anger at Liam's reaction and that damn truck. So what if I'm representing Troy? He's innocent. And Liam's own unit screwed up the investigation with rushed, sloppy police work. And by that glory-seeking prosecutor doesn't know her ass from her hand...

I was in a bad frame of mind when I walked into the kitchen to see Sean doing the dishes. He looked at me with the pizza box and pointed at the clock on the wall. 6:48 p.m. "We already ate."

I tossed the pizza on the counter and went to the fridge. No open bottle of wine.

"We're out," Sean said. "If you really need a drink, I got that twenty-year-old bottle of scotch my dad gave me."

That brought me out of my funk, and I laughed. "I *could* use a drink. It was a bad day. But not that crap." I opened the pizza box and started on a slice. As I chewed, I said, "I ran into Liam, and we went at it. He called me a sell-out for defending Troy."

Sean let the water drain out of the sink and said, "I'm sure it's tough for him to see you on the other side."

"He doesn't need you to defend him," I snapped.

"Relax, Red. I'm on your side." Sean playfully snapped the dish towel at me.

"I know. Sorry." I finished the first slice in record time and started on a second.

Sean said, "This is a tough case, isn't it? I thought we left all of this high-pressure stuff behind in Chicago. Are you sure you want to do this?"

He was right, of course. "It's just, I didn't expect to have someone so close to me get charged with murder. And the investigation is a mess. These next two months are going to be tough, but…"

"But after this case, you'll have another tough case. That's the kind of lawyer you are, Maggie. You go all out. Whether it's to convict someone or defend them."

"After this, no more murder cases. I promise." I finished the second slice and said, "I could sure use a glass of wine." Instead, I pulled out a third slice.

"How's your leg?" Sean said, pointing at me.

"Fine, why?"

"You're not that good of an actress," he said. "And you haven't been running in the morning."

"You're quite the detective." I nodded. "It's my left hip. I slipped in the driveway." I rubbed it, checking for the painful spot. Yep, still there. "I just need a few days of rest."

"No sense pushing it," Sean said. "You've worked too hard on rehab to have a setback now."

"I'll take the rest of the week off."

Sean looked at me a long moment, something else on his mind. "I probably shouldn't tell you this now," Sean said, "but kids at school are talking about this case. Today, a student in first period asked if I was married to the woman defending the coach's killer."

"What did you say?"

"I said yes."

"Alleged killer," I said.

Sean walked over to the pizza box. "This smells good," and he took a slice himself. "We had grilled cheese sandwiches and tomato soup." He took a bite of pizza. "Ian didn't say anything, but I kind of sensed that he might be getting some comments too."

"Great," I said. Kids could be brutal. I had experienced a little bit in school myself. Bullies making fun of my drunk dad, or the beater car he dropped me off in.

Sean said, "Seniors from the football team this year would have been on the coach's team two years ago when he was killed."

I was just about to tell him about the graffiti and the truck driver when my cell rang. I pulled it out of my leather satchel. "Hi, Auntie El. I'm glad you called. I was thinking about those gun shows—"

"Margaret, that's not why I called. I just got off the phone with Liam and, well, I think I need a few days to think about things. About working with you."

"What do you mean?" I was shocked. Where was this coming from?

"Well, we're a law enforcement family. We always have been. Your uncle Carl's father was the Chief of Kerry way back when, back before you were born and... I just don't like being on the other side from my children."

"Liam's the one who's making it about sides. Shouldn't we all be on the side of wanting an innocent man to be set free? Troy is innocent," I said. "And he needs you. *I* need you."

"I'm not so sure about that," she said. Then a little more heated, "Let me think about it a few days, Margaret. You said some things to Liam that...well, family just doesn't say those things." *What about the things he said to me?* I wanted to shout back, but I didn't get a chance. She had already hung up.

I stuffed my phone in the satchel and looked at Sean. "Auntie El just quit." I took my last bite of pizza. "Want to become my investigator?"

## 17

I drove to work and treated myself to an almond pastry and coffee from the shop on the first floor. I was relieved to see that there'd been no more vandalism. When I sat down at my desk and checked my emails, I found one from Carol Becker. One line. "I have more discovery waiting for you." Of course, there would be more after the search warrant at Troy and Denise's home.

I finished my pastry and coffee, then drove over to the prosecutor's office. Once again, I asked the receptionist if the elected prosecutor, Daniel Jackson, was in. "Who should I say is asking?"

"Margaret Gallagher."

A few moments later, he came through the double doors into the reception area. "Hello, Ms. Gallagher. What can I do for you?"

He was early sixties, a full head of gray hair in a white shirt and tie. Very distinguished looking, but also old enough to be thinking of retirement. I shook his hand.

"I wanted to talk with you briefly about the Weaver case."

He stood still, very formally. "Well, as you know, that matter is being handled by my chief prosecutor, Carol Becker."

"Right. I just wanted to discuss with you these press conferences…"

"As I understand it, Ms. Gallagher, you were the first one to issue a press release."

"That is true." I had done it to preempt Carol's presser. "I don't think media attention does either side any good. I will be glad to refrain if—"

He cut me off. "I will not tell Carol how to run her case. I suggest you take it up with her. Is there anything else?"

I didn't like it, but I admired him backing his own lawyer. "I'm here to pick up the latest discovery."

He pointed to the receptionist. "Amy can help you with that." He turned and walked back to the inner office.

Amy watched the whole thing and seemed to have decided to take her cues from her boss. The smile from before was gone, replaced by a scowl. "Your materials are over there." She pointed to a box next to a file cabinet.

I hauled the large box down to my car and back to the office. Probably another thousand pages, way more than I expected from the search warrant at Troy's house.

I set the box in the conference room and made a small pot of coffee. I would need some stimulant to make it through this giant waste of trees. But on the first page of documents, I saw what this actually was. Not the search warrant. These were records from the cold case homicide unit at the State Attorney General's office. I remembered they had taken up this case a year ago and one of the state investigators had recently called Troy.

I had been feeling fairly confident about our prospects at trial based on what I'd seen of the investigation. There simply wasn't much evidence tying Troy to this murder. Even the gun itself wasn't exactly...well...a smoking gun. Yes, it had been in Troy's house, but I hadn't seen any proof that it was in his possession two years ago. And without that, I didn't think there was enough to prove him guilty beyond a reasonable doubt. But this box worried me.

The first batch of records dealt with the firearm. Investigators had spoken to all the prior owners, which included the man in Dublin, Ohio, who bought the M17 Sig Sauer when it was new. The next owner in Toledo had died and her son inherited the gun. He said he didn't want it, so he sold it at a pawnshop. There was no record of the gun after that.

Next came information about Grant Schafer, the coach. He wasn't exactly the town hero, even though the team had had a very good record under him. Some current and former players loved him, others didn't. Some parents considered him borderline abusive to his players. In an interview, a man named Paul Marshall said he confronted the coach after he verbally berated his son in front of a crowd.

The main investigator for the Attorney General's office was a guy named Cameron Hykes, and he seemed to focus on four different suspects. Troy, of course. Then there was Mr. Marshall. The third suspect had been an ex-girlfriend of the coach, and the fourth a teenage girl who had dropped out of the high school after the coach had allegedly abused her verbally in class. All four had some profound dislike for Schafer, but they all had solid alibis.

Near the bottom of the box were the latest reports, the ones from this last week. They were dated after the discovery of the murder weapon in Troy's house. Investigator Hykes had gone back and interviewed seemingly everyone who was at the New Year's Eve party at Lefty's.

Nobody would swear that they had seen Troy there right at midnight, but they also couldn't say he *wasn't* there.

It was the last report that hit me like a punch in the gut. A woman had gone outside before midnight to smoke a cigarette with her boyfriend and she claimed she saw Troy leave the bar. The report quoted her. "It was, like, ten before midnight. I remember because I wanted to finish my cigarette and get back inside. We were standing by my car. I had left the lighter in it. This guy comes out of Lefty's. He's wearing a high school letterman jacket. It caught my eye because I thought it was weird that a high schooler was in the bar. But then I saw he was an older man."

Investigator Hykes had shown her a photo lineup of six men, including a picture of Troy. She picked Troy. "I'm pretty sure it's him." Her name was Kaitlyn Wynant, and she was asked for her certainty on a scale of one to ten. She answered an "eight."

Her boyfriend didn't see the guy.

I went back to an earlier folder that contained copies of the photos taken by people at the New Year's Eve party. In most of the pictures, Troy was wearing a black-and-white plaid shirt. But in one he wore a jacket. His high school letterman jacket. And the letter "K" on the front was yellow.

Either Kaitlyn Wynant was mistaken, or Troy was lying to me.

## 18

I brought the relevant discovery with me to visit Troy and watched for his reaction as he read through the reports. First the forensics on the gun. The computer database had matched the shell case markings from the shot that hurt Benny to the shot that killed Coach Schafer. Then, a forensic expert from the FBI lab reviewed the markings and concluded the same gun fired both shots.

Next, Troy read over the crime scene investigation report. He read slowly as I watched, but he showed little emotion.

Finally, I gave him the statement of Kaitlyn Wynant. He shook his head. "She's lying. I didn't go anywhere." He handed the report back to me without reading the rest of it.

"Why would she lie?"

"I don't know. Maybe she mixed me up with someone else."

I handed him the photos and said, "I didn't see anyone else at the party wearing a high school letterman jacket." Troy said nothing, staring back at me. "What will Denise say when I ask her?"

He crossed his arms. "The same. I never left." He continued to stare at me defiantly, but I could see a slight tremble in his hands. He was scared, but of what?

"My job is to help you, Troy. Everything you tell me is privileged. No one will ever hear it. I need you to tell me the truth."

"I don't know what to tell you."

I piled up all the reports and photos. "It's not your gun, and you never left the party. That's your story? That approach is going to get you convicted. A jury will never buy it."

He uncrossed his arms and leaned closer. "You're the smartest person I know, Maggie. If anyone can help me, it's you."

I pulled out the latest report by Investigator Hykes and gave it to Troy. From his phone conversation, Hykes quoted directly from Troy:

**Troy Weaver:** Like I told you before, I was at Lefty's all night. I never left. I mean… I might have disappeared into the bathroom for a while, you know. Some of that food didn't sit so well.

**Investigator Hykes:** So you never set foot outside until you left for home, sometime after midnight?

**Troy Weaver:** You got it.

Troy read the interview and handed the report back to me. "The guy made it sound like he was trying to help me…but he was locking me into a statement."

"Nobody's going to help you. Nobody but me." I decided to broach the subject I had been avoiding. It was time to get real with Troy. I said, "If they come with a plea offer, what do you want me to tell them?"

"A plea offer? Like what?"

"A typical offer in a capital case would be, plead guilty to straight murder. You'll serve a twenty-five-year minimum, but they'll take the death penalty off the table."

He sagged in his seat. "Twenty-five years?" He went silent for a moment. "Do you think you could do any better?"

"I can try. Are you authorizing me to negotiate a deal?"

Troy's face had turned pale as he mentally wrestled with the idea. Then he nodded.

For the first time, I believed Troy had done it. The gun was his. He had left the party at Lefty's and gone to Coach Schafer's house and killed him. I put the papers in my satchel and stood to leave, feeling a little wobbly. And a little mad at myself. I should have known better. Most defendants *are* guilty of something, and Troy was no different. I looked down at him in his orange jump suit, my childhood friend now looking more scared than ever. Guilty or innocent, he was still entitled to the best representation I could give him. I said, "I'll do my best."

As I turned for the door he said, "It looks bad, Maggie, I know, but… I didn't do this. I'm not guilty. That I promise. I didn't go to the coach's house."

I didn't look at him. I knocked on the door for the officer, and Troy reached across the table to grab my arm. "I know how it looks. But there are things I can't say, even to you. Just…believe me. Please."

The officer opened the door, and I walked out.

―――

I drove back to my office feeling lower than I had in a long time. I had believed in my old friend. And as a result, I had alienated my cousin and my aunt. I had neglected my own family. I had put in countless hours preparing for what? To negotiate a life sentence?

My office felt lonely. I wished Auntie El would come back. I stood looking out the window at the beautiful old courthouse in the square, thinking justice wasn't beautiful. It was cold and hard and difficult, and the system could grind you up if you didn't have others to help.

I needed my family. I felt tears welling, thinking how difficult this move to Kerry had become. But I didn't allow self-pity to rule me for long. Troy and his family were counting on me. Even if he did kill the coach, he and Denise and Charley and Benny needed my guidance. I was good at this stuff. And maybe I was missing something. Maybe there was more to this case than the gun forensics and Kaitlyn Wynant saying Troy had left the party.

Time to get to work. I had promised him I would try to get him one more visit to see his son Benny. So I drafted a motion asking the court to allow a supervised release for one hour and for the police to escort him to the hospital. I had never seen that done before, but it couldn't hurt to try.

When I finished and e-filed the motion with the court, I checked my emails. Carol Becker had sent a demand to interview Troy's five-year-old son, Charley. It wasn't the first she'd sent, but the language on this one was tougher. She said that we could either grant the interview or she would seek a material witness warrant for the kid and force him to talk.

Charley's statement was necessary to prove the gun came from Troy's house. I called Denise. She was working at Denny's and said she could meet me in an hour. "What's this about?" she said.

"A couple of things," I said. "Let's not talk on the phone."

―――――

Denise took her break and came out to my car to talk. She wore a Denny's colored shirt and blue slacks, but instead of making her look bright and cheerful, the vibrant colors just highlighted how she had aged five years in the last two weeks. She climbed in the front seat and said, "This job sucks, and I miss my boys."

"I'm so sorry, Denise. Any word on Benny?"

"I was there all night." She turned to look at me. "The doctor says his vitals have stabilized. They have these electrode things connected to his skull, and they said his brain activity is good." Her eyes shifted, looking out the windshield. "It's not so much whether he survives now, but whether he suffered any brain damage."

"And Charley…"

"My mom…" Denise placed her hand over her heart. "I don't know what I'd do without her. I couldn't keep him out of school any longer. So she takes Charley to kindergarten, then picks him up, looks after him until I get off shift. Charley's been living with her, mostly."

Sometimes the best way to deal with bad news is just to say it. I said, "The prosecutor is insisting on interviewing Charley."

"No way." Her eyebrows furrowed, and she raised her finger. "Nobody talks to my boy."

"She wants to get a material witness warrant."

"I don't care," Denise said. "I'll take him to Florida and change my name. They're not going to ruin another life."

I nodded, sympathizing. I'd do anything to protect Ian. But on the other hand, I didn't want Denise to do anything rash. Especially since leaving town would mean leaving Benny behind, which I knew would break her heart. "We have a hearing this Friday and we'll talk about this then. But I have an idea how we can soften the impact on Charley so it won't be so much of a big deal."

Denise turned her body in the car seat to face me. "Making him relive that shooting... I won't allow it."

I reached out and touched her arm. "I think we can avoid that," I said softly. "They don't really need to know any details about the shooting itself. They just want to know where the gun came from. I may be able to limit them to asking about that. And I am sure I can get a child psychologist to handle the interview, with you and me present."

"Charley's all I got left..." Her voice caught on a half sob.

"And we will protect him. I can argue the best interest of Charley, and I am sure the judge will agree with me. If not," I smiled, "You can run to Florida. I'll help you pack."

She laughed at my bad joke. "If you think he'll be okay..."

"Let me ask you another question. New Year's Eve at Lefty's. There's a witness who said she saw Troy leave just before midnight."

"No." Denise shook her head firmly—almost *too* firmly. "He was there all night."

I put my hand on her arm again. "You need to know that as Troy's wife, you can't be called as a witness against him. But I need to know the truth. If you and Troy have some kind of agreement..."

"I can't talk about this." She turned her body and looked away. "I should visit him," she said with a soft voice now. "I haven't gone once."

"I know it would mean a lot to him." We sat in silence a moment.

Then she said, "I should get back to work." She looked unsure, probably wondering if we were at the level where we hugged to say goodbye. In the end, she settled on formality and reached over to shake hands. "I can tell you are having doubts about Troy. And I am still so pissed at him. Those guns..." She shook her head. "He let Benny get shot, and I'm going to have a hard time forgiving him for that. But you need to know," she said, looking into my eyes, "Troy didn't kill that football coach. He really didn't do it." She squeezed my hand and got out of the car.

Could I believe her?

# 19

This was going to be a busy day in court, so I woke up early to go for a walk. Exercise always helped me clear my head. My hip had been feeling better lately, and I set out as the sun was rising, closing the door quietly. The birds were chirping, it was a delightful morning. I took a route past Troy's house for some reason, thinking over the day to come. Troy's car was in the driveway and the lights were all out. I walked past, toward the middle school.

At 11:30 a.m. I had a plea hearing on Frankie DeNuzzio's case. I had negotiated a good deal. He would plead to a charge of reckless driving and the prosecutor would dismiss the intoxicated driving charge. Frankie would pay to repair the damaged garage and hope his insurance company would reimburse him. He would also pay the homeowner's health insurance deductible for the ER visit, since the man had to pay five hundred dollars before his insurance covered the rest of his hospital bill. That was an unusual term for a plea deal, but paying five hundred dollars was a small price to pay to avoid all the hassles of a drunk driving conviction, especially since Oliver had agreed that Frankie would get credit for time served and not have to do any more jail time. It was my first deal as a defense attorney, and I felt pretty good about it.

The bigger challenge was earlier, at 10 a.m. A hearing on Troy's case. Carol was trying to force Denise to make Charley submit to an interview. I understood Denise's concerns, but unfortunately, the chief prosecutor did not. Carol Becker was more concerned about adding another feather to her cap and furthering her career than with the well-being of a kindergartener.

As I neared the school, my left knee began to hurt, a little pain under the patella. I realized I had pushed myself too hard and started back home. By the time I arrived, I was limping. Ugh! If not one thing, it was another.

Ian and Sean were in the kitchen eating, and I avoided them, too embarrassed to admit that I had overdone it. I stuck my head in and said, "Good morning," and headed for a shower and some pain meds.

---

There were a few reporters in the courtroom, but no cameras. Coach Schafer's mother sat behind the prosecution table and Denise sat behind me. This was her first court appearance, and as far as I knew, it was the first time Troy had seen her since his arrest. He sat next to me and kept glancing back at her, his eyes shimmering as he fought tears. Judge Blankenship called the case, then turned it over to Carol. We had two issues: whether to allow the interview of Charley and my petition for a short-term release to allow Troy to visit Benny.

"Your Honor," Carol began. "Defense counsel has been unwilling to compromise, and that is why we are seeking a material witness warrant."

The judge said, "You want a warrant to arrest a five-year-old boy?"

Carol flushed at the judge's wry tone, but she rallied quickly. "We want to interview him, Judge. Defense counsel and the boy's mother have blocked all our efforts."

"I can't say I blame them, Ms. Becker." He looked at me. "Ms. Gallagher?"

I stood. "Your Honor, we have been willing to compromise. However, Ms. Becker is insistent on some conditions that the child's mother cannot accept. And as I pointed out in my memorandum, a material witness warrant can only be issued when there is a proceeding for the witness to testify. There is no such proceeding here. The prosecution rushed this case to the grand jury, so that cannot be the basis for this warrant. And we don't even have a trial date yet, so that can't be the basis. It is improper to use the material witness statute to force a five-year-old boy to submit to an interview."

"Ms. Becker?" the judge said. "I'm not hearing anything I disagree with. She's right, isn't she?"

"We are prepared to take this case back to the grand jury for further proceedings."

"Oh no," the judge said. "I will not let you do that. Ms. Gallagher could rightly claim that as an abuse of the process." He looked at me. "What compromises did you ask for?"

"A couple of things, Your Honor," I said. "We asked that the interview be conducted by a court-appointed child psychologist, with the child's mother present. We asked that the interview only focus on the location where the gun came from. The child's mother does not want the boy to be asked about the shooting of his brother. We believe it would be too traumatic, and it has no bearing on the murder charge."

Carol argued back, "We need to ask that question on the underlying charge of child endangerment."

I cut her off. "Two things, Judge. One, we have filed a motion for that charge to be severed from the murder case and tried at a different time. Two, we will stipulate that the five-year-old boy fired the shot. Therefore, there is no need for his testimony on that point."

"I don't have to agree to any defense stipulations," Carol said.

"No you don't," the judge said. "But those sound like reasonable requests."

The judge was going my way, so I decided to press my luck. "As part of our compromise, Your Honor, I asked Ms. Becker to agree to allow Mr. Weaver to go to the hospital, in police custody, to spend one hour visiting his son, who is still in a coma."

"I oppose this extraordinary request, Judge. The risk is too great. The defendant is facing the death penalty and is an extreme flight risk. He could have accomplices ready to help him escape."

I looked at Carol and said, "You can pick the date and time. He just wants to see his son."

"We are not agreeing to that, Judge."

"Understood, Ms. Becker," the judge said. "But that's still what I am ordering. You pick the date and time within the next week and give counsel twelve hours' notice. Police shall escort the defendant to the hospital to see his son for one hour."

I glanced sideways at Carol, who, to her credit, was not pouting but taking notes about the judge's order. He looked at me and said, "Ms. Gallagher, are you still willing to go along with the terms of an interview as you outlined?"

"Yes, Your Honor."

"Very well. Prosecution's arguments for obtaining the child's testimony are valid. But rather than grant the material witness order, I will appoint a child psychologist to conduct the interview, which shall be video recorded. Only the mother may be present. I will leave it to you two counsel to decide the questions to be asked, but assuming the defense will stipulate that the child fired the shot on the child endangerment charge, no questions may be asked about that subject." He looked at both of us. "Is that all clear?"

Carol and I both said, "Yes."

The judge continued. "Regarding the motion to sever the two charges, I am going to wait on that. We have a pretrial hearing set for two weeks and I will address it then." He looked at me again. "Ms. Gallagher, is your client still insisting on his speedy trial rights?"

I glanced at Troy. "For now, he is." Rushing to trial wouldn't matter if he wanted to cut a deal, so maybe we could slow things down, but for now I wanted to keep my options open.

"Okay. Ms. Becker, draft up the order and I will sign it. Anything else? Good. We are adjourned." He stood and retreated to his chambers.

Carol stepped toward me. "I'll draft up some questions for the boy and email them to you." Her voice was measured and professional.

I leaned closer. "Did you intend to make a plea offer?"

That surprised her. "I didn't think that was on the table. My boss might go for a true life sentence." That meant life without the possibility of parole.

I shook my head. "I might be able to talk my client into a manslaughter. The evidence suggests a struggle over a gun."

Carol smiled, enjoying this. The judge had granted me everything I wanted, but now she had regained the upper hand. "So that's going to be your defense. Coach grabbed for the gun and it went off accidentally?"

"I got about five potential defenses," I said. "Talk it over with your boss." I turned back to Troy, who was chatting with Denise. I nodded a thanks to the officer who gave Troy a few seconds with his wife before taking him back to jail.

I waited for them to finish, then as Denise walked away, I gently put my arm on Troy's back. "I'll come visit you this afternoon."

He looked up with moist eyes. "Thank you so much, Maggie. I can't believe I get to see Benny again. Can Denise be there with me?"

"I'll see what I can do," I said. This was the Troy I knew, the loving father and husband. I hugged him and said, "Remember, don't talk to anyone."

---

I sat on the bench in the hallway with half an hour to kill before Frankie's hearing. I pulled my notes from my satchel to review the facts one more time.

Another attorney I had seen around the courthouse sat next to me. "Ed Caldwell," he said, holding out his hand to shake. He was late sixties, a little pudgy, and wearing an ill-fitting blue suit. "That was a nice job in there."

"You were in the courtroom?" I asked.

"Yep. I had a hearing after yours. My client is a kid who got overcharged. He's facing robbery one when it should be a misdemeanor theft. A few of us have been having trouble with the prosecutors since they hired that new chief. I liked the way you handled her."

"Thanks," I said. I put my notes back in my satchel. "Carol rushed this case, rushed the entire investigation."

"Well, the murder of the coach is the closest thing this town has seen to big-time crime. Everyone remembers him getting whacked a couple of years ago. And everyone will remember the lawyer who got his killer locked up." He leaned closer like he didn't want anyone else to hear, although we were alone. "I heard she plans to run for Attorney General when the current guy retires. She's looking to make a splash, get in front of some cameras."

"Yeah, she hasn't made a plea offer."

Jim laughed with his mouth full. "Don't expect one. She wants the trial, and all the publicity that'll follow."

I saw Oliver, the prosecutor on Frankie's case, walking down the hall. "Nice to meet you, Ed." I stood up. "I have another hearing."

"Stick it to the man," he said and laughed, which made me laugh. Ed must have been a hippie in his day, a baby boomer protester. I used to be "the man" when I was a prosecutor—the person in charge trying to maintain order in society. Not anymore.

I shook hands with Oliver. "Ready?" I asked him.

"Yes. Although I don't feel great about this."

I swallowed my frustration. I had spent a long hour talking Oliver into this deal, and I wasn't going to blow it now by losing my temper. "It's a win-win," I said. "Proving my client was above a .08 while he was driving was going to be tough. This way, the homeowner gets made whole and you still get a conviction."

"Carol didn't like it," Oliver said as we both walked into the courtroom.

"She doesn't have to try the case...and lose it," I said.

The door opened behind me, and I turned to see Frankie and his father, Dominic. I walked back to greet them.

"Great job," Dominic said. "I told you, Frankie. Listen to your attorney."

Frankie managed a smile. "Yeah, thanks, Ms. Gallagher. I really appreciate it."

"Glad to help," I said. "Step on up here to the table and we'll get this over with."

The bailiff came over to Oliver and me. "Are we ready?" We told him yes. The judge came out and started the plea hearing. Oliver told him the outline of the deal.

Judge Blankenship said, "Very well. Mr. DeNuzzio, please stand." We both did. "To the charge of reckless driving, how do you plead?"

"Guilty."

"Very well. Is there anything else before I pronounce the sentence?"

The courtroom door burst open, and we turned to see the commotion. It was Carol Becker rushing toward Oliver. They whispered back and forth for a long moment.

The judge harrumphed, not looking very pleased at the interruption. When the frantic whispers continued, he finally said, "Is there some trouble, Mr. Altman?"

"Ah…Judge, I've just learned about a pretty significant development in this matter. The man who owned the home which the defendant's car crashed into… His name was Joe Kearney, and he was hospitalized after the accident. Well, I just learned that he has died."

The courtroom went silent for a moment until I spoke up. "That doesn't change anything. While Mr. Kearney's death is tragic, it is not in any way related to my client's car running into his garage last month."

"If I may, Your Honor," Carol said, taking over for Oliver. "We would like to delay this proceeding so we can investigate the cause of Mr. Kearney's death." She looked at me. "We certainly can't rule out the possibility of negligent homicide or manslaughter charges at this point."

This was outrageous. "Your Honor, there are no facts to support any delay. Mr. Kearney suffered a panic attack after the accident. There was no physical impact whatsoever. My client has an agreement with the government, and he has already entered his plea."

Judge Blankenship glared at me. "Because your client entered his plea, is it your opinion that the State is prohibited from adding additional charges?"

"Absurd," Carol said, a little too loud.

I ignored her. "The tragic death of Mr. Kearney has no bearing on my client's driving charge. And further, this is a breach of the agreement my client has with the State."

Carol said, "New facts entitle us to re-evaluate the offer, and we can revoke it any time before it is completed."

I started to speak, but the judge cut me off. "That's enough. Because I have not technically entered formal judgment in this case, I will allow the State to revoke the plea offer and I will allow Mr. DeNuzzio to withdraw his plea of guilty on the charge of reckless driving." He looked at Carol. "I assume you will have to take this to the grand jury if you wish to file additional charges. Let's set this out for two weeks. Either bring your additional charges then or we will proceed with the current charges." He looked at me. "Any questions?"

I bit my tongue so hard it nearly bled. I shook my head. "Very well. Court is dismissed." He banged his gavel and again withdrew to his chambers.

"What just happened?" Frankie said.

I didn't tell him that the chief prosecutor just threw a monkey wrench into his case for no better reason, so far as I could tell, than to mess with me. She had taken over for Oliver, which clearly pissed him off, and then threatened a manslaughter charge, which was ridiculous. I said, "Hopefully this only pushes things back a couple of weeks. I'll talk with the prosecutor in a couple of days and see about getting our deal back in place." I tried to sound as calm and as reassuring as I could, although I was pissed inside.

As Frankie joined his father, Carol came over. "I know what you are thinking, but this isn't personal. If Mr. Kearney died as a consequence of your client's actions, we have a duty to look at the proper charges."

"He had a panic attack weeks ago," I said. I looked past Carol at Oliver, who stood there, embarrassed. No attorney likes to have their case taken away like that. "You file manslaughter on this, and we'll start a malicious prosecution suit."

Carol laughed and walked away. It was an idle threat, and she knew it. The prosecutor had all the power in this particular game, and there was nothing I could do. To Oliver I said, "It's your case, isn't it? Are you going to take that?"

"I don't really have a choice." He shrugged. "She's the boss."

## 20

Over my career I had tried not to burden Sean with the day-to-day issues in my cases, but Troy's matter was different. After dinner, and after Ian had disappeared with mumbles of the need to study for a test, Sean poured us each a second glass of wine. He said, "Something happened today, didn't it? I can tell."

"The judge agreed to let Troy visit his son in the hospital and to use a child psychologist to interview Charley, the five-year-old, with his mother present."

"That's what you wanted, isn't it?" Sean said.

"Yeah. Troy's hearing went well. But I had another hearing, a plea hearing on a driving intoxicated case." I sipped my wine. "The same prosecutor from Troy's case screwed up our deal. She took over the case from the other prosecutor, and she's threatening a manslaughter charge because the homeowner died. I think she's screwing with me because the judge took my side on Troy's case."

"That's pretty unprofessional," Sean said. "So, someone died from your drunk driving case? How bad were the injuries?"

"There weren't any. My client crashed into a guy's garage, but there was no one inside it. The homeowner freaked out and had a panic attack. We learned today that he died, but it had nothing to do with the accident. Just bad luck, although I should have checked up on him."

"How would you know to do that?" Sean swirled his wineglass and took a sip. "What do you think of this? It's pretty good, isn't it?"

I was no wine connoisseur, and he knew it. But I swirled the glass, took an exaggerated sniff and said, "It tickles my nose."

He took a larger sip and said, "I think it tastes like grapes," which made me laugh. He was good at breaking my bad moods.

"How was your day?" I said, feeling bad that I hadn't asked before.

He leaned back in his chair. "No student asked me about your case. But the principal asked for the reading list on my AP class. He said the school board wants to know what we are teaching in the English department."

"I told you not to teach the Kama Sutra."

"Funny." He rolled his eyes. "You know me. I'm about as controversial as this napkin." He held his up in demonstration.

I pointed at it. "That napkin is part of the deforestation of Ohio. You should be ashamed."

Sean had succeeded in getting me out of my own head. The dinner table used to be like this with Ian, back in Chicago. He would talk about school, about baseball—he was a big White Sox fan—and even about girls. The year before we moved he had joined the high school marching band. At one meal he told us about how he only pretended to play his saxophone because he couldn't play and march at the same time. Now he was sullen and withdrawn. How much of his behavior was that of a normal teenager and how much was because we moved here to Kerry?

Sean and I had almost finished our wine when I said, "I'll take care of the dishes." That was when Ian came out from his bedroom, looking like he was stepping out in front of a firing squad.

"There's something I need to tell you, but I don't want you to overreact. It's not that big of a deal."

Sean and I made eye contact, and I could tell that he was as clueless as I was as to what this was about. It made me feel a little better that I wasn't the only one in the dark. I said, "Go ahead."

"Well, my English teacher claims I didn't turn in my paper on *Animal Farm*, although I know I did. She's saying I might need to go to summer school."

"Because you missed one paper? That doesn't sound right to me."

"I knew you'd react this way," Ian said, crossing his arms. "Just because my grade's a little low…"

"Are you saying you're getting an F?" I almost shouted.

Ian looked at Sean. "It's not that big a deal."

"An F's a pretty big deal," Sean said. "You must have done more than miss one paper."

Ian stood before us, shoulders sunk, looking down. "I guess I didn't finish all the reading and didn't do so well on some quizzes… I've been super busy."

"With what?" I said. "You quit marching band when we left Chicago, you aren't playing any sports. How are you so busy?"

"It's not that big a deal," Ian repeated, his jaw getting tense the way it always did when he was angry. I suppose I had to give him points for not raising his voice, but I still wasn't wild about his tone. "I can make it up this summer, the teacher said."

I took a deep breath, trying to calm myself. In the mildest voice I could muster, I said, "Honey, you had almost straight As back in Chicago."

"That's right," he sneered, looking me straight in the eye for the first time all night. "*Back in Chicago.*" With that, he stormed off to his room. I heard the door slam.

When he had disappeared, Sean said, "That could have gone better."

"An F?" I said. "He's too smart for that. Is he even going to class? Can you talk to his teacher?"

"No," Sean said. "I am not sticking my nose in this. It would be completely unprofessional."

"I don't mean getting his grade changed. I mean finding out what's going on. Or is that asking too much?" I'd maybe put a little more sarcasm into that last sentence than I'd intended. Even I winced at how harsh it sounded.

Sean rose with his plate and wineglass. "Watch it, Red. I'm not your opposing counsel, I'm your spouse and partner," he said and walked into the kitchen with his plate.

"You're right. We need to come up with a solution…together," I called after him, but he said nothing, and I felt like a jerk.

I sat there, listening to the sink filling up with water. Sean was starting on the dishes. I wanted so badly to get out of the house, go for a run. But my damn knee… I knew better than to overdo it, especially when I was frustrated.

I needed a distraction or I would sit here and spiral downward even further into anger and self-blame for not seeing this coming. So I poured another glass of wine and headed for the den to work.

## 21

I spent the morning revising the complaint I drafted the previous night. It was for my clients who had been rear-ended in their Tesla: my first ever civil law case. That's why the drafting took me longer than it should have. I electronically filed the complaint with the court and then headed for the jail to visit Troy. We needed to have a serious discussion. The trial was scheduled to start soon, and if we were going to insist on his speedy trial rights, then I needed to ramp up preparation.

It took them almost half an hour to bring Troy to see me. They left him handcuffed this time, for some reason. "How are you doing?" I said. But it was obvious. He was doing poorly. He had blotches on his pale face, and he might have lost ten pounds since that first arrest.

"I'm okay. Any word on my visit with Benny?"

"I'm still waiting to hear from the prosecutor."

He nodded.

I leaned across the table to touch his forearm. "You don't need to answer this now, but I want you to think about it. If we do end up going to trial instead of taking a plea, I'm going to need a narrative for what happened that night. And that means a reason why you left the party on New Year's Eve."

Troy shook his head and pulled his arm back. "That woman made a mistake. There must have been someone else wearing a letterman's jacket." Then he looked straight into my eyes. "They're pretty common around town, you know."

It was almost defiant, the way he stared at me, like we both knew he was lying, but he wanted to show that he didn't care. It was clear he wasn't going to budge on this. I leaned back in my chair. "All right."

"That it?" he said.

"About the witness who saw you leaving? Yes. But I have other questions. I know I keep harping on this gun, but have you thought of anything else as to where it might have come from? If we can show that you bought it sometime after the shooting of Grant Schafer, that would clear you."

"I know," Troy said. "Believe me, I've tried to remember, but I honestly don't know how I ended up with it. Have you talked with my buddy Walt yet?"

"He hasn't returned my calls."

"Walt's not a big talker. Unless he's had a few beers."

"I guess I'll drop in on him at work."

Troy smiled. "He'll love that."

"Okay," I said. "One more thing. We are going to trial in a little over a month unless you waive your speedy trial rights."

Troy said, "You told me not to waive them."

"That's right," I said. "I wanted to put pressure on the prosecutor because I could see that they rushed the investigation. But now, a delay might help me conduct my own investigation."

Troy stood like he wanted to pace, but the room was too small. He tested the door, as if it might be unlocked and he could walk right on out. "I guess if I take a plea, it doesn't matter either way, right? One of the guys in here said prison is much better than this place. If I have to cut a deal, I'd rather be there than here." He turned to me. "The guy also said nobody gets the death penalty anymore."

I shook my head. "That's not true. The governor put a moratorium on carrying out the death penalty, but a jury can still give the sentence. And a new governor could restart executions."

Troy just looked at me, then knocked on the door.

We were done. "So you don't want to waive your speedy trial rights?"

He nodded. "That's right. I've watched you in court. You're better than that other woman. You can get me out of this." The door opened and the officer led Troy away.

We were going to trial in thirty-eight days. I needed to get to work.

---

The Kroger grocery store was five blocks west of downtown. Walt worked as a butcher there, and I hoped he had answers about that M17 Sig Sauer.

If I could show that Troy bought the gun after the murder, or borrowed it from someone for target practice, or any other explanation that put the gun in someone else's hands after the murder, Troy would go free. That would be a *home run* defense. A guaranteed win. But I knew I couldn't plan on that. If I was honest with myself, Troy was probably lying about the gun, just like he was lying about leaving

Lefty's on New Year's Eve. The job of a defense attorney, *my job*, was to create reasonable doubt. To get the jury thinking that it was possible Troy obtained the gun sometime after the murder. I'd clutch at any straw I could find to make that argument.

I walked through the store to the back, where the meat department was, then asked the middle-aged Asian man behind the counter if Walt was working. "Who wants to know?"

"I heard Walt can turn a rib roast into some beautiful steaks. I'll need three."

He smiled. "Glad to be of assistance." He reached into the glass counter and pulled out a nice roast. "Will this one do?"

"Perfect." As he started in on the meat, I said, "By the way, I am representing your friend Troy on his case and I was wondering if you could come by my office later. I have a few questions."

He shook his head as he sliced through the meat.

"It's pretty important," I pressed. "You know what he's going through, right?"

"I know," he said without looking up. "Everyone knows. The coach lived two blocks from my house." He finished with the meat and wrapped it up in white butcher paper.

"What I am looking for is some help finding out where Troy bought his guns. I just have a few questions. I don't expect you to be a witness at trial."

He printed up the price sticker and put it on the white paper. "Sorry."

From behind, I heard a familiar voice. "Walter?" It was Auntie El. She stepped up next to me. "Are you really going to turn your back on a friend like that? Do I need to talk with your mom?" She looked at me and said, "I used to do the books for Walter's parents." Then she looked at Walter. "I've eaten at their table many times. Amy would not be proud of you at this moment."

"I don't know anything," Walt insisted. "I'm not turning on Troy." He shook his head. "I just can't help."

I saw an opening. "Only a few questions. Troy said you helped him make some purchases at gun shows. I would like to talk with those who sold him his guns."

Walt glanced at Auntie El a long moment and sighed. "There's a show this weekend in Columbus. I was going anyway. I can meet you there."

"That would be great, Walt. Thank you very much." I handed him my business card. "Let me know when and where."

He reluctantly took the card and looked at Louise, giving her a "Are you satisfied?" look.

I walked away with my aunt. "Thanks so much, Auntie El. I really appreciate your help."

She took my meat package, looked at the price sticker, and laughed. "You paid a lot for his help. How about buying *me* some meat?"

I wrapped my arm in hers and squeezed. "Any chance you might come back to the office? We're going to trial in thirty-eight days, and I really need your help." I squeezed her again. "And I am very sorry about what I said to Liam. You know how I am. Sometimes I lose my temper."

"You should be more like me. Calm and reserved." She smiled. "I haven't chewed out your Uncle Carl in…almost three days." Then she pointed down the store. "Liam is down there, shopping with his kids. Now would be a good time to put things right."

I squeezed her one more time. "See you tomorrow morning? I'll bring the croissants?"

"Well, how could I say no to croissants?" she replied with a wink.

I winked back, tension I hadn't even realized I was carrying unwinding from my shoulders. And then I walked to the breakfast aisle, where Liam and three little ones were staring at the overwhelming selection of cereal.

"Too much sugar," Liam said. Then he looked up and saw me coming. For a second, he froze—then he gave me a cautious "What's up" nod.

"We like sugar, Dad. And there's free stickers!"

I took the box from his eight-year-old and said, "You should also point out to your dad that this cereal provides one hundred percent of your daily vitamin D needs."

"Yeah, Dad, vitamin D."

Liam took the box from me and tossed it in the shopping cart. "Go find your grandma," he said, and the kids took off running.

We were both silent for a second once we were alone, but I finally mustered up my courage enough to say, "I wanted to acknowledge those things I said…some of them weren't true, and I lost my temper."

Liam snorted. "That is the worst non-apology I have ever heard." He shook his head playfully. "How about this? I, too, might have said some things that could be construed as hurtful. And if that is the case, I express my regret."

I laughed myself, and then stepped close and hugged him. "You win—that was even worse than mine." I broke free and stepped back, getting more serious. "I know it's tough, me being on the other side. But I promise you I'm trying to serve justice by giving my clients good representation. I don't want to see someone guilty go free. I just want the process to be fair."

"Nice speech," he said. "Just don't shit all over us Podunk cops."

"Does your mother know you talk like that?" I said.

"No." He chuckled sheepishly, looking around like he was worried she might have heard him.

I turned to leave, saying over my shoulder, "Treat your cousin right and your mommy won't ever find out."

After paying, I walked out to my Ford. Even before I reached it, I knew something was wrong. Unlocking the car, I set my groceries down and stared down at the flat tire. It was only one. If it had been someone intent on causing trouble, they would have done something to all of them, *right*? I looked through the supplies in back, pulled out the air compressor, and sent out a silent prayer that it was charged enough to work.

The tire filled slowly but I was soon back on the road and heading home. As I drove, I leaned into the fact that some of my family was talking to me again. I also tried to shake off the feeling that the flat tire wasn't an accident. "Not everything has to be a conspiracy, Margaret," I told myself and then shook my head. Great, I was having actual conversations with myself now. Just what I needed.

## 22

Friday afternoon, Walt called and said he wasn't feeling well and couldn't go with me to the gun show in Columbus. But not to worry, he had the name of the dealer who sold Troy his guns. "Zack Raleigh of Raleigh Guns. I can't promise he'll talk to you, though. Gun dealers don't want to get tied up in a murder case."

Was Walt really sick? Maybe, maybe not, but he'd given me what I needed. The gun dealer who might have sold Troy the murder weapon. He said the show was at the Expo Center, which was part of the state fairgrounds north of downtown Columbus. I mentioned it to Sean, and he surprised me. "I'll go with you. It'll be fun. When we were kids, we used to go to the Sportsman's Show with my dad."

I invited Ian, but of course he said no. "Sit in a car all day, so we can go to a *gun show*?"

"It might be interesting. You are going hunting with Uncle Carl…"

"No thanks. I'd rather sit in the library and study."

Saturday morning, Sean and I drove north on Highway 71, getting to the Expo Center north of Columbus about 11:30 a.m. It was fun getting out of Kerry, back to a city. Not that Columbus was anything like Chicago, but I hadn't been on a road trip with Sean in forever. And there was a chance we could find something helpful to Troy's case. What if Mr. Raleigh said Troy bought the gun after the date of the murder? That would be the perfect defense. Of course it wasn't likely, but you wouldn't know unless you tried.

As we neared the entrance, we saw there was a fifteen-dollar charge for each of us, and they wanted cash. I rarely carried cash anymore, but Sean had some. We walked through double doors into a giant, multi-acre room with row after row of hundreds of tables surrounded by thousands of gun enthusiasts. There was the loud murmur of a crowd, and I was a little excited to see what this scene was like. A man in jeans and a white dress shirt came up to us. "Is there anything you are looking for? Maybe I can help you?"

"No thanks," Sean said, moving me forward through the crowd.

"We could have asked him where the Raleigh Guns booth is."

Sean shook his head. "He works for a dealer. Look at all these guys at the entrance." There were at least twenty-five men standing around, watching the door, approaching shoppers as they entered. "They're there to try to steer buyers or sellers to their own dealer's table. They used to do the same thing at the Sportsman's Show."

We moved further inside and started down a row that was over one hundred yards long. On each side were tables with guns, knives, swords, and all kinds of outdoor gear. I stopped at a table full of historic swords. A gray-haired man sat in a lawn chair behind the table. "Excuse me," I said.

The guy waved his hand as if he couldn't help me. "It's my boy's store. I'm just guarding his stuff while he gets lunch. You'll have to wait for him."

"I'm not a sword collector. I'm looking for Raleigh Guns. Do you know how I would find it?"

"We got some maps here," he said, rising from his chair. On the table were some official maps with very tiny print to fit in all the exhibits. He looked over the sheet. "Raleigh Guns, huh? You're in the right row. Go down that way," and he pointed, "Twenty or thirty tables down, on the right."

"Thank you, sir." We wormed our way through the crowd, past a table loaded with ancient muskets, to find Zack Raleigh. Near the end of the row we finally found him, a large man, maybe 6' 4", standing behind two tables filled with handguns and rifles.

"Howdy," he said. "What can I do for you?"

"You're Zack Raleigh?"

He nodded.

"I was wondering if I could ask you a few questions."

He glanced between Sean and me. "Shoot," he said, with no irony.

I removed a photo of Troy from my back pocket and handed it over. "I believe this gentleman bought some guns from you over the last few years. Does he look familiar?"

Raleigh barely glanced at the picture. "No."

"He's my client," I said. "He's charged with murder, and I am trying to track down information about his guns."

Raleigh held up his hands and backed up a step. "I didn't do anything wrong. I have a federal firearms license and I follow all the laws."

"I'm sure you do," I said, regretting how I had approached him. Of course, he would be nervous about getting wrapped up in a murder.

"The weapon I'm interested in is a Sig M17. Troy said he might have bought it from you, but he doesn't remember exactly when. I'm just trying to work that out."

He shook his head. "I don't know much about the M17."

Well, *that* was obviously a lie—but maybe I could use this as an opening to build some camaraderie. I got the sense that Raleigh was the kind of man who'd have more respect for me once he realized I knew my guns. I could still save this, could still get him to open up to me. I just had to play it right.

I stepped closer to the tables. "That's funny, because you have two right here." I pointed to a couple displayed for sale. "And you have the M18." I picked up another. "Here's the P320, though that's really the same gun, before the military modifications." The M17 was the contracted handgun for all the military services.

Raleigh looked at Sean. "She knows her stuff."

I motioned to Sean. "We were both issued the Beretta when we were in the service." I picked up the M17. "Heavier. I would probably go for the M18 if I needed a conceal-carry weapon. I do like the low-light sighting, however."

Raleigh smiled at me, looking markedly friendlier than he had a minute ago. *Bull's-eye.* "Give me the photo—let me take another look," he said, so I did. He took a good look. "This guy looks familiar. How long ago?"

"You sold him a few guns over the last few years."

"Yeah, I kinda remember this guy. He came in with several buddies. They were going over all my stuff. They liked that I didn't push them into anything. And that I'm a legit dealer. Some of these guys around here..." he waved down the row of tables, "some here aren't licensed dealers."

Sean said, "Would you have any records of sales?"

"I would," Raleigh said, "but not here. Back in my shop in Toledo."

I handed Raleigh a business card. "I would greatly appreciate it if you would check."

He took the card and looked at it. "Margaret Gallagher. You said your client killed someone?"

"No. He's charged with murder, but I'm trying to show he didn't do it."

Raleigh took out his phone and made a call. "Hon? Can you do me a favor? I got a lawyer here asking for information about a client. I'm afraid if I don't help her, she's gonna drop a subpoena on me." He looked at me and I nodded. *Yes, I would.* "Can you check for any sales to a guy named …"

"Troy Weaver," I said.

"Troy Weaver. I'll wait." He looked sideways at Sean, who had wandered down to the other table where the rifles were displayed. "You looking for something for yourself?"

Sean glanced at me. "If Ian is going hunting with your Uncle Carl, maybe I'll go along."

I wanted to say, "We're not swimming in cash right now after the down payment on our house and starting my practice, and you can borrow a gun from Carl," but for once, I kept my mouth shut.

Raleigh walked down to Sean, holding the phone to his ear. To Sean he said, "You were in the military? This is the Remington 700P. If you're getting in to hunting…" Then into the phone, "Okay, thanks, babe. You're sure?"

He looked at me. "I sold him a Ruger 10-22 rifle, a Mossberg 500 pump shotgun, which I bought back from him a year later, and a Stoeger M3000 semi-auto shotgun."

"That's all?"

"Yep. I remember him now, 'cause he was a repeat customer. He even signed up for my newsletter. Good dude, listened to everything I said, like he was soaking up as much information as possible. I can't believe he killed someone."

"I don't believe he did," I said, trying to sound confident. "Any idea whether he bought from anyone else? Did he say anything to you?"

"I deal with a lot of people, so I can't say for sure. But I remember he was pretty new to firearms when he first came by. He had several buddies with him, and I explained to them how things work. I always encourage people to buy from licensed dealers so they know they are getting a quality firearm. I think they took me seriously." Then he waved his hand, "But of course he could have bought other guns from anyone." He pointed down the row of tables. "You see that guy two tables down on the other side? He's not licensed. He just loves buying and selling guns." Raleigh stepped closer to me. "And you should know, as long as he is buying or selling to someone from Ohio, there's no law requiring him to keep records." Firearms laws were a complicated mix of federal and state law. But what he was saying was important. It was possible Troy bought the murder weapon from someone else who had no legal obligation to keep a record of the sale.

Raleigh turned to Sean, who was still examining the rifle. "It's one of the most popular deer rifles, but this particular one is fitted with a military grade barrel, which helps suppress the recoil. It's used, but I've test-fired it and cleaned it. Good as new."

"Where are you going to keep it?" I said to Sean.

"I'll throw in a trigger lock," Raleigh said, sensing my disapproval.

Sean looked at me again, and even though he didn't say a word, it was as if I could hear him saying, *So you don't want me to spend more time with Ian and your uncle? I thought that was the whole reason we moved out here.* I could argue back that I hadn't imagined the male bonding happening over firearms, but with everything else I had going on, was this really a battle I wanted to fight?

I said, "I'll be out at the concession stand getting a Coke."

## 23

I sat in the passenger seat, still stewing over our newest purchase. Guns were expensive. And we didn't have a gun safe. And was Sean really going to get into hunting? I strongly doubted it. But what if he did? Was I going to be a hunting widow during deer season? In the end, I couldn't control myself. "How much was it?"

"The thing about firearms is you can always sell them." Sean looked over at me as he turned on the signal and exited the freeway. "If Ian doesn't like hunting, I can get most of the money back."

"How much?"

"Three hundred forty."

It was a lot less than I expected. We sat in silence for a while. I was thinking about guns, how I had learned to use them in the army. They were tools, not evil in themselves, and yet what had they done to Troy's family? What would they do to my family?

The car turned a corner down a narrow, tree-shaded lane. "Where are we going?" I said.

Sean grinned. "I thought we could use a break." He said nothing else, until we pulled into a gravel parking lot by a beautiful, historic two-story house. "It's a bed-and-breakfast. With a hot tub."

"What about Ian?" I said.

"*Relax*," he said. "He's spending the night with Louise and Carl. We'll pick him up tomorrow." Sean parked and turned off the engine. "Unless you don't think we can afford this."

"Funny, smarty pants." I leaned over and kissed him, trying to make myself forget my anxiety over guns. "This is going to be great." If only I could let it be.

Sean held me close an extra moment. "Just you and me, babe. Did you bring your swimsuit, for the hot tub?"

"No."

He kissed me again. "Good."

---

Auntie El was sitting at the reception desk when I came in on Monday. "What are we working on today?" she said, picking up like nothing had changed. I was so glad to see her, I walked around the desk and gave her a big hug.

Coming in, I wasn't sure how things would be between us, so I'd stopped at the patisserie downstairs. When in doubt, French baking could be counted on to make everything better. "I brought pastries," I said, handing her the white bag of almond croissants.

"Beautiful." She looked in the bag. "Four? You must be hungry." She took a bite and pointed to the coffeepot on the counter across the room.

I poured a cup and pulled a chair up to her desk. "How good are you on the computer?" I asked. "I need an investigator, but I don't think Troy and Denise can afford it."

"You want me to snoop online?"

"Yes." I went into the conference room and came out with a police report from the case file. "This is a list of everyone at Lefty's on the night of the murder. You know a lot of folks in town, and I wondered if you could, you know, check on what they've been saying."

She lit up. "You mean on Facebook or Instagram?" she said, a big smile on her face. "I can do that."

"I don't want you to hurt any of your relationships. Some people might be sensitive if you ask to follow or be friends with them and they think you're just doing it for the case."

"Don't worry about that," she said, smiling. "I'm an expert."

I gave her the report, and she glanced over the list. "There must be thirty people here." She looked up at me. "And I already know a lot of them." I was counting on that. Auntie El knew seemingly everyone in town and could be my secret weapon. She would be invaluable when it came time to pick a jury. She turned on her computer and took another bite of pastry. "What am I looking for?"

"Photos, for one. The police have a bunch of photos taken that night, but I bet they don't have all of them. Anyone wearing a letterman jacket, any picture with Troy or Denise. But also, any comments about the case. I'm sure Troy had some friends there. Maybe he said something to them."

She said, "I know what you're thinking. If we can show Troy never left the party, he's innocent, right?"

"If we could show that," I said, "we win."

"But if someone else shot the coach, how did Troy end up with the gun?"

"Maybe a robber broke into the coach's house, they fought over the gun...or maybe there was no fight and the guy just shot the coach. Then the robber sells the gun to a pawnshop, or at a gun show and Troy buys it."

She pointed her pastry at me. "Liam and Patrick say that most murders are by someone who knows the victim."

"Almost always," I said, sitting down again. "I'm not ruling out the idea that it could have been a random robbery—but it's not the most likely option. The police had four suspects who knew the coach and might have had a motive. In addition to Troy, there was another father who was also upset with the coach. The other dad's name was Paul Marshall."

Auntie El frowned. "I don't know him."

"The cops also looked at the coach's ex-girlfriend. But she had a good alibi. So did Marshall."

Auntie El typed on her keyboard a moment, starting her search. Then she said, "You said there were four suspects."

"Yeah. The fourth was a high school girl who was verbally abused by the coach in health class. Apparently, it got pretty extreme. Ava something."

"Ava Robbins?"

"That's the name," I said. "Do you know her?"

"I know her father. He drove the combine for Carl a couple of years ago during harvest when your uncle was having some dizzy spells." Auntie El turned back to her computer. "Here. She's on Instagram... but it's a private account. Should I ask to follow her?" Auntie El looked up at me. "That's kind of weird, an old lady following a young woman."

"Let's wait on her," I said. "She wasn't really a serious suspect. I think she was out of town, or had some other good alibi." I stood and refilled my mug with coffee. "We'll look into her if we get desperate. For now, focus on the people at Lefty's."

I headed for my desk. "What are *you* working on?" Auntie El said.

"I need to draft some questions for the psychologist. She's going to interview Troy's younger son, Charley. The judge ordered it, but I want to make sure we protect him as much as we can."

I shut the door to my office and went to work. I came up with a bare-bones list, knowing Carol would want to ask a hundred questions. In my email to Carol, I also asked when Troy could visit Benny in the hospital. She had not gotten back to me since the court ordered the visit last week.

When I had developed a draft of my questions, I walked back to the outer office. "How's it going?" I said to Aunt Louise.

"Come, take a look."

I walked behind the reception desk to look at her computer screen. "I found a ton of photos from that party." She had copied over twenty pictures onto a PowerPoint slide show. "These are the ones I thought you should look at." The pictures were mostly showing Troy, Denise, or both of them. Troy was not wearing his letterman jacket. They looked like they were having a good time. The last photo showed Troy in the background, now wearing his letterman jacket and holding a phone. He did not look happy in this one, but those around him did. Everyone else was holding a drink.

I said, "Can you tell what time this was taken?"

"No. But I can tell you who took it." She switched over to a Facebook page. "Joyce Entwhistle posted it. You might have known her in high school. She'd be a few years older than you. I don't remember her maiden name."

I shook my head. "I don't know any of these people." It hit me at that moment that I was an outsider, even though I grew up here in Kerry. Nobody knew me and I didn't know anybody. Even back in Chicago, I didn't really connect with neighbors or members at our church. I had focused mostly on my career and Ian and Sean.

And yet we had moved here for family, and to connect with the community. I needed to start making more connections. Join some organizations, maybe the Chamber of Commerce... Except there was only a month until trial. My social life was going to have to wait.

The phone rang and Auntie El answered. "Gallagher Law Office." I liked the sound of that.

"Oh, hi, Mr. DeNuzzio. Let me see if she is in." She covered the mouthpiece and said, "Are you? He sounds angry."

"I'll take it in my office." I went back to my desk and took the call. "Hi, Dom."

"What the hell is going on, Ms. Gallagher?" He was loud, and I held the phone away from my ear. "I just heard they arrested Frankie. His girlfriend said they charged him with murder or something."

"Slow down, Dom. Who told you this?"

"I just told you, his freakin' girlfriend. He was driving his tow truck, and the cops stopped him, took him down with guns drawn and everything. They could have taken him out to the reservoir and shot him, for all I know..."

"Nobody shot him." I paused a moment to think. Unless Frankie had gone out and committed some other assault I hadn't heard about, this had to mean that there was new evidence suggesting that the homeowner's panic attack after the accident was linked in some way to his death. It still seemed like a stretch to call that murder, though. "That prosecutor must have gone back to the grand jury and charged him with negligent homicide, or manslaughter, maybe."

"That's insane. Frankie didn't do anything wrong."

"It is insane," I said. "I am heading to the jail right now and I'll get to the bottom of it."

"I can't do it," Dom said. He was silent a moment. "I can't afford to pay for a murder defense. That's gonna cost thousands, tens of thousands."

I said, "Let me find out what's going on. We'll worry about the money later. I will call you when I know more." I hung up and walked back out to Auntie El. "They charged Frankie with some type of homicide."

"Oh my gosh," Auntie El said. "Is there anything I can do?"

"Not with Frankie." I pointed to her computer. "Could you call Joyce Entwhistle and see if she has a time stamp on that photo?"

"You think it might mean something?"

I nodded.

"Good or bad?"

"Bad, I'm afraid. But either way, I need to know."

―――

Dom DeNuzzio was pacing inside the public entrance to the jail when I arrived. "What took you so long?"

I ignored him. "Is he being booked?"

Dom pointed to the officer behind the bulletproof glass. "She won't tell me."

I walked over to the woman. "I am Frankie DeNuzzio's attorney. Can you tell me what is going on?"

She looked at me a moment, clearly deciding whether to help. As a prosecutor, I was used to law enforcement readily cooperating with me. But back then, we had been on the same side. That wasn't the case now. "Just a minute," she said, typing into her computer. "He's being booked."

"Charges?" Dom had come up behind me.

"Manslaughter," the officer said.

Dom shouted, "You people are insane! He didn't do anything wrong."

I pulled Dom away from the counter. "Come with me," and I walked him over to a bench by the wall. I looked at my watch—almost 4 p.m. "He's going to have to do another night in jail. Tomorrow I'll see about bail and we'll figure this out."

Dom started toward the counter. "I can't let this happen."

I grabbed his arm and held him. "Give me twenty-four hours. Once I get the discovery and the autopsy report, I'll have a good idea what we're facing." He tried to pull away, so I dug my nails into his arm. "Dominic DeNuzzio," I barked out, like a teacher chastising a student, "this won't help your son. I need you to get control of yourself."

He finally made eye contact with me. His eyes looked wide, panicked, like a spooked horse. I wasn't even sure my words were getting through to him. But then he took a deep breath, let it out slowly, and nodded. I wrapped my arm around his shoulder. "Go home. There's nothing you can do tonight. Come back tomorrow at 10:30 a.m. That's when he'll be arraigned, and we'll get some answers." He just stared at me. "All right?" I said, and finally he nodded.

He mumbled something as he walked out through the double glass doors, but I didn't catch it. I just hoped he wasn't talking himself into going out for a couple of drinks. The last thing I needed was for him to get hauled in for drunk driving or drunk and disorderly behavior.

Now I had two clients charged with homicide. This charge on Frankie was garbage, however. Tomorrow I'd talk with the prosecutor on the case, Oliver. Maybe I could talk some sense into him.

Secretly, I doubted I'd be able to get him to back down. Because I had a feeling I knew what was going on. The chief prosecutor, Carol Becker, was behind this, and she wasn't going to let Oliver do anything that might make my life easier.

## 24

Frankie was arraigned the next morning. Carol Becker wasn't there, only Oliver. Before the judge entered the courtroom, I stepped to Oliver at the counsel table, trying to sound collegial. "What's going on with this, Oliver?"

He handed over the autopsy of Joe Kearney, the homeowner who had a panic attack and who had, apparently, died two weeks later. "Heart attack," Oliver said. "The pickup crashing into his house was the proximate cause of his death."

I quickly scanned the report. I was familiar with how autopsies were organized. Near the end, the pathologist would write the cause of death. I pointed to the relevant section. "Myocardial infarction." I looked at Oliver. "The man had a heart attack two weeks after the accident."

"Read earlier in the report," Oliver said. "He says what they thought was a panic attack may have been a mild stroke, or a heart-related event, which could have been the proximate cause of his later death. Led to his death."

"*Could* have been? You know that's ridiculous," I said. "You couldn't even persuade a civil jury on that theory, let alone prove it beyond a reasonable doubt."

He shrugged. "I'm sorry, Margaret." And he seemed to mean it. He looked tired, stressed—definitely not the look of a guy who thought he had victory in his pocket. It appeared he wasn't relishing the idea of trying this case either.

"You know I'm going to win this on a motion for acquittal before it even gets to the jury. All it's going to do is drive up my billable hours and cost my client a ton of money."

The judge entered, and my case was called first. It took twenty seconds to arraign Frankie on the reckless driving and manslaughter charges, and then I moved for his outright release with no bail. I told the judge about the autopsy report and the cause of death. He looked at Oliver. "Is that right, Mr. Altman? Manslaughter for a heart attack that happened two weeks after the accident?"

Oliver stood. "Ah, Your Honor, there are additional facts. We expect to show that the accident started a chain of events that led to the death, and was therefore the proximate cause." Oliver looked backward to the audience, where a younger man and older woman were watching intently. They must have been Mr. Kearney's family. What a horrible mistake this was to lead the family on, to make them think Frankie killed their loved one.

Judge Blankenship looked at me. "Ms. Gallagher, can your client post $1,000?"

I looked back at Dom, who nodded. I said, "Yes, Your Honor."

"Very well. Mr. Altman, call the next case."

I turned to Frankie. "You'll be out within the hour. Your dad will post the bail." I packed up my leather satchel. "Call my office and set up an appointment so we can go over this." I was wondering whether Frankie and Dom could pay for a defense on a manslaughter charge. If not, I would have Frankie apply for a court-appointed attorney. I felt for them in this tough situation, but I was in business, after all, and couldn't keep taking on charity cases. Troy's was enough for now.

Now I needed to get to the police station for the interview of Charley.

―――――

Liam had agreed to meet me at the public entrance to the station. I was standing with Denise and Charley when he came out. "Follow me," he said. I wanted to meet the psychologist before Carol Becker and the lead detective arrived, so I had asked her to come early. We walked past some office cubicles where detectives were working and then past a locker room. Finally, we arrived at the hallway outside the interrogation rooms.

"Thanks, Liam," I said. "I owe you."

"Yes, you do," he said and walked away.

The psychologist was unpacking her briefcase inside a bare white room. She was about my age, wearing jeans and sneakers and a light blue collared shirt. Her hair was brown, with streaks of gray in a short cut, and she wore large, framed glasses. She looked kind, which was a good start. And I liked that rather than introducing herself to me, her first move was to squat down to meet Charley. "Hi, I'm Carla," she said, shaking his hand. "What's your name, young man?"

"I'm Charley." He didn't shake her hand, hugging his mom's leg.

I introduced myself, then said, "Do you have the questions, Carla?"

"I do," she said. "We're in here." She pointed to the room behind her. To Denise she said, "Can you take Charley in there? I'd like to spend some time with him before we begin." She pointed to the next door down the hallway. "And you're in there." She walked in behind Denise and Charley and closed the door in my face. So much for getting to talk with her.

The next room had a glass window looking into the interview room. I assumed it was mirrored on the other side so they couldn't see us watching. Charley and the psychologist were already talking, with Denise sitting next to Charley.

A couple minutes later, Carol Becker arrived with the lead detective, Janice Evans.

"What are you doing here?" Carol said, surprise clear in her voice.

"This is the place, isn't it?" I said, innocently.

I could tell that Janice didn't like it either. "Who let you in?"

I wasn't about to give up Liam. "You have a friendly department here," I said, and led them into the observation room. Janice set up the video camera as Carol and I stood in uncomfortable silence. We could see the psychologist chatting away with Charley around a metal interrogation table, trying to build a rapport and put him at ease.

Carol and I had battled over the questions to ask Charley. She continued to insist on asking about the shooting of Benny, so last evening I made her come with me to Judge Blankenship's chambers. He had not been happy.

"My order was clear, Ms. Becker. We don't need to make a five-year-old boy relive the experience of shooting his brother." He looked at me. "Ms. Gallagher, you are stipulating to that fact, correct?"

"Yes, Your Honor."

He picked up his gym bag. "There is nothing else, I assume? I am late for my Pilates class."

Another battle won. Having the judge recognize me as the reasonable one in this litigation would be helpful when we got to trial, but I didn't like the growing evidence that Carol was too stubborn to back down without being forced, even when she knew she was in the wrong. Going up against her was going to be exhausting. Honestly, it already was.

Carol and I had settled on twenty-five questions, but the shooting and aftermath were out of bounds.

Detective Janice finally finished messing with the video camera. She turned a volume dial on the wall and the psychologist's voice became louder.

"So you like orange?" She said. "I always get chocolate, myself."

"I like chocolate too," Charley said. "Chocolate milk is my favorite."

Janice knocked on the window. Apparently, that was the sign to begin. The psychologist had been smiling and nodding during the entire introduction period, trying to put Charley at ease. It seemed to have worked.

"Okay, Charley. Like I said before, I am going to ask you some questions. And remember, you promised to try to answer as best as you can. Right?"

Charley nodded. Here in the viewing room, Carol said, "She needs to make him answer out loud."

"No she doesn't," I said. "That's why we have video."

The psychologist said, "Charley, do you have any pets?"

"I had a pet turtle, but he died. Mommy said we could get a dog someday." He looked up at Denise. "You said that."

"That's right, honey. Not right now, but we will." Denise glanced at the two-way glass.

The psychologist said, "Can you tell me how old you are?"

"Five."

"And are you in school?"

Charley nodded.

"Are you in kindergarten?"

He nodded again.

"Okay." The psychologist looked at the printed-out questions. They didn't give her much leeway to soften things if Charley reacted poorly. She said, "Is your dad Troy Weaver?"

Charley nodded.

"Do you know what a gun is, Charley?"

"Yes, my dad has some. I've seen him with them."

"Have you ever touched one?"

Charley nodded and looked at his mom.

"How many times?"

He shrugged, then looked up at us behind the mirrored window. I sensed he knew what was going on. Hopefully, Denise had made it clear to him that he wasn't in trouble. If he got scared and stopped talking, things could get out of hand.

"Do you remember the last time you touched a gun?"

Almost imperceptibly, Charley nodded again.

The psychologist looked at the window and said, "Can you answer out loud, Charley?"

He nodded. "Yes."

"Do you remember where the gun came from?"

Carol stood and said, "That's not the question. It's not whether he remembers—" But the psychologist could not hear us.

Charley said, "Is this about Benny?"

Denise reached over and took his hand. "Yes," she said. Her other hand came up to her face to hide her emotion. Denise was on the verge of tears, even if she was doing her best to hide them from Charley.

"The gun," Charley said. "You took it from me."

"That's right, honey." Denise was now stroking his hair. She said, "Do you remember where it came from?"

Charley stood up and looked at the window. "I don't want to talk about it." Then he climbed in his mother's lap and buried his face in her chest. She squeezed him tight.

The psychologist looked at us again and held up her hand, telling us to give her some time. They sat silently for a couple of minutes. Carol motioned for Janice to tap the window and get things going, but Janice shook her head. "Give her a chance."

After another minute, the psychologist said, "I know this is hard, but can you tell me where the gun came from?"

Charley's face was still in his mom's chest. The back of his head shook "no" in response.

"This is important, Charley. Where did you get the gun?" Denise gently lifted his head and turned him to face the psychologist. Tears ran down his face. He mumbled something we couldn't understand. "I need you to say it a little louder, Charley."

He was crying now. Denise's eyes were wide, and she looked right at me through the mirrored window as if she could see me. I could feel myself tearing up, seeing the pain in her eyes as her boy suffered. One boy in a coma, the other facing lifelong scars from the whole experience and from this interrogation. And there was nothing she could do. Nothing I could do, either, no matter how badly I wanted to help. I glanced sideways at Carol and Janice. Neither betrayed any emotion.

Denise squeezed Charley tight to herself and whispered into his ear. Between sobs, Charley said, "Garage."

With that, Denise stood and said, "You got what you wanted. We're done here." Then she walked out the door carrying Charley.

Carol turned to me, frowning. "I'm going to need you to bring him back. We have more questions."

"You got what you needed," I said, and started to leave.

Carol took a confrontational pose. "You don't get to tell me what evidence I need."

I would not put Charley and Denise through this again. If she refused to back down, she could take it up with the judge and we could fight it out in court.

I said nothing and walked out of the room.

## 25

I was surprised that Kaitlyn Wynant was willing to talk with me. She was the young woman who had seen Troy leave Lefty's in his letterman's jacket on New Year's Eve. Witnesses for the government are often hesitant to talk with defense counsel, afraid that anything they say might come back and embarrass them under cross-examination. And I was shocked to learn that Carol Becker had not yet met with her. Kaitlyn might be the prosecutor's most important witness, and I needed to zero in on the details of her testimony to find out how damaging she really was. If we were lucky, I might learn something that would help Troy.

She worked at a tanning salon in a strip mall northeast of town and agreed to meet me at the Starbucks across the street. She was waiting for me at the door when I arrived: early twenties, slender, with long brown hair, a delicate ring in her left nostril, and, no surprise, a great tan. We went inside and got in line to order.

"There was this guy from the Attorney General's office who talked to me," Kaitlyn said. "I have his card somewhere."

"Was the investigator named Cameron Hykes?" I said.

"Yeah, that's it. He was pretty excited when I told him what I saw."

"What *did* you see?"

"A guy in a letterman jacket leaving Lefty's."

I said, "How did you know who it was? That was a year and a half ago."

The barista interrupted and asked for our order. She was a teenager with dyed black hair and pale skin. Not the full gothic look, but almost there. "My treat," I said to Kaitlyn.

"Sweet, thanks," Kaitlyn said. "I'll have an iced cappuccino."

The barista rolled her eyes. "You mean an iced latte? There's no such thing as an iced cappuccino."

"Whatever," Kaitlyn said. She glanced at me, and I could sense her face getting red even under that tan. "They give me an iced cappuccino in Dayton, no problem."

The barista ignored her and looked at me, not saying anything, just waiting. "An iced cappuccino sounds good," I said.

"Of course it does," she said with as much attitude as Ian might give. I didn't let it bother me. Having a teenager was great practice when it came to ignoring sarcasm. "Name?"

"Sunshine," and I handed over my credit card to let the goth barista with the attitude tap it against the reader. Kaitlyn and I walked to the end of the bar to wait for our drinks.

"That was funny," she said. "Ordering what I got. Do you like iced cappuccinos?"

"I've never had one," I said. "But I didn't like her giving you a hard time."

"And your name… Sunshine. It's not Sunshine, though, is it?"

"No. Margaret. You can call me Maggie."

"That's right, Maggie. You told me your name when you called. Well, that was beautiful, Maggie."

"Thanks," I said. "If you don't mind my asking, how old are you, Kaitlyn?"

"I'm twenty-three. I got this job after high school. Then I went to beauty school for a while. But I'm a beauty school dropout." She smiled, humming a few bars of the song from *Grease*. Then her smile faded and she turned more serious. "I knew Coach Schafer. I had him for health class. He was kind of an ass. He made us call him Coach Schafer even in class…not that being an ass meant he deserved to get shot."

I said, "So you were twenty-one that New Year's Eve at Lefty's. Were you drinking?" This would be important if I needed to cast doubt on her testimony at trial.

"Yeah. I had just turned twenty-one about a month before—December 7th. It was my first New Year's Eve in a bar."

"You don't look like a beer drinker," I said.

"No, I hate beer. Ethan loves it. I drink cosmos."

"Is that what you had that night?"

"Yeah, a couple cosmos, some champagne. When the clock struck twelve, they passed around champagne bottles. It was free…after we paid the party fee. Thirty bucks each. So Ethan and I were like, we need to get our money's worth. We drank about half a bottle ourselves."

"Sunshine?" said another barista behind the counter.

I got our two iced cappuccinos, and we found a table by the window.

"How'd you feel the next morning?" I said.

"Shitty." She sipped the straw in her drink. "I was still living with my parents at the time and Dad was outside with his chainsaw cutting up a tree that had fallen in the last storm. It was like, 8 a.m. and I was like, what is he doing?"

I took off the lid on my own drink and sipped. "Hey, this is good."

Kaitlyn smiled and shrugged modestly.

"So that night, you went outside to smoke a cigarette with Ethan?"

"Yeah. Actually, we went outside to make out a little…and smoke a cigarette." She smiled, knowingly.

I chuckled and nodded. "I remember those days. Did you see the guy in the letterman jacket after you fooled around or before?"

She leaned a little closer. "I shouldn't be saying this, but…I mean, it's really important, right?"

I nodded.

"Well, Ethan was, kind of, kissing on my neck, you know? When I saw the door open and this guy comes out, I was a little worried he'd see us."

"*Did* he see you?"

"No," Kaitlyn said. "He walked over to a car and got in."

"Did you notice what kind of car?" I said.

She shook her head, leaned back in her seat, and sipped on her straw.

"Did he drive away?"

Kaitlyn looked up at the ceiling for a moment. "I kind of stopped paying attention once I realized he hadn't seen us." She smiled widely. "I told Ethan it was okay."

"And you went back to fooling around?"

"Uh-huh."

"How did you know it was Troy Weaver?" I said.

"I didn't. I saw his picture on TV later when that whole thing happened with his son getting shot, and then that cop from Columbus came and showed me some pictures and I picked him out."

"After you saw his picture on TV?"

"Yep."

I said, "Is it possible the guy in the letterman jacket went out to his car to get a lighter or something else, and went back inside? Like you told the investigator *you* did?"

Kaitlyn said, "Is that what I told him?"

I nodded.

"Well, that's how I got Ethan outside. I said, 'Let's go have a smoke.' But we never did."

"What about the letterman jacket guy? Did you see or hear him go back inside, maybe?"

Kaitlyn stirred her drink with the straw, then took another sip. "No, I never saw him again. I guess he could have come back in. We were out there, I don't know, maybe another five minutes. It was freezing cold, so we could only stay out so long. And Ethan started getting handsy…"

I laughed. "So you cut him off?"

"Yeah. It was like, only our third date. I said, 'I'm getting cold. Let's go back inside.'"

"Are you sure the guy you saw was wearing a Kerry High letterman jacket?"

"Oh yeah. I'm sure about that. I thought it was weird this forty-year-old guy wearing a high school jacket."

"Do you remember seeing him inside Lefty's once you went back inside?"

Kaitlyn looked at the ceiling again. "No. There were, like, fifty people there, maybe more. And to be honest, I wasn't paying attention to the old people there. We had a bunch of friends back in town from college and stuff, so it was a big party night for us." She slurped on her drink until it was gone.

"So the guy in the letterman jacket could have come back inside before or after you did and you wouldn't have known?"

"Yeah, probably. Like I said, I wasn't paying attention to the old folks. I told my friend McKenna about Ethan and me. She was into this guy named Jared... You don't want to hear about all of that stuff, though. I'm just saying, we were off in the corner, kind of in our own little world. I wasn't watching the door."

"I get it," I said. "I was twenty-one once." I took a long sip of my drink. It really *was* good. "Thank you for your time, Kaitlyn. You know I am probably going to ask you these types of questions at the trial next month."

"So you think I'm gonna have to testify?" She brought her hand to her mouth and nervously bit on her knuckle. "I mean, it's not like I saw anyone do anything."

"Yes. Your testimony is going to be important, but you'll be fine. Just do like you did here today. Tell the truth."

"Are you or the other lawyer going to ask me about Ethan?" she said. "We broke up last year and now he's dating my former BFF. I hate both of them now, and I don't really want to talk about all that."

I stood up to signal to Kaitlyn that we were done. "I don't know," I said. "But wouldn't it be fun to let her know what you and Ethan were up to that night?"

Kaitlyn laughed, standing up as well. "I hadn't thought of it that way, but I like it. I can tell the entire world how Ethan stuck his tongue down my throat." She winked at me. "You're pretty cool, Maggie. I mean, Sunshine."

I wished she would tell that to my son.

———

I drove back into town and pulled into Lefty's parking lot about 3 p.m. The owner had agreed to talk to me as long as I got there after the lunch crowd and before happy hour. Lefty's was a few blocks west of the downtown square and my office. I had driven by it many times, but never stopped. It was a stand-alone building, shaped a little like a Denny's, with glass windows all around. It was not a typical look for a bar and grill.

But as I walked up a couple of steps, I was surprised. The windows had a film over them to keep the light out, and inside, the place had a real bar feel. There was a hostess stand inside the door, empty now since it was between the lunch and happy hour rush. The booths and tables were all off to the right. I went around a corner to find more tables and a bar along the wall. There was one of those small bar-size basketball shooting games, a couple of pool tables and a small stage in the right rear corner. A four-person band might squeeze in if they all sucked in their guts.

The place was almost empty, but the guy behind the bar said, "Are you Margaret Gallagher?"

"Yes." I walked over to him and shook his hand. He was a big man, tall and thick, with slightly thinning hair slicked back and a gray Fu Manchu mustache. "Is Lefty your given name?"

"Harold Ames," he said. "I played a little ball back in the day. Pitcher. Can I get you something?"

"Sure. I hear you make a good cosmo."

Lefty gave me a quizzical look. "Okay…"

"One of the girls who was in here for a New Year's Eve party said you made a good one."

"I don't tend bar during the big events. My job then is to keep people from tearing down the place. Did you really want a cosmo?"

"No. How about a glass of white wine?"

"I'll give you the happy hour price, although it doesn't start 'til 4 p.m." He took a bottle of chardonnay out of a small fridge and gave me a generous pour. "You wanted to talk about the murder of Coach Schafer."

"Well, the night of the murder. Specifically, the New Year's Eve party here."

"I don't remember a thing about that night," Lefty said, handing me the glass. It was a common response. Most people didn't want to be witnesses in any case, let alone a high-profile murder.

"You know Troy Weaver, though, right?"

"Oh yeah. Troy comes in here pretty often. Good guy. I can't believe he shot the coach." He paused a moment. "You know what I *do* remember? When Troy's kid got cut from the football team. Troy came in here pissed. I mean really PO'd."

That wasn't good. But I didn't want to be surprised at trial. "Did the police ask you about Troy and the coach?"

He looked past me, thinking. "Not that I remember."

"When Troy came in that day, angry at the coach, what did he say?"

"I don't remember exactly. He had a few rounds, and then he got even more worked up. Some people get sleepy when they drink; Troy gets emotional." Lefty placed his elbows on the bar and leaned closer. "He said he was going to call out the coach, go to the AD."

"The athletic director?"

"Yeah. And I remember this. He was going to talk with some other parents. There's always parents upset with their kids' playing time."

"Nothing more specific?" I said. "No threats?"

"No, nothing like that." Lefty stood up straight and wiped a spot on the bar with a small towel.

That nervous feeling evaporated into relief. At trial, I could easily explain away a parent being upset at a coach cutting his kid. I finally sipped the wine Lefty had given me. It needed to warm up a little. As Sean taught me, white wine is ideal at forty-five to fifty degrees, slightly above refrigerator temperatures, so I cupped it in my hands. "Are you sure you don't remember seeing Troy the night of that New Year's Eve party? The police report said you remembered him being here."

"Did it? I talked to them a long time ago. And we have a lot of parties here. Especially at Christmas. I rent the place out to businesses and groups. Let me think a minute."

"He might have been wearing his letterman jacket." I took out my phone where I had downloaded a few key photos that Auntie El had found. I showed him the picture of Troy wearing his jacket and holding his phone on New Year's Eve.

"He always wears that thing," Lefty said. "I teased him about it once and he got kinda defensive. 'It's nice and warm,' he said. Personally, I think he likes reliving the glory days." Lefty scooped some ice into a glass, and using the nozzle, he filled it with Coke. "Yeah, I remember. It's coming back. I had a band from Columbus come over that night, but the drummer never showed and they said they couldn't play without the drummer. Part of the cover charge was that I was supposed to provide music all night. So I had to keep putting money in the jukebox." He shook his head in disgust. "Cost me over a hundred bucks."

"And you saw Troy?"

"Yeah, I saw him. Just before closing. He wasn't trashed, but he had had a few. I told Denise she needed to drive him home."

"Okay." I sipped the wine.

"Troy goes, 'I won't drive. But neither can Ted.' We were all standing by the jukebox arguing about what to play next and Troy goes to Ted, 'Give me your keys. Man. You're shit-faced.'" Lefty shook his head. "Ted didn't like that. I thought I was gonna have to break up a fight. I stepped in and took Ted's keys, told him I'd call a cab. Ted's divorced, you know." Like I might ask why Ted's wife didn't drive him home.

"So Troy was there near closing—which would have been at 2 a.m., right? And he was intoxicated."

"Intoxicated's a strong word," Lefty said, "especially in my work. Let's just say he was feeling it a little. As for the timing…what time *did* we close that night? I don't remember, exactly. We might have closed up early. On New Year's Eve, a lot of people leave shortly after midnight. I had a lot of staff working, and if nobody's buying drinks, I usually shut down."

"And you don't remember seeing Troy leave?"

"Nope." Lefty picked up a towel and wiped the bar again.

"Do you have a surveillance system?" I said.

"You mean cameras? No. That's what the state investigator wanted to know. He was here a few weeks ago. But there are no cameras."

I took another sip of wine and handed over my credit card. Lefty waved me off. "I got you. By the way, do you think you can get Troy off? He's a good dude, and that coach…" Lefty shook his head. "He never came in, but plenty of parents would come here after games and complain. He wasn't exactly universally loved, if you know what I mean." Lefty took a long pull on his Coke. "I played some ball in my time and I know how a coach should treat his players. That guy would yell at the kids. You could see it from the stands. It was never physical, but I wouldn't have let my boys play for him. Luckily, they were older and went through high school before his time."

"Coach Schafer won a few championships," I said.

Lefty shook his head. "It's just high school ball. Not worth putting your kids through that."

"Do you know of anyone else who might have wanted to harm the coach?"

"I can think of a few who wouldn't have minded taking a swing at him, but kill him? No, I can't think of anyone who'd have done that," Lefty said. "There was a lot of bitching during football season, but nothing that seemed dangerous." He paused a moment. "Do you think you're gonna call me as a witness? I don't really know anything."

"I don't know," I said. "Probably not, but I still don't know what the State's case is. The fact Troy was here at closing time that night may matter, or it may not." I stood up and shook Lefty's hand. "Thanks for the drink. Maybe I'll come back sometime for dinner."

"Thursdays my wife does this flattened pork chop in vinegar. It sounds horrible, I know, but we had it in Italy once on an anniversary trip. She talked the chef into giving her the recipe. It's good."

"Thanks. That sounds great." I walked to the door, relieved that Lefty didn't have anything harmful on Troy. And the fact he remembered that Troy was at the bar at closing meant he might have never left. Carol could put Kaitlyn on the stand to say that he walked outside, but not that he drove away. I would drive that point home with the jury. She needed to prove he drove away.

I stepped out of the bar and into the sunlight, disoriented for a moment. Was I light-headed from that half glass of wine?

I hopped in my car and checked my watch. 3:29 p.m. I pulled up the coach's address in Google maps and started the car, thinking over the damage Kaitlyn's testimony could do. I already knew that I could undermine any value she had for the prosecution because Kaitlyn had admitted to drinking those two cosmos and some champagne, which would have impaired her observations. And she picked out Troy's photo *after* she saw him on TV, which made the identification process suspect. And most importantly, she couldn't say that Troy drove away.

The prosecutor had the duty to prove not only that Troy exited Lefty's, but that he drove to the Coach's house, and then killed him. But all Carol had was the gun that had ended up in Troy's house at some unknown point and an intoxicated, horny, twenty-one-year-old woman who saw Troy walk out of Lefty's.

On the other side of the equation, Lefty's testimony proved that Troy had been back in the bar not much later. Was it reasonable to think he would leave the party, kill the coach and then come back to party away the rest of the night without anyone noticing anything was wrong? Maybe the prosecutor would say that's why Troy was intoxicated at the end of the night: to drown his sorrows after killing the coach. But there was no indication she was even going to call Lefty as a witness.

I pulled into a subdivision, turned right, and then a quick left, into Coach Schafer's old driveway. I looked at my watch. Eight minutes. It would've taken eight minutes for Troy to get here. Then he knocks on the door and the coach answers. They argue a few more minutes. Troy pulls a gun, or maybe the coach had the gun. They fight over it…it is down low, pointing up at the coach's neck when it goes off. Troy runs out, drives back to the bar with the gun.

The whole thing could have been done in twenty to twenty-five minutes.

*If* Troy did it. But after talking with Lefty and Kaitlyn, I was feeling more confident that I could create enough reasonable doubt for the jury to get a verdict of not guilty.

Of course, that didn't answer the real question. Did Troy really do it?

## 26

I stood alone in the corner of the patio, holding a glass of white wine. Sean was by the grill talking with Uncle Carl and Ian about hunting. It was the Saturday before Memorial Day, and my cousin Patrick had invited us to a backyard barbecue. The stifling summer weather had not yet arrived, and it was pleasant outside.

"Let's not go," I had said to Sean. "I bet it's going to be a bunch of cops and their families. They will not want a defense attorney there."

"How do you know that?"

"Because I didn't want defense attorneys at our social functions when I was a prosecutor."

"We're going," he said. "We moved here to be closer to family, and Patrick is your cousin. And by the way, I think Ian likes playing with his boys, even if they are younger."

So here I was in Patrick's backyard, drinking alone. Five minutes ago, I had been admiring Patrick's rose garden with a couple of women. They were neighbors and had nothing to do with law enforcement, as far as I could tell. But they knew who I was. "You're Margaret Gallagher, right?"

The other woman said, "You're defending Troy Weaver. I couldn't do something like that—defend a killer."

I smiled and said something stupid about the red roses smelling like grapefruit. Then I excused myself to get another glass of wine. This was supposed to be a social occasion, and I didn't want to have to defend Troy here.

I had a bad feeling this was going to be a long evening. No one wanted a possible killer's lawyer around. I hadn't expected to be so easily recognized, but I should have remembered that word travels fast in a small town.

Aunt Louise saw me by myself and came over. "Making friends, I see, Maggie."

"Funny. I was just thinking about that manslaughter case we have for Frankie DeNuzzio. I need to subpoena that homeowner's medical history."

"Next week," she said, grabbing my arm. "You can help me bring the food outside. Patrick's wife had to go to the store and buy more ice." So we went inside and I set down my wine glass. Then I helped bring out the potato salad and macaroni salad and Jello salad. Our family called everything a salad, I guess to make it sound healthier.

In the kitchen I made small talk with a couple of other women, fussing over whether we had enough paper plates, and whether we should make coffee. Mindless, friendly chitchat. It reminded me of family gatherings in my childhood, before mom died. I used to hang around and listen while Mom and Auntie El and grandma and other women took over the family events, organizing things and telling everyone what to do. Bossiness among women ran in our family.

"I've missed this," I said to Auntie El, whose arms were full of four different kinds of corn and potato chips.

A man in jeans and a white T-shirt that read Book 'em, Danno, came up and hugged Aunt Louise. "Mama, did you bake some soda bread? I haven't had any in months."

"Yes, but you only get some if you're a good boy," she said. Then she motioned to me. "This is my niece, Maggie. Maggie, this is Adam Fenwick. He's Patrick's sergeant."

We shook hands as he gave me a knowing smile. "I was a few years behind you in high school," Adam said. "You probably don't remember me, but I remember you. You had a thing with Troy Weaver, didn't you? Is that why you're defending him?"

"Adam!" Auntie El said.

"Actually, I never had a 'thing' with him other than gratitude," I said coldly. "His family took me in when my mom died of cancer." I glanced at Auntie El and then back at the prick sergeant. Auntie El looked as if she was on the verge of trying to smooth things over, but Fenwick didn't seem the least bit apologetic, and I had no interest in sticking around and listening to him justify being a rude, judgmental asshole. I picked up my glass of wine and walked out onto the back lawn, not knowing where else to go. This was turning into a disaster. I looked around for a friendly face. Sean was still by the grill with Uncle Carl and he waved at me. Ian had disappeared somewhere.

"Need a refill?" A shorter, strawberry blonde woman in jean shorts and flip-flops had walked up with a bottle of wine. She didn't wait for an answer, filling my glass, almost to the top. "I heard your exchange with *Book 'Em, Danno*. What a jerk."

"Thanks," I said and held out my hand. "Maggie—"

"Gallagher. Yes, I know. You're defending Troy Weaver. Everybody knows about that. I'm Suzanne Sheehan. I think our kids are struggling in the same English class."

She filled her own glass as I stood there at a loss for words. My defenses were up so high that I honestly didn't know how to respond to someone trying to be friendly. She held her glass up and we clinked. "My daughter Annie said the English teacher has a hard-on about grade inflation. Everybody's getting As these days, so he's threatening to fail half the class just to make a point. Annie said she was cooking up a plot with a boy named Ian. That's your son, right?"

I nodded.

"I was wondering if you know what their plan is? Annie won't tell me."

Still speechless, I stared at Suzanne, sipped on the glass, and finally said, "No idea. He doesn't tell me anything."

Suzanne laughed, a pleasant, confident laugh. "Sometimes I wish my daughter didn't tell me as much as she does." She took a drink and gestured with her glass toward the swing set by the backyard fence where a teenage girl was pushing another teenage girl on the swing. "Mine's the one doing the pushing."

"That's cute," I said. "Innocent girls playing on a swing."

Suzanne laughed. "Yeah, right. They're probably planning a bank robbery." She held up her glass and we clinked. "I'll work on Annie and you work on Ian. Maybe we can get to the bottom of their plan."

"Okay, but I promise nothing." I sipped the wine. "I just hope they don't get in trouble."

Suzanne shrugged. "Sometimes you got to stick it to the man, even if you get caught." She raised her glass in another toast. "Don't you think?"

Suzanne was a feisty one. She reminded me a little of a younger Auntie El. I clinked her glass again. "Stick it to the man," I said.

---

The sun had set and Sean and I stood on the back lawn, waiting for the fireworks. Apparently, Patrick and Liam always did a Memorial Day show in remembrance of their grandpa on Carl's side, who died in a helicopter crash in Vietnam. Sean put his arm around my shoulder and I leaned in.

Liam came out of the house. "All right, everyone. Out in the street. The show is about to begin. And don't worry about the cops showing up. We got that fixed."

The party had dwindled down to about twenty-five people, and we all filtered out to the front. As we walked through the house, Liam grabbed my arm. "In the kitchen," he said in a low voice, and I followed him without argument.

When he was sure we were alone, he said, "This is not police stuff. Simple intelligence, rumors, and gossip, mostly. Patrick and I did a little work on the side." He handed me a piece of paper. "This is a list of parents and a couple of kids who did not like Coach Schafer. You can use it for whatever purpose you'd like, but I can think of a few things I'd do."

I hugged him and kissed his cheek. "No one will know, I promise."

He walked outside to help Patrick set off the fireworks. I found Sean in the driveway and sidled up to him as the first Roman candle shot into the sky. Ian was out in the street with my cousins, and they had given him a lighter to help set off some of the fireworks. He had a big smile on his face as Patrick elbowed him in the side.

The big finale was about six roman candles all at once. Ian helped light them, and then came back to stand with Sean and me to watch them go off. I kept my eyes on him, so glad to see him looking happy, looking at home here.

Then we said our goodbyes to Patrick and his wife and Carl and Auntie El. My new friend Suzanne came up and suggested we have coffee sometime.

I had some new leads to follow on my case…and the possibility of a new friend. Not bad for a family barbecue I'd dreaded attending. Not bad at all.

## 27

Tuesday morning I found a voice message on my office phone. I recognized Liam's voice. "You might want to check your client's personal effects at the jail."

I walked over to the jail through bright sunlight. At the front desk, I asked the officer on duty for an accounting of Troy's personal effects. I wanted the list of things he had on him when he turned himself in. The officer wasn't happy, but she clicked around on her computer, then she looked back at me and made a phone call.

A few minutes passed. I said, "Is there a problem?"

"Someone will be down to talk with you." She pointed to the bench. "Have a seat."

I remained standing. Finally, the glass doors swung open and in came Carol Becker. I had no court appearances today, so I was casual in jeans and a striped blouse, but Carol was in classic prosecutor dress, a navy pantsuit. She held a piece of paper. "We were sending this over to you this week."

I took the paper. It was an evidence receipt. The police had seized Troy's letterman jacket. They had searched his house for something that had yellow fibers, but he had worn the jacket with the yellow "K" to jail when he turned himself in. It had been in jail custody the whole time.

"Where's the seizure warrant?" I said.

"We already had custody of the jacket," Carol said. "We didn't need a warrant."

I laughed. "We'll see about that." Among the motions I was going to file, I would add one to suppress any evidence from the jacket. I could make a good argument she violated Troy's 4th Amendment rights by not getting a warrant from a judge. I wasn't sure it would work, but I intended to try. That was my job now as Troy's attorney—make as many arguments as I could and hope that some stuck.

This one must have struck a chord, because Carol's smug expression cracked for a second—but only a second. She bounced back quickly. "I talked with the boss and he said there is no plea offer. But your client can still choose to plead guilty to spare his family from the ordeal of a trial, and proceed to the sentencing phase."

"Will you take the death penalty off the table?"

She shook her head, "No."

"I guess we're going to trial," I said.

That made Carol smile. I didn't have the slightest doubt that she *wanted* a trial, and the publicity that would go with it. She was the worst kind of prosecutor, one who wanted to be a politician.

She started for the door, but turned back to me. "One more thing. We don't have the report yet, but forensics has tied the yellow fibers from your client's jacket to the yellow fibers found on the gun. I'll get you a copy as soon as I have it." With that, she walked out through the glass doors.

I stood there, reeling, sick to my stomach. It wasn't just that they had Troy's jacket, which had some yellow on it. With that forensic evidence, Carol could now put the jacket—and Troy—at the murder scene. This was the prosecutor's missing piece. My mind raced, trying to think of an alternative explanation. Something I could argue to the jury. But there was nothing. Trying to suppress that jacket as evidence was now extra important.

For the first time, I could see us losing this case. Troy would be looking at life in prison, if not death row.

I might as well visit my client and break the news.

———

Troy was deteriorating. Some people handled jail better than others. I couldn't help asking, "How are you doing?"

"I'm okay," he said, sitting behind the little table. "They took me to see Benny last night."

"They did? No one told me." Carol was supposed to give me notice.

"He didn't move. I was there for an hour, and he never moved aside from the ventilator making his chest go up and down." Troy slumped back in his chair, looking at his feet.

My nerves felt like they were twisted into knots. Part of me was angry. All the evidence was pointing to the idea that he really was the killer, and I was pissed off that he'd fooled me into believing in him. But part of me felt despair, since he'd believed in *me* too—believed that I could win this case so he could go home to his family. And I was no longer sure that I could.

Now on top of all of that, I was swamped with sympathy for a dad and his ailing son. What an unholy mess all of this was.

Troy said, "One of the guys in here says I should just plead guilty. The jury won't give me a bad sentence if I take responsibility."

Leaning forward, I said, "I told you not to listen to anyone in here. They're not looking out for your best interests."

"I know, but…this one kid, he knew Benny a little. He said the prosecutor's screwing him too. Charged him with a robbery when all he did was a minor theft. He thinks the jury will treat me better if I own this."

"What's the guy's name?"

"Justin. He was in Benny's class. He's also waiting for a trial and he's really helped me in here."

Even in jail, people need friends, so I let it drop. "There's something I need to tell you, Troy. I learned today they seized your letterman jacket from the jail. It's going to come up in the trial."

"Why?" he said.

"They matched the yellow fibers on the "K" to the yellow fibers found under the coach's fingernails."

He stared back at me like he didn't understand. Finally, he said, "That makes no sense. I didn't go there."

My stomach dropped. "So you're saying you *did* go somewhere that night? Somewhere other than the party at Lefty's?"

"I…" His eyes darted around the room, like he was looking for an answer.

"I need you to be honest with me, Troy. Where *did* you go?"

He shook his head.

"Were you having an affair? I can see how that would be a hard thing to admit, but it's not worth prison."

He folded his arms. "I've never had an affair. Not then, not now, not ever."

"I drove from Lefty's to the Coach's house in eight minutes. It won't matter that you were back at the party before it ended. The State is going to show you could have shot the coach and returned to Lefty's in less than half an hour."

"I didn't drive to that asshole's." He was getting a little angry. "I didn't even know where he lived."

I said, "I talked with the girl who saw you leave the party and go out to your car. I need you to tell me where you went." He stared back in silence. "Troy, whatever you tell me is attorney-client privilege. I can't tell anyone else, even if I wanted to." Still silence. "If you don't tell me, I can't help you."

"I didn't do it," was all he said.

"Damn it, Troy, if you don't trust me, maybe you should get another lawyer."

He gave me a weak smile. "You won't quit on me, Maggie."

"Oh, you don't think so? Loyalty and trust go both ways." I stood up, anger pushing all my other feelings aside. I knocked on the door for the officer to let me out. I wasn't cut out for this, representing someone who actively worked against me.

"Thanks for letting me see Benny. I know it's probably the last time..." He started crying and suddenly I felt like a jerk. Troy had a son in a coma. Could anything in life be worse than what he was going through? Maybe he killed the coach, but it could have been an accident, or things could have gotten out of hand. He wasn't an evil man. Putting him in jail for the rest of his life or sending him to his execution…I didn't see how that could be justice. He deserved to have someone in his corner, fighting for him. Even against all the odds.

I said, "Is there anything you need, anything I can do? Get a message to Denise?"

Troy's head sank low and he shook his head. "She still blames me for Benny getting shot."

But she believed that he wasn't a killer. I remembered my conversation with Denise earlier. Yes, she was furious over what had happened with Benny, but even in light of that, she still had faith in her husband. Maybe I should try to hold on to that.

———

Back in the office, I told Auntie El about my run in with Carol Becker. She said, "I see letterman jackets all over Kerry. There must be hundreds around town. I think I still have Patrick's in our attic. Maybe the coach wore one himself. Can they really be sure the fibers were from *Troy's* jacket?"

"Those are good points," I said. I had been flustered back at the jail and not considered how many letterman jackets there were in Kerry. It was possible, and even likely, that the fibers weren't unique to Troy's coat, but could be equally tied to all Kerry High letterman jackets. That would mean Carol couldn't prove Troy was at the coach's house, only that someone with a letterman jacket was. But since Troy left the New Year's Eve party wearing his jacket, there was no denying that the matching yellow fibers would look bad to a jury. Another nail in Troy's coffin.

"It's hard to come up with a strategy until we actually see the forensic report," I said. "Did they match fibers from Troy's jacket? Did they check other letterman jackets? Have the fibers changed in the "K" letter over the years?"

"You'll need to know that," Auntie El said, walking to her computer. "Troy's jacket must be at least twenty years old. I'll check the manufacturer's website and see what I can find."

I was happy to have Auntie El back. She had opened up another whole avenue to cross-examine the government's forensic experts.

I left my aunt to work her magic and went into my office to do the more boring stuff. A death penalty case wasn't all investigation. I needed to draft several motions to file with the court before our pretrial hearing. Motions to suppress evidence because the government might have screwed up its investigation. Like statements Troy made to the police after I told the cops not to talk with him. I would argue that was a violation of his right to counsel.

And if Troy was found guilty, there would be another phase of the trial where the jury would decide the sentence, including whether he should be put to death. I needed to file motions challenging every aspect of the constitutionality of Ohio's death penalty law. Even though most of those issues had already been settled, I needed to make the arguments to preserve them for any later appeal. A person sentenced to death could appeal five or six different times, and a clever attorney could delay the execution for decades through the lengthy appeal process.

I had begun drafting my death penalty challenges a few weeks back, and my motions were already more than a hundred pages. Today I needed to work on a motion to challenge Carol's seizure of Troy's jacket without a warrant. Judge Blankenship had set our omnibus hearing for next Monday. That was when we would fight over the remaining pretrial issues. There was a knock on my door, and Auntie El stuck her head in.

"I know you're busy, but I forgot to tell you...I cross-checked all those names on that list you gave me." She was talking about the list Liam gave me at the barbecue of people who didn't like the coach. She handed me a paper. "Four of the names do not show up in the police reports." She shrugged and smiled. "Maybe one of them did it."

"That's good. Thanks." If we could show the investigation was not thorough, that might help create reasonable doubt. I didn't have to prove someone else did it or even prove that other suspects didn't have strong alibis. That was for the cops to handle. But the fact that they hadn't checked into every possible suspect was a weakness in their investigation. It might mean the murderer was still out there. At least that was the argument I would make to the jury.

Tomorrow I would follow up on those four names. Maybe we'd get lucky and find something I could use. I knew from experience it was better to be lucky than good.

## 28

"Have you served the prosecutor's office?" Judge Blankenship said.

"No, Your Honor. It's not required by the statute." I was in his chambers getting a subpoena signed. The judge needed to approve my request for Kerry High School's records about parents and students who had complained about Coach Schafer.

"I am not sure I am comfortable with this ex-parte subpoena, Ms. Gallagher," the judge said. By ex-parte, he meant that I had not told Carol.

"If you'll look at the bottom, Judge, you'll see I am having the records delivered to you. Then you can make them available to Carol and me as you see fit. Or if you deem them irrelevant, you could withhold them."

He smiled. "But if I did that, then you would appeal me."

I smiled back. "There is that." Trial judges lived in fear of being overturned on appeal. No one liked to be publicly embarrassed for being wrong.

He examined the document a little more carefully and then signed it. He handed it back and said, "How are things going for you? Moving back to Kerry, defending the accused instead of prosecuting them?"

"It's been harder than I expected," I said.

He stood up from behind his desk. "As you probably know, I had a defense practice for fifteen years before I moved to the bench. I got tired of the business side. Collecting on bills, leases, employees, all that stuff. But defending people...that came easily to me. Others, like Ms. Becker, can only be prosecutors." He put on his robe, letting me know he was heading to court, so I moved toward his door. "I think you're different, Maggie. I think you are one of the few who can do it all."

He exited through his chamber door, leaving me to ponder what he'd said. *Could* I do it all? Successful prosecutor *and* defense attorney? It was nice to hear the judge say so. Funny how a well-timed compliment buoyed my confidence.

I would need it this afternoon, trying to get four people to talk with me, the four people Liam and Patrick had identified who didn't like Coach Schafer.

Four people, any one of whom could be a killer.

---

I was standing at the window of my office, staring down at the museum that used to be the old courthouse. The high I'd felt at the compliment from Judge Blankenship had dissolved into a mild depression. The four names from Liam and Patrick had turned out to be a dead end. Two of the people who didn't like the coach were provably out of town on the night of the murder, and a third had been in the hospital with kidney stones. The fourth was a former student named Justin Cross. His parents had moved to California and nobody knew where he was.

There was a rap on my door, and Auntie El stuck in her head. "Heading home, boss." She looked at me a moment and then stepped inside.

I must have looked depressed, because she said, "Life doesn't always go your way, but we have to keep on fighting."

"I know," I said.

"No, you don't." She sat down in the chair across from my desk. "You were too little to realize it, but back in the nineties, the bank almost took our farm away, twice. Carl and I fought like hell to keep it. We both took second jobs. Your uncle was working over a hundred hours a week. I was a clerk at 7-Eleven on the late shift. Can you imagine that?" She chuckled, "One night a kid came in and said he was robbing me. He had a finger in his coat pocket like it was a gun. At least I thought it was a finger. But I didn't know for sure, and I honestly didn't care. I told him go ahead and shoot me—he'd be doing me a favor."

"You're kidding," I said. "What happened?"

"He didn't know what to do, so he left. The point is, somehow we made it, Carl and I." She stood up and moved to the door. "If you believe in something, you have to keep fighting. And despite all the evidence, I've got a feeling Troy is innocent. Things happen for a reason Maggie, and I think that's why you're back here in Kerry. To help Troy."

Then she came back toward me, around the desk and kissed me on the forehead. "And God also sent you back here to give me this job. I'm having more fun than my wedding night." She smiled and held her finger up to her lips. "Just don't tell Carl I said that."

*Auntie El!* Boy, did I love her. I decided to follow her lead and go home. I called Sean to see about dinner and he said Ian was studying in the school library and he'd bring him home. He was excited when I offered to pick up the meal.

Driving home, I remembered Lefty's Thursday night pork chop special, so I made a quick left and pulled into the parking lot.

I walked to the bar and placed my order, three pork chops, and a big basket of fries to go. Lefty wasn't there today, but a young man with a sleeve of tattoos and several earrings took my order. "Beer while you wait?" he said.

"How about a white wine?"

He filled my glass and went to the back to place my order. It was relaxing, sitting here by myself having a drink with nothing to do other than enjoy it. I couldn't remember the last time I did that, if ever.

Using the mirror behind the bar, I looked over the place. There were about twenty people eating and drinking and playing pool. A man in Wranglers and a John Deere hat put some money in the jukebox and out came a Kenny Chesney song. Sean and Ian had taken me to a Kenny Chesney concert in Chicago a couple of summers ago and we had a great time. It was back when Ian and I still had fun together.

And then I saw her, all alone in a booth. Carol Becker eating the flattened pork chop, drinking red wine and looking over some paperwork.

What the heck. I picked up my glass and walked over to her table. "Hi there, counselor," I said.

She looked up, and it took her a moment to process. Then she smiled. "Have a seat."

So I did. "What are you working on?"

She pushed the papers away from her and took a sip of wine. "I've been here less than two months, and they want me to do employee evaluations. Can you believe that?"

"It's the worst," I said. I had been a supervisor in the violent crime section of our Chicago office, and I hated doing evaluations of my employees.

She said, "You've had a few dealings with Oliver. What do you think?"

"To be honest, he's turned a little aggressive lately." It was really a shot at Carol, and she got it.

"He's doing what I tell him, so I guess that's a good thing."

"If you say so. I had a different philosophy when I was a prosecutor."

"Oh, yeah?" Carol took a bite of pork chop, and with her mouth full, "What was that?"

"We were supposed to show good judgment, not just be aggressive."

She waved her fork. "I don't disagree. But I've found that too many prosecutors—especially the young ones—are afraid of trial. They offer generous plea deals to avoid the stress of going to court."

I sipped my wine and nodded. It was a broad generalization, but on the whole, I agreed with her. "Look at us. A couple of old-timers complaining about the next generation." After a moment of silence, I said, "Now that we're buddies, let me ask you. What are you really after in the Weaver case?"

She drank from her wineglass, then gestured out the window. "I came from the cold case unit at the AG's office up in Columbus. We made this case there after the locals screwed it up. I want to see my old unit get the credit. The legislature has been trying to pull their funding."

I nodded. "It would look good for them, and for you," I said.

Carol took another bite and then washed it down with wine. "I've made it no secret. I plan to run for office someday. Ohio needs strong women to turn this state around."

"There's nothing wrong with ambition. As long as it doesn't affect justice."

She gave me a hard look and said, "Nice chatting with you, counselor."

I took the hint, getting to my feet. Before I walked away, I made a mock toast with my wine. "Just so you know, I served a subpoena on the high school for all complaints made against Coach Schafer. I wouldn't be surprised if the real killer is in there."

I walked back to the bar to wait for my pork chops, half expecting a wineglass to hit the back of my head.

# 29

Monday morning I got up extra early, and after stretching on the living room carpet, I went for a walk. My hip and knee were feeling better, but I didn't want to risk things by running. This was a big day, a big week, and I needed the extra energy I got from my morning exercise.

Lawn sprinklers turned on as the sun came over the horizon. No one was up yet, except an older woman out pruning her roses. She anticipated my question. "I have to do it before it gets too hot," she said. "Roses are like me. We both wilt in the heat."

Today was Troy's pretrial hearing, and I was thinking about my plan. I had filed over a hundred fifty pages of motions, including challenges to the death penalty. We would lose those, I knew, but I would preserve the issues for later appeal if Troy was convicted. I had also moved to suppress the letterman jacket the police seized from the jail. The big issue was my motion to sever the murder case from the child endangerment case. Carol wanted a jury to hear both cases together, thinking she could use the child endangerment to paint Troy as reckless and irrational, which would make the jury quicker to believe that he could commit murder. That's why she joined them, and it's why I wanted them tried separately.

After showering, I got to the office early. I had started a bad habit of getting my breakfast from the patisserie downstairs—a croissant for me, which meant I also had to get one for Auntie El. Then I made a pot of coffee and retreated to my office to go over my strategy one more time.

At 10 a.m., I walked to the courthouse with Auntie El by my side, at her request. "You don't have to pay me for my time," she'd said. "I just want to watch." We both stepped outside into a steamy, hot morning. I realized this was a mistake. I would be a hot, sticky mess by the time we got to court.

"Maybe we should drive," I said.

"Come on, you big baby. It's only two blocks." So we walked it. By the time we made it one block, we were both sweating. Auntie El took a handkerchief from her purse and wiped her forehead.

"I told you we should drive," I said.

I pointed to the statue of the Ohio football legend, Paul Brown. "What happened to that?" There were cracks visible at the neck and shoulders, like ol' Mr. Brown had been glued back together.

"Somebody trashed it last year," she said. "Knocked him over. He broke into pieces. Everyone was furious."

"Yikes." I was happy to have missed that mess.

Finally, we made it inside to the air conditioning. "Morning Ms. Gallagher." DeShawn was the security officer who usually manned the X-ray machines. I was becoming a regular, and it felt nice. "Good luck today," he almost whispered, maybe afraid of sounding too friendly to a defense attorney.

I was always nervous going to court on a big case, but today was unlike any other. We were the first there, and the bailiff unlocked the door to let us in.

That was when it hit me. In this room, we would decide what happened for the rest of Troy's life. Prison, the death penalty, or freedom. And I was responsible.

Nerves weren't necessarily a bad thing, they focused the mind. But I couldn't let them fog my thinking. Over the years, I had developed a strategy to deal with butterflies in the stomach. Follow a routine, focus on the little things, and do them well. I unpacked my leather satchel, setting my note pad and evidence book on the table. I pulled out my red and blue pens and my yellow highlighter. I took most of my notes in blue, but issues I needed to follow up on, I would write in red. And the yellow highlighter was to emphasize points I would make in my closing argument. The bailiff had already set a pitcher of water on the table, so I filled my glass, two-thirds full. If my hands were shaking, which was possible, I didn't want the water to spill over.

When I was finally situated, I glanced back at Auntie El, who sat behind me in the first row. "You have quite a routine," she said. "Now, let's kick some ass."

Observers had started filing in, including reporters. There was a TV camera already set up in the back on a six-inch raised platform. Denise came in, carrying Charley. I stood to greet her. "I'm so scared," she said.

"Thanks for being here. It's important." I poked Charley in the stomach and he giggled.

"I brought Troy his suit yesterday," she said, "but he's lost so much weight, it's not going to fit."

Carol came in with an older man in a suit and a woman in a dark dress: Coach Schafer's parents. She chatted with them a moment, then left them in the front row as she came forward to the table next to mine. She wore a cream-colored skirt and jacket, which was much too similar to my tan summer pant suit. We said nothing to each other.

Two officers brought Troy over from the jail. Denise was right. His brown suit did not fit. We'd have to do better at trial. They removed his handcuffs, and he sat down next to me. The officers sat directly behind us, next to Denise and Auntie El. It was standard practice, in case the defendant tried to escape.

"Ready?" I said to him.

"No."

"You don't have to do anything. Just sit there and look innocent." I wanted him to smile and relax a little, but he just stared straight ahead. Over the weekend I had visited to explain what would happen today. I told him, "Confidence equals innocence." The message had not sunk in. Troy was too scared.

A stack of papers landed on my desk, and I looked up to see Carol. She said, "More discovery."

"What? We are two weeks from trial."

"You're the one who didn't waive your speedy trial rights."

I stood up. "You're the one who rushed this investigation."

I must have been too loud. The bailiff came over. "Are we ready, ladies?"

"The State's ready," Carol said. I nodded.

Judge Blankenship came out from his chambers, and Carol called the case. The judge said, "We'll start with the death penalty motions. I have read your briefs. Do either of you want to add anything?" He was signaling to us he had made up his mind. This was not a surprise. The law was settled, and we were going to lose. The death penalty, as conducted in Ohio, was legal.

I stood and said, "We have nothing to add, and we will rely on our brief."

Carol said, "Same for the State."

"Very well," the judge said. "I will take it under advisement and render my decision in writing." He looked straight at me. "These are your motions, Ms. Gallagher. What would you like to do next?"

"Your Honor, we have moved to suppress my client's jacket and any subsequent test results from fibers of that jacket."

"Ms. Becker?"

Carol stood. "Your Honor, as I wrote in my brief, we did not need a warrant to take the jacket because it was already in the custody of the Donohoe County jail. Again, I'm willing to stand on the arguments I made in my brief."

This was the hardest part of defense work. I had asserted a theory I didn't believe in. But I had an ethical duty to advocate aggressively for Troy, so I needed to raise the issue for appeal. I stood. "Same here, judge."

"Okay. I understand both positions. What's next, Ms. Gallagher?"

"Your Honor, we are moving to sever the two charges in this case. The charge of child endangerment relates to events that occurred sixteen months after the killing of Grant Schafer. The only connection is the government's theory that the same gun was involved in both incidents. That is not a legitimate basis to join the charges. Joining the charges increases the likelihood of unfair prejudice to my client. The jury might improperly infer that a person who is reckless with a gun around children might also be likely to commit a murder. That is precisely why the prosecutor joined these separate charges in one trial."

"That is not true," Carol said. "We joined the two charges because they *are* similar. They involve the same gun and the same defendant. They both involve violence and injured innocents. And in addition, it is much more efficient and cost effective to hold one trial instead of bringing in an entire new jury and conducting a completely new trial."

This was a big issue for us, and I needed to show that to the judge. I had to win the point now, because if he ruled against me, I *would* appeal—and there was a good chance his ruling could be overturned. No judge likes that. I said, "Efficiency is not a reason to unfairly prejudice a defendant and violate his due process rights."

In a violation of protocol, Carol turned to address me. "There is nothing prejudicial in trying to—"

"Thank you, Ms. Becker," the judge said, cutting her off. "I've heard enough on this issue." To me, he said, "Ms. Gallagher, are you willing to waive your client's speedy trial rights on the reckless endangerment charge? It seems that is required if you want me to sever the charges."

"Yes, thank you, Your Honor. We will waive our speedy trial rights on that charge only." That way, the child endangerment trial could take place much later.

"Very well. Is there anything else?"

I said, "Your Honor. We are exactly two weeks from starting this trial, and I have just received more discovery from the government. I haven't had a chance to review this, obviously, but glancing at it, I see old phone records. There is no reason why I am only receiving this now, unless the government is intentionally withholding evidence and trying to disadvantage the defense. I plan to move to exclude this evidence as a sanction for discovery violations."

"There is nothing intentional here," Carol said. "It is the defense's fault that everything is rushed."

"It is not our fault. My client has a constitutional right to a speedy trial, and to due process disclosure of the government's evidence."

The judge said, "I have to agree with Ms. Gallagher here." He pointed at Carol. "I will not allow delays in discovery, even if it is through negligence and not intentional misconduct. And I will be willing to entertain a motion from Ms. Gallagher to exclude evidence if I see bad faith from the State. Am I clear, Ms. Becker?"

"Yes, judge. We are working very hard to get everything to the defense." Carol took the chastisement well. I decided to pile on.

"In addition, we are two weeks from trial and we have received no witness list, no exhibit list, no proposed jury instructions, and no proposed questionnaire for a death-qualified jury. We will be at the sixty-day time limit for trial next Sunday and the defense will not agree to any continuance. If the government is not ready for trial then, I will be moving for dismissal with prejudice."

"Ms. Becker?" the judge said. "Perhaps you should have a second attorney helping you with this. I expect to have each of these items identified by Ms. Gallagher by close of business on Friday. Do you anticipate any trouble complying with my order?"

Carol looked at me with pure hatred. "We will have it ready, Your Honor."

"Very well," the judge said, glancing at both of us, giving us one last opportunity to speak. "We will reconvene in two weeks for trial. Ms. Becker, you need not worry about witness or exhibit lists for the child endangerment charge." He banged his gavel. "We are adjourned. Oh, one more thing. I have the records Ms. Gallagher subpoenaed from the school district. I have made two copies, and the bailiff will deliver them to you both. Now we are adjourned."

"What just happened?" Troy said.

"We got everything we wanted," I said. "The judge is going to sever the child endangerment charge. And he just reamed the prosecutor." That was why he told Carol she didn't need a witness list for the other charge. Because he was going to postpone that trial.

"What about the jacket?"

I shook my head. "No. I knew we wouldn't win that. I'm creating issues to raise on appeal, if we need to. Hopefully, it won't come to that."

The officers stepped up next to Troy. "Back to jail," one of them said.

I squeezed his arm. "Today was a good day. Hang in there."

He tried to smile, but wasn't quite successful. "I know you're doing your best. A friend inside told me there will be good days and bad days at trial."

"Yes, he's right. Enjoy this one, though. Have an extra dessert."

The officer took him out the back door and a TV reporter came up. "Are you going to give a statement?"

"No, sorry. We are too close to trial, and I don't want to affect the jury pool." I walked behind the wooden bar where Auntie El was talking with Denise.

"That was great," Denise said. "The people behind us were laughing at the prosecutor."

"Yeah, she was shooting you daggers," Auntie El said.

"I felt it went well. That prosecutor talks tough, but I'm starting to think she's bitten off more than she can chew. She doesn't have much experience, and she's made some mistakes." I poked Charley in the belly again. "I'm glad you were both here. It will be important at the trial."

"I know," Denise said, "but I also need to work to pay our mortgage. I'll see if they'll let me have the night shift."

"Do what you can." I hugged her. I turned back to pick up my satchel when the bailiff handed me the records I had subpoenaed. These would be the complaints made to the school against Coach Schafer.

Auntie El and I walked through the crowd milling outside in the hallway. "I wasn't kidding," she said. "You kicked that prosecutor's ass. She is going to be looking for revenge."

"That helps us if she's focused on revenge against me instead of proving Troy's guilt." We reached the door outside, not relishing the hot walk back to the office. "We have a lot of work to do, including going through this new discovery."

I had a bad feeling about the phone records Carol had dropped on me.

## 30

The air conditioning in the building was struggling to overcome the heat, so we went to Auntie El's house. "I made a coconut cream pie and I don't want Carl eating the whole thing," she said. We drove separately out to her farm. My car thermometer read ninety-eight degrees. And the humidity was probably the same.

She made some fresh lemonade, which, surprisingly, went well with the pie. Then we spread the discovery records out on her kitchen table, sitting under the air-conditioning vent.

I saw it right away. Three weeks before the murder, Troy had made numerous calls to Coach Schafer's phone. On December 8th, there were five calls within five minutes. There were a couple of calls at two in the morning, and on another day, there were five calls around 5 a.m. I would ask Troy about it, but it appeared he was harassing the coach. Carol would definitely use this evidence to show his dislike of Coach Schafer. And the calls at all hours wouldn't do us any favors when she tried to show that Troy was reckless and irrational—maybe reckless and irrational enough to confront the coach in person.

Auntie El discovered some other bad news. "Remember that photo from Joyce Entwhistle I found on Facebook? On New Year's Eve, Troy was wearing his letterman jacket and holding his phone?"

"I remember."

"Well, I called her, and she said the time stamp on her phone for that picture was 11:33 p.m." Auntie El held up the list of calls. "Here's a call at 11:31 p.m. A two-minute call."

"Who'd Troy call?" I said.

"He didn't. He received the call, but I can't tell from whom. It's just a number." She pointed at my phone. "We could call it?"

Carol would have tracked down all the important calls. There should be police reports detailing what they found, and yet there was nothing. Why was she playing games with the discovery? I took out my phone and dialed the number.

It rang four times and then a message. "This is Benny. You know what to do." I hung up. I guess I shouldn't have been surprised.

"Who is it?"

"Benny."

"Benny? Troy's son?" I nodded, staring back at Auntie El in silence. We locked eyes a long moment, until she stood up. "Oh my gosh, I can't believe this. So do you think Benny did it? Did he kill Coach Schafer? Is that why Troy won't tell you where he went? Because he went to help Benny?"

I shook my head. "I don't know." But if Benny *did* shoot the coach, Troy's refusal to tell me where he went made sense. That was what a parent would do—cover for his son. "We can't ask Benny," I said. "He's still in a coma."

Auntie El walked to the whiteboard on the wall. She grabbed a pen to write something, but just shrugged. What could she write?

I picked up my phone and made another call.

"Denise?" I said. "Do you have Benny's phone?"

"Uh, yeah. It's in his room."

"The prosecutor gave me Troy's phone records from the night of the murder. Benny called him at 11:31 p.m. Did Troy leave Lefty's to go to Benny?"

The phone went dead. I looked up at Auntie El. "She hung up on me."

---

"What's this?" Troy said when I showed him the phone records.

"These are calls from your phone to Schafer's. Two calls on December 10th at 2 a.m." I flipped a page. "And some more calls at 5 a.m. What were you doing?"

We were in the small visitation room in the jail. Troy sat across from me and hung his head. "It was stupid. I was just…I guess, trying to mess with him."

"Did you talk to him on the phone?"

"Yeah. My first couple of calls, I tried to reason with him, but it didn't do any good. He was telling me shit about Benny that I thought was a lie. I got angry, and…" He shrugged. He looked up. "It looks bad, right?"

"It doesn't look good," I said. "Did you ever go to his house?"

"No," Troy said forcefully. "I don't even know where he lives. I never went there."

I showed him the next page in the phone records. "Here, this is a call you received on New Year's Eve, 11:31 p.m." I let him read the number the call came from. Then I showed him the photo of him at Lefty's, holding his phone and wearing his letterman jacket. "The time stamp on this photo was 11:33 p.m."

Troy stared at the photo a long time. Unlike Denise, he couldn't hang up on me. Finally, he set the photo down. "I know what you're thinking. But Benny didn't kill the coach. That's not what happened." He put his hand over his heart. "I swear to you, Maggie, Benny and I had nothing to do with this."

I picked up the photo and phone records and put them back in my satchel. "Where did you go that night?"

He shook his head.

"You went somewhere, right?"

He nodded.

"You went to see Benny."

He nodded again. "I can't tell you anything else. Denise and I...we swore to each other we would never tell." He sat up straight, defiant. "I'll go to prison for the rest of my life before I'll talk."

"All right," I said. "You're protecting Benny from something, but it's not the murder of Coach Schafer." He didn't respond. "I need you to answer this one question for me, Troy. You're protecting him, but not for the murder, right?"

"Yes. Benny didn't kill anyone, and neither did I."

I believed him. And the relief almost overwhelmed me. The last few weeks, I'd thought that maybe Troy was a murderer, and the conflict had been eating me up inside. Now I leaned closer and grabbed his hands, squeezing. "Thank you for trusting me." I began to tear up. "I hated the idea that you might be a killer."

"I'm sorry I put you through this. I guess I could have come clean sooner." He leaned back in his chair and smiled. "Have you ever seen anyone have a worse run of bad luck?" Then his smile disappeared. "But I'd gladly plead guilty if it would get Benny out of the hospital."

"Nobody's pleading guilty," I said. "I'm feeling good about our chances at trial. If only I knew where that gun came from."

Troy shrugged. "Me too. I would almost swear it isn't mine, but, you know... res ipsa loquitur."

"What?"

He laughed. "It's a legal phrase in Latin. You don't know it?"

"I know it," I said. "But how do you?"

"Justin told me. I was telling him about the gun, how it wasn't mine, and he said, 'res ipsa loquitur.' He said it means it was there, so it must be mine."

"Stay away from that kid."

"He's the one who thinks I should plead guilty."

"*Definitely* stay away from him. I can promise you this—he's not your friend."

## 31

I spent the rest of the week in my office, preparing for trial. The air-conditioning system in our old building was not keeping up with the heat, so I bought a fan and wore shorts and a T-shirt to the office. I also told Auntie El not to come in, which was a hard conversation. I had been lonely back when we had our brief fight and she stopped coming in, but there was no reason for her to suffer in this heat with me, and I couldn't afford to pay her when there was nothing to do. We were close to settling my one civil case—the couple that was rear-ended by a Tesla—and that would bring in some cash eventually, but the insurance company was holding up the final payment.

Auntie El was gracious. "Honey, I knew that when I talked you into hiring me. A few more months and the money will be rolling in. Do you think you'll need me during the trial?"

"Oh yeah," I said. "I need you back next week. We should get the list of potential jurors then, and I am counting on your input. You're my secret weapon. You know everyone in town."

On Wednesday, Carol sent over more discovery, which included follow-up police reports from the phone records. I was pleased to see nothing about the 11:31 p.m. call Benny made to Troy. Carol must not have thought it significant. I finished up about 5 p.m. and made it home for dinner.

Sean had grilled some salmon, which he and Ian loved. I wasn't partial to fish, but I went along when they had a craving.

After Sean said grace, Ian asked how my trial prep was going, which brought me out of my grumpiness over having seafood for dinner.

"I'm almost ready," I said. "I think we have a good chance. Are you hearing anything about it at school?"

"Yeah." He nodded slightly and looked at his dad. "We're hearing stuff."

I looked at Sean, then back at Ian. "Like what?" The last thing I wanted was my family suffering because of me.

Ian said, "I don't know, it's just kinda weird. You're defending the guy who might have killed our football coach, and some of the seniors don't like it." He looked at Sean again. "They've said some stuff."

Sean said, "This past week, the faculty has gotten weirder too. Most people haven't said anything to me one way or the other, but I've gotten some looks—and there have been a couple of teachers and coaches who've asked me straight out how you could defend the guy who killed their friend." He glanced at Ian. I sensed they had been talking about this for a while, and I was upset that Sean had not confided in me.

I said, "I am confident Troy is innocent. And I'm hoping to prove that at trial."

"That's what I tell them," Ian said.

"Me too. The basketball coach said, 'then why did they arrest him?'" Sean took a bite of salmon and slowly chewed, and I kept silent. My family knew the answer. I didn't need to tell them. "We're good," he finally said. "It will blow over once the trial is done." He looked at Ian and they both nodded.

"You do what you have to do for Troy, Mom. It's the right thing to do."

This was exactly what I didn't want to happen. This was worse than staying in Chicago. I made us move to a small-town fishbowl where everyone will now punish Sean and Ian for whom I'm defending. "I can't turn my back on Troy…"

"We're not asking you to," Ian said. "We can handle this. Besides, school's almost out."

Sean pointed his fork at Ian. "Tell her about your English class."

"Well, I've made this friend, and we are planning on going to the principal. The teacher says he's going to fail half the class, and we don't think that's right. There are some really smart kids in there and he's told them they're failing too."

Sean gave me one of his stares, which, over the course of our marriage, I had learned could mean a couple of things. Here, it meant, *Don't argue with Ian: listen and support him.* "That seems like a good approach," I said. "How has the class been lately?" Then I screwed up. "You've been turning your work in, right?"

Ian looked at Sean, suddenly angry. "Yes, I'm turning it in. That's not the point. It's not about me. Weren't you the one always talking about justice? Isn't that why you became an attorney? Well, this teacher is using his position to force students to accept lower grades just because he can."

He'd actually been listening to some of our dinner conversations. "Okay," I said, retreating as Sean nodded at me. I wanted to help Ian solve his problems. It was my job as his mom. For the last sixteen years, it had been my job.

Since we'd moved here to Kerry, Sean and I had been talking about letting go. It was Sean's view, more than mine, that it was our jobs as parents to let Ian have more control at this stage of his life, to make his own decisions and even fail on his own. That was how he'd grow to become an adult. I knew it was true, but I had argued the point. Yes, we needed to pull back and let him make mistakes, but we still had a duty to protect him. Sixteen-year-olds could make some terrible decisions. And now, I wanted to say that going to the principal could backfire. The teacher could single Ian out and seek revenge and he'd end up as the only student with an F. Had Ian really thought this through?

I needed to give him the benefit of the doubt, so I said, "I know you'll make the right decision." And I took a bite of salmon. I didn't like it.

---

Friday afternoon, Carol sent over the stuff the judge had ordered her to provide. This included her witness list and her exhibit list. I was pleased to see few surprises. I had talked with all her witnesses, other than the cops and the medical examiner, except for a name I had not yet seen, an assistant football coach at Northern Illinois University. His name had not been mentioned in any police report.

I called the school, got put on hold twice, but was finally put through to the football offices. "Hi. I am calling for Coach Othello Holmes?" Back on hold again.

Finally, "This is Coach Holmes."

"Coach, my name is Margaret Gallagher." I explained who I was, representing the father of Benny Weaver. "Your name is on the government's witness list, and I was wondering if you know why."

"I've been trying to figure that out myself. I just got the subpoena yesterday. But I really don't know anything."

"Did you recruit Benny?" I said.

"Yeah. That was what, two years ago? I coach the linebackers and I was recruiting from Ohio back then. The kid had some promise, and we thought if he filled out, put on about twenty pounds, he could be a baller. Outside linebacker."

"What do they want you to say?"

"We offered him a scholarship, but we pulled it back later. I think that's all they want me to say."

"Did you ever talk to Benny's father?" I asked.

"Yeah, back when we withdrew the offer. I talked to the kid first. I think he was failing some classes or something. To be honest, we don't take on kids with academic problems unless they're superstars. This kid wasn't. I told him he should go to a junior college, get his grades up, and we'd reconsider him in a couple of years. I hung up and his dad called me back. He was pretty angry."

I winced. This could be bad. "Do you remember what he said?"

"No. Just that he was angry. But dads get angry over this kind of thing. I didn't think it was a big deal. I can't believe his dad killed the high school coach."

"I don't think he did," I said. I thanked him for his help and hung up. Carol was going to use this college football coach to show Troy's motive—revenge for Coach Schafer costing Benny his college scholarship.

Around 4 p.m. my cell rang. It was Suzanne Sheehan, the friend I had made at Patrick's party. "How about getting a drink?" she said. I was excited to hear from her. I felt like we had connected at Patrick's.

"In," I said. "It's five o'clock somewhere, right?" I thought about places we could go. There was the Alibi, a place out Highway 3 where my dad used to get drunk. *No, thank you.* "How about Lefty's?"

She laughed. "No way. How about something on the *right* side of the tracks? Have you heard of Salty Chicks by the river?"

"No, but I can find it." When I hung up, I found Salty Chicks on Google Maps, along Paint Creek on the edge of downtown. A three-minute car ride. Why had I not heard of it before? I pulled up to a cute red shack with a patio full of potted flowers overlooking the water. The temperature had dropped to a reasonable mid-eighties and overhead misters pumped away. I saw Suzanne sitting beneath one.

She wore sunglasses, a pink tennis skirt, a halter top, and sneakers, like she'd just played tennis. "Did you win your match?" I said.

"No. That's why I need a drink." I sat down and the waiter was right there. I looked up at him. "How about a cosmo?" I said, thinking back to Kaitlyn Wynant's preferred drink.

"A cosmo?" Suzanne said. "I didn't figure you for a cosmo girl."

"I'm not," I said. "I don't even know what's in it. One of our witnesses was drinking cosmos when she saw something important, and I am curious how it impacted her."

"Make it two," Suzanne said to the waiter. "Drinking for justice. I'm in." When the waiter had left, she said, "So, how are you doing? Your big trial is coming up, right? It must be stressful."

"I've done a lot of trials, but this is my first as a defense attorney. And it means a lot to me personally. Troy was a very close friend when I was young."

"Wow, really?" she said. "That must be even more pressure."

Troy's case was in my head all the time. I had even dreamed about it recently, so I decided to change the subject. I needed a break. "Your daughter is Annie, right? Is she going to the principal with my son, Ian?"

Suzanne grinned. "He told you. That's great. Yeah, Annie and Ian. We talked it over, about how that could backfire on them."

"I'm so glad," I said. "I wanted to say the same thing to Ian, but I bit my tongue. We've had some tension lately."

Suzanne laughed. "Tension, with a sixteen-year-old? That's every day in my house." I'm ashamed to admit it, but I was glad to hear Suzanne struggling too. "Annie agreed she would try to recruit other kids. But I liked the fact they weren't just taking it. That teacher is on a power trip, and I hate teachers like that."

The waiter arrived with our drinks, pink cocktails in martini glasses, which we clinked. I said, "To sticking it to the teacher."

"Beautiful."

I took a sip. "Wow, this is strong. What's in it?"

"Vodka and cranberry juice," Suzanne said. "Maybe some other stuff. How many of these did your witness have?"

"She's the government's witness, and she had at least two. Of course, there's no guarantee the bartender where she was mixed them this strong, but still. I'm curious how intoxicated she was."

Suzanne smiled again. She had a pleasant, lightheartedness about her. "Okay, two cosmos. I guess we're going to be here a while."

Then her smiled faded, and she set her glass down. "I thought you should know, Annie mentioned that some people have been giving Ian a hard time over you being Troy's lawyer. I'm not sure if he mentioned it to you. Kids that age like their secrets."

"He mentioned it," I confirmed, letting out a tired sigh. "I'm not happy about it, but Ian swears he's got it under control, so..." I shrugged, feeling helpless.

"Hey, don't let it get you down," she said encouragingly. "For my part, I think it's a good thing that you're sticking by your friend. And considering how many people the coach ticked off, I wouldn't be surprised if it wasn't Troy who killed him at all."

"Got any other suspects for me?" I asked, joking without really joking at all. I'd been counting on Auntie El to know everyone and be aware of all the ties between people, but Suzanne was in a different age bracket and would have different connections, hear different bits of gossip.

"For my money, I'd say the most likely suspect is this guy my husband knows, Paul Marshall. He hated Coach Schafer. I mean, he bragged about going into the coach's office and tipping his desk over."

"I've heard of him." He was on the list of suspects I'd looked into. Sadly, he had a great alibi, but I decided I wouldn't mention that. I didn't want Suzanne to feel bad about giving me a dead-end lead. I smiled and said teasingly, "Are you ratting out your husband's friend?"

"He's an asshole, and my husband thinks so too. Apparently, during the season, before the coach was killed, Marshall's son was caught with some drugs, so the coach cut him."

"I hadn't heard that. What I heard was that he confronted the coach for berating his son in front of some fans."

Suzanne took another drink. "I'm sure he did that too. They say he was the type who liked the power of being a teacher and a coach a little too much, you know? He got off on making people feel small. Annie's English teacher might be bad, threatening to fail half the class, but I've heard the coach was worse—calling kids out directly, mocking or humiliating them in front of all their classmates. Or, if they were on one of his sports teams, in front of their teammates and even the crowds at games. Or are they called matches?" She shook her head. "I can never remember the terminology."

"For football? It's definitely games."

"Yeah, but he didn't just coach football. He also coached JV girls volleyball. You knew that, right?"

It had been part of the information in the police file, but I had paid little attention to it. Football was the prestige sport in towns like Kerry. Anything else paled in significance. But maybe that was something I shouldn't have overlooked.

"In fact, he ended up really messing up this girl who was his student a few years back."

"A girl on the volleyball team?" I picked up the cosmo and took another sip, wondering if I should pace myself with water. I wasn't used to such strong drinks.

"Yeah, that's right. Ava Robbins. She was a good girl—sweet, polite, good student. She baby sat for Annie years ago. Anyway," Suzanne lowered her voice, even though the people at the next table weren't listening. "The way I heard it, she couldn't take his treatment anymore and moved away, dropped out of school. One day, she's a girl with a bright future ahead of her. The next, she's a dropout. I never got the full story. I'm not sure anyone did. But everyone seemed to agree that the coach was to blame."

I remembered that Auntie El had come up with Ava Robbins as a possible suspect. "Thanks. That's interesting." I would call Auntie El to see if she could find Ava.

"Good," Suzanne said, leaning back in her chair. She really wanted to help me. "I was thinking I might stop by the courthouse, if you think that's okay. I've never seen a trial."

"Sure. It's open to the public. We start jury selection Monday after next, but that part is pretty boring. Opening statements are more entertaining. You hear each side's best version of their own case."

"Perfect," she said. "My schedule is pretty flexible, so I can pop in most times."

"What do you do?" I said, taking another sip. Was it my imagination or could I already feel the alcohol?

"I work at our church. I'm the Director of Congregational Care." She raised her cocktail in an ironic toast, and took a sip. "We don't have these at work."

"What does a *Director of Congregational Care* do?"

"Mostly, I visit congregants in hospitals or care facilities. I bring them communion and pray with them, if they want."

"That's cool," I said.

She finished her drink. "I've been praying for *you*," she said, which stunned me. I didn't know what to say. Had anyone ever prayed for me? After my awkward silence, Suzanne said, "Is that okay?"

"Yes, absolutely. I am honored—and grateful. I was just trying to think if anyone has ever prayed for me."

"Is there anything in particular we should be praying for? I'll get the pastors in on this too."

I said, "Whenever I go into trial, I always say a prayer myself, asking to be allowed to do justice." It was the perfect prosecutor's prayer, because that's what a prosecutor was supposed to do. I'd been wondering if that was still appropriate now that my job was defending people. Justice, in some cases, might mean my client should be convicted.

"*Do justice*," Suzanne nodded. "That should be all our prayers."

## 32

I didn't have time for Frankie, with Troy's trial a week away, but he was panicked over the prospect of serving prison time for the manslaughter charge. And I had been thinking about his case over the weekend. Something about it wasn't right, and I needed to meet with Frankie and his father, Dom.

They arrived Monday morning at 10 a.m. and Auntie El brought them into my personal office, getting them each some black coffee.

"No soda bread today?" Dom joked with her.

"Sorry," she said. "Nothing but coffee today."

I walked them into my office. "How are you doing?" I said, as they each sat across from my desk.

"I got fired," Frankie said. "The boss said there's too much liability for me to drive his tow truck." He looked hard at his father.

Dom said, "We were wondering, you know, what are Frankie's chances at trial? I mean, this all seems so extreme. Plus, I'm not sure I can afford it. What will this cost?"

This was the part of the job I hated. When I was a prosecutor, I made a salary and didn't have to charge clients. I was still adjusting to the fact I was now in business for myself. I said, "It's the same hourly rate as for the driving under the influence charge. The problem with the manslaughter charge is that I will need to do a lot more work, so I'll be logging more hours. I normally need a retainer in a case like this. But before we talk money, I have a couple of questions."

"Are you charging us now for this meeting?" Dom said.

"Yes." Dom would understand, right? As a mechanic, he charged by the hour. I got right to the point. "Dom, you had bruising on your sternum after the accident, right?"

He reflexively rubbed his chest. "Yeah."

I turned to Frankie. "But you were okay?"

"The seat belt dug into my neck a little," he rubbed his upper right shoulder and neck, "but other than that, I was fine."

My suspicion was right. I had gone for a walk Sunday morning and was thinking over this case. That's when it hit me. I was mad at myself for not seeing it sooner. Their injuries were backwards. Focusing on Dom, I said, "It's common in accidents when there is frontal damage to the car, for the driver's chest to hit the steering wheel, causing rib and sternum injuries. And I checked, that truck model did not have air bags." Then I pointed at Frankie, "And for passengers, the seat belt harness often cuts into the skin, causing abrasions." I motioned to my right neck. "The passenger's seat belt would cut in here."

Dom hung his head, like a kid caught in a lie.

Frankie looked at his dad, then at me. "It was my idea, at first," he said. "This would be Pop's third charge, which would be a felony and could send him to prison. That's why I wanted to plead guilty. My record is clean. I thought I'd just pay a fine or something."

Dom said, "We didn't expect all this craziness. But you gotta believe me. I wasn't gonna let Frankie go to prison for me. I figured if it looked bad for him at trial, I could tell the judge that I was the driver."

"That wouldn't go over well," I said. "Assuming they believed you, the prosecutor would then charge *you*, and you'd have to pay for a second trial. And if you were convicted, the judge would be so pissed at you for wasting his time with the first case, he'd definitely send you to prison." Why couldn't my clients tell me the truth? Was this what it was going to be like as a defense attorney?

"What do we do?" Dom said.

"I don't know," I said. "This is new for me." I paused, thinking of the permutations. "We could have you write out an affidavit, saying you were the driver, but the prosecutor might not believe you." I pointed at Frankie. "Do you still have any bruising, anything to corroborate your dad's story?"

Frankie pulled down his collar to show his neck. "Nothing there," I said. To Dom, "How about you?"

"Do you want me to take my shirt off?" He was serious.

"No," I blurted. "But have you seen anything in the mirror lately, like bruising? We could take pictures."

He shook his head. "No. I did at first, but it's healed."

I said, "Did you tell anyone? Or is there anyone who could testify to corroborate the bruising?"

"My girlfriend. She saw it," Dom said. And then he got excited. "And the cops… At the scene, I was bullshitting with them and one of them asked me if I was okay. I told him my chest hurt."

"Do you remember which one?"

"Yeah, I do." Dom lit up. "James Carpenter's son, Jimmy. I'll talk to his dad."

I held up my hand. "Not yet. Let me talk with the prosecutor." I was thinking about how this might play out. If I could convince Oliver that Dom was the driver, he would dismiss Frankie's case. Then he'd want to charge Dom. Except he wouldn't have great evidence of Dom's intoxication. Dom had done no field sobriety tests, and he hadn't taken the breathalyzer. And even better, Oliver would want to prove intoxication to support the *recklessness* element needed to prove the manslaughter. Oliver would have an extremely tough case. These two dummies might have stumbled ass backwards into a workable defense.

To Frankie I said, "Give me your boss's number. I'll call him and tell him you weren't driving. Hopefully, you can get your job back. But first I'll talk with the cop, Jimmy Carpenter. Let's hope he corroborates your story, Dom." I stood to signal we were done. "Have your girlfriend call me, and maybe we'll draft up an affidavit from her to give to the prosecutor, having her swear to your injury."

I walked them both out, past Auntie El at her desk, and shook their hands. "I have a trial starting next Monday, so I won't be able to do much on your case after then, but we'll start with the first steps this week. Okay?"

"Thanks, Maggie," Dom said. "I owe you."

*Yeah*, I thought. *At least twenty grand by the time this is over.* No charity case for a dad who would do this to his son.

I pulled out my phone. While it was fresh in my mind, I wanted to call my cousin Patrick. He answered on the first ring. "Are you on duty?" I said.

"No, I'm off today. I'm helping my sergeant repair his back fence. You met him at the party, remember? He's right here. Wanna say hi?"

"Hi," wasn't what I wanted to say to him. "No thanks. Listen, I'm calling to ask a favor." I realized I was being pushy. "Is now a good time?"

"Yeah, now's good. This asshole is acting like I work for him or something. I need a break."

The sergeant must be right there. I said, "This might be confidential, at least for now."

"Okay. Give me a minute." I pictured Patrick walking somewhere out of earshot of his sergeant. "Go ahead," he said.

"I got a drunk driving case, which the prosecutor turned into a manslaughter charge."

He laughed. "I heard about that. Frankie DeNuzzio. He's a pretty good kid. I like to call him when I'm on the road and we need a car towed."

"Well, it turns out he didn't do it. I mean, he wasn't driving at the time of the accident. His dad was driving, and Frankie was covering up for the old man because he had some drunk driving priors."

"That sounds like Dom," Patrick said.

"It's kind of complicated. I want Dom and Frankie to come clean, but I'm afraid the prosecutor won't believe them. Dom said something to a cop at the scene, Jimmy Carpenter. I was wondering if you could arrange for me to talk with him."

"Just a minute," Patrick said. Then he yelled, "Hey, Jimmy, come here." After a moment, I heard them talking, though Patrick must have held the phone up against his shirt, because I couldn't quite make out what they were saying. Finally, I heard Patrick say, "Just talk to her. She's my cousin."

"Hello?"

"Officer Carpenter, my name is Margaret Gallagher, and I was hoping I could ask a couple questions about Frankie DeNuzzio's driving under the influence case."

"It wasn't my case," he said. "I was just dealing with the accident. I didn't even write a report."

"Right, that's fine. This will only take a minute. Do you remember talking with Dominic DeNuzzio at the scene?"

"Yeah..." He sounded guarded.

"Did he say anything to you about having pain in his sternum or ribs?"

"What's this about?" Carpenter said. I knew he had no reason to trust me—or any defense attorney, for that matter—so I decided to lay it all out.

"Frankie wasn't driving that night. He lied about it to the first officer who arrived, to take the hit for his dad who has some priors. But Dom has now agreed to do the right thing and man up. I'm trying to find some evidence to corroborate what he's telling me. He suffered a bruised sternum, which would be consistent with a driver's chest striking the steering wheel, and he says that he mentioned having some pain there to you when you were talking at the scene. So, do you remember him saying anything like that?"

Officer Carpenter laughed. "Freakin' DeNuzzio. Yeah, he was hanging around while my partner took pictures of the crash scene. He was having trouble breathing, and I asked if he was okay. He said, 'Yeah, just a little sore from the accident.' Or something like that. But when he said it, he rubbed his chest, I think, like that's where it hurt. I'm not exactly positive, though. Things got a little wild after that."

"What do you mean?" I said.

"I was going to check on Dom, but then the guy in the house collapsed. I forgot about Dom."

So Jimmy corroborated Dom's story. Maybe I could get Frankie out of this. "Okay, thanks, Officer Carpenter. You might get a call from Oliver Altman, the prosecutor."

"That's fine," he said. Then in a lower voice, like he didn't want anyone to hear, "By the way, do you handle anything over in Harney County?"

It was east of Donohoe County, but not too far. "Yes, of course."

"My sister's boyfriend got popped over there on an assault. Could I give him your number?"

"Sure. Have him call me. And thanks for the help, Jimmy."

I hung up and walked out to Auntie El as she hung up her own phone. I said, "Paddy just helped me out again. Can I have your recipe? I'd like to make him some soda bread."

She beamed at the idea of her son helping me. "He's a good boy." Then she got serious. "But nobody gets my recipe. Buy him a six-pack of beer."

Then she walked out from behind her desk. "Come on. Since you're on a roll, let's go meet with a potential witness."

"Who?" I said.

"That high school girl suspect I told you about. Ava Robbins. She's back in town."

## 33

Auntie El told me about tracking down Ava as I drove us out of town. "I was on unpaid leave, 'cause my boss is a meanie, so I went to get a pedicure," she said, and I looked over to see her lips twitch.

"You got a pedicure? The farm lady has her nails done?"

"I'm not a *farm lady*. I'm a private detective. A good one. So…can I finish?" She gave me a cheeky look. "I'm getting my nails done, and in comes Connie Robbins. She's Ava's grandmother. She said Ava was back in town visiting, and I remembered we wanted to talk with her."

"You *are* a good detective," I said.

Auntie El had arranged for us to meet Ava at the grandmother's home. It was east of town, out toward Auntie El's farm. We pulled up a gravel driveway and walked to the door. The diminutive Grandma Robbins met us on the front porch. She had short gray hair and a worried expression. "Ava's having second thoughts. This has brought back bad memories for her."

Auntie El grabbed her by the arm and walked her into the house. "We're going to be very gentle, Connie. I told you how important this is." I left her to deal with the grandmother's anxieties, confident that my aunt would win out in the end. She could impose her will on anyone. Meanwhile, I walked into the dining room, where Ava was standing at the table. She was small and slender, like her grandmother, with long brown hair. Cute, but extremely nervous.

I shook her hand. "Hi, Ava. Thanks for meeting with us."

"Grandma said it was important, but I don't really know anything."

I motioned for her to sit and sat myself. "This won't take too long. As you probably know, I'm representing Troy Weaver, who was charged with the murder of Coach Schafer."

She nodded, her eyes wide.

I decided to go slowly, work up to things so she wouldn't get spooked. "Do you know Troy's son, Benny? He might have been in your class."

"Yeah, I knew Benny. I mean, I know who he is. It's not like we were friends—not really."

She gave a worried glance at her grandmother, and Auntie El saw it. Ava didn't want to talk in front of her grandma. Auntie El said, "Connie, do you have some lemonade or something we can get for everyone?" Again, she grabbed Connie's arm and walked her into the kitchen.

When they were gone, Ava said, "I had a boyfriend at the time. He hung out some with Benny." She glanced at the kitchen door. "They were kinda into drugs and stuff."

"Benny was?" I was shocked to hear that. Troy and Denise had said nothing about Benny having a problem with drugs.

"I think he was just getting into it. He didn't know what he was doing. She chuckled. "A big dumbshit. That's what JT called him."

"Okay…" I was still trying to process what I'd heard. Benny was into drugs. Was that the real reason Coach Schafer cut Benny from the team? I'd deal with that later. I needed to focus on Ava. "I understand you played volleyball."

"Yes." She became even more nervous, her fingernails digging into the inside of her left arm. I noticed some scars there. She saw me looking and twisted her arm over, hugging it to her chest. I realized Ava was likely a cutter. I ran into that once as a prosecutor in Chicago. A young woman suffering from domestic violence had taken to cutting her arms, trying to cope with the emotional trauma by taking control of something, even if it was her own pain, I guess. I never understood it completely.

I said, "I've heard that you had some issues with Grant Schafer."

"I didn't kill him." She sat up straight in her chair, suddenly defiant.

*Mistake.* I didn't want her to get defensive. "No, of course not. I'm just trying to find out more about him." I smiled to soften my demeanor. "I'm gathering evidence about his abuse. How he treated people."

"Okay." She seemed to accept that, slumping back into her seat. "He was an ass…a jerk. He would say mean things to people. I mean, all the time. He was bad in volleyball, but in health class…" She shook her head, shuddering a little.

"Like what?"

"I had this friend, Agnes." I must have made a face, because she said, "I know, right? Who names their kid Agnes? But she was cool. Anyway, whenever he talked about being overweight, or the impacts of obesity on health, he would call on Agnes. Just because she was heavy."

"Ouch," I said, wanting her to keep talking.

"Another one of my friends asked him why he did that, and he said he believed our parents all babied us, and we needed to be toughened up."

"Was he ever physical with anyone?"

"No," she said quickly. "He was a jerk, but he never hit anyone. At least that I know of."

Grandma Connie and Auntie El returned with a platter of cookies and glasses of iced tea. Auntie El saw me looking at her, and she shrugged, as if to say, *I kept her out as long as I could.*

Connie passed out the drinks and sat down. I sipped my drink and said, "Do you have any sugar?"

"It's already sweet tea."

Auntie El said, "Come on, Connie, show me where it is."

"Fine…" This time, Connie definitely knew what I was doing, but thankfully, she was too polite to call me on it.

When they were gone, Ava said, "Thanks. I don't want to talk about this in front of Grammy."

"I figured. So what did Schafer say to *you*?"

She glanced at the kitchen door, then back at me. "Somehow he knew that I sometimes cut my arms." She held up the inside of her left arm. "I don't know why I did it," she said, shaking her head. "But he liked to talk about mental health, and he would pick on me like he did on Agnes. I mean, it seemed to me like he did it every day. Some girls in class didn't like me, and they told everyone about it. The whole school." She picked up a cookie and nervously tapped it against the plate. "My cutting got worse because of him."

"Did you talk to Schafer, or report him? Maybe to the principal?"

"I moved away. My aunt lives in St. Louis, and I told her about all this at Christmas." Ava smiled for the first time. "She's a nurse, and she saw my arms. I guess she figured it out, but she was really cool. We both cooked up a story for my folks, how I could finish up high school there while working with her at the hospital and set myself up for a job after school." She took a bite of the cookie. "I'm still in St. Louis. I just got my own apartment and I'm working as a nurse's assistant," she said with some pride.

"That's great." I expected the ladies to return any minute. "When did you move to St. Louis?"

"It was after the coach was killed, if that's what you're asking, but I was home with my family on New Year's Eve playing Monopoly."

"Did the police ever talk to you?"

"No. No one thought I would kill the coach. Where would I get a gun?"

"Do you know of anyone else who might have had a grudge against Schafer?"

She hesitated a moment, which made me think there was someone. Then, "Nope. I mean, a lot of people hated that guy, but a lot of people liked him too. He was...what's the word for it?"

"Polarizing?"

"Yeah. Polarizing."

I didn't know what else to ask her, but I sensed she was holding back. "Did you talk to your family about him? About how he was bullying you?"

She glanced at the kitchen door again. "No. And thanks for getting Grammy out of here. I mean, my parents knew about my cutting, but…they didn't know about what the coach said. Or how some of those other girls were."

I said, "You mentioned your boyfriend. What was his name, JT?"

"Yeah, he looked a little like Justin Timberlake. At least he thought so. He's pretty arrogant."

I picked up a cookie and took a bite. "Was it tough leaving him to move to St. Louis?"

She laughed. "Yeah. But it was the best thing I ever did. He was part of the reason I had problems. *He* could be abusive too. Verbal and physical."

"I'm glad you got away. Did you tell him about the coach?"

"No. I didn't need to. He was in the same class and he saw it. He would get so pissed…"

The kitchen door swung open and the two ladies came out again, Connie holding a small bowl of sugar. She said, "Have you had a good talk? I thought we could go sit on the porch and drink our iced tea."

"Yes, it's been helpful. Thank you," I said.

"Let's go on the porch," Auntie El said, taking the bowl and spooning some sugar into my glass. With a mischievous grin, she said, "I know how you like your sweet tea, Maggie."

She was going to make me drink this sugar syrup. As my mom used to say when I was a kid, Auntie El was a *corker*.

I picked up my glass of caffeinated syrup and followed everyone out to the porch, resisting the urge to excuse myself to get back to work. I had a murder trial next week and I was nowhere near ready.

## 34

The courtroom was almost full. There were current and former high school football players in their letterman jackets filling the last two rows. Ironic, I thought, but I could use that later, reminding the jury how many people wore these jackets.

There were TV and print media and others interested in the drama. Today, they were going to be disappointed. Nothing too exciting would happen this Monday morning. Today we picked the jury.

Troy sat next to me, ashen white and shaking slightly. At least the slim suit Denise bought fit him. Two officers sat behind us, along with Auntie El and Denise. She left Charley with her mother today, so I reminded her how important his presence would be at opening statements. I wanted the jury to personalize Troy, see him as a loving father of a cute kid. However, it might be a while. Jury selection could last for days, if the judge wasn't strict about controlling time.

I handed writing tablets to my aunt and Denise so they could take notes about the potential jurors. I said, "Write down if you know them, if you've heard rumors about them, if their answers give you a bad vibe. Anything at all. This isn't an exact science."

Behind Carol in the first row sat Coach Schafer's parents. I caught a disapproving look from them as I returned to my table, and it stung. As a prosecutor, I had always been on the side of the victim's family.

The bailiff looked at me and mouthed the question, "Ready?"

I nodded. *This was it.* It was a surreal moment—my childhood friend about to be tried for murder, and me defending him. I reached over and squeezed Troy's hand. "Here we go." He tried to smile back, but could only manage something that looked like a grimace.

Typically, there was no drama during jury selection, but I had never been more nervous. And to be honest with myself, it wasn't just about Troy and the rest of his life. I had lain awake last night thinking about what this trial meant for me. If he were convicted, that would hang over me the rest of *my* life. An innocent man—at least I was pretty sure he was innocent—my friend, found guilty of aggravated murder because I hadn't been able to convince the jury otherwise.

There would be years of appeals trying to undo the mistakes I had made that led to such a bad verdict. And there would be the toll on my family…

"All rise. The Donahoe County Court of Common Pleas is now in session. The Honorable Victor Blankenship, presiding."

The judge banged his gavel and said, "Be seated. Call the case, Ms. Becker."

Carol stood in her navy, knee-length skirt and blazer. "This is the matter of State of Ohio versus Troy Weaver, on the charge of aggravated murder."

The judge looked at the bailiff. "Bring in the first twelve potential jurors."

Last Thursday, Carol and I had met with the judge to work out the details of jury selection. On Friday, Blankenship brought in fifty potential jurors and had them fill out the questionnaire we had agreed on.

Then Saturday morning, Auntie El and I sat in my office conference room to go over the answers. To start, I had to explain the jury selection process to her. She knew that we needed twelve jurors, plus a couple of alternates, in case someone got sick. I also let her know that I could challenge twelve jurors and the prosecutor could challenge twelve. These were called "peremptory challenges." And we could also challenge anyone who we had reason to believe couldn't be fair. I told her, "As a prosecutor, I looked for solid citizens, people who trusted the police. I also wanted logical thinkers, folks who weren't going to be governed by their emotions."

She thought that was funny. "So, as a defense attorney, do you want the opposite of that? Emotional criminals who hate the police?"

"I don't know." Of course, I had thought about the type of juror I would want as a defense attorney, but I was still undecided. "Some defense lawyers might do well with emotional jurors, but not me. I'm not that type of lawyer. I'm not very good at emotional appeals." I thought some more. "Maybe someone with a healthy skepticism. Someone who understands our justice system could make a mistake."

She sat there with a giant pile of questionnaires. "I'm not sure I'll be much help at finding that."

But she was wrong—she turned out to be a huge help. She knew something about half the fifty people on the list. Coming in today, thanks to her insights on the questionnaires, I had four people who were a solid yes, and six that I definitely wanted to keep off the jury.

The first twelve came in and sat in the jury box. I was allowed to ask questions first, but Blankenship announced that I would only have thirty minutes. He was insistent on finishing today. I focused my questions on whether any believed the justice system could make a mistake. That was going to be the theme of my defense. There were no dirty cops, no bad faith by the prosecutor, but a series of mistaken assumptions that had resulted in this horrible mistaken arrest. We were living in a skeptical time and in this first panel, I felt a connection with eleven of the twelve. There was just the one gentleman in the corner. He said, "I don't see how the police could have arrested him unless he did it."

I explained the different standards, how police only needed probable cause to arrest, but that a jury had to find guilt beyond a reasonable doubt. He didn't seem to care. I would be challenging him.

I asked if anyone followed Kerry High football. I was surprised that only about half of the people did. Nobody would admit to having strong opinions about Coach Schafer, however.

There was one other series of questions I asked each panel of twelve. "Did any of you go to Kerry High School?" If they did, I asked, "Did you or someone you know have a letterman jacket, like the kind in the back of the courtroom?" I pointed to the group of football players. They didn't like being pointed at.

Carol objected the first time I asked a panel. To the judge I said, "Your Honor, a Kerry letterman jacket is a key piece of evidence in this case, and the jury's familiarity with that evidence will be important." He let me ask it, and it turned out that over half the prospective jurors knew someone with a letterman jacket.

By 5:30 p.m. we had gone through all fifty potential jurors. The judge gave us fifteen minutes to review our notes and collect our thoughts, and then we would make our peremptory challenges on the record. Auntie El and Denise came forward to our table to talk things over with Troy. "Anyone have a definite no?" I said.

Auntie El handed me a numbered list of thirty-one names. "They are in descending order, from bad to good. These are people I know something about, or I got a strong feeling about from your questions."

Exactly what I needed in the moment. Organized, condensed opinions. I wanted to hug her right there. Glancing at the list, it aligned with what I was thinking. I pointed to number three. "I thought this guy was okay."

"No." She shook her head. "I've heard rumors he's cheating on his wife. And he's a thief. Our neighbor sells eggs at the end of her driveway, on the honor system. I saw him take a carton of eggs and not pay."

"Okay." I wouldn't want the guy if I were the prosecutor, but should I keep him if he doesn't respect the rule of law? I looked at Troy and Denise. "You guys?" I showed them the complete list of fifty names. The judge had removed four already because they knew either Troy or Denise, and he removed another two who said they couldn't be fair. From what they saw in the news, they thought Troy was guilty.

Troy pointed at a name. "This woman kept looking at me funny. Like she could tell I was guilty already." She was thirteenth on Auntie El's list.

"Okay, I'll challenge her." Trust your gut reaction in jury selection, I had learned.

The judge returned and Carol and I alternated our challenges until she had none left. I only used ten of mine. Then Judge Blankenship announced, "We have a jury. Twelve, plus two alternates." He looked at Carol, and then me. "Do either of you have any exceptions or objections?" We didn't. "Very well. We stand adjourned until 10 a.m. tomorrow. We will begin with opening statements."

"What do you think?" Troy whispered to me.

"It's a good group. I think you'll get a fair trial." *Just don't screw things up tomorrow*, I said to myself.

## 35

A few of the football players were in the courtroom again the next day, but none wore their letterman jackets this time. My new friend Suzanne was in the back row and made a gesture with her hands folded, like she was praying for me. I appreciated it and mouthed a "thank you" to her.

There was one significant addition in the courtroom today, a TV camera in the back on a raised platform. The blonde TV reporter from Dayton told me her station might carry the opening statements live. *Great. No pressure at all.*

Though really, how could there be any more pressure than there already was? *Focus on your routine. Don't get caught up in the moment.* I slowly unpacked my leather satchel, laying out my tools. Blue and red pens, a highlighter, tablet, the evidence code. I also set out a tablet and pen for Troy so he could take notes. I didn't want him whispering or distracting me during the trial.

Troy came in and sat down, in the same suit he'd worn yesterday. Maybe we should get him a second one. How would the jury feel about him wearing the same suit every day? At least Denise brought a different tie.

Auntie El was behind me, and now she reached over the bar to squeeze my shoulder. "Kick some ass," she said, a little too loud.

I turned and grimly nodded.

The jury was brought in, and then the judge took the bench. He thanked them for their service and gave some preliminary instructions about how to do their job. Then he said, "You are about to hear opening statements. I want to caution you that these are not evidence. These statements are an opportunity for counsel to give you a summary of what they think the evidence will show. Because the State of Ohio has the burden of proof, the prosecutor, Ms. Becker will go first. Ms. Becker?"

Today she wore black slacks and a white silk blouse. She confidently walked to the jury box, and all fourteen jurors stared back intently. Each had been given a pen and small tablet for note-taking.

"Ladies and gentlemen, a year and a half ago, the defendant," she turned and pointed at Troy, "left a New Year's Eve party at Lefty's Bar and Grill, slipping out, thinking no one would see him leave. He drove ten minutes to the home of Grant Schafer, the coach of the Kerry High football team, and shot him with a handgun, the bullet entering through his throat and lodging in the back of his brain. Then the defendant went back to party the night away at Lefty's. He thought he got away clean." She paused a moment. "But someone *did* see him. You will hear from the young woman outside the bar who will positively identify the defendant as the man she saw sneaking out of the bar before midnight."

I watched the jury intently, looking for their reaction. It was an advantage for the prosecution to go first, creating that first impression that I would have to work hard to try to undo. The jury kept glancing at Troy, as if trying to imagine him as a murderer.

"Why did the defendant kill Coach Schafer? The defendant's son, Benny, was a star on the Kerry High football team, with a college scholarship offer. And then his grades went bad. So bad he was removed from the team. The coach told him, 'You're a student first.' But the defendant didn't like that. He was irate. He wanted Coach Schafer fired. He went to the high school's athletic director, then the principal. He tried to stir up other parents. He confronted the coach on the sideline before a game, yelling so loud the crowd could hear it thirty yards away in the stands."

I wrote on my tablet for Troy, "Is that true?"

His head sank and he nodded.

"He made harassing phone calls, calling Coach Schafer late at night, early in the morning, trying to make his life miserable. You will see those phone records yourself." She paused and looked back at Troy. It was a tactic I had used myself as a prosecutor. I wanted the jury to see *accusation* in my look at the defendant. To see I wasn't afraid of the killer, to see my disdain.

"And then, even worse news came for the defendant. His son's scholarship to Northern Illinois University was withdrawn, costing the family a benefit worth over eighty thousand dollars. That was the final straw."

Carol walked to her table and picked up the M17 Sig Sauer. She walked back to the jury. "The case went unsolved for a year and a half, in part because the police weren't able to locate the murder weapon. The defendant had the motive, but there was nothing to clearly tie him to the murder. And then two months ago, a tragedy. In the defendant's own home, a five-year-old boy accidentally shot his older brother, Benny. The same Benny who was failing his high school classes and was removed from the football team. The young man fell to the kitchen floor, along with this gun. The police came to the scene and seized that gun, and did what they always do when they find a gun at a crime scene…"

I stood, "Objection. We talked about this, Your Honor…"

Judge Blankenship cut me off. "Sustained. Ms. Becker, you are treading on dangerous ground." Last Thursday I had cautioned Carol against bringing up Benny's shooting. It would be unfairly prejudicial, I argued. The judge told her she could mention how and why the police found the gun, but she could not call that shooting a crime. Which she just did.

"Yes, Your Honor." She turned back to the jury, her wings clipped slightly. Just what I hoped for—a blow to her confidence. After a deep breath, she continued. "The police seized the gun and conducted ballistic testing on its shell casings. It turns out that gun, the defendant's gun, is the same gun that shot and killed Coach Schafer."

This was her big moment, and despite me getting in that objection, it was obvious that it landed. The jury looked at Troy. I had seen it before as a prosecutor and I saw it now. There was condemnation in their eyes and their mind was made up. Not completely, of course. They would listen to the evidence, try to be impartial, but the rest of the trial was going to be an uphill battle for me.

Carol wasn't done. "The night of the murder, the defendant wore his high school letterman jacket." She walked to her table and picked up a large plastic bag that contained Troy's jacket. She brought it back in front of the jury. "This yellow *K* on the defendant's jacket is very important because yellow fibers were found under Coach Schafer's fingernails—embedded there while he struggled with his killer." She held up the coat. "Forensic testing matched those fibers to this jacket—concrete proof that the defendant was at Coach Schafer's house and shot him in cold blood."

Another point for Carol. She slowly carried the jacket back to her table, letting the jury digest the latest bombshell.

As she returned from her table, she continued. "After this case went unsolved for over a year, it was referred to the unit in the Attorney General's office responsible for cold cases. An investigator in that unit called up the defendant and asked him about that New Year's Eve. You will hear the defendant lie, saying he never left Lefty's bar. You will hear it in his own voice…"

"Objection! Your Honor, this is a blatant discovery violation." I could feel my face turning red. "I have received no recordings from the government. Not one. And now the government is saying it has such a recording and will be playing it for the jury?"

Carol said, "May we approach, Your Honor?" It was clear she didn't want the jury to hear this.

The judge waved us forward. "I am confident we have provided this recording to the defense," Carol insisted.

"We have received no recordings, Judge," I said. I was furious. Such a blatant discovery violation was so inexcusable that I was struggling to formulate a sentence. "I want to go on the record and move to exclude all references to any statements by my client. I am going to seek sanctions against Ms. Becker—"

"Hold on, Ms. Gallagher," the judge said. "Let's confirm whether or not this recording was turned over in discovery. We'll go back on the record, and Ms. Becker, I am going to caution the jury to disregard any mention of a recording, for now. If it turns out you provided it in discovery to Ms. Gallagher, I will allow you to offer it into evidence. But if you did not provide it," he pointed his finger at her, and I glanced at the jury to make sure they saw it. They did. "If you did not provide it, I am going to exclude it from evidence as a discovery violation."

Carol said, "I know we turned over a verbatim transcript of that recording." She glanced at me, wanting me to confirm that.

The judge gave me an inquiring look too. "Yes," I said, "I have a police report with my client's statements. But I have no audio recording."

The judge turned to Carol. "Very well. You may mention the statements, but not the recording. Understood?"

"Yes," she said, then under her breath to me, "I'm sure we gave you the recording."

I went back to my table, still angry, but also pleased. I had been able to interrupt Carol's flow a second time. I had caught her in an inexcusable violation of the rules *and* had the judge wag his finger at her in front of the jury.

The judge said, "Ladies and gentlemen of the jury, again, I am going to instruct you to disregard something the prosecutor has said. For now, you must disregard any discussion of a recording of statements by the defendant." He looked at Carol with obvious disapproval, and I struggled to hide my smile. "Ms. Becker, you may continue."

"Thank you, Judge." She turned to the jury. "So, ladies and gentlemen, at the conclusion of the evidence in the case, I am going to ask you to find the defendant guilty on the charge of aggravated murder of Kerry High football coach Grant Schafer." She turned and walked back to her table.

I let her sit at her table a long moment, the courtroom silent. I wanted everyone, the jury, the judge, the members of the audience, all to bask in that disastrous, anti-climactic finish. I wanted them to think that if Carol could screw up her discovery, what else could she screw up? I waited so long, the judge had to prompt me. "Ms. Gallagher," he said. "Your turn."

## 36

I stood slowly and walked to the jury. I said nothing at first, taking the time to look at each one, letting them feel the gravity of this situation. "You have already seen it this morning. The government has made mistakes in this case." I turned and looked at Carol. I wanted the jury to look too. I wanted them to lose respect for her, to begin to suspect her trustworthiness. "The gun that shot Grant Schafer *was* found in Troy Weaver's home. But it was found a year and a half after the crime in question. Essentially, that's the government's case. You will not hear any evidence about Mr. Weaver buying that gun, about him ever using that gun, or even possessing it during that stretch of time. So when did he buy it? Could it have been three months ago at a gun show? Six months? You will hear nothing on that point, even though the government must prove Mr. Weaver possessed that gun on December 31st, a year and a half ago."

I moved a few steps to my right, standing in front of different jurors. It was important to move, to make each juror feel I was talking to him or her, while avoiding making them feel uncomfortable or under scrutiny. "Did Mr. Weaver even visit the home of Grant Schafer? The prosecution has to prove he was there, but you will hear no evidence of that fact. No one saw him in the neighborhood, and none of his fingerprints were found at the coach's house. Sure, there are the yellow fibers, but what the government told you isn't the full story. The prosecutor said the three yellow fibers under Grant Schafer's fingernails came from Troy Weaver's letterman jacket. But those fibers are the same in *all* yellow letters in *all* the letterman jackets that are produced by a company known as Stapleton Products. How many people in Kerry wear a letterman jacket? How many other schools in Ohio or Pennsylvania have yellow letters? When you hear the witnesses, you will conclude this evidence is almost worthless."

"Objection," Carol said. She was trying to interrupt me the way I had her. "Counsel is making an argument."

"Sustained," the judge said. "Move along, Ms. Gallagher."

I pretended like nothing had happened. I didn't want to lose my momentum. "There is the fact my client was upset with Grant Schafer over the dismissal of his son from the high school football team. We will not dispute this. But you will also hear evidence of other parents unhappy with the coach's style and treatment of some players. Complaints made to the athletic director and the high school principal. Why is unhappiness with the coach a motive for my client, but not for anyone else?" I looked with disdain at Carol again, wanting the jury to feel my aggravation at the way she'd jumped on the idea of Troy's guilt.

"There is one other element to the prosecutor's opening statement that I want to correct. At the New Year's Eve party at Lefty's, it is true my client went outside. He was seen by a young woman who was celebrating that night, having a couple of drinks, stepping out to kiss her boyfriend. She wasn't particularly focused on a forty-year-old man walking outside. What she saw was my client going to his car. But she did not see him drive away. She can't say that he left. As she herself will testify, he might have come outside for a smoke and gone back inside. In other words, there is zero evidence that Troy Weaver drove away from Lefty's that night."

I walked over to Troy and stood by him. "Because of a couple of coincidences, the government has leaped to false conclusions, putting Mr. Weaver here in a nightmare position of having to defend himself against charges for a crime he did not commit."

I patted his shoulder and then walked back toward the jury, suddenly worried that patting his shoulder was laying it on too thick. Too late to take it back now. I just had to keep going. "At the conclusion of this trial, I am confident you will see this case as the farce that it is."

I walked back to Troy and sat next to him, feeling like I had blown it. I had always been the reasoned, logical attorney. This last touch felt over the top. Too emotional. Too theatrical.

Troy leaned over and said, "Thank you."

Judge Blankenship waited for me to sit down and collect myself. Then he said, "Ms. Becker, call your first witness."

No time to beat myself up. "The State calls Kerry Police Detective Janice Evans."

This was the short-haired blond detective I had confronted at the hospital two months ago. She entered from the hallway as if she was listening at the door, professionally but not formally dressed, wearing tactical pants with plenty of pockets and a white polo shirt with a Kerry PD logo on her chest.

She began her testimony by describing her background and experience as a cop, including working two years as a detective. That meant she had been a detective a mere six months when she got this case. When the preliminaries were over, Carol got to the meat. "Can you tell us what happened on the night of December 31st and the morning of January 1st?"

"Well, that evening, New Year's Eve, the department was stretched pretty thin. New Year's Eve is always busy, but there was also a power outage earlier in the night and a streak of vandalism downtown. Everyone was called out. I was working on a property damage case when my sergeant sent me on a possible homicide call."

"Where was this?" Carol asked.

"The home of Grant Schafer. A patrol officer had already arrived and found a dead body."

"What did you find when you arrived?"

Janice said, "I found a white male lying on a carpet in the entranceway to his home, in a pool of blood."

Carol walked to the witness stand and handed over an 8x11 photo. "For the record, this is marked as State's Exhibit 2. Can you tell us what this is?"

"This is a photo from that morning, taken by the crime scene technician."

Carol said, "Does it accurately depict what you saw there?"

"Yes."

"I move to admit Exhibit 2."

I stood and said, "No objection." There was nothing I could do to stop it. The gruesome photo was coming into evidence. It showed the entryway of the coach's house, with him lying on a blood-soaked Turkish-style carpet. It was exactly the kind of dramatic image that would have an impact on a jury...but with this piece of evidence, Carol had been by the book, as had Janice.

Carol handed it to the jury and waited while each juror looked at the photo and passed it down the row. Only when they finished did she continue. "When you arrived, how did you find the front door?"

Janice said, "The patrol officer showed me exactly how it was when he arrived. It was ajar."

"Was there any sign of forced entry, like the door had been kicked in, or jimmied with a burglary tool?"

"No. The door was undamaged." Carol offered another photo into evidence showing the door in good condition.

Then she moved forward in time to Benny's shooting. "Were you called to the defendant's home on March 21st this year?"

"Yes, I was," Janice said. "There had been another shooting. The defendant's son had been shot. When I arrived, he had already been taken to the hospital."

Carol stood, holding a handgun, the murder weapon. It had a trigger lock in place to make the gun safe to handle. She said, "What did you find there?"

Janice said, "I asked the defendant's wife where the gun was that had shot her son." Janice looked at a report in her hand. "Denise Weaver was her name. She pointed to the kitchen counter, where I retrieved a 9 mm handgun." She glanced at the report again. "Specifically, a Sig Sauer, M17 handgun."

"What did you do with that gun?" Carol said.

"I seized it and made it safe. Then I logged it into evidence."

Carol came forward again. "For the record, I am showing the witness what is marked as State's Exhibit 1. Is this the weapon you seized?"

"It is."

Carol moved it into evidence. "One last thing, detective, did you seize a shell casing from the scene?"

"Yes, I did." Janice turned to the jury. "When a semi-automatic gun like this is fired, it discharges a shell casing. I seized that shell casing and turned it over, along with the gun to our forensic unit."

"And why did you do that?" Carol said.

"Our ballistic experts can compare it to shell casings from other incidents to see if this gun was involved in a previous crime."

Carol looked at the jury a moment, then walked back to her table. She would have to call the ballistics expert to tie the gun to the murder. "No further questions," she said and sat down.

My turn. There was not much I could do here. This evidence wasn't in dispute. My goal was to discredit the detective and this investigation. I stood to begin my cross.

"Ms. Gallagher?" the judge said. "We've been going for two and a half hours. Let's take lunch. We will reconvene at 1:30 p.m."

The bailiff escorted the jury out, after which the judge withdrew. Then the observers headed out to get some food. The officers took Troy back to the jail for his lunch, and after a few minutes, only Auntie El and I were left. I planned to sit right here and work through lunch, even though I had already prepared my cross of Janice. This was going to be one of the pivotal moments in the trial—perhaps my best chance to discredit the investigation.

But first, I needed to eat. Over the years, I had learned the toll that a trial took on the body and mind. Fuel and hydration were key to surviving and excelling in a long trial. I reached into my leather satchel and pulled out the banana I had brought...except it was smashed and had turned a gooey black. *Great.* Auntie El saw it and laughed.

"Here." She handed me a peanut butter and honey sandwich. Unlike my father, she always remembered that I preferred honey to jelly. She came around the bar and sat at the table next to me. "I figured you might be too distracted to think of lunch."

I grabbed her forearm and squeezed. "Thanks. I would be lost without you."

She set a thermos on the table. "And a civilized person needs milk with a peanut butter sandwich." Then she unwrapped her own sandwich and took a bite. With a full mouth she mumbled, "Now, how are we going to tear that detective apart?"

## 37

"Detective Evans, you were promoted to detective shortly before you were assigned this case, correct?"

She squirmed in her seat, and I sensed she wasn't used to being cross-examined. "Four months before," she said.

I sat at my table to ask questions. I only liked to move toward the witness if there was a tactical reason, like she was being evasive and I needed to exert control. Or perhaps to break up monotony for the jury. As politely as I could, I said, "So this was your first murder case?"

"Yes."

"And there was pressure to solve it, because Grant Schafer was something of a local celebrity."

She smirked, relaxing a little as she started to think that this might be easy. "There's always pressure to solve a murder."

I stood. "How many murder cases have you had since this one?"

"None," she said quietly.

I looked at the jury. "Your one and only murder case." I picked up a stack of papers. "Did you go to the high school principal and request a list of parents that had complained about Coach Grant Schafer?"

She looked at the judge, then back at me. "We spoke to the principal…"

I held up the papers, wanting the jury and Janice to think this was the list. "But did you obtain a list of all the parents and all the students that had been so dissatisfied with Mr. Schafer that they filed a complaint?"

She didn't look like she wanted to answer, but she knew she had no choice. "No, we didn't."

"So you have no idea how many names are on this list."

"No."

I returned to my table, standing by it. "Now, let's talk about the firearm. The last known owner was an Akron woman who purchased this gun from a gun show, correct?"

"Umm…" She fumbled with the stack of reports she had brought to the witness stand.

"Objection," Carol said, standing. "This is beyond the scope of direct exam."

I started to respond, but Judge Blankenship cut me off. "Overruled. You asked about the firearm, Ms. Becker, and this is the lead detective. I'm giving Ms. Gallagher some leeway."

This was what I had been working for since Troy's arrest. I had treated Blankenship with respect and I had been reasonable, not overstating things, not fighting needlessly like Carol. I had tried to make the judge's life easier, all toward this end. Judge Blankenship giving me *leeway*.

I said, "Detective Evans, going back to the firearm. If it will help, the report is dated January 7th."

She fumbled through her paperwork a moment. "Yes, I've found it. The last known owner was from Akron."

"Did you go to any gun dealers to see about sales of this firearm?"

She said, "There is no duty for dealers to keep records of guns sold in state." Her tone was smug, pleased that she could sound more knowledgeable than me.

"But many dealers *do* keep records. Did you even try?"

"Not to my knowledge."

"You didn't even try." I leaned back on the table. "So that means you didn't talk to the dealer who my client buys his guns from?"

Detective Evans looked at Carol like she might help. But there was nothing she could do. "No."

"Do you even know the name of the dealer my client bought his guns from?"

She nervously glanced sideways at the jury. *Yes, Janice, they are watching you.* "No."

"Did you visit any gun shows, talk to anyone?"

"No."

"Did you visit any pawnshops to see about recent sales, or to see if there had been any thefts of guns?"

"No."

I picked up the same papers as before to use as a prop again. I said, "Do you even know how many pawn shops and licensed gun dealers are in Donahoe County?"

She shook her head.

"I need you to give a verbal answer, for the record."

"No," she said louder, with a little anger. I was embarrassing her, and she wasn't happy about it.

I set the papers down and walked toward her. "After about a year, this case was still unsolved, correct?"

"Yes."

"And it was taken from you and given to the Attorney General's cold case unit out of Columbus, right?"

"It wasn't exactly taken from me…"

"The cold case unit didn't take it over?"

"They came to help us."

Standing between the detective and the judge, I said, "And the prosecutor there," pointing at Carol, "Ms. Becker, she was in charge of that cold case unit, correct?"

"Objection," Carol said, standing. "This is not relevant."

Perfect. I wanted the jury to hear my explanation. "It is relevant," I said to the judge. "It shows a motive on behalf of the cold case unit and Ms. Becker to rush this case, trying to solve it at a time when the state legislature was threatening to pull the cold case unit's funding."

Blankenship rubbed his hands together a moment. "I'm going to sustain the objection. Let's move along, Ms. Gallagher."

"Yes, Your Honor." I didn't mind letting the question drop, since the jury heard my explanation. Maybe a little doubt was creeping into their minds about the prosecution's motive.

I turned back to Detective Evans. "Did you attempt to get any video surveillance evidence from Lefty's Bar and Grill on New Year's Eve?"

The shift of topics left the detective a little confused. "Umm...I don't believe we did," she said as she fumbled through reports.

"It would have been helpful, wouldn't it, to have video evidence of everyone who came and went that night?"

The detective looked at Carol again before turning back to me. "Um, yes, if there was video, it would have been helpful. But I want to say there was no video."

I pointed at her stack of reports. "But you don't know for sure, do you?"

"Not at this moment," Janice admitted.

Now I walked to the end of the jury box and put my hand on the bar that separated me from them. From that position, I turned to face Detective Evans. "You said there were no signs of forced entry at Grant Schafer's home."

"Yes, that's right," she said.

"Do you know whether he regularly kept his door unlocked?"

She looked at Carol, then sat up a little straighter, trying to regain some authority. "It was evening, so like most people, I suspect he locked his doors."

"Really?" I said. "You *suspect*? Do you know how many people in Kerry regularly keep their doors unlocked?" I looked at the jury and raised my hand, sending them a signal that I didn't lock my door. A couple of jurors nodded along with me and one raised her hand.

I turned back to Detective Evans, who said, "I lock my doors."

"But you have no idea about Mr. Schafer, do you?"

"I don't think it's important."

I shook my head in disgust. "You mean it wasn't important whether someone could have entered his house by simply turning the knob, without damaging the door?" She stared back at me, not answering. "Or whether he opened the door and let in someone he knew?"

"I don't know," was all she could say.

I stared at Detective Evans a long moment. Then I walked back to my table to look at my notes. I had one more point I wanted to drive home, but I couldn't remember it. *Oh yeah.*

"Did you do any investigation to learn how many people in Kerry have a letterman jacket?"

"No."

"Do you know how many letterman jackets have been issued in Kerry over the years?"

"I don't."

I walked toward her. "There are a lot of jackets, aren't there?"

"I guess so."

"Maybe fifty or sixty kids on the football team each year. Baseball, basketball, track, wrestling... I could go on with the sports. And graduates from previous years." I turned to look at the jury. "Coach Schafer was also the JV volleyball coach, wasn't he?"

"Yes, he was."

"Perhaps there were students or parents of volleyball players who might not have liked him."

She didn't answer. I shook my head and walked right up to her. Trying to sound incredulous, I said, "You simply don't know how many students or parents had trouble with Coach Schafer—or how many of them might have had letterman jackets of their own." It wasn't a question and again, she just stared back at me. I let it linger a moment. "The fibers you found could have come from *any* letterman jacket, correct?"

"You'll have to ask the fiber expert."

"Oh, I will." I looked at the judge and said, "No further questions."

As I walked back to my table, Troy gave me a slight head nod. Behind him, Auntie El was beaming.

Carol called one more witness for the day, the deputy medical examiner who had conducted the autopsy. There was not much in dispute, so I had little damage I could do with my cross-examination. He described the cause of death, a gunshot that caused the coach's bodily functions to cease. He also testified that, based on the body temperature, the death would have occurred between 11:30 p.m. and 2 a.m. I wanted the window to be as wide as possible, but he was pretty adamant that the latest the shooting could have been was 2 a.m., "Maybe 2:30 a.m. at the outside," he said.

I then approached him in the witness stand, having two more points I wanted to make. "Doctor, you just testified about the trajectory of the bullet. Could you please step down here, in front of the jury, so we can do a little demonstration?"

He looked at the judge, who nodded that it was okay. I said, "Using your hand as the gun, could you show the jury where the gun might have been when it was fired?"

"Assuming the deceased was standing when shot, it would have been about here." His fist was near his sternum, pointing up through his neck. "The bullet lodged in the back of the skull, so the angle would have been about eighty degrees."

I said, "You are using your hand as if Mr. Schafer held the gun. In your job, do you ever do autopsies on suicides?"

"All the time," he said.

"When a person attempts a suicide with a gun, do they ever miss, or flinch at the last moment?"

"Yes. Of course. As a medical examiner I don't see self-inflicted injuries where the person survives, obviously, but I have handled a number of suicides where the person's aim was poor, or perhaps the recoil from the gun caused the bullet to go somewhere other than intended even though the shot was still ultimately fatal."

"Do people ever shoot themselves in the heart when committing suicide?"

"It's rare, but I have heard of it."

"Thank you. You may retake your seat." When he had, I said, "Earlier, you testified that it was plausible, based on the three small yellow fibers under Mr. Schafer's fingernails, that there had been a struggle between him and an assailant, and that is when the gun went off."

"Yes."

"You found those fibers under the nails as part of your autopsy, right?"

"Yes."

"But it is possible those fibers were under his fingernails long before the shooting?"

"Yes, that is possible. I can't tell you when the fibers lodged under his nails."

"No further questions," I said, and sat down.

Carol jumped to her feet. "Doctor, have you ever seen a suicide where a person shot themselves through the neck and into their brain?"

"No, I haven't."

Carol finished, and the judge adjourned court. "It has been a long day. We will reconvene tomorrow morning at 10 a.m." The jury was escorted out and then the judge disappeared. Then I felt a tug on my sleeve. I turned around to see Denise.

She was angry and crying at the same time. She waved a piece of paper. "They just gave me this. It's a subpoena for Charley. He's supposed to testify tomorrow."

I looked at Carol, standing by her table. She was watching us. She said, "I told you the boy would answer all my questions." Then she walked from the courtroom.

## 38

I called Sean to let him know I would be home late and spent a few more hours getting ready for Carol's witnesses tomorrow. I also called Denise and arranged to talk with Charley tomorrow morning before court convened. I knew he would say the gun came from their garage, but was there something else he might reveal? Better to find out before he began his testimony. And maybe I could help him get ready for the experience, help lessen any trauma that might come from testifying against his father.

Sean was watching a baseball game on TV when I came in. "How'd it go?" he said. "The news said you scored a few points, but the media never gets things right."

I plopped on the couch next to him. "It went well," I said. "Their lead detective left me some low hanging fruit, and the prosecutor screwed up a few times in her opening statement, but it's going to be a fight." I kicked off my shoes and rested my feet on the coffee table. "How's the game?"

"Guardians are getting killed," Sean said. "Ian's in his room, *studying*," he said, making air quotes. "Although maybe he really is. His English final is tomorrow."

"He was going to the principal this week, right?"

"They didn't go," Sean said. "He got some other kids to join with him. You remember that girl from Patrick's party? Her and a couple of others. Ian said they're going to wait until after the final and see if he fails anybody. The teacher's been letting students turn in late papers for partial credit."

"So, it might all work out," I said, relieved. I had been feeling guilty for dumping all the parenting burden on Sean, but with my focus on Troy and his case, I had no time to spare. That didn't stop me from worrying about Ian, though. I'd wake up in the night with a sense of panic, questions racing through my head. What if he failed? Would he have to do his sophomore year again?

"He's going to be okay," Sean said. He clicked off the game and turned to face me. "I talked to the remedial English teacher about this guy. Apparently, he does this every spring. He tries to scare the kids, but then softens up in the end. He's still a hard grader, but he doesn't fail kids…as long as they try."

Sean scooted over, picked up my left foot, and massaged my arch. "Oooh." I leaned back and closed my eyes. "Nice…"

"What's up for tomorrow?"

I opened my eyes. "Charley is testifying. I'm worried about how Carol's going to handle him. Maybe I should talk to the judge…"

"Sorry I brought it up," Sean said. He squeezed his thumbs into the underside of my foot.

"Ouch," I said.

"Stop worrying. For just tonight, forget about Troy, and Charley, and everything to do with the case. Lean back, close your eyes... Enjoy my magic touch."

"I will not say no to that."

---

It was just before 8 a.m. when I knocked on her door. Denise answered right away. "I didn't sleep at all last night," she said, stepping aside for me to enter. "I am still so angry."

"It will be all right." I followed her into the living room. "I didn't sleep either. But I'm going to talk with the judge this morning and make sure he protects Charley."

She sighed, some of the tension dropping from her shoulders as if I'd taken a weight off of them by reminding her that she wasn't in this alone. "I appreciate that," she said.

"Is he here? We don't have much time before we need to get to court."

She yelled, "Charley, get in here." He came running through the kitchen door, but stopped when he saw me. Then he ran to his mom and grabbed her leg. "Remember what we talked about, Charley? Maggie is trying to help Daddy and me. She just wants to ask some questions."

He hid between her legs, peering out at me. "Hello, Mr. Weaver," I said in a deep voice, trying to be funny. It didn't work.

"We don't have time for this, Charley," Denise said. She lifted him up, carried him to the couch, and she sat down with him in her lap. "Go ahead," she said to me.

I sat next to them. "You get to testify in court today, all right? That's the place you were yesterday." He stared back at me. "I'm going to ask you the same questions you'll be asked later, just so you can practice, okay?" He still didn't answer, staring at me with big eyes. How could I overcome his fear? "This is a chance for you to help your dad and your brother…"

"Benny?" he said, lighting up.

"Yes, Benny, your mom, your dad. Can you do that?"

He nodded, still uncertain but getting more enthusiastic now.

"Good. I want to ask about the gun you found in the garage." He wasn't being particularly verbal, so I thought of a new strategy. "Can you show me where you found the gun?"

He nodded and jumped off his mom's lap, then looked up at her to see if it was all right. "Go ahead," she said. Charley ran to the front door. "The garage is through the kitchen," Denise said, sounding confused.

"This way," Charley insisted and walked out the front door.

We both followed. Denise said, "Maybe that morning he went through the outside garage door?" We followed Charley out the front door, waiting for him to turn toward the garage, but he went across the driveway. "Where are you going?" Denise said. Charley didn't look back, crossing the lawn to the neighbor's garage. "Charley," Denise yelled. "Did you get the gun there?"

He nodded, then walked to a side door of the neighbor's garage. He turned the handle, but it was locked. We both joined him at the door, peering through the window into the dark garage. Denise knelt down to Charley's level, grabbing his shoulders. "You got the gun from this garage?"

"Yeah."

"How'd you get in there?"

He shrugged. "It was open."

Denise grabbed Charley and squeezed him tight. "Do you know what this means?" she said to him. "It belongs to Mr. Cross. It wasn't Dad's gun!" She looked up at me. "I was so wrong. I didn't believe Troy, but he was right. It wasn't his gun." Denise stood, still holding and hugging Charley. "Oh my gosh…"

"Let's go back inside," I said, fighting back the excitement. Had we just won the lottery? This was too good to be true. "I have a bunch of questions."

Denise and I stood there in the neighbor's yard, grinning at each other. The whole case was built around the police finding the gun in Troy's home. But if it wasn't Troy's gun, they'd have to dismiss, right?

## 39

Carol didn't begin the day with Charley as a witness. Instead, she called the FBI ballistics expert. He testified about the NIBIN system, a database that contained data from millions of shell casings from crimes all across the country. A shell casing from the gun that shot Benny matched a shell casing from the gun that shot Coach Schafer. After that initial match, this expert did his own analysis and confirmed it. "I have no doubt the same gun fired both shots."

There wasn't much to cross him on. As an FBI expert, he wasn't involved in the case, other than this one examination. I said, "These two shootings were over fifteen months apart. Do you know where the gun was during that time?"

"No. I have no way to tell that from my examination."

"Can you tell where the gun came from originally, who the previous owners were?"

"Sorry." He smiled, knowing what I was doing. "All I can tell you is these two shell casings match."

"So none of your testing was to determine who fired the shots, correct? For all you know, I could have fired the first shot, and Ms. Becker here could have fired the second shot."

He laughed. "Two lawyers? It wouldn't surprise me." The whole courtroom thought that was funny.

"No further questions," I said.

Next, Carol called a forensics expert from the state crime lab. She testified in detail about the crime scene, which wasn't really a big focus of mine, other than the lack of evidence pointing to Troy. But then Carol got into the fibers the medical examiner found under Schafer's fingernails. She compared them with the fibers from the *K* letter on Troy's jacket. "The patch is produced by a company separate from the jacket maker," she testified. Carol handed her Troy's jacket, marked as Exhibit 5. "The patch here," she said, "is made of chenille thread." She looked at the jury. "That's silk thread. The color is known to the manufacturer as 'sunshine yellow.'"

Carol said, "And what about the threads found under the victim's nails?"

"It is the same fiber, chenille and a spectrometer reading confirmed it has the exact same pigment as the thread on this jacket."

On cross-examination, she was beautifully honest. "I can't say whether the victim chose to let someone into his home or whether the door was unlocked." When I turned to the fiber evidence, she said, "No, I can't say the threads from the under fingernails came from the *K* on this jacket."

I rose from my table and walked toward the jury, watching them as I asked my question. "So the thread could have come from another jacket?"

"Yes."

"It could have come from something besides a letterman jacket?"

"Yes."

"Anything containing chenille thread in sunshine yellow?"

"Yes."

"No further questions." I walked back to my desk, watching the jurors to see if they would document those answers in their notebooks. They did.

In her opening statement, Carol had oversold the importance of the yellow fibers, and the testimony of her own witness had just shown how inconclusive that evidence really was. Hopefully, it was enough to have the jury second-guessing everything Carol had stated as a fact.

She rose quickly to change the subject. "The State calls Charley Weaver."

*Here we go.* This could be the trial. How would Charley do?

Denise was waiting in the hallway. The bailiff brought her in with Charley holding her hand.

Before court this morning, I had raised the topic with the judge and Carol. I wanted her to agree on the record to be gentle with Charley. Carol didn't like the suggestion that she didn't know how to behave. "I have six nieces and nephews. I know how to handle kids."

Judge Blankenship said, "I will take over the questioning if I'm not satisfied, Ms. Becker." He also agreed with me that Denise could sit in a chair next to the witness stand.

But on entering the courtroom, Charley let go of Denise, walking by himself through the swinging gate and up to the stand. He sat down on the chair and disappeared from view. He was too short to be visible, and the courtroom erupted in laughter. The judge pointed at the bailiff. "Get a phone book or something."

So we all waited a few minutes while the bailiff scrambled for a booster. Denise sat next to Charley, talking quietly to him, until the bailiff returned with a cardboard box full of books. "It's all I could find," he said. He put the box on the witness stand chair and Charley climbed on it, visible now to everyone.

"That's better," Judge Blankenship said. He leaned over his bench toward Charley. "Can you tell us your name?"

"Charley." He said it loud and clear. Charley was no longer afraid.

"Is it Charley Weaver?"

"Yes."

"Charley, do you know the difference between telling the truth and telling a lie?"

Charley nodded. "Yes."

"And you promise to tell the truth here?"

Charley held his hand up like he was taking an oath. "I do." Again, the crowd laughed.

Carol walked up to the witness stand. In a sugary sweet voice, she said, "Charley, I'm going to ask you some questions, okay?"

He nodded.

"How old are you?"

"Five."

"Are you in school?"

"Kindergarten," he said.

"Have you ever seen your father with a gun?"

"Yes."

"Do you know how many times?"

Charley shook his head. "No."

Carol stepped to the left, between the judge and Charley, so the audience could see him. "Have you ever held a gun?"

Charley wasn't having fun anymore. He glanced at his mom. "Yes."

"Can you tell us about that? Where did that gun come from?"

"The garage."

"Okay, thank you," Carol said. She looked at the jury a long moment. This was a key part of her case. "Can you tell us where in the garage the gun came from?"

"It was in a big brown box, on the floor."

Carol got down on one knee, trying to get at Charley's level, but she was actually below him now. "Was it in a gun safe?"

Charley shook his head. "A box," and he held his arms out as far as his little arms could stretch.

"What did you do with that gun?" Carol asked.

"I brought it home."

Carol glanced at the jury again. "You mean, you brought it from your garage into your house?"

Charley shook his head again. "Our neighbor."

At least one juror gasped, as did people in the audience.

Carol stood up. "I'm sorry. Let me ask it again. Where did the gun come from?"

"Our neighbor."

Carol looked straight at me, accusation in her eyes, like I had put Charley up to this. Then to Charley, "You are now saying this gun came from your neighbor?" The sugary sweetness from before was gone. Her voice was harsh now, like she was talking with an adult. "You told the psychologist it came from your garage."

"Objection," I said, standing. "Counsel has a transcript of that interview, and Charley's answer was one word. Garage. Not *my* garage."

"Sustained," the judge said. "Rephrase your question, Ms. Becker."

Carol had to be reeling. She glared at me again. "Did you talk to anyone about your testimony, Charley?"

"Yes."

"Who?"

He pointed at me.

Carol said, "Let the record reflect the witness is pointing at defense counsel."

"What did she tell you to say?"

Charley glanced at his mom, then in a clear voice, "She told me to tell the truth."

After Charley's revelation this morning, it was easy to guess that Carol would accuse me of witness tampering. So I had spent an hour with Charley, prepping him. I said it to him at least three times. "Remember, Charley, the most important thing is to tell the truth."

"Did she tell you to say the gun came from the neighbor?"

He shook his head. "I took them there." He pointed at me again. "She asked me to show her where the gun came from. I took her there."

"What's this neighbor's name?" Carol said in a snarky voice. It was clearly an inappropriate way to talk to a five-year-old, and the judge scowled at her.

Charley looked at Denise, who said, "Mr. Cross."

"Mr. Cross," Charley repeated, smiling. "Can my daddy come home now?"

Carol looked back at me a third time. I smiled and mouthed the word, "Surprise!" Then I stood and said to the judge, "Perhaps we should take a break, Your Honor."

"That's a good idea." He looked to the jury. "Ladies and gentlemen, it's almost noon. We will take our lunch break now, returning at 1:30 p.m. I will remind you not to talk with each other or anyone else about this case." He banged his gavel. "Counsel, see me in chambers."

# 40

"Have a seat." The judge motioned to the two leather chairs before his desk as he removed his robe. Neither Carol nor I sat. "What are we going to do?" he said, looking at Carol.

I waited for her to attack me. I could tell she wanted to, but she held back. "This could have been avoided if we had been allowed to interview the witness as planned."

"What are we going to do *now*?" the judge said. "The jury will be back in ninety minutes."

Carol was flustered. "I need to fully cross-examine the witness," she said. "I think the jury sees what he's doing. He's protecting his father." She looked at me. "I'm not saying you did this, but his mother—"

Time to protect Charley. He wasn't lying and an aggressive cross-examination could only harm him. "I've contacted the owner of the house, Mr. Cross. His home has been empty for a long time. He currently lives in a senior rehab facility, but he's agreed to let the police search his garage."

Carol pointed at me. "Have you been in there?"

I ignored her, turning to the judge. "I think the government's case is almost over, and I will be making a motion for a summary judgment. There is simply no evidence my client possessed the murder weapon, let alone that he went to the victim's home on the night of the murder."

"I'm not done yet," Carol said. "I will want to finish my examination of that boy, and we need to talk with Mr. Cross."

In an impatient voice, the judge said, "Again, what do we do *now*?"

I said, "I suggest we adjourn for the day and Carol and I go talk with Mr. Cross. Like I said, he's happy to cooperate."

The judge said, "It's your case, Ms. Becker. I'm not going to tell you how to run it. But I will grant a recess for this afternoon if you want to do as Ms. Gallagher suggests."

Carol glanced between us, not liking that she had lost control. But she had no choice. "The police are going to conduct the search. You will not be permitted inside."

I smiled at her, but said nothing.

---

Archibald Cross arrived in a gray, beat-up Chevy Impala driven by a younger woman. I was waiting in Denise's driveway and walked over to him. "Hi, Mr. Cross. I'm Margaret Gallagher. We spoke on the phone." We shook hands.

He looked to be early seventies, bald and overweight. He struggled to get out of the car. Then the driver got a walker out of the trunk for Mr. Cross. Earlier, Denise had told me he was kind of prickly, but that she and Troy had always gotten along with him. He broke his pelvic bone in a fall last November and had been in a facility since, with Troy taking care of his lawn. "Using *his* lawn mower," Denise had noted. We locked eyes, both knowing what that meant. *This was not over.* Carol would argue to the jury that Troy had access to the garage, and therefore could have hidden the gun there himself.

Mr. Cross introduced me to the young woman, Cammie. She was thick-boned, with bad teeth and a hard look, like she'd had a hard life, and she didn't seem to trust a single one of us—not me, not Carol, not even Denise. She said, "I'm not comfortable with this, Dad. You know how the cops are." Cammie looked at the four police cars in her father's driveway. "They have a warrant, right?"

Mr. Cross smiled and shook his head. "There's nothing in there but my Malibu and a bunch of tools. And a whole lot of Miller Lite. I wish they would let me have some at the care center." Then, more seriously, he said, "I have no idea how a gun got in there."

Carol walked quickly toward us at the bottom of the driveway. "Thank you, Mr. Cross, for granting us access to your garage." She tapped his shoulder and pointed up the driveway, where Janice was waiting. "We'd like to ask you some questions."

I said, "We agreed we would *both* talk with Mr. Cross."

"I agreed to nothing," Carol said.

Cammie grabbed her dad's walker and held it in place. "If my dad's going to talk to anyone, it's Ms. Gallagher, here." Either she had decided to take a liking to me, or she *really* didn't like the police.

I said, "You should be here too, Cammie."

"Thanks." She liked that. She urged her dad back toward her car so he could lean against it. "Standing for long is hard on him."

He leaned on the front quarter panel, using the walker for balance. Janice then came down the driveway to join us. After presenting the search warrant, the first thing she said was, "Do you have a key to the door?" Cammie took it out of her jeans pocket and handed it over. Janice then gave it to a uniformed officer who walked back up the driveway.

Carol asked Mr. Cross, "How long have you been away from your home?"

"I broke my pelvic bone last fall. It was the day of the Ohio State, Michigan game." He shook his head in disgust. "Stupid. It was halftime, and I was outside with the leaf blower when I stepped in a hole and went down."

Janice said, "The neighbor boy said he got into your garage and found a gun."

"I don't know how. I don't own any guns. Got rid of 'em the year Lisa left me." He looked at Cammie. "What was that, ten years ago?"

"Something like that."

"How would Charley get into your garage?" Carol asked.

"I don't know," Mr. Cross said. "You'll have to ask *him*."

Carol turned to Cammie. "You had a key, so you had access. Who else did?"

Mr. Cross said, "This isn't about Cammie. This is about Troy, right? He's been mowing my lawn for me since I went into the care place. He had access." He was protecting his daughter, but then must have realized he was pointing his finger at Troy. "But like I said, I didn't have a gun. And Troy wouldn't shoot anyone."

"So Troy Weaver had a key?" Carol said.

"Yeah."

Janice held a recording device, but was also taking notes. She looked up and said, "And he's had a key since you were injured last fall, correct?"

"That's right."

"Did he have it before then?"

Mr. Cross looked at me, like I might have the answer. Then at Cammie. Finally, he said, "Yes, we exchanged keys a while back, in case one of us had an emergency or something. I don't know when, though."

I said, "So it could have been after the murder of Grant Schafer."

Mr. Cross understood what I was doing. "Yes, I can't say for sure Troy had my key before the murder."

I said, "Did anyone else live with you or have access to your garage?"

Mr. Cross shook head. "Not since Lisa moved out."

"Visitors?" I said, getting a dirty look from Carol. She didn't like me taking over. *Too bad.*

"Yeah, family. Cammie here, she's my daughter-in-law. And her boys sometimes, Justin or Billy, if they needed a place to crash. Their dad's in prison, been there three years come September, so it wasn't him. David, my oldest son, lives in Dallas and comes home for Christmas or Thanksgiving. But nobody brings guns."

I glanced up the driveway and saw at least six officers walking into the side door of the garage, including my cousin Liam.

Mr. Cross said, "I'm not in trouble, am I?" He looked at his daughter-in-law, who had not wanted to cooperate. If I figured things right, Cammie's husband was the one in prison, which explained her distrust of the police.

"You're not in trouble," I said, and then was cut off by Carol.

"We appreciate your cooperation, sir. Just a few more questions about Mr. Weaver. Did you ever socialize with him, have barbecues or anything?"

"Not really. We'd talk in the driveway, stuff like that." He thought a moment. "He would have a beer with me once in a while. I'd be working in my shop in the garage, listening to a Guardians game and he might come chat."

"In the garage?" Carol said.

"Yeah. But it's not like he brought a gun."

I saw Liam walking out of the garage now, holding a box. He waved at Janice, who walked up the driveway toward him. He wore rubber gloves and pulled a cell phone out of the box.

I pointed up the driveway. "You see that box? Is that familiar? Little Charley said he found the gun in a box."

Mr. Cross shook his head. "I got a lot of shit boxed up. I don't know. I'd have to look inside."

Carol yelled at Janice to bring the box down the driveway. When she arrived, Janice said, "They found this box on the floor by your work bench. Does this look familiar?"

Mr. Cross looked inside. "Yeah. My rag box. I keep old T-shirts and socks in there to clean my hands, wipe up oil drips, stuff like that."

Janice held up a cell phone in a plastic evidence bag. "We found this cell phone in there. Is this yours?"

It looked to be an older model iPhone. "Not mine," Mr. Cross said. He took his own phone out of his back pocket and showed it to us.

Time for me to drop a plausible theory on Carol. She wasn't likely to dismiss the case, now that she could show Troy could have had access to the gun, but I had to try. "Maybe it's the coach's. Somebody robs him, then panics for some reason. The robber happens to be in this neighborhood and looks for a place to hide the gun and phone." I looked at Mr. Cross. "Did you always lock your garage door?"

"I can't say always. Usually, though."

I turned to Carol. "You need to dismiss this."

She locked eyes with Janice a long moment, like they were telepathically communicating as they tried to think of a way out. Then she squared up with me. "Your client did this and I'm dismissing nothing. He had access to the garage, and it's the only logical explanation."

The *only logical explanation*. Hardly. I just gave her another, and I could think of five more. I would be making them to the judge, and if he didn't dismiss, I'd be making them to the jury.

## 41

Judge Blankenship agreed to return to the courthouse, and we met in his chambers after 7 p.m. Carol began by saying that she wanted a delay in the trial. "It will take at least twelve hours to download the phone, and then we'll need to analyze the data."

I objected. "You have other evidence you can put on in the meantime." We had the advantage now, and I wanted to press it.

"I'll give you tomorrow morning, Ms. Becker. In the meantime, you might consider another way of resolving this case." He was telling her to make me a generous plea offer. He sensed her case falling apart. "We'll reconvene tomorrow at 1:30 p.m. I'll have the bailiff notify the jury."

She stared back at the judge, but said nothing. Then, as we walked out of his chambers, she said, "The county prosecutor has authorized a deal. Tonight only, your client pleads to manslaughter with a five-year minimum."

I looked at my watch. "I can't talk to him tonight." The jail did not allow visitors this late, and I couldn't make a deal without his consent.

"Tomorrow, then." She started down the hall. As she walked away, she said, "A guilty plea. You have until we get the phone data."

I stood there, alone in the courthouse hallway. It had been a long day and my brain was fuzzy, so I sat down on a bench to think. Didn't we already have data from the coach's phone in the discovery?

I opened my leather satchel and took out a notebook that contained my summary of the evidence. Sure enough, the cops had gotten the phone call and text message data from the coach's phone company. So what else could there be on his phone that was not in the phone records? Photos, videos, maybe content from some other apps like emails or WhatsApp. Probably nothing that would hurt Troy.

So, should he take the deal? *Five years in prison.* Actually, state law mandated credit for time served, so with the two months he's already done, and then credit for good behavior in prison, he would end up with less than four years total. Compared to the prospect of life in prison that had been keeping me up nights, it was a pretty good deal. But I was more convinced than ever he was innocent. It was not Troy's gun. Just terrible luck that Charley brought it from Mr. Cross's garage and shot Benny with it. Carol had dug in her heels, and I had a feeling that she wouldn't let this go, even if the phone didn't give her anything useful, but her case was getting weaker by the day. Maybe we should roll the dice with the jury.

Except there was no guarantee they would do the right thing. I thought back over the jury trials in my career. Almost always the jury did do the right thing. *Almost* being the key word. I usually preferred trying cases to a jury rather than a judge because twelve citizens working together were smarter and more rational than even the best judge. But there were a couple times I had seen a jury vote based on emotion and not evidence. Maybe they elected a presiding juror who bullied the other jurors, or more likely, I had done a poor job of presenting evidence so they could understand it. It was impossible to say because the jury deliberations were secret.

What it all meant was, there were no guarantees the jury would see it my way.

"Gallagher." I looked up to see Deputy Prosecutor Oliver Altman.

"What are you doing here so late, Oliver?"

"In court all day," he said. "Just picked a jury in a robbery case. What about you?"

"Meeting with Judge Blankenship. It turns out the murder weapon didn't come from my client's house, but the neighbor's."

"Holy shit," Oliver said. He sat down next to me on the bench. "Is Carol going to dismiss?"

I shook my head. "She offered manslaughter with a five-year minimum."

"Hmm," he said. We sat in silence as he thought about that. "Are you going to take it?"

"What would you do?" I liked Oliver, and I honestly wanted his opinion. I had not made friends with any defense attorneys in town who I could talk this over with. This was a huge decision, and I was afraid of giving Troy poor advice.

"She lost the murder weapon," Oliver said. "I don't see how they convict." He thought another moment, then added, "Don't tell Carol I said that."

I smiled and waved my hand like I was swatting away his concerns. "Don't worry. I appreciate your honesty. By the way, did you hear from Officer Carpenter about the DeNuzzio case? You know that ridiculous manslaughter charge?"

He brought both hands up to his forehead. "What a mess."

"I can prove the father Dominic was driving," I said. "He and Frankie will swear to it. Frankie's injuries are consistent with him wearing the right side seat belt and Officer Carpenter and Dom's girlfriend will corroborate Dom's injuries."

Oliver held his hand up to stop me. "I believe you. Send me affidavits from everybody. Something I can use. I have to persuade Carol to let me drop the case, and you can imagine what that'll be like. But I'm going to need Dominic to plead guilty to the drunk driving."

I was exhausted from Troy's case, but Oliver had been in trial all day too. Now was a good time to press negotiations. "You don't have any evidence of Dom drinking."

"He's still looking at manslaughter," Oliver said, a little exasperated with me. "Do you want me to charge that? He crashed into a house!"

"We might plead to a careless driving."

"That's just a traffic ticket," Oliver said. Suddenly, he stood up. "I'm too tired for this. Send me the affidavits. When I'm done with this robbery trial, I'll give it some thought. But the father is going to have to plead to a crime. Driving under the influence, reckless driving… maybe I'll keep the manslaughter."

*Nice bluff.* We both knew he couldn't prove a manslaughter charge. "I'll work on it this weekend," I said, standing myself. "Affidavits from everybody and I'll get them to you Monday." I had pushed him enough. Time to let him think about how weak his case was. I patted him on the shoulder. "Let's both go home and get some rest."

———

I slept great after such a hectic day. No worrying about Troy, or about Ian. And since there was no court this morning, I didn't set the alarm.

I woke up at 7:30 a.m. and decided to go for a run, my first in several weeks. Sean and Ian had already left for school, so I was all alone. After stretching and warmup, I stepped outside into a cool morning, overcast with no humidity.

I felt great the first few blocks and had to force myself to go slow. *Don't hurt yourself again.* I began to think about the trial and how well things had gone. Charley's testimony was so powerful. The decision about the plea offer seemed easy now. I would recommend that Troy not take it. Of course it was a gamble, four years of his life versus the rest of his life in prison, or even death, potentially. But I felt good about our odds. After showering and breakfast, I'd go to the jail to talk it over.

I turned the corner and started across the street, and then, as so often happens, everything changed. I heard it before I saw the truck. I couldn't be sure, but it looked like the same one from outside Village Subs. It came barreling toward me, engine revving. At the last moment, the driver swerved to avoid me, but it was too late. I stepped onto a grate which caused my ankle to snap outward, the shock and anger at myself hitting before the pain, and I went down. I had sprained my ankle before and I knew I had done it again. The sharp pain came, even worse than I expected. I sat there in the street, watching it swell before my eyes. *But I needed to visit Troy.*

"Are you okay?" A man in a Jeep stopped, rolling down his window. "That looked bad. Those damn kids. Always causing problems."

I winced. "Does that mean you saw who was driving?"

He shook his head. "Not exactly. The windows were tinted, but I do know the truck belongs to Pete Cafferty's boys. He owns the autoshop off Crimson."

I had no idea who that was or why they'd try to run me off the road. On a whim, I asked, "Any chance they play football?"

The guy smirked. "Not anymore. They graduated a couple years ago. They're normally pretty harmless."

"Thanks for the info." I was pretty sure they were the same ones from before and I now suspected that one or both were the ones who graffitied my office door. I stood and balanced on my good foot, ready to soldier on. But after one step, I went right back down. My left ankle could not bear any weight. This was a bad sprain.

The Jeep driver hadn't left yet. "Want me to call an ambulance?"

I was a mile from home and didn't have my phone. Sean had left for school. "Yes," I said.

## 42

The medic loaned me his phone on the ride to the hospital, and I called Sean. He was with Ian, just pulling into the high school parking lot. "I'll come right now," he said.

"No. It's going to be awhile." I remembered spraining my ankle back in basic training. The base doctor had insisted on X-rays, which took some time. "If you could pick me up in about two hours… I'm headed to the ER."

"It might be broken," the medic said when I gave him back his phone.

"No. I've sprained it before and it feels the same." At least the pain was the same, sharp and intense. It was more swollen than my last sprain…but I couldn't really spare the bandwidth to worry about that. Not when I had so much else on my mind.

It was now 8:15 a.m. Maybe two hours at the hospital, then back home to get dressed. I could still meet with Troy before court and explain the plea offer to him. And there was Charley. I needed Denise to bring him to my office so I could prep him again before Carol's further examination. I was afraid of the damage she might do to the young boy.

When we arrived at the hospital, they wheeled me in on the gurney, right into an examination room. The doctor came in almost immediately. He looked at my clothes and said, "Out for a run?" He removed my shoe and sock, pressing hard with his thumb. "Can you feel that?"

"Yeah, that hurts."

"It might be broken," he said.

"I don't have time for that," I said, which made him chuckle. After a half hour, they wheeled me into an X-ray room, covered everything except my ankle with a lead blanket and took some pictures. Then back to the examination room. Things had moved along pretty swiftly up to this point, but I should have known that was too good to last. I ended up waiting for another half hour.

At long last, the doctor finally returned. "Good news and bad news," he announced. "The good news is that the break is clean, so we don't need to do any surgery or insert pins or anything." Damn it. So there *was* a break.

"What's the bad news?"

He grinned and said, "It's broken." I didn't laugh. I was thinking about what this meant for the trial. "And of course there's also a bad sprain. I can write a prescription for some painkillers if you want them."

"I don't." Hell no. I needed my head clear.

He shrugged, as if that was what he'd expected me to say. "In that case, ibuprofen, ice, keep it elevated and stay off of it."

They fitted me with a plastic boot and gave me crutches, along with a lecture about giving it six weeks to heal before starting rehab.

I didn't have the heart to say I knew about rehab. I had been doing it for a year.

After the nurse adjusted the crutch height, I hobbled out to the front desk to take care of paying only to realize I didn't have my credit card. I felt tears of anger and frustration welling up. Troy needed me, and here I was, fumbling around at the hospital, the pain overwhelming my ability to think clearly. Why did I go for a run? The trial would be over in a week, and I could exercise then.

"We can send you a bill," the clerk said, taking pity on me as I wiped my eyes. I glanced at the clock behind the desk and saw it was only 9:30 a.m. Sean might not arrive for another hour. I stood up from the chair and felt the blood rush to my ankle, the pain getting even worse, making my teeth clench. With my luck, I'd end up with a dental injury by the end of this.

I needed a distraction…and suddenly, I found myself thinking of Benny, still lying unconscious in this very hospital. *I could visit him.* I had an hour to kill before Sean arrived, and then I could report to Troy how his son was doing. What a blessing it would be for him if there was good news. So with my ankle roaring in pain, I crutch-walked down to the elevator.

On the third floor, I asked the desk nurse for Benny Weaver's room. Her jaw dropped as soon as I said his name. "How did you know?"

"Know what? I was in the ER. I'm a family friend and thought I should visit. Why? Did something happen?" *Oh God, please don't let it be bad news…*

"His vitals spiked this morning. We think he might be waking up."

I stared at her a moment, trying to grasp the enormity of what she said. Benny was waking up. "Have you called his mom?" Denise should be here.

"Yes. She's on her way."

My mind flooded with thoughts. "Is he okay?" I said. "I mean, is there…you know, any damage?"

She knew what I meant. *Brain damage.* "It's too early to tell. There will be a lot of tests. He's not even fully awake yet."

"Can I see him?"

She shook her head. "Restricted access for now. If his mom says it's okay, then yes." She pointed behind me to some seats and a couch. "The waiting area's over there."

I hobbled over, glad to sit and put my foot up on the coffee table, letting the blood drain and release some of the pressure and pain.

My mind was racing with the ramifications of Benny waking up. Denise and Troy could get their son back. And Troy's case…Benny could be Troy's alibi! He could corroborate that Troy didn't go to the coach's house.

Of course, Carol would say it was just another son lying for Troy. But at this point, Benny didn't even know his dad was charged with murder. He had no incentive to lie. At least not yet. If I could get Benny's statement *before* he knew about the charges, Carol couldn't attack him.

I sat there waiting for Denise to step off the elevator. After almost fifteen minutes, there she was, carrying Charley. "Denise!" I yelled, struggling to my feet.

"Maggie! What are you doing here?" She looked at my crutches. "What happened? Are you okay?"

"It doesn't matter," I said. "I heard about Benny! What amazing news! But before you go in there, we need to talk." I was rushing my words, knowing she wanted to see her son. "I know Troy went to see

Benny on the night of the murder. He can help Troy with his case if we handle this right…"

"No!" she almost screamed at me. "You are not bringing Benny into this!" She hugged Charley tight to her chest and rushed past me toward the nurse's desk. To the nurse she said, "Do not let her into Benny's room," pointing at me. Then she continued down the hall.

The nurse at the desk stepped out from behind the desk, as if to physically block me from following Denise.

*She must be a mom.*

---

Sean brought me home and helped me take a quick shower, which was awkward and painful and difficult.

My rushing made it worse. "Take it slow," Sean kept saying, but I ignored him, even when I almost fell off the edge of the bed while putting on slacks. "You're lucky it's your left ankle."

"Yeah, things are really going my way."

"It's your *left* ankle, so you can drive." Oh. He was right. "And we need to talk about the fact that you didn't tell me about this driver harassing you."

I closed my eyes, not wanting to get into it now. "I didn't put it together until a little while ago."

"You could have gotten seriously injured, Maggie. Or worse." Worry and condemnation were rolling off Sean in waves.

"You're right and I'm sorry. I didn't think there was any connection to my cases. It's not like this is Chicago." I knew I was being defensive but thankfully, Sean didn't call me on my shit.

He wrapped his arms around me in a tight hug and kissed the top of my head. "You're right. This isn't Chicago, but that doesn't mean bad things don't happen here too, Ms. Defense Attorney. I'll let you finish getting ready."

When I was finally dressed, he walked with me out to my car and stood by as I fumbled my way inside, putting the crutches in the back seat. The big boot fit under the dashboard, barely.

"I'll follow you to your office, just to make sure you're okay," Sean said.

"No, I need to go to the jail and meet with Troy."

"Okay. Before you go, I just thought of something." He rushed back inside and then returned with a Tupperware container. "You haven't eaten yet, and it's almost noon." Two pieces of leftover pizza.

"Where would I be without you?" I said, tears welling for the second time this morning as I leaned out to kiss him. Forcing the tears away, I put the car in gear. I needed to meet with Troy before they brought him to court.

## 43

So much for that plan. By the time I got to the jail, they were already taking Troy to court, leaving me to hobble my way to the courthouse.

"What happened, Ms. Gallagher?"

"Don't ever exercise," I said to DeShawn, the security officer. He took my crutches and helped me through the metal detector.

"You don't need to go through this in the future. Just your briefcase."

"Thanks." I rushed as fast as I could down to the courtroom, which was full. A couple of reporters perked up when I entered, maybe sensing a story in my injury.

Troy was waiting at our table. "What happened?"

"No big deal," I said. "I slipped going for a run this morning. Did you hear from Denise?"

"No." He looked behind us where she had been sitting. She wasn't there.

"When I was at the hospital, I checked on Benny. The nurse said he is close to regaining consciousness."

"He's waking up?" He grabbed both my shoulders.

"Maybe. I didn't see him. Denise was there with Charley, so hopefully she can give us a report."

Troy let go of me and sank back into his chair, stunned, tears forming in his eyes. Two months of stress and worry finally finding a release. "My Benny…" he gasped, then covered his face with his hands.

The officer guarding Troy leaned over the bar. "Is everything okay?"

"We think Troy's son is coming out of his coma," I explained.

He seemed genuinely moved. "That's great, Troy."

"Where's Charley?" It was Carol, standing behind me. "I am not done with my direct exam."

She said nothing about my crutches, nothing about Troy sobbing like a baby. "Sounds like you have problems," I said. I had my own challenges without worrying about hers.

"Fine." Carol smiled wickedly. "And by the way, the plea offer is revoked. I'll get you copies of the phone forensics when I have them." She flounced off and sat down at her own table.

Carol must have some new evidence from the phone. Something damaging enough to make her withdraw the plea offer. I turned to my client.

"Troy, I need to ask you some questions."

He nodded and wiped his eyes, working to pull himself together.

"They may have found the coach's phone in your neighbor's garage—near where Charley found the gun."

He winced, and I could tell he knew what I was going to ask.

"Did you send the coach any text messages, or did he take any pictures of you?"

His head lowered, and he muttered some swear words. "Yeah, I texted him."

The bailiff came over to my table. "Are you ready?" I glanced at the clock on the wall. It was 1:30 p.m.

"No," I said. "I broke my foot this morning and I haven't had a chance to confer with my client." I glanced sideways at Carol, watching. "And Carol's witness isn't here yet."

"That's okay," Carol said. "I'm ready to go."

The bailiff said, "The judge wants to get things moving. I can give you about three minutes."

"Thanks," I said, as he went to tell the judge in chambers.

"What's in the texts, Troy?"

"It's bad," he admitted. "I might have made some threats. I wanted to mess with him, you know? I mean, he ruined Benny's life."

"Threats?" I repeated, thinking. It depended on what he said, but the jury might understand that. His son had lost a scholarship. I wanted to get more details, but there wasn't enough time. There was something more pressing we needed to discuss. I said, "If Benny recovers in time, he could testify that you came to help him that night—"

"No," Troy said forcefully. "We're not bringing Benny into this. You don't need him."

"I *do* need him." I grabbed his hand. "We can't gamble on this. He's your alibi. You have to help me, Troy."

He shook his head. "Nope. I promised."

"Promised who?"

"All rise," the bailiff said. "The Donahoe County Court of Common Pleas is now in session. The Honorable Victor Blankenship, presiding."

"Be seated. Are we ready to bring in the jury?"

Carol stood and said, "May we approach, Your Honor?"

I picked up my crutches and hobbled up to the judge alongside Carol. He frowned, looking genuinely concerned. "What happened, Ms. Gallagher?"

"I went for a run this morning and broke my foot. As a result, I haven't been able to talk with my client about the prosecutor's plea offer." I wasn't going to bring up that I thought some of the coach's former players were trying to intimidate me.

Carol cut me off. "I revoked that offer, Judge, so it's off the table. I asked to come up here, off the record, to discuss the fact that my witness, Charley Weaver, is not here." She looked at me like it was my fault.

The judge didn't miss a beat. "I'm sure you can get some officers to go find him. Let's proceed with your next witness."

I said, "Your Honor, I understand that the government has completed its forensic analysis of the phone recovered from the neighbor's garage. Yet, I don't have any of the results. I cannot be expected to proceed without having all the relevant discovery."

"That seems fair," he said. "Ms. Becker?" His voice took on a harder note. "I have granted you two delays now. I am not inclined to give a third. Where is the discovery?"

"It is being collated and copied, Judge. I hope to have it for Ms.

Gallagher later this afternoon. I am prepared to go forward with a witness that has nothing to do with the cell phone."

I started to object, but he cut me off. "We will proceed, but I am going to give Ms. Gallagher latitude. If she needs to re-cross this witness at a later time, based on the new discovery, I am going to allow it."

We returned to our tables and Carol said, "The State calls Kaitlyn Wynant." She was the tanning salon clerk who saw Troy leave Lefty's.

She took the stand, wearing a yellow sundress and looking more tanned than seemed humanly possible. I had expected Kaitlyn to be Carol's last witness, her attempt to finish strong with evidence that Troy could have driven to the coach's house. But now she was probably going to use the new cell phone evidence to finish.

She began her direct examination, going slower than usual, maybe killing time until her staff brought the cell phone discovery. Eventually, she got around to Kaitlyn standing outside the bar on New Year's Eve and seeing Troy walk out of Lefty's.

"And where did he go?"

"He walked to a car and opened the door."

Carol was standing up by the witness stand. She said, "Is that man here in court?"

Kaitlyn pointed. "Yes, he's the man sitting over there at the table."

"Let the record reflect the witness is pointing at the defendant. No further questions." Carol walked back to her table.

I remained seated at my table and got right to the point. "Did you see what happened next, Ms. Wynant? What that man did after opening the car door?"

"No, I didn't."

"Can you tell the jury why you were outside on that cold night with your boyfriend?"

"He's not my boyfriend anymore, but…we went outside so we could, you know, fool around."

"And he was kissing your neck when you saw the man in the letterman jacket."

"Yes, he was pretty handsy." That brought some laughs from the crowd, and Kaitlyn smiled. She was enjoying being the center of attention.

"When you later identified my client, it was because you had seen him on TV, correct? That night, you weren't too interested in what he looked like."

"Yeah," she admitted readily. "To be honest, I don't remember seeing his face that night. I just remember that jacket, and then seeing him later on TV."

"Did you see this man drive away?"

"Nope. Once I thought it was clear, Ethan and I went back to fooling around."

I said, "Is it possible he went out to his car for something and then went back inside?"

"I guess it's possible. I mean, I wasn't really paying attention to him."

"And you'd been drinking, hadn't you?"

"I had a couple cosmos and some champagne. Ethan was drinking beer, but I don't like beer."

"And a cosmo is a cocktail with vodka, correct? A pretty strong drink."

"Oh, it's strong all right. But I don't know what's in it."

"Thank you," I said. "No further questions."

As Kaitlyn bounced down from the witness stand, smiling at me, the courtroom door opened and in came Liam and a younger man holding a box.

Carol stood. "Your Honor. This is the discovery we discussed." She didn't want to describe it further since the jury was still present. "I would request a short break so we can provide the materials to Ms. Gallagher."

"Very well. We'll take ten minutes." The judge disappeared, and the bailiff escorted the jury out.

Liam came forward and took the box from the younger man, turning toward me. "We printed out all the relevant items on these," he said, holding up a full three-ring binder. "And the whole data set is on these two DVDs."

"How am I supposed to watch this?"

Liam saw the boot and the crutches under my table. "What happened?"

"Broke my foot." I took the DVDs and held them up. "These don't do me any good. I don't have a DVD player."

"Not even on your computer?"

"Nope."

"You can borrow my laptop; it's in my car. I'll go get it."

Dropping discovery on me like this, in the middle of trial, was completely unacceptable. When the judge returned, I would make an argument that it violated Troy's due process rights. Simply put, there was no way we could go forward with the trial until I had gone through everything.

I opened the binder and started flipping pages, Troy looking on with me. Then Carol came over. "We put yellow stickers on all the messages from your client to make it easier to find them." I ignored her, taking my time. The binder began with downloaded emails from the coach's phone, but while he had plenty of emails from various teachers and students, none of those were from Troy. My ankle was throbbing and my mind wandered to it. Did I have some more ibuprofen? *Focus, Maggie.*

And then I saw an email from "JT49." It was full of expletives, how JT was going to "F*** up" the coach for picking on his girlfriend. "And thanks for f***ing me up too." I thought of my interview with the girl, Ava, who moved to St. Louis because the coach harassed her. She said her boyfriend was upset with him. And the boyfriend went by *JT*.

Troy looked at the email address. "Maggie, that reads like it was written by my friend in the jail, Justin. He talks just like that. And sometimes he calls himself JT."

"That's the guy who wanted you to plead guilty, right?"

"Yeah." Troy leaned closer. "He's also been asking about the coach's cell phone, wanting to know if the police had it. I told him no."

"Well, they have it now." This guy *had* to be Ava's boyfriend.

"Maggie…" Troy leaned back in his chair, a shocked look on his face.

"What is it?"

"Justin's last name—it's Cross. Do you think he could be Archie's grandson?"

We stared at each other as the significance sank in. Finally, Troy said, "He's in trial right now for robbery."

Justin Cross would have had access to his grandfather's garage. And he had a motive to kill the coach. I picked up my crutches and stood. "Maybe I can talk to him."

I started to leave and Carol said, "Where are you going? The judge is going to want to start."

I ignored her. If I was right, we had found the real killer.

## 44

I took a seat in the back row of a mostly empty courtroom. Justin's mom, Cammie—the daughter-in-law of Archibald Cross I'd met the other day—sat directly behind her son. Oliver, the prosecutor, was questioning a uniformed police officer on the witness stand, but Justin wasn't paying attention. I'd tried to be quiet, but the crutches had made some noise when I'd entered, and he had turned in his seat to look back at me. He was about twenty years old, with short curly blond hair. I didn't think he looked much like Justin Timberlake, but I was hardly an expert. I was pretty sure that this JT was bigger. I wondered if he had played football for Coach Schafer.

Cammie saw me and came to the back row. "Hi, Ms. Gallagher," she whispered. "What are you doing here?"

"We had a break in our trial, and I just thought I'd pop in. How's Ed Caldwell doing?" Caldwell was Justin's attorney. I had run into him in the courthouse a few times over the last month. He was in his mid-sixties, still doing indigent defense work. A decent enough guy, from what I could tell. Not much of a fighter, but he knew the courts back to front and he worked hard for his clients.

"He's okay. Public defender," she said, like that was all the explanation needed.

"Is Justin going to testify?"

She shook her head. "Justin wants to, but so did my ex-husband, and now he's in prison. Mr. Caldwell and I talked him out of it."

The courtroom door opened and in came Liam. He leaned down next to me and whispered, "The bailiff is looking for you. And I left my laptop on your table."

To Cammie, I said, "Could you have Mr. Caldwell come see me when he gets a break?"

"Sure, I guess."

I stood and left the courtroom with Liam. "Do you have some ibuprofen?"

"Hurts, huh?"

"Yeah." The door closed behind us, and I stopped in the hallway. "Liam…"

"What is it?"

"I think I know who killed Coach Schafer."

"You think it's the kid in there, Justin Cross," Liam said, like he had thought of it too.

"He didn't like the coach picking on his girlfriend in health class. And the garage where the gun and cell phone were found? That's his grandfather's house."

"Everyone in the PD knows Justin," Liam said. "He's been trouble since he was a kid."

"There's more. In the discovery you gave me, I found a threatening email he sent to the coach. And..." *Should I tell him the rest?*

"And what?"

"And he's been buddying up to Troy in jail, trying to talk him into pleading guilty." Liam locked eyes with me, and I could tell we were on the same page. I said, "Did anyone check to see if he had an alibi on New Year's Eve?"

"You know it's not my case," he said.

"I know. But Troy didn't do this." I placed the tip of my crutch on the top of his shoe and pressed slightly. "Don't make me hurt you," I said, which brought a smile. "You can do the right thing here, Liam. And besides, I'm your favorite cousin."

"Do you want me to get you some ibuprofen, or do you want me to solve a murder? I can't do both."

"I guess you better solve a murder, then."

"I'm Carol's next witness. That's why they wanted me to find you. The judge wants to get going."

"Okay. Testify first. Then solve the murder."

---

We were in Judge Blankenship's chambers. "Your Honor, I haven't even begun to go over this last-minute discovery," I said. "There's no way I can proceed today."

The judge frowned. "I'm sympathetic, Ms. Gallagher, but we need to keep things moving."

"I don't want to file the motion, but my client has a due process right to evaluate all the new discovery. I need more time."

The judge didn't like that, but he knew I was right. He turned to Carol. "What other witnesses can you call today without getting into the cell phone evidence?"

"I can wait to offer the texts and videos until tomorrow," Carol said, feigning cooperation, "but I could authenticate the phone with the detective who found it, and I can call the forensic expert who downloaded the data. I also have an officer out looking for Charley Weaver."

I chose not to tell Carol where he was. Denise and Charley should be with Benny, not here.

Carol looked directly at me. "Just so you know, there are threatening text messages from your client and the victim shot video of your client saying he was going to kill him."

*Great. Troy and his big mouth.* "Do I have copies of *all* the photos and videos that were stored on the phone?" Maybe Justin had done something similar.

"Yes," Carol said, then immediately started hedging. "That is, I think so. I will double-check." She had already gotten in trouble for not giving me the audio interview of Troy, and we both knew it wouldn't go well if the judge thought she'd held something else back.

"Okay, we have a plan," the judge said. "And Ms. Gallagher, I assume the State is almost finished with their case. Do you plan on offering a defense?"

"I might have a couple of witnesses. It will depend on what I find in this latest discovery."

"Very well. Let's go back out there and finish up today. If we end early, that will give you more time to review the discovery. I expect it will be a late night for you, Ms. Gallagher."

I limped back out to the courtroom, the audience all watching as we retook our seats. Carol called Liam O'Brien. As he took the witness stand, I handed the three-ring binder back to Auntie El. "Could you go through this and look for anything important?"

"Like what?" she said.

I shrugged. "You'll know it when you see it."

"After this witness." She smiled and added, "I've never seen my boy testify."

Liam was sworn in, then gave a recitation of his training and experience. He was a much better witness than the case officer, Janice Evans. He was relaxed and professional, explaining how the police had searched Archibald Cross's garage. "In a large cardboard box, I found a cell phone."

Carol showed him the phone in a plastic bag. "For the record, I am showing the witness State's Exhibit 19. Is this the phone you found?"

Liam took it. "Yes, it has my mark from when I placed it into the secure evidence locker."

"Thank you," Carol said. "No further questions."

I would have liked to approach Liam on the stand, but I remained seated because of my ankle. I looked back at Auntie El, who winked. "Kill him," she said.

Time for a little fun. "Detective O'Brien, would you please tell the jury how we know each other?"

He looked at them. "Well, we are cousins. Ms. Gallagher and I used to chase frogs together when we were kids. And we would argue about almost everything."

Most of the jurors smiled at that. A murder trial was serious business, which could wear jurors down. It was nice when a moment of levity arose. "The chance to cross-examine my cousin is too delicious to pass up," I said, playing it up with a big smile. "Let me remind you, you are under oath. And with that in mind, Detective O'Brien, wouldn't you agree that I won most of those childhood arguments?"

Liam winked at the jury. "I don't think she won any of them."

I waited for the laughs to subside. Then I asked, "Can you tell us why the police searched Mr. Cross's garage?"

"As I understand it, Charley Weaver said that was where he found the murder weapon."

"So the murder weapon and Grant Schafer's phone were found in the same place—the neighbor's garage."

"Yes."

"And this phone was found in a big cardboard box."

"Correct."

"And Charley said the gun was in a big cardboard box. Charley was right, wasn't he?"

"Objection," Carol said as she stood.

"Sustained." I knew it would be, but I didn't care. The jury knew Charley had been right.

"One more question. Was the phone checked for fingerprints?"

"I understand it was submitted for prints, but I don't know the results."

"No further questions."

Carol quickly moved to the Kerry PD's phone forensics specialist. He explained how he'd extracted the data from Coach Schafer's phone.

As her last question, she stated, "The phone was checked for prints. Do you know the results of that?"

I could have objected. This witness wasn't the prints expert. But what was the point? He said, "I understand there were no usable prints found on the phone."

When I had no questions on cross-examination, Carol said, "I have no further witnesses today."

"Very well." Judge Blankenship said. To the jury, he added, "Ladies and gentlemen, we will adjourn for the day. Please be back here tomorrow. We will start early, at 9 a.m."

Troy leaned close. "Can you call Denise before I go back? I need to know what's going on with Benny."

"Of course," I said. I felt awful for not thinking of that earlier. Troy had sat here through the afternoon with no updates on his son. Technically, it would be a violation of jail rules for Troy to talk on my phone, but given the circumstances, maybe they'd let us slide. Catching the eye of the officer, I told him what I was doing, and he gave me a slight nod. With that, I dialed Denise and put it on speaker.

"Hello?"

"Denise? This is Maggie. I am here in court with Troy on the speakerphone. We wondered if you could give Troy an update."

"Oh, honey! Benny's doing so good. He's moving around, mumbling things... I can't understand him, but the doctors say his brain waves are great. They think he could be conscious soon. I wish you could be here."

"Me too," Troy said, tears forming again. "My Benny..."

"My mom's here," Denise said. "She's going to take Charley, but I'm staying the night. They think he could wake up anytime."

"Okay." The officer motioned that Troy needed to go back to jail. "I got to go, babe. But things are really going well here. Maybe Maggie can tell you about it later."

"This will all be over soon," Denise said, "and we'll be a family again. I love you."

"Love you too."

Troy wiped his eyes on his coat sleeve. He turned to the officer. "Thank you, man. You have no idea…"

"I have two boys," he said. And then, in mock seriousness, "Now let's go."

As Troy left, Auntie El came up to the table and sat in his seat. "Maggie, what can I do to help?"

"Go back to the office and go through this stuff." I pulled the computer Liam had given me out of my bag and handed it to her. "Check these DVDs. Carol said there's video of Troy threatening to kill the coach."

"What are *you* going to do?"

"I need to talk to a witness. I may have figured out who killed the coach."

She nodded, like she expected that. "What took you so long?" Then she gave me that great big Auntie El smile.

First, some ibuprofen if I could find it. Then, Ed Caldwell. Would he let me talk to his client, Justin Cross?

## 45

Oliver came out of the courtroom as I approached on my crutches. "What happened to you?" he said.

"Don't ask." I was already tired of hearing that question. "Are you finished in there?"

"Yes. We rested. The judge wanted to do closing arguments tomorrow morning."

"Are Ed and Justin still in there?"

"Yes. Why?" Oliver was suspicious.

"It has nothing to do with your case," I assured him, then I limped into the courtroom. Ed was at his table, talking with Justin. An officer sat patiently on a bench, waiting for them to finish before taking Justin back to jail.

I walked up. "Ed, I was wondering if I could interview your client briefly. I just received some discovery on my case and thought he might have some useful information." I knew Ed would say no. But from what Troy had said, Justin might be arrogant enough to want to talk with me. He'd been pumping Troy for information about the phone, after all. He had to know that I was a better source.

"What's this about?" Ed said, turning around. "And what happened to you?"

"Some bad luck." I waved my hand like it was nothing. "Like I said, Carol just dumped new discovery on me, and it mentions your client."

Ed shook his head. "I don't think so. Maybe when our trial is over. Helping you isn't going to win him any points with the prosecutor's office."

"I'll talk to her," Justin interrupted. "I got nothing to hide." He turned to the officer. "Can you wait a few more minutes?" The guy shrugged. He wasn't in any hurry.

Justin stood and leaned on the table. "Go ahead and ask me your questions."

"Did you have a girlfriend named Ava?"

"Maybe. Why does it matter?"

I needed to be careful here, and not to tip my hand too soon.

"Well, I understand Coach Schafer harassed her in health class."

"You're trying to come up with another suspect besides Troy." He smiled, confident now that he thought he knew my motive. "She's a bitch. It wouldn't surprise me if she did it."

"You tried to protect her, though, didn't you?"

"Sure. I mean, she was my girlfriend, for a while. 'Til I dumped her."

"Did you play for the coach?"

Justin's cocky grin gave way to a scowl. "He made up some lies and cut me."

"So you didn't like him either."

Ed interceded. "Wait a minute. I'm not going to let you insinuate that my client killed the coach."

"It's okay," Justin said. "Yeah, I didn't like him. He was an asshole."

"Did you wear number forty-nine?" I said.

"How'd you know? Did you see me play?"

I had guessed from his email address. For some reason, people, including my husband, used their glory-days jersey numbers in their email addresses. "JT49" was Justin.

I said, "Why did you want Troy to plead guilty?"

He smiled at that. "He told you, huh? 'Cause I think he did it. I mean, he had the murder weapon. And I know you can do less time if you cut a deal."

"Did you know Troy's son, Benny?"

He looked at his attorney, like he was finally having second thoughts about talking with me, though his smile didn't waver. "Poor Benny. What's it been, two months in a coma? Too bad."

I don't know why I asked it. Just a hunch, I guess. I had nothing to lose—and I wanted to see his reaction. "You were with him that New Year's Eve, the night of the murder, weren't you?"

The reaction was even better than I'd hoped, as all traces of the smile dropped away. He actually looked nervous as he stood up straight. "We're done here." He looked at his attorney again and then turned toward the officer. "Let's go."

As they walked out of the courtroom and back to the jail, I called after him. "There's no statute of limitations on murder."

Justin Cross turned and stared at me. I held his gaze.

*Yeah, I know it was you.*

---

Back at the office, I called home and told Sean not to wait up. He immediately sounded concerned. "You're pushing yourself too hard. You've got a broken ankle, remember?"

"It's a broken foot. The ankle is just sprained."

"Oh, that's much better," he said sarcastically. "And do you remember that thing called sleep? This is just like Chicago."

I grimaced knowing I needed to make peace with my husband, but now wasn't the time. "You're right, but I have to get through all the discovery that just landed in my lap. Judge Blankenship won't grant me a delay, which means I'm working late."

There was silence at Sean's end and I resisted the urge to check to see if he'd hung up. At last, he blew out a loud breath. "Just don't stay up too late."

"I promise."

Luckily, Auntie El had a large bottle of ibuprofen. "I need it when my arthritis acts up," she said. Then she brought me to her desk, where she had cued up the video of Troy. "It's not good."

They were in the high school parking lot. Troy was about twenty feet away. "Don't come any closer," the coach said.

Troy kept coming. "You think you can hide from me?" He stopped about five feet away. "You think a camera's gonna change things? How many lives have you ruined? I know for a fact Benny isn't the first."

"You need to quit harassing me or I'm going to the cops."

"Somebody needs to stop you." Troy stepped closer. "If there weren't people around, I'd do you right now." He pointed his finger like it was a gun. "Watch your back, 'cause I'm coming."

As Troy walked away, Schafer narrated. "That was Troy Weaver, the father of Benny Weaver. Near the end of the season, I released Benny Weaver and some other kids from the football team for drug use. Troy has been harassing me ever since. Today is December 16th." The video ended there.

I looked at Auntie El. "Not good."

"This was two weeks before the murder," she said. "Any chance you can keep it out of evidence?"

"Probably not." But I would try. "Anything else on the DVDs?"

"A lot of photos and some videos," Auntie El said. "But nothing that seemed relevant." She hesitated a moment. "There was one picture I wanted to ask about." She scrolled through a bunch of photos. "Here, look at this football team photo. They took it in front of that Paul Brown statue. Is Benny in this? I don't know what he looks like."

The date on the picture was November 14. I had only seen Benny briefly, but I was sure he wasn't here. He was cut before then. Next, I scanned it for Justin Cross. There were about twenty kids, but I didn't see Justin anywhere. I suspected he was kicked off the team at the same time as Benny. *Two drug users.* That lined up with what the coach said about running a clean program.

"This isn't the whole team," I said. "It's only twenty kids."

"Just the seniors. After the season, the seniors get their picture in front of the statue. It's a Kerry High tradition. Patrick has his senior football picture up in his house."

We still had the binder full of emails and texts to go through. "Let's go in the conference room and spread out. I can put my foot up, and maybe we can order dinner."

"I already did," Auntie El said. "Your uncle is bringing some fried chicken and a couple of beers. I'll drink yours if you don't want it."

Auntie El to the rescue again.

---

Of course, Sean was still up when I got home around 11 p.m. He was watching the local news as I hobbled in. "How are you doing?"

I plopped on the couch next to him and put my leg on the coffee table. "Just about the longest day of my life," I said. My ankle throbbed, but I was getting used to the pain. The fatigue, however, was almost overwhelming.

Sean said, "Are you keeping your ankle up?"

"Not really. I need a box or something under my table in court. It hurt the whole day. But we're almost done. We might even finish tomorrow."

"How are you feeling about it?"

Before I could answer, Ian came into the room. "Hi, honey," I said. "I haven't seen you in a while." He looked at my boot, then at the crutches on the table. He turned and almost ran back to his room.

I looked at Sean. "What was that?"

"You know," he said. And I guess I did. "Here you are, injured again. It was hard enough on him the last time. You could have been killed in that accident, you know. And then all that rehab you went through, all the pain. He watched all of that. Now it happens again?"

"I know…" I shouldn't feel guilty about another injury—after all, it wasn't like I'd done it on purpose. "I hate being the cause of more trouble for Ian, especially when I have no idea how to comfort him." Our relationship was getting worse and it was my fault.

Sean reached out to squeeze my hand in what felt like solidarity. "Do you want me to talk with him?"

I shifted closer to him so I could lean my head against his shoulder. "No. I need to do this. We need to clear things up between us." Should I do it now? Go into his room and talk it out? Just the thought of standing up made me want to cry. I was too tired. If I tried to go in there now, I'd probably say something stupid and make everything worse. *I need sleep.* "I'll talk with him tomorrow."

After the trial. We would finish tomorrow. Carol's phone evidence, my witnesses, closing statements, maybe even the jury verdict. Troy's future and freedom were on the line.

## 46

When the jury had taken their seats, Carol offered State's Exhibit numbers 20 through 24. These were text messages sent by Troy to Coach Schafer. The first two asked for a meeting with the coach, explaining how devastating it was for Benny to get cut from the football team. It was the last two that hurt.

Exhibit 23: **If you cared about your kids, you wouldn't treat them like this. I hope someday, someone treats you the same way. Maybe it will be me.**

Exhibit 24: **You piece of shit. Don't even have the courage to meet me in person. I heard what you did to the Marshall boy. How many kids are u going to screw?!?!? I'm gonna mess u up bad!!!!!!**

The judge allowed Carol to read the texts out loud. Then she handed them the printed versions to take into deliberations.

Next she offered Exhibit 25. "Objection," I said. I picked up my crutches and stood. "Your Honor, there is insufficient authentication of this video. We don't know if it is accurate. Was it altered in some way? The government has failed to show this video correctly depicts the event as it occurred. Also, the last half of the video contains a hearsay statement of Mr. Schafer that is inadmissible."

"Thank you, Ms. Gallagher. While the authentication was not ideal, I believe that goes to the weight of the evidence. You are free to argue to the jury that it is not reliable. Concerning the hearsay objection, I am overruling that as well. I believe it is admissible to show the effect on speaker." He looked at Carol. "You may proceed."

Carol had set up a large movie screen with a projector connected to her laptop. She wanted Troy to appear life-sized as he threatened coach Schafer. The bailiff dimmed the lights and then she played the video. The audience, including the news media, could see it as well. I kept my eyes on the jury. When the lights came back on, they were all staring at Troy.

It was the most powerful moment of the trial.

"The State rests," Carol said.

Judge Blankenship said, "Let's take the jury out for a moment." The bailiff led them into the deliberation room. Then Blankenship said, "Ms. Gallagher, before you make your motion, we have the matter of the unfinished testimony from Charley Weaver. I could strike his testimony, since you did not have the chance to cross-examine him."

I stood and said, "I'm willing to waive my cross."

The judge nodded. "I thought you might. Now, go ahead and make your motion." This was standard practice in a criminal case. At the conclusion of the government's evidence, defense counsel always moved to dismiss.

"I move the court at this time for a judgment of acquittal. The government has failed in its burden to submit sufficient evidence whereby any reasonable jury could find guilt. They have offered nothing more than a motive. There is nothing placing my client at the scene of the crime, nothing placing the murder weapon in his hand at any time. In fact, the evidence actually points to Mr. Weaver's innocence. After the crime, the gun was not in his possession, but in his neighbor's garage."

My temples were throbbing in time to the pulsating in my foot, but I pushed through. "And Mr. Weaver has an alibi for the time of the murder, which the government has not refuted. The best they can show is that sometime on New Year's Eve, Mr. Weaver might have been seen going out to his car. And this is from a young witness who readily admits that she was under the influence of alcohol and distracted by her boyfriend. Her identification is worthless—and pointless, since even she makes no claims to having seen him drive away.

"Your Honor, the government has utterly failed in its burden, and you should grant my motion to set Mr. Weaver free." I sat back down, knowing what the answer would be.

"Thank you, counsel. I am going to deny your motion. At this time." Interesting that he said, "At this time." That seemed to imply he agreed with me that the government's case was weak. He said, "Do you intend to offer a defense?"

"Yes, I have a few witnesses, Your Honor."

When the bailiff brought the jury back, I said, "The defense calls Kerry High School Principal David Boudreau."

I had only spoken with him on the phone and was surprised to see how young he was. About my age, with sandy blond hair and wire-rimmed glasses. I asked him the typical preliminary questions to familiarize him to the jury. Then, "Mr. Boudreau, as part of your duties, do you deal with unhappy parents?"

"Unfortunately, yes."

"Did you encounter parents unhappy with the football coach Grant Schafer?"

"I did."

"How many?"

"Well, at the time of Coach Schafer's death, I had been principal for five years. Over that time, I received some verbal comments, some complaints over the phone, and of course some in writing."

"Did you bring the ones in writing, like I asked you?"

"I did." He reached for a manila folder at his feet and brought it up.

I slowly rose, grabbed my crutches, and hobbled up to him. I took the folder and looked at them. "How many written complaints are here?" I asked.

"Nine."

"Could you estimate how many complaints you received in total? Whether in person, on the phone or in writing?"

"Just from parents?"

I looked at the jury, trying to appear surprised. "Were there other people unhappy with him?"

"Yes."

"And who were these other people?"

"Students, other coaches and some teachers. Grant had a…strong personality."

"So in total, during your five years as principal before the coach's death, how many complaints, would you estimate?"

"I couldn't say for certain," he hedged.

"Just give me a ballpark figure, then."

"Maybe thirty?" I had the feeling he was lowballing it, probably not wanting to admit how lax he'd been, allowing Schafer to bully the people around him. But the number he'd been willing to admit to was bad enough on its own.

"*Thirty complaints*," I said, looking at the jury. "During the investigation, did the police ever ask you to provide these written complaints?"

"Not that I remember."

"Thank you. Your Honor, I'd like to offer these into evidence as Defense Exhibit 1."

"Objection," Carol said. "Hearsay."

"Sustained."

I looked at the jury and shrugged, as if to say, "I tried." They would see Carol as the obstructionist. And even if they couldn't read the complaints, they now knew they existed. Troy wasn't the only one who'd had a grudge against the coach.

Carol had no cross-examination of the principal. Next, I called Harold Ames, otherwise known as Lefty. The big man with the Fu Manchu mustache took the stand. He was not happy.

"Thanks for coming in, Mr. Ames."

"I didn't really have a choice, did I?"

"Nope," I said. "You are the owner of Lefty's Bar and Grill?"

"Yes, me and my wife."

"And those great pork chops on Thursdays—that is her recipe, right?"

He smiled at that. "Yes, that's right. Y'all come down next Thursday and give 'em a try."

A few jurors smiled at that. I said, "Are you familiar with my client, Troy Weaver?"

"Yes, I know Troy. He used to come in quite a bit. Good guy." He nodded toward Troy. It was one of those unexpected moments in a trial that could help. The jury seeing that a respected citizen thought highly of Troy.

"I would like to call your attention to that New Year's Eve about sixteen months ago. Do you recall Mr. Weaver being there?"

"I do. We had a party that night, with a cover charge. Of course, I was very busy, but I do remember Troy being there around at closing time. So was his wife, Denise. Troy got into it a little with another customer who had too much to drink. Troy wanted the guy to take a cab. Like I said, he's a good guy."

*Perfect.* "No further questions."

Again, Carol had no cross-examination.

I stood and said, "The defense intends to call Justin Cross, but I understand he is currently in trial in Judge Yost's courtroom."

"Objection," Carol said, standing herself. "This person is not on the defense witness list."

I said, "Your Honor, this is a result of the last-minute discovery that Ms. Becker dropped on me."

The judge looked at the jury. "Ladies and gentlemen, now is a good time for our afternoon break." The bailiff ushered them into the jury room, then the judge pointed his two fingers at Carol and me. "In my chambers."

Getting Justin Cross on the stand was going to be tricky. He was on trial in another courtroom, for one thing. And his attorney would almost certainly want to protect him by asserting his Fifth Amendment rights against self-incrimination.

Troy's future might depend on what happened next.

## 47

Blankenship wanted Judge Yost and Ed Caldwell to join us. So, while we waited for them to arrive, he made me tell him about my injury.

"I'm sorry, Ms. Gallagher. I know how difficult that can be. I once tried a case with kidney stones. If there's anything you need from us…"

There was a knock and Judge Yost entered, along with Justin's attorney. "Thanks for coming, gentlemen," Blankenship said.

"Luckily, my jury went out to deliberate before lunch," Yost said. "So we are available." He was a younger judge, with longish brown hair, known for riding his bike to the courthouse in the morning.

Judge Blankenship turned to me. "Why don't you tell us what this is about, Ms. Gallagher?"

But Carol spoke first. "This witness was not on the defense witness list. It is improper for him to be called at this late date."

"As I said, these are facts I learned from the prosecution's late discovery. If she can put on newly discovered evidence, so can I."

"Go ahead, Ms. Gallagher," the judge said, giving Carol a warning look that said, *don't interrupt.*

I slowly stood from the chair where I had been sitting. I didn't like Carol hovering over me. "Mr. Cross sent a threatening email to the victim which I just received yesterday in the discovery. And Mr. Cross is the grandson of Archibald Cross, the man who owns the garage where the murder weapon was found."

There was silence. The judges exchanged glances, then looked at Justin's attorney. Blankenship simply said, "Ed?"

Ed Caldwell had remained near the door. Now he stepped in closer to us, giving me a harsh look in the process. He knew I was trying to pin the murder on Justin. "My client just received the subpoena this morning in the jail. I have spoken with him about this." He hesitated. "These are very unusual circumstances. I have advised him of his rights against self-incrimination. I have gone over what he believes would be his testimony…and against my strong advice, he wants to take the stand. But first he wanted me to check on one thing."

He turned and looked at Carol, then at me. "Judge, I don't believe I can say anything further in the presence of counsel. It would be a privileged communication, but one I think you must hear."

"Counsel, would you give us a minute?" Blankenship said to us.

We both stepped out into the hallway. Carol said, "What do you think that's about?"

I shrugged, but I thought I knew. *And it's my fault.* When I met with Justin earlier, my last comment had been telling him that I knew he was with Benny the night of New Year's Eve. If Benny was awake, he could contradict Justin's testimony. He would want his lawyer to find out how Benny was.

I limped around the corner and back into the courtroom to get my cell phone. Then I called Denise. "Make sure you don't tell anyone how Benny is doing," I said.

"Why not?"

"I can't explain now, but it could impact our case. And tell the hospital to not release anything."

"They won't. They're paranoid about privacy and stuff."

I hung up and went back to Carol. The judges and Ed Caldwell were still inside, discussing the matter. Invoking Justin's Fifth Amendment rights was not as easy as TV made it seem. If Justin were to invoke, he would have to go before the judge and, in private, explain how his testimony would incriminate him. Only then would the judge grant him the right to refuse to testify. But his statement to the judge could never be used against him. It would never be known to anyone but the judge.

I hoped it wouldn't come to that.

After almost thirty minutes, the door opened, and Judge Yost brought us back inside. Judge Blankenship said, "We will bring Mr. Cross up from the jail and we will clear the courtroom. Then, on the record, I will consult with Mr. Cross about whether he wants to invoke his rights." This was a tricky legal area, and I could see that the judge wanted to make sure he had a clean record so an appellate court couldn't overturn him. "If he declines to testify, I will send the jury home and I will have an in-camera meeting with Mr. Cross to check the validity of his assertions."

The bailiff was already emptying the courtroom when we returned.

The media members were not happy, complaining about a violation of their First Amendment rights.

Then in came Justin Cross from the jail, still dressed in civilian clothes from his own trial. Ed Caldwell stood waiting for him between Carol's table and mine. Justin glanced back at Troy with a cocky smirk. *Good.* I was counting on his arrogance.

Judge Blankenship said, "Mr. Cross, you have been subpoenaed to testify in this matter, State versus Troy Weaver. You are present with your counsel, Ed Caldwell. Mr. Caldwell has told me you are currently in trial in another courtroom on a robbery charge. Is that correct?"

"Yeah."

"I have cleared the courtroom to ask you, on the record, whether you wish to assert your right against self-incrimination, or whether you will honor your subpoena. Before you answer, you should know that if you decide against testifying, I must examine you, in private, to determine whether you have a legitimate claim that you might incriminate yourself." He looked at me. "Counsel, have I stated the issues correctly?"

"I believe so, yes," I said.

"Yes, Your Honor," Carol said.

"Very well. Mr. Cross?"

Justin looked back at Troy again. This time with menace. "I have nothing to hide, Judge. I'd love to testify."

"Very well. Bring in the public and the jury."

———

Justin took the stand and was sworn in. I knew this was going to be dangerous. Justin wasn't here to pump me for information like earlier. He wanted Troy convicted so he would be in the clear.

This was the kind of witness I liked to confront face-to-face, but because of my ankle, I remained seated at the table, at least for now. "Mr. Cross, how old are you?"

"Twenty."

"Do you go by Justin?"

"Sure, you can call me that. I have a lot of names."

"Is one of them JT?"

"Yeah." He turned to the jury like a polished witness. "People think I look like Justin Timberlake." He smiled at them. "I wish I had his money."

"Did you play football for Grant Schafer?"

"I guess I did, for a while. I quit my senior year." He smiled at me. We both knew he was cut by Schafer, and he was daring me to prove it. I couldn't. Yet.

"What was your number?"

"Forty-nine."

"Did you take health class from Grant Schafer?"

"Yep."

"Did you have a girlfriend in that same class, Ava Robbins?"

"Yeah. But not anymore. I dumped her."

"At that time, did you think Coach Schafer picked on Ava Robbins?"

Justin squirmed slightly. "She had some mental problems, and he kinda made fun of her."

I picked up the paper copy of his threatening email. "How did you feel about that?"

"I thought it was *unkind.*" He smiled at that answer. "We were still together then."

"Did you send him an email, telling him that was unkind?"

He shrugged, nonchalant. "Could be."

I picked up my crutches and hobbled forward, holding the document. "Your email address is JT49. Did you send him this email?" I handed it over.

Justin read it, then glanced at his lawyer sitting in the first row. "Probably." The cockiness was wearing off now.

I turned to the Judge. "I will offer Defense Exhibit 2." Carol had no basis to object. Then I read the email to the jury:

**"You talk tough to girls in class asshole. Picking on the fatties and on my own GF. I guess I'm gonna have to f*** you up. And by the way thanks for f***ing me over too."**

I said, "What did you mean by, 'picking on the fatties?'"

"I don't remember." He was going into evasive mode. I looked at the jury to make sure they saw it.

"Did Grant Schafer pick on any overweight students?"

"Like I said, I don't remember."

"But you do remember him picking on your girlfriend?"

Justin shook his head. "You know, I remember she was a headcase, but I don't remember him picking on her specifically." He looked at the jury to see if they bought it. They showed no emotion.

"But it made you angry enough to threaten to 'eff up' Mr. Schafer."

Carol stood and said, "Objection. Leading question."

"Your Honor, given the circumstances and the witness's evasiveness, I request permission to treat him as hostile."

"Granted," he said.

This was big. I could now ask leading questions to control Justin's testimony. And the judge essentially agreed that Justin was being deliberately evasive.

Still standing next to Justin I said, "You were so angry with Mr. Schafer you threatened to 'eff him up,' didn't you?"

"Like I said, I don't remember that."

"To 'eff up' someone means to harm someone physically, doesn't it?"

The smirk was long gone. He was sorry he took the stand, but there was no backing out now. "Not necessarily."

"Oh, okay. Then tell us how exactly you intended to harm Coach Schafer, if not physically?"

"I just wanted to scare him."

"You wanted him to *think* you were going to physically harm him."

"Is that a question?" he said, trying to reassert some control.

"Yes," I said, stepping closer to him. I could feel the tension in the courtroom, and I wanted the jury to see I had no fear. It was like my old days, cross-examining a violent criminal. "You were so angry, you wanted Coach Schafer to think you'd harm him, correct?"

Now he smiled again, trying to change the mood. "You know how it is. Sometimes you send a text or something when you're angry and then later you regret it."

"I bet you regret it now," I said.

"Objection," Carol said. "Ms. Gallagher is badgering the witness."

"Withdrawn," I said. Keeping my eyes on Justin, "'And thanks for effing me up too,' you wrote. You were referring to Coach Schafer cutting you from the football team."

"I don't remember."

"Football was so important you put your jersey number in your email address. It was your senior season, your last year of high school football, and Coach Schafer cut you."

Justin pointed at Troy. "He cut his son, Benny too. Ask him about that."

I leaned on the witness stand, even closer to Justin. I wanted to provoke a reaction. Justin took the challenge, leaning in himself. We were only a foot apart. Quietly I asked, "Why did he cut you?"

Pure hatred in his eyes, he hesitated. Then he leaned back in his seat and folded his arms. "I don't remember."

I looked at the jury. They were with me. A couple leaning forward on the edge of their seats. I picked up Defense Exhibit 2 to read again. "You were so angry, you wrote to him, and I quote, 'I'm going to have to eff you up.' And yet here, under oath, your testimony is that you don't remember why you were angry, why he cut you?"

He smiled and shrugged. "Sorry."

On my crutches, I hobbled over to the end of the jury box. "Your family lives here in town, don't they?"

"Some do," he said, confused by the change in topics.

"Your mom does?"

"Yes."

"And your grandfather?"

Now he knew where I was going. Troy must have told him where Charley found the murder weapon. Justin just stared back.

"Your grandfather, Archibald Cross, lives here in town, correct?"

Justin nodded.

"I need you to speak out loud, for the record."

"Yes," Justin gritted out. "He lives in town."

"He lives alone, correct?"

"Yes."

"But sometimes you visit him, don't you?"

"Not in a long time."

"And you've been in his garage, haven't you?"

"Actually, I don't think so."

"Do I need to call your grandfather in here as a witness?"

He shrugged. "I guess it's possible."

"The same garage where little Charley Weaver found the murder weapon."

His eyes darted to the jury, then back to me. "I don't know anything about that."

I turned to the jury and in a mocking voice I said, "You don't know anything about that." I took my time making eye contact with each juror. Then to the judge I said, "No further questions."

## 48

There was not much for Carol to do on cross. She knew about Justin's criminal record, although the jury did not. They didn't even know he was facing a robbery charge. So she tried to make him sound like an upstanding citizen. She asked where he worked. "I am currently looking," he said. Then she asked where he was on the night of the murder. He glanced sideways at the jury, a little nervous. "I was out with some friends, you know, partying."

In an attempt to mock me, Carol said, "Did you kill Coach Schafer?"

Justin laughed. "No. Of course not."

"No further questions," and she went back to her table.

It was a good ending for Troy. Of course Justin would deny murdering the coach, but she made explicit what I had only hinted at. I stood and said, "Your Honor, I have a couple of questions on redirect." I limped forward to the jury box again. I wanted Justin to look at me and the jury at the same time as he answered. "So, you deny shooting Coach Grant Schafer."

"Yeah. That's ridiculous."

I ignored Justin and looked to the jury. They were all looking back at me. I said, "Tell us the names of the people you were out with that New Year's Eve. Tell us your alibi."

The jurors' eyes all shifted to Justin. His discomfort was palpable. "That was a while ago. I don't remember."

"You don't remember. This was less than a year and a half ago. Have you ever been checked for memory problems?"

"Objection," Carol said.

"I withdraw the question." Then I faced Justin again. "Can you give me the names of *any* of your friends? I'd like to ask them what they remember."

"Like I said, I don't remember who I was out with. It was New Year's Eve, so I was probably drinking. That's why I'm having trouble remembering." He smiled slightly, thinking that was a clever answer.

"Just so I am clear, you don't remember who you were with, and you were drinking heavily?" He didn't respond. I let his non-answer hang in the air a long moment, then I said, "Nothing further."

"You are excused," the judge said. Justin got off the witness stand and glanced toward the door. Two large officers stood there, trying to appear unobtrusive. Justin was in custody and facing serious time for robbery. They were not going to take any chances on him escaping. He walked between the two tables, then instead of heading out the door, he walked down the aisle between the benches and through the back exit, where the in-custody defendants would go.

It was a great finish. Surely the jurors would understand that he was not an ordinary witness who was free to leave.

The judge said, "Ms. Gallagher, call your next witness," bringing me out of my reverie.

"Just a moment, Your Honor." I leaned over to Troy and whispered, "I'm ready to rest. We could call Archibald Cross, but I'm afraid he might try to cover for his grandson."

Troy nodded. "Yeah. His son is in prison. He'd do anything to protect Justin."

"And then there's Justin's girlfriend, Ava. All she could do is confirm Justin was upset about how Schafer treated her." Not to mention she was in St. Louis and it might take a week to get her here. "His threatening email is better than any testimony from Ava." I patted his shoulder, then I turned back to Auntie El. "Where's Liam?" I mouthed. It was a long shot, but I had hoped he would find something out about Justin.

She shrugged. "Sorry."

I stood and said to the judge, "The defense rests."

"Very well." Judge Blankenship looked at his watch. It was almost noon, a perfect time for a lunch break. But he said, "Let's proceed straight into arguments. Ms. Becker?"

Carol seemed surprised too. But she didn't hesitate. She walked up to the jury carrying a yellow notepad. She began with the physical evidence. Describing the crime scene, how police found the body. She talked about the trajectory of the bullet, the undamaged door into Schafer's home. Then she recounted the testimony of her second most important witness, Kaitlyn Wynant. "The night of the murder, in the exact time window when Coach Grant Schafer was gunned down, the defendant was seen sneaking out of the party at Lefty's, by himself, and going to his car. And then as you heard from the defendant's own witness, Lefty himself, the defendant reappeared at the bar later, as if trying to conceal the fact that he ever left."

She tried to explain away the location of the gun. "As you all heard, the defendant had access to Mr. Cross's garage."

"Objection," I said, standing. "There is no evidence of that." While standing in his driveway, Archibald Cross had told us that Troy mowed his lawn and had access to the garage. But Carol never called Archibald as a witness. It had been a glaring mistake on her part. I was glad now that I hadn't called him.

Nevertheless, the Judge ruled against me. "I will rely on the jury to remember what facts were presented as evidence. Continue, Ms. Becker."

Carol knew I was right. She had screwed up. To recover, she turned to her best evidence, setting up the giant screen to replay the video of Troy threatening the coach.

It was torture to listen to it and watch it again. When the lights finally came back up, the jury was staring at Troy. It was powerful evidence. Carol reiterated Troy's comments. "'Somebody needs to stop you,'" she said, walking over to stand by Troy. "'If there weren't people around, I'd do you right now.'" Then she pointed her finger at the jury, the way Troy had done in the video. "'Watch your back, 'cause I'm coming.'"

She paused, turned, and stared at Troy for a long moment. Then she walked back toward the jury. "From the defendant's own mouth. Ladies and gentlemen, on that New Year's Eve, Troy Weaver planned to take revenge against the man who he blamed for ruining his son's future. He created an alibi by going to a New Year's Eve party. He stole the gun from his neighbor, thinking no one would ever be able to trace it back to him. Then he drove the short distance to Grant Schafer's house. He entered. Holding the gun down here," using her hand as a pistol near her stomach, "He fired one shot, directly into the coach's neck, the bullet lodging in his brain. As you heard from the medical examiner, the coach died almost instantly."

She turned to look at Grant Schafer's family members in the front row. The jury would surely be sympathetic to them.

"Justice demands that Troy Weaver be held accountable. I ask you to return a verdict of guilty for the aggravated murder of Grant Schafer."

She returned to her table and sat down. I remained seated for a moment, thinking this was it. My last chance to help Troy. Almost every night since the trial began, I had lain awake in bed, thinking about this moment. What would I say? Of course, I had prepared my statement. And as Carol talked, I took notes. But I didn't need them now. I knew what needed to be said.

I slowly rose, picked up my crutches, and hobbled up to the jury. They sat waiting, pens and paper ready in case I said anything wise. Silently, I said a little prayer. *Help me, Lord.*

"Ladies and gentlemen, Troy Weaver sits here, an innocent man, having had the full weight of the government brought down on him in the greatest example of injustice I have seen in my career."

"Objection," Carol said. "This is not argument, but counsel testifying herself." She wanted to interrupt me like I had to her.

"Overruled. Continue, Ms. Gallagher."

I kept my eyes on the jury the whole time. "What evidence places Mr. Weaver at the home of Grant Schafer?" I waited a few seconds, making eye contact with each juror. "None. That's right, the government cannot show that Mr. Weaver went there. They say that someone wearing a letterman jacket was there—but how sure can we be that that was Troy? Plenty of people in this town own letterman jackets. People like former football player Justin Cross. Did anyone see Troy there? No, they did not. Remember the witness at Lefty's, Kaitlyn Wynant? She was honest with you. All she could truthfully say was that she saw an older man in a letterman jacket walk out of Lefty's toward his car. She couldn't say whether he drove away or went back inside. She couldn't even say that man was Troy Weaver. She just assumed it after seeing Mr. Weaver on TV after he was wrongfully arrested."

I liked to move a little when addressing a jury, but it was hard with the crutches. I took a step back, which was a mistake. I stumbled slightly, using my right crutch to steady myself. It was embarrassing. I sheepishly said to the jury, "Never go for a morning run in the middle of trial," which brought a few smiles. *Good*. At least some were still with me.

"So there's no proof Mr. Weaver went to Grant Schafer's home. Similarly, there is no proof that Mr. Weaver ever touched the murder weapon, let alone fired the fatal shot. Remember the testimony of Charley Weaver? The government thought he was going to say he got the gun from his father. Remember that from Ms. Becker's opening statement? They believed it was Troy's gun." I turned and pointed at Carol. "She was the most surprised person in the courtroom when Charley said he got the gun from his neighbor's property."

She stared back coldly. *That's right, Carol. I'm going to blame you.* "The gun was located in the garage of Mr. Archibald Cross. In a horrible mistake, Troy's young son Charley found that gun and brought it home, but from the time of the murder—sixteen months ago—that gun had been in Mr. Cross's garage." The gray-haired woman in the back of the jury box nodded with me.

"How do we know? Because Grant Schafer's phone was found in that same garage. In fact, it was found in the same large box that Charley had described." I waited as a couple of jurors jotted notes. "Really, the government presented only one piece of meaningful evidence, and you deserve to have me address it. I'm talking about the video that Coach Schafer took of Troy Weaver. It was not pretty. Mr. Weaver thought his son was poorly treated by the coach and he reacted poorly himself. But how many parents of athletes have lost their cool and acted like a jerk? Does that make him a murderer?"

I crutched back to stand by Troy, to physically show I believed in his innocence. And there, sitting next to Auntie El, was Liam. In his hand were police reports. Dirt on Justin, it had to be. He held them up for me to take. I shook my head slightly. *You're too late.* The judge would never let me reopen the case at this point.

I turned to the jury. "Ladies and gentlemen, that video is the *only* evidence that even suggests Mr. Weaver had anything to do with this case." I paused a moment. "And remember what high school principal David Boudreau testified? That in the time he served as principal prior to the murder, he received from parents and students over thirty complaints against Mr. Schafer. And that's to say nothing of other complaints that might have gone directly to Mr. Schafer without going through the principal. So why single out my client?"

From my leather satchel, I removed a large piece of poster paper, which I had folded into a square. I liked to use props in my closing arguments. "I want to talk to you about the most important legal rule you will apply in this case." I unfolded the paper and held it up. In black marker I had written, *Reasonable Doubt.* "In a few minutes, the judge is going to give you instructions about how to decide this case. And the most important instruction tells you that to convict, you must believe Mr. Weaver is guilty *beyond a reasonable doubt.* The judge will tell you that reasonable doubt is doubt based on common sense and reason. It requires proof that an ordinary person would be willing to rely on in the most important of their affairs."

I set the paper on my table and pegged my way back to them. "Would you send Mr. Weaver to prison, based on nothing more than a threat? Because that is all the concrete evidence the prosecutor has laid before you." Time for the big finish. I took a breath.

"Let me suggest that you follow the evidence. *All* of it. And apply your common sense and reason. That's why our jury system is so important, because it takes power from individual government officials," I pointed at Carol, "and gives it to citizens like yourself. Power to make the most important of decisions: whether someone is guilty and should lose their freedom or even their life. So if you consider *all* the evidence, you must consider all those who made threats against Coach Schafer. Something which the prosecution has entirely failed to do. You need to consider another person in particular who made such threats. That person is Justin Cross. The coach picked on his girlfriend. The coach cut him from the football team. So Justin wrote an email threatening to eff up the coach." The gray-haired lady in the back was furiously scribbling notes. Good.

"It was only sixteen months ago, but in his testimony, Justin Cross claimed he couldn't remember much of anything, didn't he?" I said it with as much snark as possible. "And importantly, he couldn't remember the names of his friends he was supposedly with on the night of the murder. Unlike my client, Troy Weaver, he could not provide a single name of anyone who could corroborate his claim that he was elsewhere. That means he has no alibi whatsoever." I hobbled over to the bailiff, who had placed all the physical evidence out on a table in case we needed it during argument. I picked up the murder weapon. I had intended to carry it back to the jury, but that was impossible with the crutches.

"And now the most important fact." I held up the gun and reminded them. "State's Exhibit number 1 did not originally come from Troy Weaver's house, like the prosecutor told you in her opening statement. This murder weapon came from the garage of Justin Cross's grandfather. Common sense and reason suggest that it was placed there by the killer."

I set the gun down and walked back to the jury. "Who murdered Grant Schafer? Was it Justin Cross? Was it one of the thirty people who are known to have made complaints against the coach? Was it a random act committed by a stranger? Because the government rushed its investigation, we cannot answer that question, at least right now. But you don't have to. You, the jury, have one job, and that is to decide whether there is such overwhelming evidence of my client's guilt that common sense and reason require you to convict him. Ladies and gentlemen, the truth is, the evidence is so *under*whelming, so nonexistent, that common sense and reason require you to vote *not* guilty. Because Troy Weaver killed no one. Any other verdict would be a travesty."

I looked over the jury, hoping for some acknowledgement, some encouragement. But they all sat stone-faced. Even the gray-haired woman in the back row.

I limped back to my table, feeling like I had blown it. Troy said nothing. He was watching Carol stand for her rebuttal argument. Ohio law allowed the prosecutor to have the last word, so I was done. I barely could make myself listen to her through the pain in my ankle. If they came back guilty, could I live with it? I grew angry watching Carol stand there, trying to persuade the jury of a lie.

From behind me, Liam handed up the police reports he had shown me earlier. "Read these," he whispered.

# 49

After Carol finished her short rebuttal argument, I stood. "Your Honor, I have an urgent matter. May we approach?"

At the bench, in whispered tones so the jury couldn't hear us, the judge said, "I am ready to give final instructions. What is it, Ms. Gallagher?"

"Your Honor, I just received some important evidence. Evidence that I could not have found until after receiving the late discovery from the government. I would like to go on the record and ask to reopen my case."

Carol didn't like it. "I strongly oppose this. The defense has rested. If she thought there might be additional evidence, counsel could have asked for a continuance."

"If you had conducted a thorough investigation—"

Judge Blankenship cut me off. "Hold it, ladies." He turned to me, a little anger in his voice. "I am not going to reopen this case. And I am not going to delay jury instructions or deliberations." His expression softened slightly. "But what I will do, Ms. Gallagher, is once we have a verdict, if you still want to make a record, I will allow you to do so."

I stared back at the judge, trying to understand the implications. He was saying, if Troy was found guilty, I could make a record for appellate purposes stating why, under the law, I was entitled to reopen the case. It wouldn't change anything with this jury, but if we lost, it might help on appeal. It might get Troy a new trial. It wasn't ideal, but I would have to live with it.

Carol and I went back to our tables, and the judge gave the jury their instructions for deliberation. When he defined "reasonable doubt," several jurors looked at me. At least they were paying attention.

It took almost ten minutes to give the instructions, but they weren't that complicated. It was a one count, aggravated murder trial. Did Troy pull the trigger or not? That didn't mean the deliberations would be easy. Twelve unique citizens all had to come to a unanimous agreement. It could take days.

The bailiff led the jurors back to their deliberation room. He would order them lunch, and then they would decide Troy's fate.

The judge said, "Counsel, we have your numbers. We will call when we have a verdict." He banged his gavel and said, "We are adjourned."

Immediately, Liam and Auntie El were at our table.

Liam said, "Janice is here, and she's ready to testify."

"Too late," I said. I held up the reports. "But this is good. If the verdict goes badly, I think I can get a new trial with this."

"What is it?" Troy said.

Liam took over. "New Year's Eve, there was some vandalism downtown. The Paul Brown statue was torn down and a couple of storefronts were broken into."

Troy's eyes went big. "You know who did it?"

"Not officially. But we were all called out that night. It was messy. Janice responded to Main Street and saw Justin Cross sitting on a bench in front of the pharmacy, drinking a beer."

"But nobody else?" Troy said.

He seemed tense. Was he thinking of Benny? Did Benny and Justin tear down the statue together? That might explain his stubborn protection of his son and his refusal to admit where he went when he left the party that night. The Paul Brown statue was revered in Kerry.

I said, "We're not worried about the statue. Across the street was the Pawn USA store. Someone broke into it and stole a gun."

"Not just any gun," Liam said, "but a Sig Sauer handgun. The same type that killed Grant Schafer."

"Why are we just finding this out now?" Auntie El said.

Liam and I exchanged a look. I said, "Because Carol rushed this case."

"It must have fallen through the cracks," Liam admitted. "Nobody checked the PD's case management system for stolen guns. Not that it would have shown much. The pawnshop records are pretty bad. There's no serial number and they couldn't tell us the model."

I said, "But Justin was seen there, sitting across the street. That would have been powerful evidence." Then I quickly said, "I'm not blaming you. This is great work, and I really appreciate it. The timing's not your fault."

We sat in silence as people continued to filter out of the courtroom. I noticed Denise still sitting on the bench, her eyes wide and scared. Maybe she was thinking of raising her two boys alone.

Troy said, "So, what are my chances?"

I was never good at predicting juries, and I didn't want to lie. "We've got a good case."

"It was a powerful closing," Liam said guardedly. He had seen enough juries himself to know better than to make a prediction.

"Well, *I* know," Auntie El said. She waved her hand like it was a foregone conclusion. "You don't need to be a lawyer or a police officer to figure this out. It's *common sense*. I bet Liam that they will be back with a verdict inside of two hours." She looked at her watch. "3:16 p.m."

"But with what verdict?"

"One hundred percent, super-duper innocent," she said, beaming. I was both pleased and worried at her faith in me as a lawyer.

I sensed movement behind me and turned. It was Carol. She held out her hand. "You try a hard case."

I handed her the police reports. "You can read these while we wait for the verdict. And you might want to start a grand jury investigation of Justin Cross."

---

I was able to talk with Denise before she headed back to the hospital. "Thank you so much, Maggie. You did a great job. I know those people will do the right thing and we'll have our family back again."

Now there was nothing to do but wait. I drove back to my office and parked, feeling a wave of exhaustion come over me. I checked my phone and saw several text messages. My new friend Suzanne had been in the courtroom:

**Great job. Let's have a drink to celebrate later, and you can tell me about your leg.**

And Sean:

**It was on TV. Wow! That's why I never argue with you. Awesome!!**

Then Ian:

**You did good mom.**

I needed that. A trial lawyer has all the insecurities of an actor, only with much more on the line. Here the stakes were literally life or death. *Did I do enough?* I was not in a good position to judge my own performance. And of course, my husband and friend wouldn't tell me I sucked. But I'd take what I could get.

Patrick and Liam had joined Auntie El in the office, waiting for me. She gave me a powerful hug as I walked in, almost knocking me backward. "I am so proud of my family right now," she said. Then she grabbed Patrick's cheek and pinched it.

"Ow." He pulled away.

"Even my little baby. Tell her what you did, Patrick."

"Nothing, really," he said. "It's just that, I arrested Justin Cross a year ago. He was smoking a joint and throwing rocks at cars on the highway."

"Fine lad," Liam said sarcastically.

"He and three other dicks. His buddies. I gave the names to Janice, and she is tracking them down right now. Maybe one of them will remember Justin breaking into the pawnshop."

Liam said, "Janice feels terrible. She feels like Carol used her."

"She did," I said. I snapped my fingers. "Any chance one or more of his buddies are related to Pete Cafferty?"

Patrick gave me a funny look. "Yes. How did you know that?"

I waved him off, promising we'd talk about that later. I wasn't entirely sure if Justin had put them up to harassing or if they'd done it on their own. That didn't matter now. I didn't want to dwell on Carol or Janice or anyone else. I was surrounded by my family. "I want to thank you guys. Because of all your help, Troy has a fighting chance." I began to tear up as the stress and anxiety I'd kept tightly strapped down finally began to bubble up.

Auntie El saw me getting emotional. "We'll have a big barbecue at the farm to celebrate," she said. "Then we can all talk about how great we are. But for now, how about some soda bread?" She lifted the loaf from her desk and held it up.

Liam rubbed his hands together in anticipation.

"I'll wait to have some until after the verdict," I said, and started for my own office. I needed to be alone.

I closed the door, hobbled around my desk and collapsed into my chair. There was nothing more to do. As the stress melted away, the tears came. And I let them.

## 50

There was a knock on the door, and Auntie El burst in. "It's the court!" She disappeared a moment and came back with a box of tissues and a hand mirror. I must have looked a mess. "Take a few minutes," she said, "but not too long. The jury is back." Then she broke into a big grin, pointing to her watch. "3:02 p.m. I win."

"Let's see what they say before we celebrate." I cleaned up my face, and then Auntie El drove us back to the courthouse in her pickup. We passed the Paul Brown statue and the Pawn USA store. "I hope we get that guy," I said.

"Don't worry," she said. "I made Liam promise. He's out helping Janice right now."

Before we went inside, I remembered to call Denise.

"Benny's awake," she said. "Is Troy there?"

"Not yet. We have a verdict and we're all going back to court." Then I realized what she said. "Benny's awake? Is he okay?" Perhaps it sounded harsh, but we had all been concerned about brain damage.

But Denise said, "Yes. Thank God, he's okay. He's talking. Everything's great." Then in a muffled tone. "I haven't told him yet." She meant, she hadn't told Benny about Troy's trial. "Do you think I should come, be there for the verdict?"

"No," I said. "There's nothing for you to do. If he's acquitted, I'll bring him to you."

Auntie El had just pulled up in front of the courthouse. It was a zoo with satellite TV trucks and media and members of the public all over the steps. To Auntie El, I said, "Benny's awake, and he's okay." She banged her fist against the car horn and slapped my shoulder.

"Ouch."

"Now, for the perfect day, we just need a not guilty verdict…so I can win my bet."

I climbed out of the truck and slowly made my way up the courthouse steps. A reporter along with a cameraman came over. "How do you feel about your chances?"

"Good. We are very confident the jury will see the truth and find my client innocent." I chuckled to myself. Juries don't find *innocence*. They find guilty or not guilty. It had always bothered me as a prosecutor when defense attorneys referred to "findings of innocence." And now I was doing the same thing.

As I entered the courtroom, it seemed different, more chaotic. Media and members of the public were milling about and talking loudly. In the back, I saw Suzanne. She gave me a thumbs-up and I waved. Troy came in between two officers looking glum, like he had resigned himself to a life in prison. Or maybe even a death sentence.

"I just spoke with Denise," I told him. "She said Benny's awake."

"What?" He grabbed both my shoulders. "Benny's awake? Fully awake?"

I broke into a wide grin. "She said he's doing great, talking and everything."

He stared at me a moment, and then fell back into his chair, tears filling his eyes. He began to sob as two months of pent-up stress and worry came pouring out. "My God…" he said, covering his face with his hands and rocking gently back and forth.

"Is everything okay?" One of the officers on the bench behind us leaned forward.

"Troy's son just came out of his coma," I said. The man stood and placed his hand on Troy's shoulder in a reserved, cop-style show of emotional support. Nice.

"I'm happy for you, Troy," he said.

The bailiff came over. "Are we ready?" He glanced at Troy crying and laughing, maybe thinking he was reacting to all the stress.

"Ready," I said. But I wasn't. I had never experienced a swirl of emotions like this. Over-the-top happiness for Benny, anxiety for the verdict. Media and the public surrounding us… Carol was at her table looking composed on the surface. But I knew better. If she was anything like me, she would be anticipating the end of her career if she lost. And after the way she'd handled this case, I had no sympathy.

I leaned over to Troy as Auntie El handed up some tissues. "Here, wipe your face. Just remember, if it goes bad, we have good grounds for appeal." I was trying to convince myself as much as Troy.

"I don't care," Troy said. He wiped his eyes and blew his nose. "I really don't. I've been praying that Benny would be okay. A trade, him for me. I'm good with that."

*I* wasn't okay with it, but there was no point arguing now.

The judge took the bench and the courtroom went quiet. "All rise. The Donahoe County Court of Common Pleas is now in session. The Honorable Victor Blankenship, presiding."

"Be seated," he said. I looked behind at a packed courtroom. How many of them wanted Troy's scalp? Had I persuaded any of them of his innocence?

The bailiff brought in the jury, who all looked somber, keeping their heads down. The judge said, "Who is the presiding juror?"

The gray-haired lady in the back stood. "I am, Judge."

"Have you reached a verdict?"

"We have." She held up a piece of paper and the bailiff took it. He walked across the courtroom and handed it to the judge. The silence and tension were thick. I put my hands in my lap so no one could see the tremors.

Judge Blankenship said, "The defendant will rise." I grabbed Troy's elbow and pulled him up. We stood together as the judge unfolded the paper and began to read. "We the jury, having been duly impaneled and sworn in the county Donahoe of the State of Ohio, find the defendant, on the charge of aggravated murder…" He paused for a moment and looked at the observers, then he looked at Troy. "Not guilty."

I felt weak and might have fallen over if Troy hadn't immediately pulled me into a hug. "You did this," he whispered in my ear. "It's over, isn't it?"

"It's over," I said, squeezing him back. I looked at the jury over his shoulder. Every one of them was watching us. Most were smiling. I mouthed the words, "Thank you," and the gray-haired lady nodded back.

Troy finally pulled back, and his smile faded. "What about that other charge, the reckless endangerment?"

I laughed. I had almost forgotten about it. "Remember? They thought it was *your* gun and that Charley got it from you. But we disproved that. They'll drop that charge. You are a free man, Troy." I hugged him again.

An officer came up behind us and asked Troy to come with him back to jail, which I found funny. The judge had ordered Troy released, but I was vaguely aware that the jail wanted him to sign some forms, and Troy would need to get the clothing he was arrested in. This was my first acquittal, so I didn't know all the procedures. It seemed absurd, and I started to argue, but Troy said, "It's fine, Maggie." With a big smile, he added, "I can say goodbye to a couple of guys."

"Stay away from Justin," I warned him.

The officer said to me, "You can pick him up at the sally port behind the jail. Give us about half an hour." Then he leaned closer and made a point of shaking my hand. "You did a great job, by the way. He's really innocent, isn't he?"

"Yep."

"And just so you know, Justin Cross was found guilty on his robbery charge."

As Troy walked back to jail one more time, I sat back in my chair and leaned the crutches against the table. Both Carol and the judge had left the courtroom, but half the crowd remained. A reporter came up from behind and asked if I was going to hold a press conference.

I hadn't even considered it. Before I could answer, Auntie El said, "Yes, she is. On the front steps in fifteen minutes." Then she wrapped her arm around my shoulder. "We're in business now and this is great publicity."

I grabbed her hand and kissed it. I loved my aunt. "Can I borrow your truck?" I said. "After I hold your press conference, I need to take Troy to see his son."

She handed me her keys and kissed the top of my head before letting out a punch-drunk chuckle. She said, "What a day."

## 51

I felt numb, sitting in Auntie El's pickup truck behind the jail, waiting for Troy. After all the stress and tension, I was thoroughly enjoying the quiet. My phone buzzed, a text. It was Dominic DeNuzzio.

**Any word on my case?**

Did he even know I was in trial? I put my phone away, thinking over these last two months. *No more murder cases.*

But no, who was I kidding? I'd loved it. I thought of Auntie El and her comment. I was "in business," and there were a lot of billable hours in a murder trial. I just wouldn't represent any friends. The pressure was too great.

I took out my phone again. I was in business and Dominic was my client, so I dialed up Oliver, Dom's prosecutor. "Congratulations on the Justin Cross robbery," I said. "What's he looking at, six years?"

"Thanks," Oliver said. "Seven years with his record. And I heard he might be facing another sixty or seventy years, thanks to you."

"Yeah, I'm pretty sure he killed the coach. Listen, my client Dom DeNuzzio is calling about his case..."

"Geez Gallagher, can't you even give me a day to let me enjoy my win?" He was only half joking.

I laughed. "What about me? It's been less than an hour since I got my verdict." Through the windshield I saw Troy step through the jail door. I honked the horn and he saw me.

Oliver said, "Carol's already left for the day. She stormed in and stormed out. Didn't say anything to anybody."

"So you're the winner in the office," I said. "That means you should be free to make a deal. I bet I can talk DeNuzzio into a careless driving charge, plus full restitution for the damage to the house."

He sighed. "I don't really care, except he lied to the cops. I can't reward him for that. Have him plead to a reckless driving charge and I won't seek any jail time. Forty hours of community service."

Troy climbed in the passenger seat, still with a big grin. To Oliver I said, "Okay, that seems fair. I can probably talk him into that." In fact, Dom would be thrilled with that outcome. "We'll talk Monday about the community service. I'm thinking twenty hours," I said, then hung up.

"Who's that?" Troy asked.

I waved my hand dismissively. "Another case. Ready to go?"

He hadn't changed out of the suit he wore throughout the trial. The clothes he had worn to the jail two months ago were in a bag on his lap. "They didn't have my letterman jacket," he said. "Do you think I'll get it back?"

I laughed. "With everything you've been through? Yeah, you'll get it back. It's still in evidence. I'll check on Monday."

We headed for the hospital, past Lefty's and a couple fast-food restaurants. Troy said, "You know, I could use a bite. There." He pointed at a Wendy's. After two months of jail food, Troy gorged himself on a double Baconater hamburger, fries, and a large frosty. And of course, I couldn't let him eat alone.

At the hospital, I had planned to drop Troy and head home, but he insisted on me coming up with him. "You are part of our family, Maggie. We owe you everything." And I wouldn't mind talking with Benny. If the time was right, maybe he could tell me about Justin Cross.

We walked into the hospital room, and Troy practically leaped on Benny. Charley was on the bed too, and all three Weaver boys embraced in one of the sweetest moments I had ever seen. Denise sat nearby, tears rolling down her cheeks. She came over and hugged me. "I can't believe this, Maggie. You did it." She pulled back to watch her boys. "We are a family again."

Troy stood, picked Charley up off the bed, and gave him a big squeeze. "You did all this, Charley. You were a hero in court." He looked at me, "Wasn't he, Maggie?"

I limped closer. "Charley, you were a great witness." He smiled wide, looked at his parents, then grabbed Benny's hand. It seemed he couldn't get enough of his big brother.

Troy said, "Benny, this is my lawyer and close friend, Maggie Gallagher. We went to school together, and she just saved me in court. Saved us."

I reached out and shook his hand. "Nice to meet you."

Benny sat up against his pillows, wanting to talk. "Mom said you proved that JT did this. Thank you."

"They're still working on the case. There's not enough evidence yet. Maybe we can talk about it next week." I was dying to get his story, but now I just wanted to leave their family alone to enjoy each other.

"JT hated Coach. Mom said you knew about the Paul Brown statue. That was his idea. We tied a chain around it and pulled it down with a stolen car." He shook his head in shame.

"You don't have to tell me this," I said.

"I already told my folks." He glanced at Charley, weighing what he should say. "After we did that, I was like, 'what am I doing?' I didn't even like JT or the other guys. And tearing down Paul Brown... I just took off, started walking. I called Dad, and he came and picked me up."

I looked at Troy. "The 11:30 p.m. phone call at Lefty's."

Troy nodded.

"You could have told me," I said, and instantly regretted it. Scolding him now didn't do any good.

"It was my fault," Denise said. "We made a pact we wouldn't tell anyone. Everybody loves that statue."

"It wasn't anyone's fault but mine," Benny said. "I screwed up my whole senior year." He rubbed Charley's head and pulled him close to the bed. "You're never gonna do dumb stuff like that, are ya?" And he began tickling his little brother.

I said, "When they release you, we can talk more. There might be little bits to the story that will help. And I'd rather interview you than let the police do it. Nobody needs to know about the statue."

"Talk to Kyle Langers," Benny said. "He was tight with JT, until dude stabbed him. Kyle said something about Ava, and JT jammed a butcher knife into his thigh. I bet Kyle will talk."

"That's good, thanks. I'll pass it on." I turned to Troy. "Time for me to go."

He grabbed me, and we hugged for a long, long time. Through tears, he muttered something about God sending me back to Kerry. About my mom, and us being family. "We are always here for each other. No matter what."

"No matter what," I said, when I finally broke free.

"We'd love to meet your son," Denise said. "Maybe next weekend, you guys can come over."

"That would be great."

Limping down the hallway on my crutches, I felt like I was floating. The pain was still there, but it didn't register. I had won many trials, but I had never felt like this.

---

Saturday morning, Sean was in the den grading his students' final papers and I was at the kitchen table with a cup of coffee, scanning the news on my phone. I was a little ashamed for enjoying all the attention.

Last night I had texted Liam to go interview Kyle Langers, the guy Justin stabbed. This morning I got a reply:

**Done. A gold mine. Thx. Tell you later.**

So the tip paid off. Hopefully, they'd have enough to charge Justin Cross.

I heard steps in the hallway and looked up as Ian came in, his hair mussed from sleep. "Morning," I said.

He mumbled something and turned to walk out.

"Hey," I said, with a little too much force. He froze, and I winced. I didn't want this to turn into another argument, so I softened my tone. "Can we talk a minute?" He stayed still, not looking back. "I just want to apologize," I said. "I know this move has been really hard, starting over in a new town…"

He spun around. "You don't get it, do you? It wasn't the move. I mean, I wasn't happy about it, but that's not what really bothered me." He glanced at my leg in the boot, resting on a kitchen chair. "It's like, you've been in constant pain for the last three years. Taking pain pills, walking on a cane…now the crutches." He came into the kitchen and sat across the table. *He finally wants to talk about it. Thank God.*

"I've healed from those injuries," I said. "I was back to running, and then this. It's just a minor break…"

He scoffed, crossing his arms over his chest. "You still don't get it. I mean, you almost *died*. The idea that I might lose you… We're in this new town, Dad and me don't know anyone…" He shook his head. "I can't really explain it."

"It feels like you've been pushing me away," I said.

He looked at me for a long moment. "I guess I have." Then he looked down at his hands on the table. "I don't know. Maybe I thought it'd be easier to have some distance so it wouldn't hurt so much if I *did* lose you."

My heart broke. "You're not going to lose me." I reached across the table and grabbed his hands. "You're the most important person in my life and I'm not going anywhere. In fact, there will be times you'll wish I would go away."

He laughed at that and nodded. "I know. Believe me."

That made *me* laugh. "You can talk to me anytime, you know that? We all need somebody when things get hard."

"Oh man," he said, leaning back and running his hands through his hair. "If ever there was someone who should take her own advice. You're the queen of doing everything yourself and shutting everyone out."

"You're right." I hung my head in mock shame, but he truly was right. "You know what? I learned that lesson while I was working on this case. I never could have done it without Auntie El. Without my cousins Liam and Patrick. And without you and your dad."

I fumbled with my crutches, trying to stand. I *so* wanted to hug him. And my boy Ian sensed that. He came around the table and met me in an embrace I had needed for so long. We stood there in the kitchen, tears flowing, my eyes closed in pure pleasure. I didn't want to let go.

"Hey, Dad," Ian said. I opened my eyes to see Sean in the doorway, beaming. We both reached out to him, and he stepped into our embrace as my crutches toppled to the floor.

Wiping the tears from my cheeks, I smiled at the both of them. "Right, so how about some breakfast?" I started to bend to retrieve my crutches, but Ian beat me to it.

"What did I just say, Mom, about you doing too much?" Ian grabbed my crutches and leaned them against the wall out of my reach. "Sit back down. You too, Dad. I got this." Ian bustled around the kitchen pulling things from the fridge and setting a pan on the stove to heat before placing bread in the toaster.

Sean pulled his chair close to mine and wrapped his arms around me before leaning in to whisper, "Does he know how to cook?" I shook my head—at least, I didn't think so—and we shared a chuckle as we watched Ian. I knew that no matter what he ended up making or how it tasted, I'd eat whatever he put in front of me. I wanted to bask in this moment.

Ian set plates down in front of us and I was surprised to see the eggs looked properly cooked and the bread was nicely toasted. Biting into the eggs, I smiled at my family. This was exactly why I returned to Kerry. For moments like this. I knew that there would be times when this kind of peace would be in short supply, so I intended to savor this moment while I could.

# END OF THE MIDWEST LAWYER
## MAGGIE GALLAGHER LEGAL THRILLER BOOK 1

*The Midwest Lawyer, April 24, 2025*

*The Bloodied Client, December 18, 2025*

PS: Do you love legal thrillers? Then keep reading for exclusive extracts from **The Bloodied Client, Small Town Judgment,** and **Small Town Trial.**

# ABOUT PETER KIRKLAND

Loved this book? Share it with a friend!

**To be notified of Peter's next book release please sign up to his mailing list, at**
www.peterkirklandauthor.com

## ABOUT PETER

Peter Kirkland grew up in Beaufort, South Carolina. As a kid, Peter loved history and learning about his area. One year in school, he was given a project to research a few South Carolina law cases and the precedents they set and their effect on people's lives. This research project lit the flame for his passion for law and creating a more equal justice system since. Soon after this, Peter began reading legal thrillers voraciously and enjoyed the legal maneuvering and justice found within. As an adult he has continued researching the law and understanding the system and its effects on individuals. A few years ago, he decided to try writing his own legal thriller.

Now a full-time writer, he uses his research, passion for justice, and real case studies to bring together courtroom dramas with deep, rich characters, and gripping twists and turns. New to the industry, Peter would love to hear from readers and other authors and invites you to connect with him through:

## BLURB

***A teenage girl is charged with the unthinkable…***

The crime? The brutal murder of her own parents. The prosecution's argument seems airtight. But small town defense attorney Maggie Gallagher senses something isn't right…

Months earlier, Zoey Conrad had already faced her worst nightmare when two men broke into her room. In the terrifying struggle that followed, one intruder ended up dead. The judge declared it self-defense and dismissed the charges, allowing Zoey to rebuild her life in their small town. But now, with her parents found murdered under disturbingly similar circumstances, the evidence against Zoey quickly piles up.

Maggie knows Zoey and she wants to believe the girl is no killer. Yet the more she learns about the twisted life the Conrads led, the stronger her compassion for Zoey grows. But the deeper she digs, the worse things get. Especially since Maggie's own son has gotten personally involved.

As the prosecution builds an ironclad case and the clock ticks down, Maggie must race to expose the truth. If she fails, Zoey's fate is sealed—and an innocent life could be shattered forever.

Get your copy of ***The Bloodied Client***
**Available January 15, 2026**
**(Available for pre-order now)**
www.peterkirklandauthor.com

---

## EXCERPT

### Chapter One

You expect warning signs before a disaster. Sirens. Gunshots. Clouds rolling up on your perfect blue sky. But I was sure my sky was all blue, no clouds, no sirens. Nothing out of its place—at least, that I could see.

The Dunlaps were in for a quick probate issue—Emily Dunlap and her son Ken. Emily's husband George had passed on unexpectedly in a car crash, and I could see that her grief was still raw. She looked past me, not at me, as I talked through our business. My office had a nice view of the old courthouse, but I doubted she noticed it in her state.

"Mrs. Dunlap?"

She focused her gaze on me to show she was listening. Ken gave me the nod, so I went on.

"Most of the estate was in both of your names: the house, the business, your Atwood Lake cabin. There's no paperwork you need to worry about to transfer those assets. Same goes for—"

Ken cut in. "His retirement account?"

"Yes, that as well." Emily was back to staring past me, and I found myself frowning as I went on. "All his accounts were in both of your names, with the exception of this one." I held out the statement for her to see, but she didn't look at it. Ken reached out instead. Was he a little too eager? I thought back to an old case I'd once prosecuted, a son who had stolen his mother's estate. Sold it all out from under her while she stewed in her grief.

Ken smiled. "Uh, Ms. Gallagher?"

I realized I was holding onto the statement, clutching on tight as he tried to take it. But he wasn't the kid from that long-ago case, and Emily wasn't that sad, helpless mother. She had her sisters and cousins to lean on, and Ken was a good kid as far as I'd seen.

*You're not a prosecutor anymore,* I reminded myself. *And not everyone is a crime waiting to happen.*

I let go of the statement and cleared my throat. "It's an investment account, and it's just in your husband's name. Same goes for your Lexus, and your son's truck. I've prepared an order for the court to sign, to transfer those over. You should be through probate by the end of this month."

Ken let out a tight breath and sagged with relief.

"So we give this to the judge, and that's it? We're done?"

I could sense his fatigue, so I offered a smile. "I'll take care of that part. You're essentially done. All I need from your mom today is her signature here." I'd prepared applications to put the titles for the Dunlaps' two houses solely in Emily's name. Now I passed her a pen, and she signed them without reading.

"So that's all you need?" She seemed relieved too, glad to be done with this and with my office.

"That's all," I said, then searched for some words of comfort. "Your husband did a great job securing your future. He made this easy as easy could be."

Emily laughed then, a soft, broken sound. She blinked, then she stood. "Yeah. That was George."

The Dunlaps filed out and Auntie El bustled in, in one of her trademark loud floral blouses. I'd thought about asking her to tone down her wardrobe—we were a law office, not a car lot—but clients liked her. She put them at ease. And she cheered me up too, a bright splash of color to pep up my day.

"So sad," she said, when the Dunlaps were gone.

I sighed. "I know. How old was he, sixty?"

"Sixty-one, far too young. Damn those drunk drivers." Auntie El set about straightening my desk. I winced, thinking back to Dad's drinking days, all the times I'd had to confiscate his car keys. There'd been a few times I hadn't caught him fast enough, and only by God's grace had he come home okay.

Auntie El stepped back, done with her straightening. "You have Edie Endicott coming by later. She has some more questions about her 'divorce.'" She did bouncy air quotes, and we both groaned. Edie had been coming every week for a while, testing the waters on her maybe-divorce. "And you've got the Batchelder custody hearing, so you'll want to get down to the courthouse by four."

"Get me their file," I said.

Aunt Louise fetched the file, and she freshened my coffee. "You ever wish you'd get a splashier case? Like when Troy was charged with killing Coach Schafer?"

I shuddered at the memory. "That case was messy in a lot of ways. Don't forget, it started when his son almost died."

"But it was exciting. You live for a challenge. I've known you all your life, so don't act like you don't."

I thought again of the Dunlaps and their dull probate case, and how I'd flashed back to the Mulligan fraud. Had some part of me wished for a monster to fight? I did love a challenge, no doubt about that. But Troy's case had been awful. Folks had been hurt. I shuddered, remembering how hard it had been on Troy and his family.

"No one gets traumatized in probate court."

"But does it stir your soul?"

I swiveled my chair around to look out the window, at the old courthouse with its closely-cropped lawn. No one heard cases there anymore, not since the new courthouse went up down the road. But still, when I looked at it, I always sat straighter. It reminded me why I did what I did.

"My soul's fine," I said. "Now, go on, get." I put on my "gruff sheriff" voice to show I was joking. Auntie El huffed, hands on her hips. Then, with a shake of her head, she went out, grumbling the whole way about stubborn people. I watched her go, smiling, then got back to work. I was fine with these types of workaday cases, and finer still with leaving at five. No long nights holed up in my office, desperately digging for contradictions in witness statements. No tossing and turning, losing sleep over whether I'd done everything I could to save my client's life. With these cases, I could rest easy—and have time to relax. I'd made it home every night last week to a hot dinner, and I expected this week to play out the same.

Get your copy of *The Bloodied Client*
**Available January 15, 2026**
**(Available for pre-order now)**
www.peterkirklandauthor.com

**BLURB**

*Every small-town hides something...*

When seventeen-year-old Jason Demers is accused of pushing his girlfriend from a third-floor balcony in quiet Autumn Harbor, the case seems clear-cut. Eyewitnesses. Circumstantial evidence. A town ready to see him locked away.

But criminal defense attorney Spencer Dunn—once a forensic scientist—knows better than to trust appearances. Something about Jason's case doesn't add up. And the deeper Spencer digs, the more unsettling the picture becomes.

Jason swears he's innocent. His powerful, enigmatic father wants the case buried. And someone in town is working hard to keep the truth from surfacing.

As Spencer unravels a chilling web of secrets, betrayal, and long-buried grudges, he realizes this case is far from ordinary. It's dangerous. And the closer he gets to the truth, the closer danger gets to him.

Because in Autumn Harbor, justice comes at a price—and Spencer might be the one to pay it.

Get your copy of ***Small Town Judgment***
**Available July 24, 2025**
**(Available for pre-order now)**
www.peterkirklandauthor.com

---

**EXCERPT**

**Chapter One**

My client, Jason, couldn't sit still at the defense table. His right leg was pumping up and down, and he seemed unable to stop it. He looked anxiously around the courtroom. His mother, Mary Ann Demers, sat in the first row of the gallery. She waved to her son and smiled, but he didn't appear to notice.

Just a few days earlier, she'd sat across from me in my office, her nails bitten to the quick, the skin on her cheeks red and cracked. She'd asked if we could meet early on a Saturday morning so she wouldn't miss too much work. "What exactly does this mean?" she'd asked.

The petition from the DA's office had landed on my desk like a bombshell, right after I'd taken on the case. The prosecutor wanted to try Jason, charged with throwing his girlfriend off a third-floor balcony at her mother's home, as an adult.

As Mary Ann leaned forward, I'd felt the slightest burning sensation in my nose: bleach. Apparently, even at the start of the day, she couldn't escape her job running a laundry. I was no expert when it came to women's clothing, but the simple shift she had on was worn, and I was sure it had been inexpensive in the first place. She and Jason lived on the poorer side of town. I wondered how she had scraped together the money for our fees.

"Well, to begin with," I told her, "in Juvenile Court, the focus is on rehabilitation rather than punishment. If a young person has a drug problem, he'll get treatment. If he has anger management issues, he'll get therapy. The court can be creative in looking for solutions other than incarceration. Most kids get probation and help rather than jail. On the other hand, if a juvenile is bound over to adult court and convicted, he's usually sent to prison."

Mary Ann blanched. "You mean Jason will be locked up with real criminals? He didn't do this. I swear to God he didn't do this. He's in love with Lara."

I'd promised Mary Ann I'd do everything I could to keep Jason's case in Juvenile Court. I didn't share with her my knowledge that the judge assigned to the case, Randolph Waters, had bound over a lot of juveniles, including several kids younger than Jason. There was no point making her even more upset.

I hated the idea of trying kids as adults. If it were up to me, I'd push the ceiling for Juvenile Court to twenty-one, maybe even higher.

Teenagers just didn't have the maturity and judgment that warranted decades-long punishment for their mistakes.

If I lost this hearing, Jason could be crushed by an adult criminal justice system he didn't belong in. He could be an old man before it was done with him.

"The judge will be coming out in a few minutes," I said to Jason. "As I told you before, once he's in the room, you've got to remain calm. You can't do anything that will make him think you have a violent streak or that you could lose control of yourself."

The boy's appearance was everything I could have asked for: clean-shaven, his sandy hair pulled back in a ponytail. I'd told Mary Ann to have him wear a dress shirt and slacks, no suit jacket. I didn't want him looking any more like an adult than necessary. "Yeah, whatever," he said. "Is Rachel going to testify? I don't see her here. She saw me leave that night before Lara fell. She knows I didn't do what they say I did."

Rachel, Lara's sister, had told the police a very different story than Jason claimed. I didn't know why he thought she would vouch for him. I didn't want to agitate him now by telling him that she wouldn't.

I shook my head. "We're not going to get into that today. This hearing isn't about whether you're guilty or not. It's only to decide where you'll be tried."

Jason continued to scan the courtroom, apparently looking for Rachel.

"Listen to me," I said. "The prosecutor is going to try to convince the judge that you deserve to be tried as an adult. She'll bring up whatever she's learned about you that looks bad. You're charged with a serious crime, and she'll say she has witnesses that establish probable cause to believe you did it. You've got some things on your record, and she'll talk about them. No matter what she says, you can't show any anger, and you can't act out. If you do, the judge will hold it against you." I'd been telling him pretty much the same things for the past hour, but I was concerned that he wasn't paying attention.

"All rise," the court officer intoned.

Judge Waters walked slowly from the door to his chambers to his seat on the bench. His thinning white hair was combed straight back. He looked down over his hawk nose at the people in the courtroom, disdain in his eyes. It was clear he thought he was superior to everyone in the room. "You may be seated," he said, his tone suggesting he was granting us a favor.

"Oh shit," Jason whispered behind his hand.

I put my arm around him and spoke softly in his ear. "Keep it together. We're just getting started. Stay calm, and let me do the talking."

The judge turned to the prosecutor. "I'll hear you, Ms. Forester."

Lucy Forester was one of the older assistant district attorneys in the Juvenile Court and a lifelong resident of Autumn Harbor. "Your Honor, this matter concerns the adult Class A crime of attempted murder," she began. "The victim, currently in intensive care, may not survive. If she dies, we will be seeking a murder charge. If culpability is established, the least charge would be Class B aggravated assault. Therefore, the State asks the Court to bind over the defendant to be tried in adult court."

She looked over her glasses at the judge. "The victim was nearly killed after being struck on the head with a heavy object and pushed from a third-floor balcony to the ground. She sustained a traumatic brain injury and is currently in a coma."

She pointed to Jason. "This accused is well-known to the local police. He has a record of drug offenses and is currently in a drug diversion program. In addition to his substance abuse problem, he's been picked up many times for underage drinking. In this court he's been adjudicated of vandalism, namely throwing eggs at a house and striking the homeowner. The original charge was assault and battery, but that was dismissed by the prosecution."

*He never should've been charged with that in the first place,* I thought.

Ms. Forester raised her voice slightly as she reached the conclusion of her statement. "I mention those facts, Your Honor, because they reflect on the character of the accused and show that he has already been afforded leniency by the Juvenile Court. Despite that, we find him back here today. His attack on Lara Reed is just the latest escalation in his behavior."

I stood. "Objection, Your Honor. The present charge has not yet been tried. Absent a conviction, it cannot be held against my client."

"Sustained," Waters said. "I'll hear from you, Mr. Dunn."

Jason's leg was pumping again. I put my hand on his shoulder and gave it a squeeze.

"Your Honor, I'll begin with the language of the United States Supreme Court in *Miller v. Alabama,* citing and reaffirming earlier holdings: 'Youth is more than a chronological fact. It is a time of immaturity, irresponsibility, impetuousness, and recklessness. And its signature qualities are all transient.' Youth's problems are *transient,* Your Honor. That's why we keep juveniles in this Court, where we can address problems of immaturity with tools other than incarceration and punishment."

I looked at Jason. I pictured him trudging from his cell to an exercise yard in an orange jumpsuit, surrounded by hardened criminals. The image made me feel sick.

"Jason has a prior record, but no history of violence, only hitting someone with an egg—probably accidentally—when he was thirteen. As Ms. Forester noted, his substance abuse problem is currently being addressed with therapy. My client is, of course, presumed to be innocent of the crime with which he's been charged. If evidence develops that he did play some role in causing Lara Reed's injuries, the Juvenile Court is the best place to address the issue."

The judge sat stone-faced. I couldn't read what was passing through his mind.

"I have filed a brief, Your Honor, addressing the published findings of neuroscientists and forensic psychologists with respect to what the Supreme Court has termed the 'mitigating qualities of youth.' Juveniles' brains are incompletely developed, including the prefrontal cortex. As a result, they lack impulse control in emotionally arousing situations and are prone to risk-taking. They are more susceptible to peer influence than adults. And, significantly, they have a greater capacity for change than older individuals due to the plasticity of their brains. Indeed, the research shows these same qualities are present in what might be called emerging adults through the age of twenty-one and beyond. For that reason, it should not affect the Court's decision that Jason is approaching his eighteenth birthday."

I put my hand on Jason's shoulder again. "The last factor I mentioned, capacity for change, is the reason we have the Juvenile Court. The research demonstrates that trying juveniles as adults does not reduce juvenile crime and leads to poor results for the juveniles involved. Compassion rather than retribution is called for, Your Honor."

I sat down. The prosecutor rose with her rebuttal. "We recognize that the defendant is entitled to the presumption of innocence, Your Honor. However, the witness statements we've attached to our brief establish probable cause to believe that Jason Demers committed the crime of attempted murder."

A woman behind me choked back a sob. Mary Ann, I presumed.

"Under the bind-over statute," Ms. Forester continued, "the Court is required to take the existence of probable cause into account. Jason has shown consistent poor judgment. If he is convicted, public safety will require commitment to a facility more secure than any dispositional alternative available to the Juvenile Court. It's true that we keep most juveniles in this Court. However, the legislature in its wisdom has provided that under appropriate circumstances someone under eighteen should be tried as an adult. This is such a case."

Judge Waters shuffled his papers into a pile. "You have put together some impressive research, Mr. Dunn."

It was never a good sign when a judge began his decision by complimenting the lawyer on his brief. My heart sank.

Sure enough, Waters continued, "However, this young man has already had the benefit of the leniency and the help that the Juvenile Court can provide. He is charged with a heinous offense, attempted murder. I am ordering him bound over to the criminal court to be tried as an adult. Court is adjourned."

The ruling hit me harder than I'd expected. I should have prepared Jason and Mary Ann better for this. I clenched my jaw, keeping my face neutral, though I felt the turmoil bubbling over inside. Jason could be buried inside the penal system before his life had even begun.

Maybe I should've called witnesses. The truth was, I hadn't been on the case long enough to know how Jason was regarded in this community. I'd have to double down at the bail hearing. I needed to be at my best for that. I couldn't let Jason down.

He looked defeated. "Does this mean I'm going to prison?"

My eyes narrowed. "No." Not yet, anyway. And not ever, if I had anything to say about it. "I'm going to try to keep you at home with your mother until your case is tried. Let's go talk with her."

Mary Ann had apparently dashed out of the courtroom as soon as the judge ruled, and she was waiting for us on the sidewalk in front of the courthouse. Her eyes were moist, and her mascara had run. She was dabbing at her face with a tissue. "What's going to happen now?"

"When Jason first appeared in court, the judge ordered him released to your home, where he needs to stay except when attending school or his drug program or working with you," I said. "That's still in effect. In a couple of days, we'll have to appear in criminal court, where the judge will set bail. Once that's posted, Jason can remain at liberty until the trial." I turned to Jason. "Your mom told me you've been making all your appointments in the drug diversion program. Will your counselor give you a good recommendation?"

"Yeah, I think so."

I nodded. "I'll call him to see if he'll come to the hearing."

My cell rang. Seeing Leah's name on the screen, I answered and said, "Honey, hold on for a minute, will you? I'm with my client."

I pressed the phone to my side and turned to Jason and his mother. "This is my wife. I've got to talk with her. I'll call you at home tomorrow to get the information that I'll need for the bail hearing."

After hasty goodbyes, Mary Ann and Jason walked toward their car. He was dragging his feet. I couldn't blame him. This had been a bad morning for the both of them.

I raised the phone to my ear. "Sorry about that. The judge bound my client over to adult court."

"Oh, honey, I knew you were concerned that might happen. It sounds like a tough case, no matter what. I just wanted to tell you I'm thinking of you. That young man's lucky to have you on his side."

"Thanks. I've got to get to the office. We'll have a bail hearing in a couple of days, and I have a lot of files to look over. I think I should be able to get home by around seven, though."

"Sounds good. Love you."

"Love you too."

Demonstrating that things weren't always what they seemed to be was a lawyer's stock-in-trade. To win this case, I'd have to make a persuasive argument that Jason didn't do what he'd been accused of. But the witness statements Forester had filed with the court made a strong case that he did. And the crime was awful. The victim was his girlfriend, someone he supposedly cared about. If he could bash her on the head and throw her three floors to the ground, what else was he capable of? While I still didn't believe he should be tried in adult court, I was afraid this kid might be a ticking time bomb, just waiting to go off again.

Get your copy of *Small Town Judgment*
**Available July 24, 2025**
**(Available for pre-order now)**
www.peterkirklandauthor.com

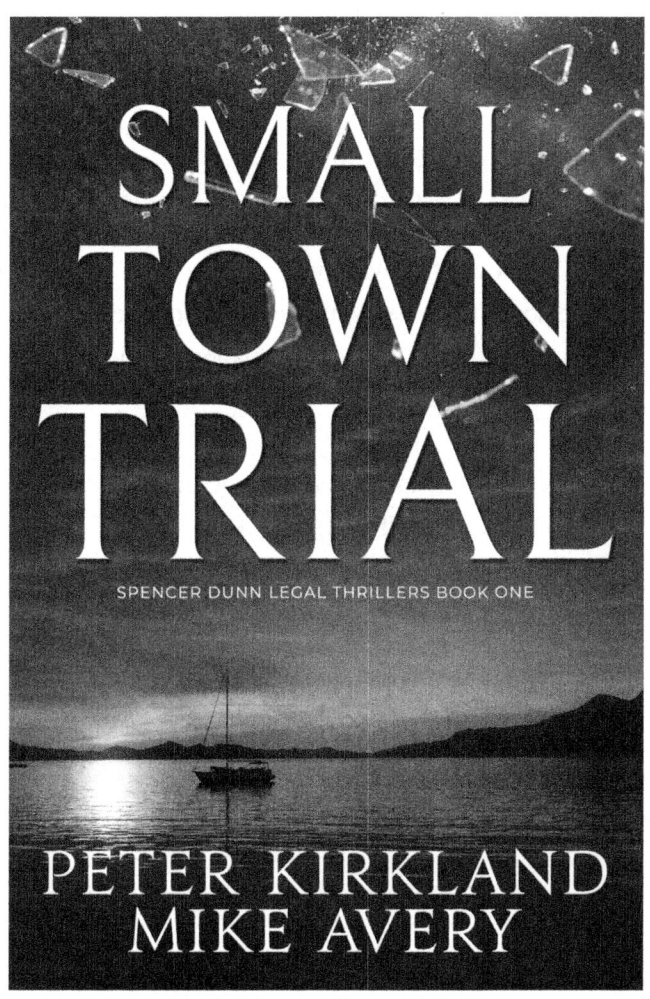

**BLURB**

*Murder in a sleepy coastal town… Can attorney Spencer Dunn keep his head above water?*

When beloved mayor turned state senator Carlton Osborn is found dead on his boat, the prime suspect is the only other person on board: his pregnant teenage girlfriend, Amber Vega.

Struggling to restore his self-confidence after a string of personal and professional losses, Spencer Dunn isn't eager to defend a young woman who is almost certainly guilty yet refuses to follow his legal advice. But once Spencer starts digging, he realizes this case isn't as simple as the police are making it out to be.

Spencer doesn't know the meaning of the word "quit," and he's willing to ruffle some feathers in his quest to uncover the truth. But in the course of unraveling the mystery of Osborn's murder, he's making some very powerful enemies…

**Grab your copy of *Small Town Trial* (Spencer Dunn Legal Thrillers Book One)**
**eBook**
**Paperback**
**www.peterkirklandauthor.com**

---

### EXCERPT

**Chapter One**

Judge Callahan was staring at me over the top of his glasses, and I reached up to adjust the volume on my hearing aids. I wasn't used to wearing them yet, and figuring out the correct volume for different situations was a work in progress. Thankfully, the low-level whistling that had been tormenting me since I put them on this morning went away, and my shoulders went down a notch.

With a nod to my client, I dropped my prepared speech onto the counsel table and walked slowly toward the jury box. I stopped a few feet from the railing at the front of the box and waited a moment. My eyes moved slowly from juror to juror. They stared at me impassively. I could read nothing on their faces.

"A prosecution like this is a terrible experience for the Williams children," I began. "At a time when they should be able to rely on their parents for stability and support, intolerance and vindictiveness define their family life. Their father filed criminal charges against their mother. Their private lives have been invaded by a public trial. The possibility of their mother's conviction has imperiled their ability to feel secure and protected. Thank goodness this is finally coming to an end. What that end will be is up to you."

I couldn't believe my client's ex-husband had talked the prosecutor into filing charges for criminal restraint. Maybe he was a major contributor to the DA's reelection campaign. I wasn't yet sufficiently connected in Autumn Harbor to know. I had to hope the jury found the charge as ridiculous as I did.

"Mary Williams was excited to take her children on an adventure in Canada. It was a special trip. Kids love to visit their grandparents. Grandparents let them get away with stuff their parents are strict about—candy, TV, you know what I mean." I looked at the jurors old enough to have grandchildren and smiled.

I gestured in Mary's direction. "Mary planned the trip properly. She got an agreement from the children's father to take the children out of the country. That's the responsible and respectful thing to do, and that's what she did." I was starting to find my rhythm, though I still felt shakier than I liked.

"When Grandpa suggested they spend a couple of days at his cabin in the woods, it promised to make their adventure even more exciting. Mary didn't need her ex-husband's permission for that. She was entitled to change her day-to-day plans in Canada. She had the right, as the custodial parent, to manage the trip as she saw fit." So far, so good.

"Then, suddenly, when they were in northern Ontario, there was an emergency. You can't plan for emergencies. They come out of the blue, and you do the best you can. Sometimes everything goes well. Sometimes it doesn't. When people are stressed and upset, they're not always able to manage things perfectly. But this is life. We have to make allowances when someone's plans are upset by unexpected and frightening events."

Judges generally kept their expressions neutral during arguments by counsel. Judge Callahan, a senior jurist with white hair and a pink complexion, was no exception. I got a little nod, however, from His Honor on the nature of emergencies.

I pursed my lips and cocked my head. "That's what happened here. Grandpa got sick. Very sick. He had to be airlifted to a hospital." I shook my head. "What could be more alarming? Imagine it. The helicopter lifts off, taking Mary's father away." I raised my arm, mimicking the takeoff, and looked past it toward an imaginary sky. "Mary doesn't know if she's about to lose him. She wants to get to his bedside as quickly as possible. Maybe these will be the last few moments she has with her father."

I walked back to the defense table and stood behind my client, my hands on the back of her chair. "In that dire moment, Mary does the best she can for her children. She arranges for them to be looked after by a longtime friend of the family, someone who babysat Mary herself when she was a child. She sends a message to the children's father, explaining the situation. She informs the kids' school and their karate and music teachers that they will be absent, and why. She contacts the parents of her daughter's friends to say her upcoming birthday party will need to be rescheduled. She does everything she can think of to keep the children's life as normal as possible while she's on her way to the hospital."

Shaking my head, I resumed my spot in front of the jury box. "Those are not the actions of someone who is engaged in the criminal restraint of her own children to infringe on their father's rights." A couple of the jurors shook their heads in response, and I felt—though didn't show—a surge of optimism. "As you've heard, Mr. Williams never got Mary's message. There's no evidence that was her fault. As I said, in an emergency, sometimes things go off course. Was Mary trying to deprive her ex-husband of time with the children? Certainly not. In fact, in the message she sent him, she suggested he take an extra weekend with the kids to make up for the time he would be missing." That, too, seemed to get a positive response from the jurors.

"Mr. Williams complained that Mary didn't confirm that he received her message. In an ideal world, where she wasn't worried to death at her father's bedside in the hospital, she might have done that. Her failure to do so under the circumstances here can hardly be considered a criminal act."

I turned and pointed at Mr. Williams. He was the kind of person whose resting face betrayed arrogance. I hoped that the jurors assigned that frame of mind to him. "He didn't do everything perfectly either. He might have checked with the school, the karate and music teachers, or the parents of his children's friends to see if they knew what was going on. If he was as worried as he now claims he was, wouldn't you expect him to reach out to anyone and everyone who might have the slightest bit of information? He called *no one*." I paused to let that sink in. "No one. Not until three days after he missed his weekend—just one day before Mary and the kids arrived home—when he called, again, not the school or other parents, but the police." The idea of going the better part of a week without checking on a child's welfare was so alien to me that I still found it hard to imagine... though I knew all too well that plenty of parents did far worse to their kids.

"The prosecutor has tried to suggest that Mary had a history of keeping the kids with her on their father's scheduled weekends. But in fact that only happened on two occasions. Once, one of the kids had a stomach bug, and Mary thought he wouldn't do well on the hour drive to the father's place. The other time was soon after the divorce, and the child had a meltdown and didn't want to leave home. Two incidents over the whole time the parents have been separated is hardly a pattern. It doesn't demonstrate disregard for the other parent or for the law. Young kids get sick. They throw tantrums. The same things might've happened at the father's house. In his concern for the children's health and feelings, Mr. Williams might well have delayed returning them to their mother until things calmed down."

I paused and gave another small shake of my head. I was glad I didn't handle matrimonial disputes on a regular basis. Too often they ended up as battles between parents in which the children were the principal victims. "Managing visitation issues in a divorce isn't easy. It takes patience and understanding. The parents have to be willing to give each other a break when problems arise—which can be a challenge when emotions run high. But," I emphasized, "the most important thing is the children's welfare. The Williams children were well taken care of in Canada. They were worried about their grandfather, but they were safe and nothing bad happened to them. And hopefully they're fine now, despite the stress and publicity of this trial. But they won't be fine if their father's vendetta against their mother is successful."

I grimaced. "No. A prosecution like this is not the way to resolve minor problems that arise during a divorce. There is no evidence here of the criminal restraint of children. There is no evidence that Mary intended to deprive Mr. Williams of his right to spend time with his children. There is no evidence that she intended to violate any law. A guilty verdict would be a travesty of justice."

Time to wrap this up. I hoped I'd made all my points persuasively.

"It's up to you to set this family back on the right path," I said, trying to press my sincerity into each juror's heart. "The path of mutual respect, understanding, and cooperation. You can do that with a verdict of not guilty. That is the correct verdict under the law and, equally if not more important, the one that will protect the welfare of the Williams children."

I sat down. Mrs. Baynard, juror number four, the gray-haired schoolteacher in the front row, stared at me with an expression so stern, so angry that I wanted to turn away. I waited a second, then looked down and folded my papers into a pile. I couldn't tell what her reaction meant. Was she angry at me? Why? While the prosecutor was getting to his feet for his closing argument, I reviewed everything I could remember. I couldn't imagine what might have set Mrs. Baynard off… unless something had been said during the trial that I missed because of my hearing issues. I didn't think so—I'd been carrying spare batteries every day, just in case I noticed my hearing aids giving the slightest bit of trouble—but if I had, it was too late to do anything about it.

**Grab your copy of *Small Town Trial* (Spencer Dunn Legal Thrillers Book One)**
**eBook**
**Paperback**
**www.peterkirklandauthor.com**

Printed in Dunstable, United Kingdom